Field of Generations

Suzanne Burrus

by
Suzanne Burrus

Note for Librarians: A cataloguing record for this book is available from Library and Archives Canada at www.collectionscanada.ca/amicus/index-e.html
ISBN 1-4120-9580-8

Printed in Victoria, BC, Canada. Printed on paper with minimum 30% recycled fibre.
Trafford's print shop runs on "green energy" from solar, wind and other environmentally-friendly power sources.

TRAFFORD
PUBLISHING™
Offices in Canada, USA, Ireland and UK

Book sales for North America and international:
Trafford Publishing, 6E–2333 Government St.,
Victoria, BC V8T 4P4 CANADA
phone 250 383 6864 (toll-free 1 888 232 4444)
fax 250 383 6804; email to orders@trafford.com
Book sales in Europe:
Trafford Publishing (UK) Limited, 9 Park End Street, 2nd Floor
Oxford, UK OX1 1HH UNITED KINGDOM
phone +44 (0)1865 722 113 (local rate 0845 230 9601)
facsimile +44 (0)1865 722 868; info.uk@trafford.com
Order online at:
trafford.com/06-1335

10 9 8 7 6 5 4 3

Acknowledgment

Without my sister, Sherry McVeigh's, study of the genealogy of our family, this novel would not have emerged. I thank both her and my mother, Alpha Cochems, for their hours of reading and rereading and their encouragement. Much appreciation to my sons, Kelsey and Trent, his wife, Karen, my daughter, Brandi, and her husband, Chris Otten, for their support and input throughout the writing of this book. My special thanks to our friend, Dixie Moore's, artwork for the cover. And to friends: Dick and Maxine Wilson, Carol Smith, Yvonne Howard (to name just a few) who emboldened me to get the darned thing done, thank you.

The clouds of time creep across
the field of generations
leaving one row of golden grain
illuminated by the sun a while
and then move on to give
another row its time to shine.

⇒ 1 ⇐

1751

Elizabetha dashed to the ship's stairwell and flew down it straight into the arms of someone at the end of it. She gaped up in trepidation, blood pounding in her ears. Stern blue eyes met hers. They belonged to a man too young for such severity.

The young man's expression changed, which confused her until she realized it was because he'd smiled.

"*Entschuldigen Sie bitte.* I'm sorry I startled you," he said. His brow knitted. "Are you all right?"

She nodded. Her racing heart paused a moment as if catching its breath. Her eyes felt so huge she was sure there wasn't enough skin to hold them in place. She blinked just to see if she could. She tried to control her panting and gulped.

She'd only wanted a breath of fresh air. The pulsating sea of German emigrants who'd been herded aboard the *Nancy* were crammed between the decks of the great ship for the long journey to America. The din of hundreds of voices jabbering at once, children screaming, oldsters moaning, had beat upon her eardrums. The reek of rancid sweat, musty oak, and other foul odors she didn't care to identify had seared her nostrils and stung her eyes. She'd just had to get outside, but two sailors had almost discovered her on deck and she'd raced back down.

With a tilted head, the young man gazed at her, studying her with a quizzical glint in his blue eyes. "How old are you?"

There was nothing wrong with his words she supposed, but something about his question rankled. What had her age to do with anything?

She straightened her long, magenta skirts and tugged her bodice down in front. She thought about saying she was fifteen—others had thought she looked older, but instead she confessed, "I'm eleven, almost twelve."

As the words left her mouth, she wished she had lied about her age. She pulled herself up as straight as she could and faced him. "You don't look all that old yourself."

"I'm a lot older than you. I'm sixteen, almost seventeen."

Was he mocking that she'd said almost twelve? "A worldly man, are you?"

His jaw tightened, and a dolorous flicker that crossed his gaze almost made her regret her flippancy. "Where is your family?" she asked.

"My older brother and I came alone. Our parents said they were too old and would miss their home too much. They and our younger sister stayed behind. My father said he didn't want to leave his church." He lowered his head and clenched his teeth. "Truth is they couldn't afford for us all to come."

When he looked up, his searching gaze stripped her soul clean of further malice. She couldn't help feeling pity for him. It must have been difficult to confess his family's poverty. Why had he?

His expression softened and he said, "I saw you and your family once on the riverboat coming down the Rhine, then again in port in Rotterdam while we were waiting to board the *Nancy*. My brother and I are situated not far from your family. I noticed you make your way through the crowd and wondered where you were going."

Had he intended their collision? He was quite sweet after all.

Her father appeared out of the throng. His forehead crinkled. "Thank God. There you are, Elizabetha. I've been searching frantically—."

"I'm sorry, Papa." She hoped the young man wouldn't say she'd been up on deck.

He didn't. Instead he stepped forward and shook her father's hand. "Martin, Sir, Martin Kimberlin, my brother and I boarded the Rhine boat at Wuttemburg."

Elizabetha fiddled with a stubborn wisp escaping her lappet cap as she studied the young man. His dark, wavy hair was long and disheveled. The heavy cotton breeches, unbuttoned waistcoat, and white full-sleeved shirt he wore were clean enough though crumpled. There was a run in one of his hose and a sole coming loose on one shoe. Tidiness was not a priority on board, nor was it even possible. He had a determined air about him. Probably six inches taller than she, solidly built with good, strong features.

"*Ja, Ja, Ich bin* Wilhelm Kirstaterin. I see you've met my daughter." Her father glanced down at her and smiled. His gaze turned to the young man. "We boarded at Durlach. Lutheran, I presume."

"Yes, I am Lutheran, very much so."

"*Gut, gut.*" Her father's smile broadened.

Elizabetha wondered why being Lutheran always seemed so important to other Lutherans. She didn't believe in any of it since her grandfather had died when she was nine and everyone at the funeral had cried, except her. Why were they crying? If her grandfather was going to heaven, they should be happy for him. It was obvious that they must not believe in heaven. It was all just a sham.

Elizabetha and her escorts wound their way through the maze of people in separate small groups huddled together with their bedding and travel chests close beside them around the vat of fetid water. A scattering of men around the vat dipped brass pans, pottery, and wooden bowls full of the vile liquid to take back to their families. Elizabetha hated that water, but there was nothing else to drink.

When her mother was in sight, her father said, "Go on to your mother Elizabetha, I'll chat a moment with Martin. He turned to Martin and said, "I was a shoemaker in Durlach. I made a good-enough living, but America, now that's the place to be." His gaze dropped to Martin's feet. "By the way, I want you to feel free to come around and see us, Martin. I'll fix that shoe for you."

Martin glanced at the errant sole and grinned. "I'd like that, Sir. *Danke.*"

Elizabetha glanced back at her father. She loved his easygoingness. He was tall and lean and enjoyed talking about the new world and shoemaking. He enjoyed talking, period. She knew they would be a while. Her father seemed to like this Martin. She glanced at Martin. She liked him, too. When he wasn't arrogant, he was sweet.

She turned her attention forward. She hoped Martin wouldn't think of her as a child. Why hadn't she lied about her age? He *was* handsome. He seemed so determined and sure of himself. She vowed to make him notice her as a woman. After all, she was officially a woman, her mother told her so when her monthlies came earlier this year. She hadn't thought of herself as any sex until then. Maybe being a woman wouldn't be so bad after all.

Her petite mother, Rebecca, wore a gray, wool dress. A few ringlets escaped her cap. She was perched on one of their travel chests carefully packed with their belongings and the dried and salted foods they would consume on the long journey. One small chest was devoted entirely to her father's shoemaking materials.

Her four-year-old brother, Toby, clenched their mother's skirts in his tiny fist. His cheeks were wet from tears. Their mother comforted him. Elizabetha guessed he'd received a scolding and was seeking forgiveness.

She thought her mother a handsome woman with dark, curling hair and lavender eyes. When people said she resembled her mother, Elizabetha was pleased, but she didn't want to be like her. She loved her mother, but her mother seemed weak. She never stood up for herself. She just went along with whatever Elizabetha's father said.

Rebecca wished her daughter would settle down and learn her woman's place instead of being so curious and questioning everything. It would only lead to heartache. At least Elizabetha seemed to relate to Wilhelm. That pleased Rebecca except when one took a stance on some issue and the other one took the opposite side. She hated those arguments—debates as they called them. She wished Wilhelm wouldn't encourage Elizabetha to debate. It really wasn't fitting for a young lady.

"I'm so glad you're back, Elizabetha. I was worried about you. There's so much confusion."

"I'm sorry, Mama, I'll stay near. I promise." Elizabetha wiped a remaining tear from Toby's cheek. She was always sorry when she worried her mother, but then, her mother worried at everything.

"I know you will. Toby has also promised to stay near." Their mother tousled Toby's dark hair and winked at Elizabetha. "Where's your father?"

"I, er, ran into a nice young man, Mama. Papa even liked him. I could tell. Papa stayed to talk to him."

Elizabetha settled herself on her cot and took her writing materials from her small travel bag. She held the inkpot in one hand lest it should spill. It was the last she had. She opened her journal and set the events of the day to paper. At the end, she skipped a few lines and boldly wrote:

P.S.
Eleven, July 1751
Today, I met the man I will marry, Martin Kimberlin.

⇒ 2 ⇐

Martin came to visit Elizabetha's father alone the first day. On the second day, Martin brought his brother.

"Mrs. Kirstaterin, Wilhelm, I'd like you to meet my brother, Johanne." Toby hugged Martin's leg. Elizabetha stood. "Oh, and let's not forget Toby and, of course, Elizabetha."

Elizabetha noticed Johanne was taller and thinner than Martin but had a strong resemblance, the same dark hair and eyes so light blue they reminded her of steel.

Toby played on the floor at the feet of the men as they discussed everything from religion to politics to philosophy while Elizabetha helped her mother wash the family laundry in a large pot and hang the clothes across the travel chests the men weren't using. She tried to listen in as best she could. She wanted to join the conversation and was relieved when her chores were finished.

Her mother settled on her cot and began the mending stashed in her sewing basket.

Elizabetha pulled her cot closer facing the men, eager to join the conversation.

After several attempts to offer her opinion, she grew infuriated as Martin changed the subject each time. He was treating her as a child not fit for the serious discussions of men. She decided to try a new tack and put on her Sunday-best smile. "What will you do when you get to America, Martin?" She asked sweetly.

Martin contemplated her. "I will be a farmer, like my father. I'll find a place with limestone soil. My father says it's the best. I'll rotate the crops to keep the soil healthy: first hay, then corn, next tobacco, then wheat or barley, and use plenty of manure." He stopped speaking. A sheepish expression shifted his features as if he thought he'd gone on too much.

"And what else?" she asked not wanting to lose his attention.

"Else? Well, a church. I'd like to build a Lutheran church like the one my father loves in Germany, wood-frame all white-washed with two towers in front with tall steeples. One day when I've earned enough, I'll bring my parents and sister to America." He smiled at her.

Martin turned his attention to her father. "But enough about me. What are your dreams, Wilhelm?"

Her father stretched. "That's easy, a shoemaker's shop, of course—."

Elizabetha tuned out her father and tried to recapture the warmth she'd felt while Martin spoke to her.

* * *

The following week, Johanne was struck down with influenza. The next week it turned into pneumonia, and Elizabetha knew Martin was worried. Since his brother's illness, Martin had come alone only once a week. She hated all the misery and wished they were already in Philadelphia. In Philadelphia everything would be all right.

But there still remained a lot of water between the ship and Philadelphia. She felt the sea seethe as a summer storm swirled the *Nancy* in the peaks and valleys of its waves like a paper boat bobbling in a swift river current.

She spotted Martin threading his way toward her family.

The ship heaved up on a massive storm wave and slapped back down, and so did the scant contents of her stomach. Martin lost his footing and almost landed in the lap of a large woman in a red shawl squatted on her worn, wooden travel chest. He made apologies to the woman. When he was upright again, he saw Elizabetha watching and managed a sheepish smile.

"How is Johanne?" her father asked as Martin approached.

Elizabetha's heart sank at the tenseness about Martin's eyes and dark smudges beneath them.

"No better. Johanne can barely get up. He's sleeping now. The woman in the group next to us said she'd watch over him. She's most helpful."

"Let us all pray for Johanne," her father said.

Elizabetha joined in as each stood in a circle upon the deck with feet set apart to brace against the roiling sea beneath. They clasped one another's hands. Martin stood next to her. Martin's hand was warm in hers in spite of the chill that permeated the air. She was pleased he was holding her hand even if it was only in prayer.

Elizabetha peeked at Martin by her side. With eyes closed, he seemed oblivious to the clamor and chaos of the others all about them. Her father's eyes were closed, as were her mother's. They, too, seemed lost in their private prayers.

Intent on her mission of prayer, Elizabetha tightened her eyelids and uttered, "God, please spare Johanne." Martin squeezed her hand. She squeezed his back, careful to keep her gaze lowered. She felt like a hypocrite. Praying did not come easy for her. She had only done it for Martin's sake.

The ship rose on a mountainous wave and slammed down the other side. People all around her clutched at their sick loved ones to keep them in their cots.

"Oh, dear God," her mother cried out and pulled Toby close.

Elizabetha's father put his arm around her mother and held her to him. Toby buried his face in her skirts.

Martin still held Elizabetha's hand. "Don't be afraid," he said.

She glanced around at all the apprehensive faces surrounding them. Fear permeating the ship turned her knees to a quivering mass like pudding her mother stirred at home. "Are we going to sink?"

"No, no. The storm will pass soon." Martin's steady gaze held hers. Her heart calmed its wild beating as Martin whispered, "You have the loveliest eyes. I can't decide the shade of blue, they're like the very sky."

"They're azure, my mother says." A hot flush rushed up her neck to her cheeks.

"Azure," Martin said. "In all the pain, fear, and miseries around us, something as lovely as azure is like a beacon shining on life. Glory to God for azure."

Elizabetha's heart throbbed. The warmth from his hand spread through her whole body like honey on a warm biscuit. "Martin, I love you," she blurted.

His mouth slacked and his eyes widened, eyebrows arched. "Oh, Elizabetha, I'm sorry—I didn't mean—you're just a child," he stammered.

She instantly realized he had just been trying to calm her fears of the storm by distracting her thoughts. Mortified, she pulled her hand away.

The ship reeled again, throwing sick and healthy every which way. Martin's gaze darted back to where his brother lay, then back to her.

"Elizabetha, I'm so sorry if I made you think—I must get back to my brother."

"I know. I'll be all right." She straightened her skirts trying to regain her composure then added, "My thoughts go with you."

She watched Martin wind his way through the emigrants, sometimes falling into one as the ship lurched in the storm. She wished she'd said prayers instead of thoughts. Martin would have liked that better. Why couldn't she be more devout?

Martin tucked his brother in for the night and sat with him until Johanne fell asleep. Martin kicked off his shoes and settled himself on his own cot. His thoughts drifted to Elizabetha's avowal of love. He smiled. She was a pretty and perky thing, but she was far too young. He felt awful that he'd led her to think he was interested in her that way. Someday she would grow up into a lovely woman. He rolled over. She'll have beaus flocking all around her, if she learns her place.

* * *

The following day, Elizabetha and her father made their way to Martin and Johanne's space. A woman was beside Martin. They were attending to Johanne who was broom-thin and pallid.

Elizabetha felt her stomach turn as she neared enough to see what they were doing. The woman held a wooden spatula and was scraping at Johanne's frail body as Martin turned him and stroked him with a wet cloth.

Elizabetha moved nearer to her father who put his arm around her and whispered, "Lice plagues everyone, but especially the sick."

When Martin and the woman finished, they pulled Johanne's shirt back down and tucked his blanket around him. Johanne had a coughing spasm for several moments. Martin used the wet cloth to wipe yellow-green sputum heavily laced with blood from Johanne's mouth. Martin and the woman glanced up at Elizabetha and her father.

"This is Katrina," Martin said. "The kind woman I told you about. Katrina, I'd like you to meet my friends, Joseph and his daughter, Elizabetha."

Katrina's large frame equaled Elizabetha's father's height. Her shoulders were as wide as well. Though her hard mouth smiled, she seemed severe. Yet, there was a gentleness in her eyes that belied her stern exterior.

Katrina wiped her hands on the soiled pinafore protecting her dress and made a small curtsy. "*Guten Tag.* Pleased to meet you." A young boy coughed somewhere behind her. Katrina turned toward the sound, her broad brow rutted. "There are so many who are sick, so many," she said, shaking her mobcap from side to side. "*Entschuldigen Sie bitte.* I must see to my son." She gestured toward the boy who'd coughed.

Katrina knelt beside the cot of her son, not much older than Toby. Katrina dipped a dirty blue rag into a pan of gray water and wiped her son's forehead with gentle strokes.

Martin was saying, "Johanne's getting worse. He needs a doctor." Martin studied his brother and his shoulders sagged. He sighed and turned to Elizabetha and her father. Martin's brow was furrowed and the smudges under his eyes were even darker.

"We'll pray with you," her father said.

Elizabetha wished she could believe prayer would help.

⇒ 3 ⇐

The following day, Elizabetha knew the praying hadn't helped. She and her father stood beside Martin as his brother's body was about to be given up to the sea. The woman Katrina and her family were on deck. Her son had also died in the night. Elizabetha's mother had remained below with Toby.

A breeze ruffled wisps of Elizabetha's hair and blew them across her face. She glanced up at the clear, cerulean sky and shielded her eyes from the brightness. A sea gull wafted on the breeze. Land was near, yet not near enough for Johanne.

Martin's mouth sagged at the corners. His eyes brimmed with unshed tears.

The Captain removed his hat and said a prayer aloud for the gathered mourners.

Martin lowered his head. His lips moved in silent prayer.

Solemn crewmembers lifted the slats where Johanne and the younger boy lay and tilted them over the railing. Their bodies slithered into their silent resting site.

Katrina, tears flowing down her cheeks, put her large arm around Martin's shoulder and hugged him. Elizabetha marveled that the woman could give comfort to others despite her own loss. She vowed to have such strength herself.

Later that day, Martin came to Elizabetha's family's area. His shoulders drooped. Elizabetha wished she could comfort him.

Her father clasped Martin's shoulder. "What will you do now, son?"

Martin took a deep breath and slowly let it out. "I haven't the money to pay my sea freight. I've just come from selling myself to the Captain for resale to redeem my debt for passage, and Johanne's." He lowered his gaze.

"Oh, Martin. No!" Elizabetha cried. She turned to her father for help. "Papa?"

"Perhaps the Captain would allow me to give security for your debt. Let me try," her father said.

She glanced at Martin, hoping he'd see the sense of her father's offer, willing him to accept it.

"No," Martin said, jutting his chin in the air. "I can't allow you to assume my debt. It will only be for a few years."

"I wish you'd reconsider."

"No, Wilhelm, I must bear my own burden, but I thank you."

Elizabetha searched Martin's face for some sign of yielding. None was there.

Martin's jaw was firmly set. "The Captain told me tomorrow the *Nancy* will dock in Philadelphia. All males fifteen and over will be taken ashore to the city court to take the oath to become British citizens and rowed back to the ship." Martin glanced at each of them as if already saying his goodbyes. "The paying passengers will be allowed to disembark. I'll remain behind with the other redemptioners."

"I have a cousin in Lebanon, Henry Hamblen, a silversmith. That's where we're going. Please write to us there and plan to visit us when your indenture is ended," her father said.

"I will." Martin seemed to be ignoring Elizabetha's gaze on purpose.

She resented his stubbornness. She so wanted him to stay. A few years was an eternity. Would he even remember her? She vowed she would dream of him every day. The force of her will might reach him and make him think of her.

* * *

Elizabetha had closed her eyes and held her breath as the cloud of white dust to delouse the passengers settled over her as she debarked the ship.

Her father had left the family on the dock with the travel chests as he searched for a hackney coach that would take them the ninety miles to Lebanon. Her mother stood amidst the family baggage and comforted Toby who clung to her skirts.

Despite wobbly legs still feeling the sway of the sea, Elizabetha stood outside the circle of chests and twirled around trying to take the whole scene in at once. The port of Philadelphia teemed with noise. Pedestrians and horsemen darted everywhere. It was an exciting tumult.

Her father returned with their means of travel. The driver helped her father load their travel chests, and the Kirstaterin family climbed inside the coach.

On the ride to Lebanon, Elizabetha turned her head to the side window and feasted her eyes on the lush greenery lining the road.

She glanced across the coach as Toby's head bobbled on his thin shoulders as he struggled to keep his eyes open. Soon he was fast asleep on their mother's lap.

Elizabetha turned her gaze to the window and thought of Martin. Was he enjoying being on land again? Was he gazing out at similar scenery? Elizabetha felt her own eyelids growing heavy. She dreamed of Martin.

She awoke when the coach stopped and her father said, "We're here."

Her father bounded out of the hackney, lifted Toby down, and assisted his wife.

Elizabetha clamored out the other side and came around the coach just as a large, rotund and red-faced man and a plump matron with a button nose and red hair came through the front door of the two-story hall and parlor house and fussed over their guests.

After embracing them, Elizabetha's father introduced his cousin Henry Hamblen and his wife, Polly. Henry kissed Rebecca and Elizabetha's hand and shook Toby's.

Toby beamed with importance. His brow knitted in a puzzled frown. "What shall I call you, Sir?"

"Why, you may call us Uncle Henry and Aunt Polly, lad." Uncle Henry's large belly shook as he chuckled.

Aunt Polly giggled behind her lace handkerchief.

Elizabetha decided she would use the word "quaint" to describe them in her journal.

The Kirstaterins were ushered into Uncle Henry and Aunt Polly's home and shown their sleeping quarters. The Hamblens spared no measure making the Kirstaterins feel at home and welcome.

Elizabetha admired the delicate white lace curtains framing the west-facing window in the bedroom she and Toby would share. Pink roses in a white vase perched atop a small writing desk matched the roses on the white of the bed comforter. Elizabetha settled her things into the chest of drawers and placed her journal and ink on the desk.

After putting Toby's things away, she settled at the desk and opened her journal to the entry she'd made that she would marry Martin. She traced his name with her finger. Think of me, Martin. Think of me.

≫ 4 ≪

Saturday afternoon a month and a half later at the Hamblen's home, Elizabetha heard a commotion in the hall outside her and Toby's bedroom.

Toby burst into the room, red-faced and panting from dashing up the stairs. "That new friend of yours is here," he said. "Anne, is here, come."

Elizabetha tousled Toby's hair. "Come on, I'll race you down," she said.

Young Toby hurried down the stairs on his spindly legs. Elizabetha was careful to stay just behind him so that he could be the winner. When they reached the bottom, Toby exclaimed, "I won, I won."

"So you did, and fairly, too," Elizabetha said.

Toby darted into the parlor to find their parents to boast of his triumph.

Elizabetha followed behind and found her mother and father chatting with her new friend, Anne Sanders, and her parents.

The mauve balloon curtains were raised at the sash windows, and the sun streaked in making elongated squares of light on the green and mauve carpet centered on the wooden floor.

Anne's father, a business partner of Uncle Henry, emulated aristocracy with his hand on the fireplace mantle and his body inclined toward his wife.

"Hello, Mr. Sanders," Elizabetha said.

"Afternoon, Elizabetha," he answered.

"Mrs. Sanders," Elizabetha said as she nodded to Anne's mother who held her long-fingered, delicate hands one on top of the other on her lap in refined repose in a straight-backed chair. Anne's family's hair was as blond and straight as Elizabetha's family's was dark and curling.

"Elizabetha." Anne's mother inclined her head toward her.

Aunt Polly came into the parlor with a tray. "It's chocolate-covered *lebkuchen*," she announced. "Because I know how you children love gingerbread, and small beer with just enough alcohol content to kill any bad things in the water. We all remember the water on those awful ships."

Uncle Henry was close on Aunt Polly's heels to assist in any way he might.

Aunt Polly wrinkled up her button nose. "Just you sit down on the Windsor, Henry, I can handle this."

Their eight-year-old redheaded twin boys exploded into the parlor. Elizabetha expected they'd been wrestling again by their flushed, freckled faces.

Elizabetha and Anne shared the sofa while Aunt Polly served the treats.

Elizabetha savored a sweet bite of the rich gingerbread. "Remember when we first met, Anne? It was just a few weeks after we'd arrived at Uncle Henry's, and you and your parents came to pay a visit. I just knew we would become best friends."

"Me too, and we're so lucky that your Uncle Henry shares the cost of a tutor with my father. Learning English with you is such fun," Anne said.

"I remember that first day. You were so shy."

"But you took me under your wing." Anne reached over and squeezed Elizabetha's hand.

"Yes. I always seem to understand others needs," Elizabetha

said. She wondered why no one ever understood hers. Why did she always have to see the other person's side of things? Sometimes she wanted to be totally selfish.

Elizabetha slipped her hand into her pocket and felt Martin's letter. Her father had allowed her to read it, and she was anxious to share it with Anne.

"Why don't you girls go outside for a walk while the sunshine lasts," her mother said as if reading Elizabetha's thoughts.

Anne and Elizabetha grabbed their woolen cloaks and dashed out into the November-chilled afternoon. They strolled along the dusty road peppered with leaves from the red and orange-leafed maple and elm.

They arrived at their favorite spot, a grassy knoll not far from Uncle Henry's house. They wrapped their cloaks around their full skirts and reposed under a large, brown oak that defiantly hung onto its russet leaves. The faint smell of rotting ferns wafted on the air. Elizabetha removed a stone from beneath her bottom and flicked it into the undergrowth. The girls squealed when three ruffed grouse flew out from the bushes.

After the last of their giggles died away, Elizabetha took Martin's letter from her pocket, unfolded it with care, and read aloud:

Twenty-five, October 1751
My dear Wilhelm,
Bear with me while I bring you up to date. After the paying passengers had debarked, we redemptioners were taken to the dock. The buyers milled around and evaluated us. I watched a slight figure of an old man in a dusty black frock coat and tricorne hat pause at each redemptioner and examine each one.

The old man held his arms behind his back at the elbows and plodded down the line till he got to me. He looked me over. I stared right back at him. He hesitated and adjusted his rimless glasses on his hooknose. He spat and wiped his chin with his sleeve and asked if I were Lutheran. I said I was, and he asked if I knew farming. I said I did, and he spat again. He glanced down the rest of the row of redemptioners.

The old man told me to follow him. We stood in the line in front of the Captain's makeshift desk of a cargo crate. After the old man talked to the Captain, he turned to me and said he was sorry my brother had died, but for two passengers I'd have to serve five years to redeem our fares. I agreed and we signed a contract to that effect that he shoved into his coat pocket. He motioned that I should follow him.

I loaded my belongings onto the old man's wagon. One of the two wagon horses at the other end turned his head and snorted at me as I jumped on. Thus, began my indenture.

The old man's farm is in Scott County, Virginia, and it took nearly a month to get here with the slowness of the wagon horses. His name is Mr. Klaus. And Mrs. Klaus is as sweet and homey as her husband is cantankerous. I think she is the shortest grown woman I've ever met, and she is a bit wide. Her kind blue eyes twinkle out from her merry face. I guess it's her humor that allows her to take in stride her ornery husband, but he is a devout Lutheran and Reformed Lutherans living nearby meet at his house every Sunday. I enjoy the company of this group. The Klauses' eldest son was taken by pneumonia, like Johanne, and the younger sons are not old enough to be of much help. The Klauses' have been good to me and treat me as a son. So I am in good hands, and you needn't worry about me.

It was most difficult to write home to my parents in Germany about Johanne's death, but at last that dreadful deed is done.

I hope this letter finds you and your family well and settled in Lebanon. Give my best to Mrs. Kirstaterin, and, of course, Elizabetha and young Toby. I look forward to your return letter.

With deepest affection,
Martin

Elizabetha folded the letter and put it back in her pocket. She sighed. "Do you think he cares for me?"

"Oh, Elizabetha, he sent his best didn't he? It must be wonderful to already have met the man you're going to marry. I wonder if I'll ever meet my someone." Anne lay back in the grass. Elizabetha stretched out as well and gazed at the cirrus clouds pointing their lacy fingers in all directions. "At least he remembered my name. I must make plans of how to get him to notice me when he returns. I'll have five years to perfect my strategy. I'll be sixteen by then and full-grown. I hope you will find your husband, too. I'll find one for you, if need be."

⇒ 5 ⇐

1756 Five Years Later

Anne Sanders walked into her father and Elizabetha's uncle's silver shop to bring her father's dinner that he'd forgotten. She'd packed extra for herself so they could eat together. Her straight blonde hair was piled up and tucked under her braided straw hat. She'd sewn the pale blue ribbons on to match the dress that her father had ordered made for her. It was the color of her eyes, he'd said.

John Sanders sat behind the desk in the small office to the left of the entrance. Anne waved in at him but stopped a moment to say hello to Elizabetha's father in his shoemaking shop across from her father's office.

Mr. Kirstaterin was engrossed in welting a work boot. A three-inch globe filled with water stood on the table between him and the window to magnify the light for his work.

Anne poked her head into the doorway and said, "Don't stop what you're doing, I just wanted to say hello."

Wilhelm Kirstaterin glanced up from his project. "Hello, Anne, I'm glad you stopped. It's good to see you. Is Elizabetha with you?"

"I've come alone to join father for dinner. He forgot to bring his."

"Have you met the silversmith journeyman, yet?"

"No, I haven't. I won't take any more of your time, I know you're busy." She turned from the door to go to her father's office and collided with a young man she hadn't seen before, knocking them both off balance.

The young man grabbed her shoulders to steady her. His sandy hair was wavy and a tress had fallen across his forehead. His fiery, dark sable eyes were intriguing. "Excuse me, are you all right?" he said.

"It's my fault, really. I wasn't looking—."

"No, the fault is mine," he broke in. "I'm Joseph Blakemore, journeyman. Please accept my apologies."

"I'm Anne Sanders. I've come to have dinner with father." She nodded toward her father's office. "As for the apology, I insist we at least share responsibility." Usually reticent, she didn't know where her nerve came from.

He grinned displaying his straight white teeth. "If you insist. It's a pleasure to meet you, Miss Sanders," he said with a slight nod of his head. "I'm afraid Mr. Hamblen is waiting for me to fetch his acid, so I must excuse myself. Perhaps I'll see you again."

"Perhaps." She knew she would make a point to have dinner with her father more often.

Joseph Blakemore turned to go about his duties and Anne's gaze followed his tall muscular build as she sauntered toward her father's office.

All through dinner, Anne caught glimpses of Joseph Blakemore working with Mr. Hamblen and darting here and there for supplies. Occasionally he caught her eye and smiled. Her heart raced each time.

After six weeks of visiting the shop, Anne was delighted one Sunday when Joseph asked her father after church if he could call on Anne at home.

Later that afternoon, Joseph and Anne conversed with her parents in their parlor.

"So tell me about your family, Joseph. We don't have much

time to chat at the shop," her father offered.

"My father, Edward Blakemore, came from Wales and settled in Virginia. He died when I was fourteen and his will appointed a Mr. Michael Dillon to act as my guardian. He was to teach me reading, writing, and the trade of tailor." Joseph paused and glanced at each attentive face. "I was inept with the needle, and my older brother, named Edward for our father, became my guardian and taught me the trade of silversmith." What he didn't say was Mr. Dillon had beaten Joseph's knuckles raw with a willow switch for his ineptness. Joseph apprenticed for only seven months when one day, anger overwhelming him, he had seized the switch from Mr. Dillon and broke it in two. Joseph had vowed to never fail again. Never would he be intimidated by another man. "When I attained twenty-one years, three years ago, I inherited the land and slaves my father left in his will. My mother has remarried."

Anne admired Joseph's confidence as he'd leaned forward as he spoke, his fiery, dark eyes intent.

"You are a converted Lutheran?" her father asked. "I hadn't seen you at St. Paul's until a few Sundays ago."

Joseph straightened. The blush started at his neck and crept up to his cheeks as he answered, "Yes, er, when I found out Anne, and her family, was Lutheran, I decided to join. It's not so different from the Anglican religion."

"John Sanders, I'm afraid you're embarrassing our guest," Anne's mother admonished.

Her father's brow knitted. "My apologies, Joseph. I didn't mean to make you uncomfortable. You're a fine young man and have my permission to call on Anne at any, well, reasonable time."

Welsh, Anne thought. That explains the fire in his eyes. Anne's mind kept repeating Joseph's words "... when I found out Anne ... was Lutheran, I decided to join .... " Perhaps she had met the man she would marry like her dynamic friend Elizabetha had. Dare she hope?

* * *

On a Saturday several months later, Joseph called on Anne and asked her to accompany him into town on some errands he must complete. Anne was exhilarated to be by the side of the handsome Joseph as they sauntered into Lebanon.

The summer breeze bore the sweet aroma of wild flowers and grass. Birds chirped gaily from the trees along the lane as if to share with the world the very happiness beating in Anne's heart. Joseph took her hand as they strolled, and Anne could not imagine any more contentment than this moment.

Joseph carried a sack of silver items he had polished at home and was to deliver to several town businesses. The silver clinked together in a tinkling tune of merriment against Joseph's thigh as he walked.

The first delivery was a candelabrum to a dry goods store for window display. Anne waited outside and admired the fabrics draped in the front window of the shop. Green silk brocade held center stage with an ecru crepe to its right and a peach silk damask to its left. Joseph placed the candelabrum in the center of the brocade. It made an elegant display. The slight, dapperly dressed owner clapped his small hands together in delight.

Moments later, Joseph exited the shop and admired the effect of the candelabrum against the fabrics. He turned to Anne. "I just have one more stop at the tavern to deliver tankards, and then we'll be free to enjoy the day."

Anne again waited outside while Joseph made his delivery. She stood to the side of the entrance and glanced up the street thinking about Joseph.

A large beer-smelly man lurched into her as he stumbled out of the tavern. His bleary leer made her uncomfortable. His frock coat and waistcoat were unbuttoned and the front of his shirt was saturated in stale beer. His scraggly-whiskered chin held telltale signs of foam.

"'Lo there, pretty lady," he slurred. His rank breath made Anne turn her face away.

"Wha's matter? You too good to speak?" He grabbed her shoulders.

She backed against the building, her heart beating in her throat.

Joseph erupted from the door and spun the drunkard around. Joseph's eyes were coal black and deadly. He shoved the sot against the wall beside Anne.

Anne leapt away into the street. She had never seen such fiery hatred in anyone's expression to match the one Joseph wore.

The drunk swung at Joseph's head, missing it completely.

"Don't ever lay a hand on my lady," Joseph snarled through his teeth as he struck the lout square in the nose. He kept hitting the man over and over even as his victim slithered down the wall.

Anne screamed, "Joseph."

Joseph's arm was drawn back for another strike and poised there in suspension as her scream seemed to seep into his conscience mind. He sprang erect and turned toward Anne. A wild animal glared out from his eyes. Joseph rubbed them with his fingers, and the animal disappeared.

Anne couldn't speak. She trembled fitfully and couldn't stop it.

Joseph bounded to her side and encircled her with his arms until she stopped shaking. "I'd better get you home."

Anne nodded her head as he took her elbow and led her away.

They were half the way home when he stopped, turned, and placed his hands on her shoulders. "Anne, I'm so sorry you were frightened. I just can't bear your being exposed to such ugliness as that drunk." He took her in his arms. "I want to protect you always. I love you."

He loved her. He wanted to protect her. She didn't understand what had come over him in town—maybe it was his Welsh heritage—but it had disappeared quickly. He loved her. That was all she needed to know.

* * *

The following week, Elizabetha twirled Anne around her family's parlor, their full skirts almost upsetting her mother's open three-shelved cupboard display of porcelain Chinese vases.

"Anne, I'm delighted for you," Elizabetha said. "How did he ask you to marry him? Did he ask on bended knee?"

"It was more of a statement than a proposal. He simply said, 'Marry me, Anne'. Of course, I said yes. When Joseph had asked to speak to my father earlier, I had hoped marriage was the purpose. I'm so happy. We'll be married when I turn eighteen next year." Anne clutched Elizabetha's shoulders and hugged her again.

They plopped down on the sofa holding hands and grinning. "Just think, Anne, someday we'll both be married. Won't it be fun to watch our children play together while we chat over tea?" Elizabetha hunched her shoulders together. "In the evening after supper, one of us and her husband will join at the other's home to play whist and afterward, will carry their sleepy children back home to their beds," Elizabetha said gazing off into the future.

"Yes, and on Sundays we'll all go in our carriages together to St. Paul's church. Later, we'll go on a lovely picnic," Anne added.

"Oh, Anne, it will be so wonderful." Elizabetha clapped her hands. She thought of Martin. She grew quiet and gazed out the window in a dreamy trance. Soon his indenture would be over and he'd be coming to visit. Would he notice her? Had he found someone before she had a chance? Dreaminess changed to worry.

"Elizabetha, what's wrong?" Anne asked.

"Oh, Anne, Martin only thinks of me as a child. He's probably already found someone. I'll be an old maid."

Usually Elizabetha was the stronger of the two, but this time Anne put her arms around her friend. Kindness always made Elizabetha cry. She could stand up to anything but that. She buried her face in Anne's slim shoulder and sobbed.

⇒ 6 ⇐

The same month of Anne's engagement, Martin's ears perked up at the Sunday meeting of the Reformed Lutherans in the Klaus home when he heard Thomas Bryant tell of the seventy-five Lutheran families that had settled in Mount Airy, Virginia. Martin had heard of this before, but Thomas had been there.

Thomas had become Martin's best friend over the past five years. He was a jovial sort who always had a kind word and a helping hand. He was a year younger than Martin. It seemed to Martin that Thomas looked to him for approval as if he were an older brother. Thomas had red hair and a fair, freckled complexion that always took on the hue of his hair when he was excited, like now.

"I had been hired to help get a dozen milk cows back that a man by the name of Adam Cook had come to buy for the Mount Airy settlement. It's tucked in a fertile valley on the upper reaches of Reed and Cripple Creek surrounded by the Blue Ridge Mountains. The area is a sea of rolling hills and is heavily forested with oak, maple, basswood, and pine." His eyes widened. "I saw white-tailed deer, red and gray fox, wild turkey, quail, ruffed grouse all for the taking and not many people to do the taking," Thomas said, his face rosy with excitement.

"And what of the people? Are they all German Reformed Lutheran?" Martin asked.

"Yes, so I'm told. I met many of them. Most of them had come down from Pennsylvania. They are mainly farmers. There is good limestone soil in Mount Airy Adam told me. They took right to me. I helped a group of them erect a barn."

"It sounds like just the kind of place where I'd like to settle. One day I'll join them," Martin said.

A pounding knock reverberated through the door. Mr. Klaus opened it and John Dustin, a burly trapper from the Lutheran meeting group, burst inside. He was in his thirties with soot black eyes and dusky skin. He yanked off his flop hat and drew a deep breath before speaking. "I've just come from the Bush's' place. Indians killed Mr. Bush and his wife, scalped them both. Their four children are nowhere to be found. It looks like they were taken captive. The trail is not too cold, but I'll need help when I track down those blasted Indians. Who will come?"

Martin and Thomas both stood at once. Mr. Klaus grabbed three rifles and handed one each to Martin and Thomas, keeping the third for himself.

"No, Mr. Klaus, you'd best stay and protect your own," John Dustin said. "Martin, Thomas, and I will go. The Indians have a good start. It will be a hard trek."

Mr. Klaus glanced at his wife who had entered at the commotion. He hesitated an instant, but his wife's distraught face seemed to decide him. He put his rifle back on the rack. "Before you go, let us pray for God's guidance," he said.

Martin was the first to kneel. The others joined.

"God, we beseech you to look after those lost children and grant swiftness and courage to these three men in the task before them."

"Amen," they all said in unison.

Martin and Thomas donned their hats, grabbed their coats, and pulled them on over their waistcoats. The three men nodded eager agreement and rushed out of the house running toward the Bush's' homestead and the path of the dastardly Indians' retreat.

On the trail, Martin and the others settled into the familiar straight-legged walk with legs swinging from the hips and bodies leaning forward as they fell into each next step. The soft rustling of the fallen pine needles and maple and oak leaves beneath their feet harmonized with the rhythmical sounds of their breathing.

John Dustin stopped from time to time to study the path for signs of the Indians' passage.

From the setting of the sun, Martin guessed they had walked about three hours. "I keep thinking about those four children," he said. "The Bush's son was near grown, wasn't he? And those three young girls, if those dirty Indians have harmed them—."

"I know, Martin, I know," Thomas said.

John halted. "Quiet, I think I heard crying."

Martin and the others listened. Sure enough Martin heard a young girl sobbing. He noticed movement through a stand of beech up ahead on the right. He pointed it out to the others. It was an Indian. Martin, John, and Thomas edged closer and readied their rifles. A barred owl hooted his harbinger of death in the distance.

Three Indians stood together in a clearing, and a fourth squatted at the startings of a campfire. The four children were huddled together on the ground several yards away. The other ends of the long ropes around their waists were tied together around a beech tree.

The oldest girl looked about ten. She had golden hair and her blue dress was torn at the shoulder. Her younger sisters of perhaps eight and six were towheads. The youngest nursed a scraped knee. The oldest tried to calm the sobbing of her sisters. The blond, teenaged boy glared menacingly at the Indians talking and laughing together.

The Indians wore deerskin leggings, breechclouts, and moccasins. The bronzed skin of their upper bodies glistened in the last glow of sunlight. The stout Indian stood between one tall and one shorter companion. The youngest brave tended to the fire. Between his palms, he twirled a stick set in the hole of a small wood piece to coax a spark into the dry leaves.

"We'll run in, each shooting at one Indian, and surprise them. I'll take the left, Martin the middle, and Thomas the right," John whispered. "Ready, go."

With readied rifles, the three men ran. Martin was in the lead. He fired at the Indian in the middle who went down in a heap. The two Indians on either side went down as Martin headed for the fourth. The young brave pulled out his knife.

Martin felt as if he and the Indian were in a slow motion dance together under water. Martin didn't feel his feet touch the ground. His legs thrashed through the sea-like air toward the Indian. The Indian floated up to a standing position. The scalps hanging from the Indian's deerskin breechclout undulated. The steel-like glare of the Indian's eyes vied with the glint of his knife.

There was no time to reload. Martin whacked the butt of his rifle into the Indian's head, sending him sprawling. Martin jumped on him. He grabbed the Indian's knife. He drew it hard across the Indian's throat. The red man's eyes were wide with disbelief. A thin crimson line of blood formed across his throat. The blood soon pooled around his head. A non-seeing stare revealed that life had oozed from his body.

It had all happened so quickly. Martin had never killed anyone with a knife. In fact, before shooting the first Indian, he'd never killed anyone with anything. The shock of seeing the blood form across the Indian's throat had made it all too real. It had been a necessity, Martin told himself. He stood and threw the Indian's knife to the ground. His hands shook. He took a deep breath and turned.

Thomas stared down at the dead Indian and then up at Martin with glassy eyes, his mouth agape. He was panting. "You cut his throat." He studied Martin's face. "Were you scared?" Thomas's body trembled. He shook so hard he dropped his rifle. "*I* sure was," Thomas said and sank to the ground.

John kneeled beside him and put his hand on Thomas's shoulder. "Of course he was scared, Thomas. So was I. Everyone is scared in combat."

"But you're—you're not shaking like me."

"Breathe in and out slowly. It will help."

Thomas inhaled deeply and slowly exhaled.

Behind Thomas, Martin did the same.

"It's always best to get the fighting over quickly and then put it behind you, quicker," John said. He rose and strode to the children.

John cut the ropes from the children. The boy shook Martin's hand as Martin approached the group with Thomas at his heels. Tears escaped down the boy's cheeks which he whisked away with the back of his hand before thanking the other two men. The girls hugged each other, their brother, and the men.

Martin sat the girls down on a log and kneeled before them on one knee with his other leg bent and rested his arms across it. "I don't know how to ask this, but did those Indians hurt you?"

The sisters glanced back and forth at each other and at Martin. Their brother stood at the end of the log.

"One hit me," the youngest said. "'Cause I cried. I fell down and hurt my knee." She lifted her hem and stuck her leg toward Martin to show him the damage.

"That's too bad." He kissed his fingertips and touched them to her knee. "Here's a kiss to make it better, but that wasn't exactly what I meant."

"They made us run fast and yanked on the ropes," the eight-year-old said.

"Oh dear, but still—."

The lad of fifteen sauntered to Martin. "They didn't hurt them the way you mean, Sir, just scared them and roughed us all up, nothing else."

"That's a relief." Martin rose.

"We saw our parents lying on the ground. Are they dead?" the ten-year-old asked.

Martin settled back down to his knee. "I'm afraid so, honey."

The boy hit his fist hard into his open hand. "I knew it. I'm glad you killed those damn Indians."

His sisters held each other and sobbed. The boy went to them and put his arms around them. "I'll look after you now," he told them.

Martin rose and helped John and Thomas drag the bodies of the Indians into the woods. When they returned, they put the Indians' campfire to good use. They fed and comforted the youngsters as best they could.

The next morning, the men took the children to stay with the Johnson's' who lived near the Bush homestead. Later that day, they buried the parents in the Bush family cemetery.

That night as Martin lay in bed, the scene at the campsite replayed itself in his mind. Martin got up and paced. He reached for his Bible on the chest of drawers and opened it in search of consolation. He turned to *Mark* 11:23: "For verily I say unto you, that whosoever shall say unto this mountain, Be thou removed, and be thou cast into the sea; and shall not doubt in his heart, but shall believe that those things which he saith shall come to pass; he shall have whatsoever he saith." Martin thanked God for the strength He had given him.

⇛ 7 ⇚

In June, Martin bought a road horse with the freedom dues Mr. Klaus had paid him. Mr. Klaus had embraced him as did Mrs. Klaus. She made such a fuss over his leaving that Martin promised to come back and visit after he returned from Mount Airy where he planned to buy his land with the rest of his money.

Thomas accompanied Martin on the two-day journey to Mount Airy, and they spent several days scouting around for the perfect two hundred acres Martin could afford.

Martin found his land near Reed Creek. Willow, oak, beech, maple, and basswood lined the east bank of the creek. An open area sprawled behind the forest.

Martin bent down and clumped a handful of the fertile soil. He inhaled its earthy scent. He stood and surveyed the florid array of mountain laurel, rhododendron, and dogwood. A pair of gray squirrels scampered after one another up the trunk of an oak and ruffled through its leaves. "This is it. A bit of heaven on earth," he said. He knelt on the moist, rich earth and thanked God for His bounty.

Martin and Thomas paced off two hundred acres, piling stone markers at the corners. They stopped in at Adam Cook's homestead, the man Thomas had met. Adam's homestead was next to the land Martin coveted. Martin would ask if the land was already claimed.

Adam Cook welcomed Martin and Thomas and invited them into his home. He had a slight limp they were to learn he'd acquired in a losing battle with an enraged bull during his youth. He was about thirty with dark hair and eyes. He was soft spoken and made Martin feel as if he'd known Adam for years. Adam's wife, Sally, was pretty with dimples and curly blonde hair, but properly shy and reserved.

After chatting awhile, Adam Cook accompanied Martin and Thomas to the site Martin had selected. He assured Martin the land was available. "We're always glad to see new German Lutherans move to our settlement. It is our hope that one day we'll be able to attend our services in a real church. Right now, that forest along Reed Creek is our meeting place," Adam said.

"Well, I won't be moving in right away. I must first go back to Pennsylvania to visit some special friends I met on the ship to America, but when I do come here, I will one day build that church," Martin avowed.

After registering and paying for Martin's land at the Fincastle County office, the three returned to the Cook home. Adam and Sally insisted Martin and Thomas have supper and stay the night.

The ride back to Scott County was a quiet one Martin realized when Thomas broke into his thoughts of the church he would build.

"Do you have a girl in Pennsylvania?" Thomas asked, his red hair flaming in the bright sunlight.

"No, actually I was thinking about that church." Martin's thoughts turned to Elizabetha. She'd be sixteen by now.

"Well, you have your freedom, your land, and a church to build to boot," Thomas said.

And I'll be needing a wife Martin thought. He wondered if the pretty Elizabetha was awash in beaus as he'd predicted. "Thomas, I've been thinking, I've decided to go on to Lebanon. Will you tell the Klauses that I'll be gone a few months?"

"Sure, I will. Good luck to you, Martin. I'll see you when you get back."

Martin shook Thomas's hand and rode off toward Lebanon wondering if Elizabetha had learned more ladylike, God-fearing manners.

* * *

Two weeks later, Martin stopped at a tavern on the way to Pennsylvania and received directions to Lebanon.

He arrived at dusk the following night and searched the shops, remembering that Wilhelm's cousin was a silversmith. He grinned as he noticed a shop with a shingle hanging beneath Henry Hamblen, Silversmith that read Wilhelm Kirstaterin, Shoemaker. The shop was whitewashed with blue trim. Black shades covered the door and left window. The right window was uncovered and Martin could see a candle on the worktable inside.

Martin poked his head around the door. Wilhelm Kirstaterin was cleaning up the day's work. His tall frame looked even leaner than Martin remembered. A few strands of gray were mixed into his dark hair at the temples and he now wore eyeglasses, but otherwise, he appeared the same as Martin remembered. "Hello, Wilhelm," Martin said.

Wilhelm gaped at Martin for a moment. Recognition descended on him. "Martin, is that you? Let me look at you. My word, you've grown into a fine young man. Why, you're all filled out. How are you, lad?"

"Fine, Wilhelm, it's good to see you again."

Wilhelm grabbed Martin's shoulders with both hands and shook him, or tried to; Martin was well muscled and several pounds heavier than Wilhelm and as tall.

"You've come at a fine time. We're having a party at the Sander's home. Elizabetha's friend, Anne Sanders, is bringing her fiancé for everyone to meet. They're having a bit of a wing-ding with friends and neighbors, even a fiddler."

"I'm really dusty from the road; perhaps I'll take a room at the tavern."

"Nonsense, you can freshen up at our home, it's just on the way, and I'm sure I have something you can borrow to wear. The family will be so pleased to see you."

Martin led his horse as they strolled along the main street, passing a variety of shops lined on either side. Two blocks past the last of the shops, they turned down a lane with half a dozen homes.

Wilhelm stopped in front of a white wood-frame house of two stories. "We're here," he said. "Come in."

Martin tied his horse to the rail fence in front. They walked the flower-lined path to the house and entered. Wilhelm left Martin in the guest room and returned with a set of clothes for Martin. "While you change, I'll put your horse in the barn. It isn't far to the Sanders' home. We can walk."

The shirt Wilhelm provided fit well enough, and the waistcoat, unbuttoned, would do. Martin felt poured into the breeches and hoped he wouldn't have to bend over for anything.

It was a short walk as Wilhelm had said. They entered the Sanders' home into a hall with stairs to the upper floor at the far end, a large parlor on the right, and a large hall on the left where a fiddler played and guests danced. Martin was anxious to see if Elizabetha was still as high-spirited.

⟫ 8 ⟪

At the dance, Joseph Blakemore willed himself not to ogle Elizabetha. He cursed himself again for his attraction to her. After all, this was Anne's and his engagement party, delicate and refined Anne, but he couldn't help watching Elizabetha gliding around the dance floor with a young man. Maybe it was the wide set of her eyes that made him feel she could see right down to his soul. Or maybe it was the dark ring that encircled her irises that made her gaze so hypnotizing.

He had never met a woman like her. His own mother had been cold and withdrawn, especially after the death of his father, and sweet, fragile Anne relied on him, but Elizabetha was so full of life, and she held opinions on everything—opinions like his own, as if their souls were matched. They'd had some wonderful discussions since he'd met her.

But, he could never hurt Anne. He loved her. He had sworn himself to protect her and he would, but Anne didn't care for serious discussion. It was just that Elizabetha mesmerized him with her curiosity and her philosophy so similar to his. He would not allow himself to think what if he had met her first? He would have one dance with her and that would be that.

The dance ended and the young man escorted Elizabetha off the floor. Tom Clingman was making his way over to her, but Joseph reached her first.

Elizabetha accepted Joseph's request to dance. She'd liked him immediately when she'd met him several months ago. Besides her father, he was the only man she knew that didn't mind when she expressed her opinions. Joseph's soul was a kindred spirit it seemed she'd known forever. In their discussions that she so enjoyed, he seemed to know what she was going to say before she said it.

His expression now seemed sultry with his sensuous mouth drawn up in a one-sided half-smile. It made her uneasy. She didn't know why. Anne had said that Joseph told her he enjoyed Elizabetha's vivaciousness. Perhaps he was just amused by her.

She saw her father enter the hall. A handsome stranger was behind her father. My God. It was Martin. She drew herself closer to Joseph, gave her head a flirtatious toss, and laughed with abandon at his comment on the fiddler.

With her peripheral vision, she noticed one of Anne's eyebrows go up. She would have to explain to Anne later. Right now, she wanted Martin to notice her.

Joseph's half-smile widened to a full grin and he said, "You look beautiful tonight, Elizabetha." His hand tightened around her waist. His gaze riveted on her. She glanced over to see if Martin was watching. He was.

The music ended and Joseph bowed and kissed her hand before leading her off the floor.

Anne motioned him over.

Elizabetha turned her attention to her father and Martin's approach. The manliness of Martin stole her breath, and her heart beat faster. He's actually here she thought. She turned away a moment to gather her composure. She heard footfalls behind her, affixed what she hoped was a beguiling smile on her lips, turned, and offered her hand. "Why, Martin, is it truly you after all these years? Whenever did you arrive?"

Martin held her fingers, bowed, and brushed his lips over the back of her hand, sending an electrical shock through her being.

She slowly fanned and batted her eyes, tricks she never imagined she'd ply. How easy it came. She'd always wanted to be appreciated for brains not beauty, but not tonight.

"Elizabetha, how good to see you." Martin said.

He was more handsome than she remembered. She couldn't help noticing the well-defined muscles of his calves and thighs in his snug breeches. His dark hair was tied behind, and a curling shock crossed his forehead. His face no longer a boy's face, but a man's chiseled features. His gaze never left her.

"What a lovely young woman you've become." His blue eyes glinted like steel. A smile played around the corners of his mouth.

Perhaps he was mocking her. "You've grown some yourself. How grand to see you," she said.

"May I have the next dance? Or is there a line ahead of me?"

He *was* mocking her. Damn him.

Elizabetha's mother and Toby joined the group. "Martin, It's wonderful to have you back with us," her mother said.

"It's good to see you again, Mrs. Kirstaterin." He bowed and kissed her hand.

She smiled and smoothed her still dark hair.

Toby reached his hand out to shake Martin's. "I remember you from the ship I think, but mostly from your letters Papa reads to us. Nice to see you, Sir."

"Toby, what a fine young man you've become. What are you now, eight, nine?"

"Nine, Sir." Toby held himself up to his full height nearly to Martin's shoulder.

"Good man," Martin said. "And call me Martin, please."

"Yes, Sir, I mean, Martin."

The brash Tom Clingman strode over to Elizabetha and asked her to dance. He extended his hand to her as if confident she would be dying to dance with him. She thought, but Martin asked first, then changed her mind and accepted Tom's hand. She'd show Martin. How dare he mock her?

Tom twirled her around the floor. Martin stared after them.

When the dance ended, Tom had barely led her off the floor when shy and skinny Jimmy Shackly asked for a dance. She immediately accepted. She felt beautiful and flirtatious under Martin's scrutiny.

Martin was struck by the beauty Elizabetha had grown into. He couldn't keep his gaze off her as she gracefully glided around the dance floor. He was having a hard time paying attention to what was said to him. He nodded absent-mindedly to Mrs. Kirstaterin's comment on the party and studied Elizabetha. She seemed to be deliberately taunting him with her eyes. She snuggled closer to her partner. Martin's hand inadvertently clenched. His blood seemed too warm for his body. He had to get outside.

Elizabetha observed the scowl come over Martin's face. He said something to her father, bowed to her mother, and went out the door. Perhaps she'd gone too far. What if he was leaving? As soon as the dance ended, she plied her fan and excused herself for a breath of fresh air. Jimmy Shackly nodded his uncertain acquiescence.

Outside, others from the party gathered in small groups of three or four people. Elizabetha scanned the guests and spied Martin alone at the side of the yard leaning against an oak, his foot braced on its trunk. She was relieved he hadn't left. She strode over to him.

His brow crinkled and his gaze was stern as she approached. "You certainly seemed to be enjoying yourself in there. Which one is your special beau?" Martin asked.

"Why, Martin, I can't believe my behavior could bother you. I'm just a child, right?"

"You seem to have grown up, at least outwardly. You didn't answer my question."

"What would you care if I had a beau? You've always been so mean to me." Elizabetha stomped her foot at him.

"I'm sorry if you think I've been mean. I didn't intend that. I asked if you had a beau because, if you don't, I'd like to become better acquainted, if I may." His brow smoothed and his gaze softened.

"Oh, Martin, of course you may." Elizabetha blushed at her forwardness. "How long can you stay?" she asked.

His foot dropped from the trunk. He grinned. "No longer than six weeks, I've just come from buying some land in Mount Airy. I promised to return to the Klaus farm afterward. My friend Thomas told them I'd be delayed a few months because I was coming here."

"Martin, it truly is good to see you," Elizabetha said.

"We'd better go back inside before your parents get worried, and I really would like that dance."

"You shall have all the dances. I promise."

Martin took her hand and led her to the house. He was back, and he had remembered her. She had six weeks. Life was good.

➤ 9 ◄

The first week of Martin's stay at the Kirstaterins, he told them all about his term of indenture and the friends he had made, especially Thomas. He told them of his property in Mount Airy and the poor children whose parents had been killed by Indians. This last part pleasing Toby the most as Toby insisted Martin go into detail about the rescue. Martin skimmed over the killing of the Indians as best he could.

All through the telling, Elizabetha kept visualizing the brave and handsome Martin defending those poor children against the savage Indians. From time to time, she glanced at his tanned face and muscular build and imagined him in shining armor, his strong arms lifting her up to his white steed and riding off with her. She would turn her face to his, and he would plant an ardent kiss upon her lips as the horse charged forward.

After the first few days of Martin's storytelling, the family and Martin played whist and dominoes together in the evenings, and though the game playing was pleasurable enough, Elizabetha began to wonder if she and Martin would ever have time alone.

By the third week, Elizabetha and Martin were allowed to

have the parlor to themselves after Toby went to bed. Her parents busied themselves with tasks in the hall or upstairs.

This evening, Elizabetha and Martin played dominoes. As Elizabetha finished making her move, Martin took her hand and held it, gazing at her. He kissed her hand then released it.

Elizabetha held her breath the while; her gaze fixed on the candlelight flickering across Martin's chiseled features and highlighting his dark brown hair. How long she'd waited for this moment. How often she'd lain in bed dreaming of the day he'd show her some sign of affection, and now, at last, that day had come. She placed the kissed hand in her lap and covered it with her other hand, fearing the touch of his kiss there would evaporate from her skin.

Martin's gaze locked with hers, and they remained in silent enrapture.

She heard her father come down the stairs and knew he was snuffing out the candles in the hall. She still could not bring herself to break her gaze away from Martin's.

Martin broke the spell by standing as her father came into the parlor.

Her father said, "Mornings come early, Elizabetha, time you got your rest."

It took a moment before her father's words pierced through the mist fogging her brain. Elizabetha excused herself and drifted up the stairs.

As she lay in bed savoring the feel of Martin's kiss imprinted on her hand, she kissed the spot and held the hand close to her heart. She drifted off, dreaming of Martin.

In the parlor, Martin paced the length of carpeting while Wilhelm studied the dominoes and lowered himself onto the brocade sofa. Martin paced back and stopped, placing his hand on the back of the chair Elizabetha had just occupied. He must speak his mind to Wilhelm, now. "Sir," he began.

Wilhelm's eyebrows arched.

Martin stopped, surprised at his own formality. "Wilhelm," he began again. "I would like, er, to ask your permission to, er." Why were his thoughts jumping about so?

"Yes, lad, what is it? Go on," Wilhelm said.

Elizabetha's azure eyes swam before Martin's vision. He must get hold of himself. He rapped his open hand on the chair back to clear his mind. "I wish to court Elizabetha."

Martin suspected a flicker of a smile playing at the corners of Wilhelm's mouth.

"Of course, but, Martin," Wilhelm said. "I thought that you already were." Now the smile was evident.

"Well—I hadn't officially asked permission," Martin stammered.

"Well, now you officially have it." Wilhelm grinned as he rose, clasped Martin on the shoulder, and shook his hand.

* * *

The next evening after supper, Martin asked Elizabetha to go for a walk.

Outside, on their way up the lane, Martin said, "Last night I asked your father for permission to court you and he granted it. Do you grant it, Elizabetha?"

Her heartbeat quickened. "Oh, yes, Martin, yes. I was beginning to fear you only wanted to be friends, until last night." She stroked the back of the hand he'd kissed.

He reached for the hand and held it as they strolled.

After a while, Elizabetha stopped, spread her skirts upon the ground as she sat, and glanced up for Martin to join her. He sank to the ground beside her. For several minutes they said nothing as they admired the soft reds and oranges of the sunset spreading across the evening sky.

"It's a beautiful sunset," Elizabetha said at last.

"Almost as beautiful as the ones in Mount Airy, you should see it—and smell it there—the aroma of mountain laurel, rhododendron, and dogwood all around, the lush green forest by Reed Creek, the tilled farms with their earthy scent of rich loam—I can't wait to show it to you," Martin said.

"Hmm," Elizabetha uttered. She sat up straight. "Speaking of not being able to wait, I've just found out Anne and Joseph have set the date for their wedding. It is to be next month. Isn't that wonderful?"

"That's great news. I'm sure they'll be very happy together. Joseph and I hit it off from the first, and Anne is very sweet." He gazed at Elizabetha. "Your eyes remind me of the sunsets in Mount Airy: clear sky-blue background dappled with the red and gold reflections of the sunset."

For an instant, Elizabetha's mind was torn between Anne's wedding and Martin's compliment. The compliment won.

The sun was about to descend below the horizon. Martin rose, helped Elizabetha to her feet, and kissed her as she stood—a long, lingering, sweet kiss. Elizabetha closed her eyes and leaned into him, wanting more. Fire was spreading through her whole body from where his hands touched her shoulders.

Martin chastised himself for the burning in his loins. A God-fearing gentleman did not take advantage of a young lady. He gently pushed her back and took her hand. "There'll be time enough for kissing when we're married."

That night in bed, Elizabetha dreamed her pillow was Martin and awoke to find it crumpled under her, her face buried in it. The rest of her sleep was fitful.

⇒ 10 ⇐

Elizabetha couldn't believe six weeks could fly by so fast. She and Martin had spent many hours together getting to know one another. She had remained on her best behavior. Her parents seemed pleased with her and Martin's new relationship. Martin was to leave this morning.

Elizabetha put on her favorite pink cotton dress. She leaned over before the mirror and pinched her cheeks before going downstairs.

She was too apprehensive to taste the breakfast of sausage, eggs, and baking powder biscuits. She washed the last of it down with a gulp of buttermilk and hoped for a moment alone with Martin before he left.

Martin stood and said to her parents, "It's time. I must be on my way. Thank you for your hospitality."

They all rose and followed Martin out to the yard and his waiting horse. After saying their goodbyes, Elizabetha's mother, father, and brother, Toby, discreetly went inside.

Martin kissed Elizabetha's hand. She held his in both of hers.

Martin gazed at her a full minute before speaking. "I'll come back for you, Elizabetha. I promise. I'll write when I can come."

"I'll be waiting. I promise."

Martin mounted his horse and peered down at her. Elizabetha placed her hand on his calf and gazed up at him. He looked so dashing on his horse.

He reached his hand down and smoothed her hair, caressed her face, and held her chin.

Elizabetha reached for Martin's hand, kissed it, and held it against her cheek. How could she let him go now that she had his love? She knew she must. It would just be a short while. She'd count the days till his return. At length, she disengaged his hand with one last kiss. "Write soon," she said.

"I will." Martin rode off quickly as if not to have a chance to change his mind.

* * *

Martin smiled as he approached the Klaus farm. Soon he could retrieve his belongings and return to Elizabetha. He inhaled the summer air and imagined he smelled the warm sweet lavender scent of her deep chestnut hair. She was still spirited but such a lovely creature. She would become content and subdued once he made her his wife.

His attention focused on a group of men gathered in front of the house. I wonder what's going on? They look agitated. Martin urged his horse to a gallop.

As Martin alighted from his horse, Thomas approached him. Trapper John Dustin hailed Martin and turned to the others, "Here's another brave lad experienced in killing Indians to join us."

"What's going on?" Martin asked.

"It's the Indians and French. War's been declared. Colonel Washington's been appointed Commander in Chief of the Virginia militia to defend the Ohio Valley," John Dustin said. "We're joining the fight in two days time. Are you with us?"

Before Martin could answer, the usually silent Nathaniel Burke added, "The French are trying to keep fur traders and settlers out of the interior. The Shawnee are allied with them. The

British, with the Cherokee's help, are trying to get the French out of the valley." Nathaniel gulped. "There have been attacks all over. The Scranton and the Morgan places have been raided. They're all dead." Nathaniel took a long breath after his tirade.

"Are you with us, Martin?" Thomas asked.

His new country needed him. He chased the scent of lavender from his mind. "Yes, I'm free of indenture, I've got my land set, and my affairs are in order." He didn't say—except for Elizabetha. I'm sure she'll understand. I'll write her at once.

* * *

At noon several weeks later, Elizabetha met her father at the door when he came home for dinner. She had to know if he brought mail. His eyes twinkled. Elizabetha knew Martin's letter had arrived at last. "Oh, Papa, don't tease. It's come, hasn't it?"

"Well, let's see," he said as he reached into his coat pocket and held a letter toward the light from the window as if to see it better. "Why, yes, I believe this does have your name on it."

Elizabetha squealed, grabbed the letter, and tore it open.

Her mother poked her head around the hallway wall and said, "Elizabetha, can you help me and hold Toby while I get a sliver out of his knee?"

Elizabetha hesitated. Martin's letter had arrived. She was anxious to read when he would be returning. Reluctantly she tucked the letter into her pocket. "Of course."

In the kitchen, Toby writhed under Elizabetha's hands as their mother dug at the sliver site with a paring knife.

"Ouch, ouch," Toby wailed and jerked his knee free.

Elizabetha grabbed her brother's leg and forced him to be still.

"Got it," their mother exulted.

Elizabetha left her mother soothing Toby's wounded pride and read the letter to herself as she joined her father in the dining area. She gasped as she read:

So, I know you will understand that I must join in the fight to stop the French and Indians from attacking the British and colonists in their efforts to keep us out of the interior. It won't take more than a few months ....

Elizabetha clenched her hands to her face and sobbed, still holding the letter. How could he do this to her? She'd waited so long for him. She couldn't wait any longer. Didn't he love her more than anything in the world, as she did him?

Her father turned and embraced her. "There, there, Elizabetha. What is it? Have you bad news?"

"Oh, Papa, he's not coming. He's going to fight that damnable war. I can't bear to wait for him another minute. He promised—." She stopped, lifting her tear-stained face to her father realizing the possibility of the very worst, she said, "What if something happens to him? What if he's killed?"

"He's a strong, determined lad. If I know Martin, nothing's going to keep him from you. This war won't last long. The British are sending more troops. It will be settled soon."

"Oh, Papa, I hope you're right. I couldn't bear it if you're wrong." Elizabetha smoothed the crumpled letter, folded it, and put it in her pocket before drying her tears. Her father handed her his handkerchief and she blew her nose. "*Danke,* I'll be all right now. He will come for me soon. I know he will. He promised."

⇒ 11 ⇐

1758

September 6, Martin, Thomas, and the Virginia Regiment under Major Lewis reached the swelling forces of General Forbes Army at Fort Ligonier which was halfway between Fort Bedford from which Forbes Army had come and Fort Duquesne which General Forbes planned to attack.

The retrenchments of a low breastwork of horizontal logs surrounded the inner fort for protection and refitting of the army. The inner fort was square with pointed bastions at the corners. Inside the square were storehouses, officer's barracks, a powder magazine, and troop barracks.

Thomas glanced around the fort, his cheeks reddened to the hue of his hair in his excitement. "I'll bet we'll see lots of action soon," he said.

Martin smiled at his friend. Thomas was anxious to get to the fighting. Martin knew it was because Thomas was afraid and wanted to get it over with. Martin would be glad to get it over with himself. He thought again of Elizabetha and hoped he would soon be able to return to her and make her his wife. He could almost feel the touch of her hand on his calf the last morning he saw her.

Martin and Thomas's unit was assigned to a barracks with some of the forces that arrived before. "Looks like we're in with some Scottish Highlanders by the looks of those bagpipes," Thomas said to Martin as they claimed two empty wooden bunks.

A giant, craggy-framed Highlander nearby stood and introduced himself in a booming baritone. "I'm MacPherson, welcome to our party. You boys are with the Virginia Regiment, eh?"

Martin nodded and shook MacPherson's huge hand. "Glad to meet you, I'm Martin and this is Thomas," he said gesturing toward Thomas.

"Good to meet you, MacPherson," Thomas said.

"Have you been here long?" Martin asked.

"About two weeks. Some more of the militia are already here, from Maryland and Pennsylvania."

"Have you seen any action since you've been here?" Thomas asked.

"We sure have." MacPherson's resonance resounded through the barracks. "Fort Ligonier may be made of earth and timber, but she held up as we fought off several severe attacks by the French and Indians about a week ago. This fort's to be the staging area for the final assault on Fort Duquesne. We Highlanders and you colonists will be heading out on a scouting expedition in about three days," MacPherson said. "You boys better rest up while you can."

* * *

Three days later Martin, Thomas and their Virginia Regiment under Major Lewis, along with the Maryland and Pennsylvania Regiments, a nearly equal number of Highlanders under Major Grant, and a number of Indian scouts left Fort Ligonier and marched on the scouting expedition toward Fort Duquesne.

Four days later, the Indian scouts reported to Major Grant that they were about ten miles from Fort Duquesne, so Major Grant positioned the main body of troops and sent Major Lewis'

Virginia Regiment to lie in ambush five miles from the fort. Ensign Chew of the Virginia Regiment took twenty men to scout around the fort in an attempt to draw some of the French and Indians into Major Lewis' waiting ambush.

Martin and Thomas stayed ready through the night. They rested on their buttocks on the ground with knees bent, sharing an oak trunk for support of their backs. They faced the direction of the fort with their weapons across their laps. "I wish something would happen soon. I hate this waiting," Thomas whispered.

"I know. Try not to think about it."

"It's been hours."

"Lean your head on the tree and try to get some sleep. I'll keep an eye out. Then you watch while I doze."

Thomas tilted back against the tree and clenched his eyelids closed. "Please, God, let's get it over with," he whispered.

"Amen," Martin concurred. He wondered how long it would be before he could return to Elizabetha. He imagined running his fingers over her smooth, alabaster cheek.

The next morning Ensign Chew and his men and Major Lewis' men returned to tell Major Grant that he wasn't ten, but more than fifteen miles from the Fort.

An enraged Major Grant moved the troops to within sight of the fort under cover of darkness and sent a detachment of Virginians ahead. At dawn, the unsuccessful Virginians straggled back, many lost in the woods. The confused detachment left behind to guard the supplies moved forward. Major Grant ordered the bagpipes played from atop a nearby hill to regroup his men. The pipes shrilled over the still valley.

The troops reorganized, Major Grant and his Highlanders led the army to the open plain in front of the fort.

"Seems strange there's no movement from the fort," Martin said to Thomas marching at his side.

"I know. My skin still crawls from that eerie skirl of those bagpipes," Thomas said. "I just want it over and done."

The French, like angry hornets, swarmed the point attacking the Highlanders while Indians rained a murderous fire on the colonists from the cover of the forest. Men scattered and ran.

"They're retreating," Thomas yelled. "Dear, God, get me out of here."

Martin and Thomas fled with the others in the undisciplined withdrawal. Their countrymen fell wounded or dead all around them. A searing pain tore into Martin's right thigh. Blood oozed from the wound. He hobbled forward.

Thomas reeled in front of Martin and fell to the ground. Blood spurted from Thomas's throat. Martin bent to hold Thomas's head as Thomas tried to speak. Only a gurgling emerged. Thomas lay still, his eyes fixed in a sightless stare.

Martin lowered Thomas's eyelids with two fingers and let his forehead drop onto Thomas's chest. He wept. The lad had been so anxious to get to this fight. His fear of fighting was over for him now. He was gone.

Another stinging agony struck Martin's left shoulder.

MacPherson lifted Martin to his feet as if he weighed no more than a girl. "Let's get to Fort Ligonier," MacPherson bellowed.

Only four hundred and fifty of the original seven hundred and fifty men made it back to the fort Martin would later learn. Martin collapsed inside the gates and MacPherson hauled him to a makeshift hospital and dumped him on a table. Someone stood over him with a knife and probed into his thigh for the lead ball. Everything went black.

The next morning Martin awakened in his own cot. MacPherson towered over him. Martin tried to raise himself, but the pain was too much. The gaping hole in Thomas's throat and his staring eyes flooded Martin's memory.

MacPherson pressed Martin's shoulders back down. "You'll not be getting up for a few days. They dug out the lead, but you won't be fit for much for a while."

A month later, Colonel Washington arrived at the fort with his Virginia Regiment. The now swollen Forbes Army would soon take Fort Duquesne and the Ohio Valley would be in British hands. The war would be over for Virginia. Martin determined to go to the Klaus homestead, get his belongings, and claim Elizabetha. The death of Thomas haunted his mind.

Martin reached under his shirt and pulled out his Bible. He kept it close to his person since the death of Thomas. He propped his knapsack under his head and stroked the leather cover of the Bible. His father had given it to him before Martin and Johanne had set out for America. It was all he had left of his family, except his memories. One day he would pay for the passage of his parents and sister to America. Thomas's death had brought back the memories of the loss of Johanne.

Martin had felt utterly helpless to prevent either death. If only his faith had been stronger, God might have saved them. He vowed to follow every law in God's divine teachings. He randomly opened to *Mark* 9:23 and read the words of Jesus to the father of a sick child: "If thou canst believe, all things are possible to him that believeth." He chanced on *Mark* 11:24: "Therefore I say unto ye, What things soever ye desire, when ye pray, believe that ye receive them, and ye shall have them."

Martin tucked the Bible beneath his shirt and gazed at the ceiling. If mankind could just have enough faith, there could be perfection right here on earth. He would do his best to inspire such faith.

⇾12⇽

Elizabetha finished writing and closed her journal just as she heard her father come in the front door. She wore her green cotton dress flared over panniers for the special occasion of her eighteenth birthday. She rose and turned to greet her father and froze in disbelief at the second person hanging his coat and hat on the pegs. "Martin!" she squealed. He'd come back to her. Thank you, Martin; thank you for not dying. Her father had been right. Martin's determination had brought him back to her. Elizabetha ran toward Martin.

He grabbed her hands and twirled her around, his gaze feasting upon her. He brought both her hands to his lips and kissed the palms. They stood with arms outstretched and fingers intertwined for several moments, gazing at each other. "I was beginning to fear I'd only imagined you," Martin said at last.

Her father grinned. "See the fine birthday present I've brought home for you. He magically appeared on the shop doorstep as I was leaving."

"Oh, Papa, no present could be better." Elizabetha's heart pounded in her chest. "You must be starved, Martin. I'll add another place." Elizabetha led Martin to the table. She fetched another setting and arranged it beside her own at the table.

Elizabetha's mother and Toby entered the room. Her mother's hands fluttered to her cheeks. "Martin, it's really you."

Toby marched over to Martin and shook his hand. "Good to see you, Martin."

"Thank you, good to see you, too."

Martin strode to Elizabetha's mother and kissed her hand. "It's nice to see you again, Mrs. Kirstaterin. You look lovely as usual."

"Oh, Martin, you needn't flatter me, it's Elizabetha you're courting." She smiled. "It's wonderful to have you back with us. Come and sit down for supper."

Martin held the chair out for Elizabetha's mother and for Elizabetha. He seated himself next to her. Toby sat across the way, and her father took his place at the head of the table. He asked Martin to give the blessing.

While Martin summarized the past two years through supper, Elizabetha couldn't keep her gaze off him. His dark hair was tied in back. His jaw seemed even firmer. There was a hardness to his features that she hadn't seen before, faint creases at the corners of his eyes as if from squinting at the sun, and perhaps the war had left those slight furrows in his brow.

Martin passed the platter of beef to her father, and Elizabetha couldn't help noticing the muscles in Martin's upper arm bulge beneath his shirt. She couldn't believe Martin was here at long last.

Martin spoke of the death of his friend, Thomas, and had to stop a moment to compose himself. He glossed over his own wounds.

"Martin, no." Elizabetha's mouth gaped.

"Don't worry. I've healed fine." His firm hand squeezed hers under the table.

* * *

The week before Christmas, Martin and Elizabetha wed in a simple ceremony in her parents' home, with her family, Anne and her husband, Joseph, Anne's parents, and Uncle Henry's family present.

Elizabetha wore her best Sunday dress for the wedding, pale blue with elbow length sleeves trimmed in white lace and matching lace at the top of the bodice. She'd applied the juice of crushed berries to her cheeks and lips. Using lampblack, she'd highlighted her lashes and brows. Everyone said she looked beautiful. She felt beautiful.

The hall was bathed in golden sunlight. Cut wild flowers in glass vases sat on the center of the table and on several other small tables in the room. A pair of large vases of gladioli waited on the floor on either side of the place where she and Martin would repeat their vows. Ladder-back chairs for the guests had been located to form an aisle between them down which she would proceed.

At her mother's signal, Elizabetha glided on a sunbeam down the aisle. Martin waited at the other end with the Reverend Henkel from St. Paul's in Schaefferstown. Reverend Henkel's thick mane of dark hair bobbled as he nodded to them that the ceremony would begin.

Standing beside the Reverend, Martin made a cutting figure in his snug, beige breeches, waistcoat, and narrow-tailed coat. His hair was neatly tied back at the nape of his neck.

She felt she was dreaming as she repeated her vows. Uttering the words, "I do," she gazed into Martin's eyes, trying to grasp the reality of their marriage. At the conclusion, Martin held her hands and imparted a chaste peck on her lips.

After the ceremony, Joseph and Anne congratulated the newlyweds. Anne kissed them both on the cheek and Joseph shook Martin's hand.

Joseph bent, holding Elizabetha by her shoulders, and kissed her cheek. She thought his kiss lingered a tad too long. He straightened. "You're a beautiful bride," he said. She felt a slight apprehension at the intimate tone of his voice. Elizabetha glanced from Martin to Anne. They hadn't seemed to notice. Was it merely her imagination?

Elizabetha and Martin, as bride and groom, were the first to fill their plates in the parlor at the sideboard laden with a medley of English and German cuisine provided by Elizabetha's mother and Aunt Polly.

The fare starred roast beef, small venison medallions, potato dumplings, sauerkraut, breaded trout in butter and lemon, boiled carrots in butter, rhubarb sauce, several cheeses, and heavily fruited Queen's cake. The aromas mingled in the air inviting all to partake.

Elizabetha took small portions. She was too excited to eat. She noticed Martin did the same. They sat on two Windsor chairs under the parlor window, the afternoon sunlight swaddling them in warm golden hues. They were both more interested in gazing at each other than what they were putting in their mouths. Was he as happy as she was?

Through the evening, Elizabetha smiled so much her cheeks ached. She was Martin's wife.

After the guests left, Martin and Elizabetha retired. Martin's wife, Elizabetha said to herself again, trying to absorb the title.

At the dressing table, Elizabetha, wearing only her shift, stroked the brush through her long hair. Martin stood in his nightshirt behind her, intent on her image in the mirror.

As Elizabetha lowered her head and brushed her hair forward, Martin's fingertips caressed the nape of her neck. She felt a tingle in her lower spine as if he'd touched her there as well.

Martin moved to her side and raised Elizabetha by her shoulders, turning her to him. He smoothed her hair at the sides and his hands caressed the contours of her face as he beheld her. She'd waited for this moment for so long. She trembled with anticipation. His hands slid down her throat to her upper arms and drew her toward him. He lowered his head, his mouth hovering above hers. Elizabetha couldn't bear the slowness, his teasing mouth inches away. She met his lips and fused into his embrace. Before entering their marriage bed, Martin snuffed out the candle.

The next morning was Sunday. "Wake up, sleepyhead, it's time to get ready for church services," Martin said.

Elizabetha rolled onto her back and pulled the quilt over her head. A smile played across her mouth as she remembered the night before. Martin had been so sweet and gentle, almost too gentle. She'd hoped for more passion, but he knew it was her first time, maybe later.

The last thing Elizabetha wanted to do this morning was go to church. "Can't we miss just this once, Martin?" she pleaded.

"Miss God? Certainly not. Does He forsake us, even just once? Come on and get dressed, I'll wait for you downstairs."

Elizabetha heard the door close. She tossed the quilt away and forced herself to get out of bed. Why did Martin have to be so pious?

⇻•13•⇺

Two months later, Martin lifted Elizabetha by her waist and danced her around the parlor. "A baby," he said. "That's wonderful news."

He returned her to the floor. His brow furrowed. He paced. "Now that we're going to have a child, it's time for us to get our own place." Martin stopped pacing and glanced at Elizabetha. "These past months I've been working for your father, I've saved enough for us to move to Mount Airy." He resumed pacing. "I'll start farming the land I bought. I'll build the church." He stopped again and turned to her, beaming. "You'll love it there, Elizabetha."

"Mount Airy—the church—farming? Why, I—I thought we'd stay here, in Lebanon," she said.

"You remember my telling you about my land and all my plans. Surely, you thought we'd go there one day, didn't you?"

"No, no I didn't. I thought you'd changed your mind when we married. I thought you were content here. Oh, Martin, I don't want to move. When the baby comes, I'll need my mother. I don't want to leave my friends, to leave Anne." Tears streamed down her cheeks.

Martin hugged her close and gazed down at her. He wiped the wetness from her face. "There, there, don't think about it now. We'll wait until the baby is born. That will give me more time to accumulate extra money."

And more time for Elizabetha to find a way to dissuade him.

* * *

Seven months later, Martin paced the parlor. His father-in-law paced the other direction. "Hasn't it been a long time?" Martin asked.

"It sometimes takes awhile, especially with the first," Wilhelm answered.

Half an hour later, Martin and Wilhelm resided on the sofa, their elbows on their knees and chins resting on their fists.

Martin finished counting the blue squares on the paint-laden canvas carpeting for the third time and moaned, "It's three hours since the midwife arrived. What can be taking so long? What if something's wrong?"

An infant's wail rang out from the upstairs. Martin rose to his feet, peered upward, thanked God, and waited.

Wilhelm stood by his side.

Elizabetha's mother stepped out of the birthing room and shouted down the stairs. "It's a girl," she said. "They're both doing fine. In a few minutes you can come up and see them, Martin."

Elizabetha cuddled the tiny infant with its blanket snuggled around it and cooed, "Hello, Beth. You were a long time coming, but now it was worth the wait."

Elizabetha remembered Martin's words, "We'll wait until after the baby is born." She knew she'd have to deal with the move to Mount Airy soon. For an instant, she regretted Beth was already here.

Six weeks later, Elizabetha lay Beth down in her cradle and turned to Martin poised at the fireplace in the parlor. Once again she pleaded, "Haven't we been happy here? Why must we move to Mount Airy? I'll be so lonely there not knowing anyone." She took her handkerchief from her sleeve. She was prepared to cry if need be.

"You won't be alone. Joseph and Anne will be coming with us," Martin stated triumphantly. "When he turned twenty-one, Joseph had received acreage on the Clinch River near Mount Airy. He's decided to settle there to farm it. I've been helping him with his farming skills and in return he will sell me, for a fair price, half of the dozen slaves he inherited."

"Slaves?" Elizabetha was stunned.

"I know. It will take getting used to, but it's the way of things in the South Joseph says. Besides we will certainly need the extra hands for the farm. And you'll have help in the house. His uncle's been looking after them for Joseph." Martin smiled broadly at her with outstretched arms. "Isn't it grand? Now you have no reason not to agree," he said.

"Anne is going?"

"Yes, yes." His arms engulfed Elizabetha, pressing her to his chest.

Elizabetha knew she had no more excuses. Martin successfully removed them all. They were moving. She sighed. "All right, Martin, we'll go to Mount Airy."

"Elizabetha, you'll love it there. Really you will. We'll leave in the spring." He kissed her forehead.

Martin seemed so happy. Surely she would come to love it there in Mount Airy. She'd simply have to be happy. After all she had Martin at last. She had his baby.

* * *

The scrubbed clean smell of April usually invigorated Elizabetha, but not today—today they would begin their trek to Mount Airy. Three robins hopped along the young grass blades gathering the worms that bloomed out of the earth—each worm plucked from the familiar surroundings of home much like she was about to be.

Martin and Joseph loaded the two Conestoga wagons with their families' belongings as Elizabetha and Anne handed various bundles up to them. Elizabetha and Anne had begged and borrowed from their families as much furniture and household items as they could fit into the large, deep-sided wagons. Atop their cargo, the men deposited mattresses and blankets so they could sleep inside and lashed the babies' cradles behind the wagon seats to keep them secure and within easy reach of their mothers. Sash windows for the homes they would build were cradled amid blankets and padding.

When everything was stowed, Elizabetha turned. Her father stood with his thumbs tucked in the sleeve holes of his waist-coat. Her mother, holding Beth, dabbed her eyes with the hem of her sleeve. Elizabetha embraced each of them. She hugged Toby who was already much taller than their mother.

"I'll miss you all so much. I promise I'll write often. Goodbye." Elizabetha managed to turn away before the tears welling in her eyes tumbled out.

Drying her eyes with her sleeve, she stepped on the stool to climb into the back of the covered wagon. Joseph hastened to her side and aided her ascent, holding her hand even after she was seated. He gave her hand a slight squeeze before releasing it and sauntered off to Anne's side. Why did his actions unsettle her so?

Elizabetha's father held Anne's baby, Hannah, until Anne was seated and handed the nine-month-old up to its mother.

While fighting back her tears, Elizabetha's mother handed seven-month-old Beth up to Elizabetha's arms.

Elizabetha's father put his arm around her mother's shoulder as he said to Elizabetha, "Have a good journey and keep well. We love you." Tears glistened at the corners of his eyes.

Martin shook Elizabetha's father's hand and Toby's. He hugged her mother then settled himself on the wagon seat.

As the assemblage pulled out, Elizabetha and the family left behind waved goodbye until they were out of sight of one another. Elizabetha's tears cascaded down her cheeks. She'd never been away from her parents before. How she would miss them. She wondered when she would see them again, or Toby, still just a boy.

Elizabetha tucked sleepy Beth into the cradle which would gently sway with the lumbering wagon's gait. She climbed onto the seat beside Martin. The three of them would be alone now in their own home with no family around them. She glanced at the Blakemore wagon in front. At least they would have friends there—Bthere in that strange new place called Mount Airy. She hoped she would love it as much as Martin did. She would. That was all there was to it. Wonderful experiences would be waiting for her there. She would put it all in her journal, each new day like a fresh sheet of paper. It would be exciting to see how she filled the pages.

⇻ 14 ⇺

The wagons jostled along the Great Philadelphia Wagon Road through the fertile Lebanon valley in the colorful Pennsylvania Dutch countryside. Farms and livestock dotted the serene landscape along the way. Every so often, Anne peeked around the side of the wagon and waved her hand at Elizabetha, who imagined Anne must be feeling as forlorn and disenchanted with all the dust and grime the wagons churned up as she was.

Stopping just before sunset, they camped beside a small stream. While Martin and Joseph unhitched, fed, and watered the oxen, Elizabetha and Anne gathered wood for the fire, tended to the babies, and prepared a stew of potatoes, carrots, rutabaga, and salt pork.

Martin and Joseph started a blazing fire and sauntered off to more manly business, leaving the women to their duties.

"I swear, Elizabetha, this is certainly not my idea of how a genteel woman should be spending her time," Anne complained as she stirred the concoction over the open fire as she balanced Hannah on her hip. "I just wish we could have stayed in Pennsylvania." A large owl hooted, and Anne jumped, almost upsetting the iron pot of stew.

"How very much I agree with you," Elizabetha concurred. "At least when we get to Virginia, we'll have help from the slaves." She wiped her apron across her eyes which watered from the smoky fire.

"That can't happen soon enough to please me," Anne said.

While supper simmered, the men located wooden chairs around the fire and all ate from tin plates balanced on their laps.

After eating, the men lolled around the fire as the women washed the dishes in the stream, and put the babies to sleep before they joined the men to relax before the fire, something they sorely deserved Elizabetha thought as she plopped down, exhausted.

Anne brought her mending with her and began with one of Hannah's nappies, sewing up a frayed hem.

Martin rose and excused himself and headed into the woods behind camp.

Joseph turned to Elizabetha. "I've missed our discussions. It's been a while since we could talk. Martin seems to resent your participation."

"Martin doesn't believe women should talk about anything but motherhood and fashion, I'm afraid."

"I know he's literal in his interpretation of the Bible. I've been anxious to hear more about your thinking on religion, though."

Elizabetha's blood surged through her body in anticipation of one of their favorite subjects. "As I've said, before, I can't accept the concept of a supreme power. It goes against all logic. If God is *absolute* good, God would have no concept of evil; therefore, either evil is good or God is not absolute, and—. "

Elizabetha didn't see Martin approach from behind. "Elizabetha," he barked.

Her body jerked in reaction and nearly toppled her off the chair.

"It is not fitting for a woman to involve herself in other than women's concerns, especially denouncing God of all things."

"But, I—," she stammered still shaken by the intrusion.

"I forbid you to involve yourself in the affairs of men or speak of God other than as directed in the Bible."

"Forbid, Martin?" She was stunned.

Martin glared at her and, in a preachy roar, said, "1 *Timothy* 3:8-15: '... But I suffer not a woman to teach, nor to usurp authority over the man, but to be in silence. For Adam was first formed, then Eve....'"

She opened her mouth to reciprocate but glimpsed Joseph nodding his head sideways, his lips silently mouthing the word "no" as his eyes warned her.

She clenched her teeth and glared into the fire, the heat of her anger boiling her blood. Joseph was right, it would do no good to protest. Nothing would ever change Martin's mind on the issue. She had been eager to discourse with Joseph like they used to before they all had married. Joseph would never forbid her to speak. She should have married him. What was she saying? He was Anne's husband.

Martin took his seat beside Elizabetha.

Anne kept her head lowered, her sewing needle darting in and out of the cloth.

Joseph rose to tend the fire.

Elizabetha's anger slipped away as she observed how gracefully Joseph moved, every muscle under control. He threw on the last of the wood and squatted in front of the fire to adjust the logs with a stick. His muscular body was silhouetted against the flames, his profile as handsome as a Greek god's. Her gaze followed his every move. When he rose and turned, he surveyed her as if he knew what she'd been thinking. She lowered her gaze and fiddled with her sleeve. Why had she been watching him?

* * *

They crossed the Potomac River at Evan Watkins Ferry and followed the narrow trail across the up county to Winchester and on through the Shenandoah Valley of Virginia between the Blue Ridge Mountains on the east and Allegheny Mountains on the west.

They jostled onward on the bumpy and sometimes extremely narrow road through widely scattered hills and crossed the James River at Looney's Ferry where the Appalachian Range made a southeasterly thrust to touch the Blue Ridge Mountains. After Big Lick, the road went on with diminishing ruggedness. At Fincastle, The Great Road turned eastward, and they followed the Wilderness Road southward instead.

Anne jostled uncomfortably in the wagon as they continued on the Wilderness Road until they arrived in the second month of travel at Evansham where they followed Ingles Trail. With assistance from the map Joseph's uncle had sent him before they left, they successfully arrived at Clinch River.

The woods approaching Joseph's land loomed dense and dark. They came upon an open area and Joseph stopped the wagon.

Anne peered over the rugged precipice with a fifty to sixty foot descent to the river. "Is this where your land is?" she asked incredulously.

"No. The land is a few miles north of here, but isn't this a beautiful spot? We must have picnics here. It's breathtaking."

It took Anne's breath away to be certain, but she was relieved they wouldn't have to live here.

As they drove further, they came upon more woods and the river smoothed. Along the east bank where the seventy-five acres on which Anne and Joseph would live, it was level. Across on the west bank sprawled the four hundred acres that Joseph would farm. All Anne could think of was that they hadn't seen evidence of other human beings for miles.

⇉ 15 ⇇

As the work on the buildings began, the fur trapper Tom Kilgore, rugged and blond, and his swarthy friend Charles Boren had arrived from Tom's homestead about five miles south of Joseph's place. They had seen the wagons and joined in with the clearing of the land and participated in the plans for building, offering suggestions to lessen the heat inside the house, such as high ceilings, putting the chimney on an outside wall, and placing the kitchen off the main house.

The slaves had been delivered, and the one called Sarah had taken quickly to young Hannah. Anne was pleased. Sarah was petite with unusually fine features. Her head was covered by a blue gingham cloth with long ends twisted and wrapped around and tied in front with ends tucked into the coil. She wore a faded dark blue handmade blouse with white twine run through the neck hem, gathering the scoop neck and tied in front. Her tan cotton skirt was covered in front by a long white apron.

Anne and Elizabetha, holding Beth, sat on ladder-back chairs under an oak far back from the bonfire the men had started to burn the debris they had cleared from the land. Behind them, the men stood discussing their plans. Anne shielded the harsh midmorning sun from baby Hannah's face. The heat and humidity shimmered together. It wore on her nerves. "I dread the coming of summer," she said.

Sarah's sixteen-year-old daughter, Prue, presented tin cups and a pitcher of small beer to refresh them. She wore a bandana on her head like her mother, a bright red skirt and a white blouse. She offered the tray to each one while she kept her gaze lowered.

Tom Kilgore took a cup from Prue's tray and said, "I'd build a stockade if I were you, Joseph. It'll help keep the Indians out." He slaked his thirst with noisy gulps.

"Indians," Anne exclaimed. "Are there many around here?"

Tom swiped his sleeve across his mouth. "Sure are, Ma'am. Why just over a month ago some Cree Indians attacked my place, and if it weren't for my own stockade, might have overrun us, but we held 'em off," Kilgore said.

Charles Boren added, "They're fond of taking scalps for the bounty they get from the British for 'em if they're French, or the French if they're British. Likely take 'em before the victim's even dead. For the most part the Indians don't bother settlers, but every now and again they get their dander riled and start up."

Anne shuddered and clutched Hannah close. "Joseph, you must build a stockade. Please, promise me." She couldn't bear the thought of savages touching her Hannah. She wished she'd never agreed to come here. She didn't like anything about this wilderness. She started at every branch that crackled for fear it was a bear. Now she'd fear it was an Indian.

"Yes, Anne, we will. We'll begin it today," Joseph moved to her side. "No Indian will bring harm to my gentle wife or daughter." He stroked Anne's cheek with the back of his hand and smoothed his daughter's hair.

Joseph and Martin felled pine as the other men arranged the logs horizontally, one on top of the other, to a height of about ten feet. They packed mud in the crevices, leaving holes about every six to eight feet along the wall to allow for the placement of rifles. A platform was built around the inside with stairs leading up so shooters could kneel there and aim through the holes.

Gates were installed at the south and east ends. And a crude bridge erected across the river at the east gate.

The hall and parlor house was made of riven siding from local oak, split out with a froe and maul Joseph and Martin had brought along for the purpose. Joseph and Sarah's husband, the slave Gim, a tall muscular black in his early thirties, gently removed the sash windows from the wagon. The slave quarters were of unhewn logs chinked with mud. Anne was relieved the construction was finished and they could sleep indoors again.

* * *

Two days after the completion of the building, Elizabetha was glad that she and Martin and their slaves and Anne and Joseph and company left the Blakemore Fort and traveled the day's journey to Martin's land in Mount Airy to build Elizabetha and Martin's homestead.

The wilderness unraveled into a rolling valley of grassy hills nestled in the sentinel of the Blue Ridge mountains. Martin selected the highest hill amid his acres as the site for their home.

Elizabetha did have to admit it was beautiful. Mountain laurel, dogwood, rhododendron, trailing arboreta, and violet littered the graceful hills and mountains.

The farms of the seventy-five previous German settlers encircled their acreage. They would not need a stockade here. It was a peaceful valley with many neighbors near.

Adam Cook limped ahead of a half-dozen German Lutherans that came to assist. With so many to help, the two-story house and the slave quarters were completed in less than a month, and Anne and Joseph readied to return to their wilderness fort.

Anne hugged Elizabetha. Tears streamed down both their faces. "Take care of yourself, Elizabetha. I will miss you so much," Anne said.

"And I will miss you." Elizabetha wiped away her tears and straightened her skirts. "So now we carry on our married lives. Not exactly as we'd planned, is it?"

"Oh, Elizabetha, how will I survive the wilderness? I miss

Philadelphia and all our dreams. I'll be so lonely without you."

"Now, now," Joseph said. "It's only a few hours ride to visit. We'll see each other often." His dark gaze fixed on Elizabetha.

She wished he wouldn't look at her like that. What if Martin or Anne noticed?

Joseph took Anne's elbow, assisted her into the wagon, and settled beside her. The slave Sarah and her daughter, Prue, were inside the wagon tending to baby Hannah. Gim, the largest of the four black men, ushered the other three into the wagon. The men wore different colors of breeches and hose and white shirts open at the neck with sleeves rolled up on their arms to varying heights. They wore various shaped straw hats. Gim climbed into the back, and they were off.

Elizabetha waved goodbye to Anne until the wagon was out of sight. Martin moved to Elizabetha's side and put his arm around her.

"I'm worried about Anne. She's so fragile and refined." Elizabetha said. "I don't know if she'll ever fit into the wilderness out there at Clinch River."

"God will look after her. We'll pray for her. God will look after us all." Martin turned to the house and strode inside. Elizabetha gaped after him. Prayer was his answer for everything. Why couldn't they all just have stayed in Lebanon? She gathered her skirts and stomped inside.

Martin stood in the huge hall admiring its vastness as she entered. "Do you know why we built this room so large? So the Lutherans along Reed Creek can meet here on Sundays. We can all worship indoors instead of the forest until I build a real church."

"I see. Don't I have any say in the matter? Isn't it my home as well?"

"Of course it is. Don't wrinkle up your nose like that. It will all work out fine, you'll see. It will be a while before I can build the church. Land clearing and planting crops must come first."

"Always that church," Elizabetha mumbled.

Martin didn't seem to hear and continued, "Tomorrow I'll go to the county office and apply for our Importation Right of fifty acres apiece. Adam Cook told me that we can build a cabin on another four hundred acres and plant hay, thereby acquiring the land by cabin rights. We'll plant hay on the rest also, the following year corn, then tobacco. I'll start the slaves on making benches. We'll stack the benches along the wall over there for the Sunday meetings."

Elizabetha realized Martin was oblivious to her presence in his planning. The farm, the church, everything seemed to be more important to him than she was. She tramped to the parlor.

As Elizabetha entered the parlor, the slave Sudie was cooing to Beth while rocking her. Sudie was proud of her ability to sooth the baby. She glanced up and smiled at Elizabetha. Sudie was a full-figured, plain-looking girl in her twenties with a complexion somewhat lighter than the other Negroes. She had a wide, flat nose splattered with freckles. Sudie adored Beth and had confided to Elizabetha that she wanted a passel of babies herself.

Elizabetha meandered over to the drop-front desk across from the fireplace and plopped down. Glancing at Sudie, she wondered if she'd ever get used to the idea of owning slaves. She'd never imaged herself as mistress, but she guessed Martin was right in that they needed assistance with the planting and all, and she was grateful for the help in the house and with the baby. After all, she and Martin did provide them with clothing, shelter, and food. Yes, they amply repaid them for their services. She would look after them. Martin certainly was too busy to pay anyone any mind. She opened her journal and poured her frustration with Martin onto the pages.

⇒ 16 ⇐

1761

In the Kimberlin parlor, Elizabetha enjoyed debating the philosophy of the French writer Voltaire with Joseph. Martin had gone to instruct the overseer, Charles, whom Martin had hired. Anne was tending to Hannah upstairs.

So seldom did Elizabetha have an opportunity to discuss things with Joseph. They had to take advantage of the times Martin wasn't present. At least Anne didn't mind if they had discussions in her presence. Elizabetha did feel a little guilt about sneaking behind Martin's back, but he was so unreasonable about women not discussing such things, it was very little guilt.

Joseph thoughtfully brought her the books he'd finished reading when he and Anne visited. She had to keep them hidden away beneath her shawls in the chest of drawers. Martin wouldn't approve of her reading those kinds of books either.

The front door slammed shut and Elizabetha's hand took flight from her lap with fright at the suddenness. Joseph reached out and took her hand in both of his and gazed at her. He squeezed her hand and smiled.

Martin called to them from the hall. "I'll be right in. Get ready for whist."

Joseph tenderly rubbed the back of Elizabetha's hand and released it, his sable eyes still peering into hers. She regretted when he let go of her hand. She broke her gaze away from Joseph's as Anne descended the stairs and Martin entered.

* * *

The following month was Martin's twenty-sixth birthday. Elizabetha had invited Anne and Joseph, Adam and Sally Cook, the Swansons, Kirstens, Bentleys, and Hawthorns from the Lutheran congregation.

Elizabetha, in stays and petticoats, was pleased with the up-sweep of her hair that Sudie completed with ringlets trailing down the nape of her neck. She gazed out the window. Joseph and Anne's carriage pulled up outside. Joseph assisted Anne's descent. Anne was heavy with child and stopped for a deep breath before waddling to the house. Joseph kept his hand at her elbow to steady her. "Sudie, go on down and tend to Anne. I can manage to dress alone."

Sudie nodded. "Yessem."

About twenty minutes later, Elizabetha decided on the wine-colored gown with white lace trim. She draped it over the dressing screen.

A rap sounded on the bedroom door. "It's Joseph. I've brought wine."

She stepped behind the dressing screen. "Come in."

She peeked around the corner as Joseph entered the bedroom carrying two glasses of wine.

"Martin isn't home yet," Elizabetha said from her concealment.

"I know. Sudie told me. I thought you might like a glass of Madeira for the festive occasion."

"Where's Anne?"

"She's lying down in the guest room. The trip was hard on her. She's having a hard time in her condition with all this heat. Sudie is with her."

Elizabetha reached her hand from behind the screen to take

the wine glass. "Thank you for the wine." She peeked through the space between the panels of the screen. Joseph wore tan breeches and a dark brown waistcoat. His white shirt enhanced his deeply tanned skin. His wavy, sandy hair, tied behind, was a fitting crown for his bronzed complexion.

Joseph gazed at the screen as he took a sip, almost as if he could see through it. He turned and sauntered toward the window.

Joseph reminded Elizabetha of a mountain lion she had seen once, moving with languid ease, contented in its own magnificence and with the control of muscle that made one know he could instantly pounce on his unsuspecting prey at any given moment.

She took a sip of the Madeira and stood the glass on the small stand beside the screen. She lifted her dress off the screen and lowered it over her head. She fumbled at the hooks in back. "Damn hooks," she mumbled. She wished she hadn't sent Sudie away. She stopped and took another sip and set the glass down.

She felt Joseph's presence behind her. "Let me help you," he said. She turned her head slightly. His dark eyes blazed from his handsome face. She snapped her head back around.

Joseph's fingers lightly brushed her skin as he moved the ringlets off her neck, his touch sending tingles down her spine.

He fastened the hook at the waist of her dress, ascending with methodical slowness. Her excitement heightened. When he reached the top hook, he gently rearranged her ringlets down her neck, sending a quiver through her body.

She sighed. She didn't dare move, didn't dare look at him.

He turned her toward him. Lust filled his gaze.

Elizabetha knew at any moment he would take her in his arms and kiss her. Worse yet, she wanted him to kiss her. It hadn't been her imagination. Joseph did covet her.

His arms surrounded her. His lips were on hers. She knew she should twist away but couldn't make herself do it. In spite of herself, she returned his passion, ashamed of herself all the while.

At last, she tore her mouth free. "Joseph, we mustn't."

"I know." He kissed her again, harder. His tongue probed her open mouth. She felt weak-kneed. She had to stop this.

"Joseph, please, don't." She pushed herself from him.

"I'm sorry, Elizabetha—no I'm not. I can't help myself. I've wanted you a long time. I feel deceitful, but I can't help it. You're so intelligent, and vibrant, and beautiful." He reached for her again.

She ached for more of Joseph's kisses. He awakened more in her than Martin ever did. Passion, that was it.

Joseph was passionate when he discoursed and passionate when he kissed as well. They were dangerously alike.

The front door slammed. "I'm home," Martin called.

"Joseph, we must forget this ever happened." She straightened her dress and smoothed her hair.

"I'll never forget," Joseph said.

She peered into his dark gaze. She wouldn't forget either. She gathered what was left of her dignity and strode from the room.

⇒ 17 ⇐

Later that evening at the party, Elizabetha chatted with Sally and Adam Cook. Elizabetha worried that Anne and Martin would notice that Joseph blatantly stared at Elizabetha whenever he thought no one was watching. The lust in his eyes seemed so obvious to her. How could anyone not notice?

Elizabetha glimpsed Anne sitting in the wing chair grimacing and rushed to her side. "What is it, Anne?"

"I think I'm in labor, Elizabetha. It's a month too early. The travel must have escalated things." Pain tightened Anne's features again.

"Let me help you up to your room," Elizabetha said.

Joseph appeared at her side, concern disturbing his handsome face. He lifted Anne and carried her upstairs.

Elizabetha found Martin and asked him to clear the guests and to send the slave Big Jim for the midwife. She found Sudie in the kitchen. "Please, come with me." They arrived in the guest room, just as Joseph put Anne on the bed.

"We'll take over now," Elizabetha said. "Go down with Martin and bring the midwife when she arrives. Tell Phoebe to boil some water and bring fresh linens." The lust in Joseph's eyes had been replaced with worry. Before leaving, he bent over his wife and kissed her forehead.

When he was gone, Elizabetha and Sudie removed Anne's clothes down to her shift. Anne was perspiring heavily. Her face scrunched into multiple puckers with the next pain. They were coming closer together. Anne squeezed Elizabetha's hand with each contraction. Where is that midwife? Elizabetha fretted.

She soaked a cloth in the basin water and wiped Anne's forehead. Finally, the midwife arrived at the same time Phoebe brought in the hot water and linens.

Mrs. Gruner was the epitome of efficiency, her hair tucked in a bun at the nape of her neck, not a single strand dared escape. Her pinched nose made Elizabetha wonder how she could breathe. Mrs. Gruner's beady brown eyes peered at Elizabetha then at the pile of linens Phoebe set on the table beside the hot water. "Are these all you have?" Mrs. Gruner asked in a nasal snap.

"Phoebe, fetch more linens, please," Elizabetha said with all the syrupy sweetness she could muster.

"Yessem," Phoebe answered with an exaggerated curtsy, her apron billowing around her chubbiness. She gave Elizabetha an extravagant grin of wide lips accompanied by a crinkle of her button nose. Mrs. Gruner received a disdainful glance as Phoebe left the room.

Elizabetha stepped back so Mrs. Gruner could examine Anne. She'd love to give Mrs. Gruner a piece of her mind, if Anne didn't need the midwife so desperately. She'd be needing the old crone herself probably.

"The baby is definitely coming," Mrs. Gruner announced.

Anne's pains came more sharply. Elizabetha held Anne's hand. Anne squeezed Elizabetha's fingers with unbelievable strength. As soon as the pain subsided, Elizabetha removed her wedding ring and checked for damage. To her surprise, there was no bleeding. She stuffed her ring into her pocket.

"Don't push," Mrs. Gruner ordered.

Anne's face contorted and reddened. She glared at Mrs. Gruner.

Anne grabbed Elizabetha's hand again and her moan escalated into a piercing scream.

Elizabetha and Mrs. Gruner helped Anne into a vertical position onto the birthing stool.

"Push," Mrs. Gruner ordered. "Push."

With a grudging glare at Mrs. Gruner and a guttural grunt, Anne delivered a slimy, squirmy, baby girl into Mrs. Gruner's waiting hands. The midwife dangled the baby by the heels and slapped her behind. The lovely screech of her first cry filled the air. Elizabetha heaved a sigh of relief.

After Mrs. Gruner tied and cut the umbilical cord, Elizabetha and Sudie helped a shaking Anne back into bed. Mrs. Gruner bathed the baby and wrapped her in clean linens.

Blood gushed from Anne and soaked the sheets.

Elizabetha gasped, her hand at her throat.

Mrs. Gruner handed the baby to Sudie and rushed to Anne.

The afterbirth erupted with more blood. At length, Mrs. Gruner stemmed the bleeding. All of the linens Phoebe had brought had been needed.

Elizabetha and Sudie changed Anne's blood and perspiration-soaked shift to a clean one of Elizabetha's.

Mrs. Gruner placed the baby girl in Anne's arms. Dark smudges beneath Anne's eyes contrasted sharply with her ashen skin.

Mrs. Gruner took Elizabetha aside. She folded her hands across her waist and peered down her long nose at Elizabetha. "This delivery took a lot out of her. She shouldn't be moved for a couple of weeks until she recovers her strength."

"Thank you so much. I'll look after both of them," Elizabetha said.

"It would be best if I stayed the night with her to be sure the bleeding has stopped," Mrs. Gruner announced.

"Of course, I'll have Sudie bring you a cot. Is there anything else you'll need?"

"Well, perhaps a cup of tea and a bite to eat would be nice—if you can spare it."

Elizabetha winced at the affront. "I'll have the cook, Phoebe, bring it up to you." Elizabetha swished around and swept out of the room.

After asking Sudie to bring the cot and bedding to Mrs. Gruner and bedding for Joseph to sleep in the parlor, Elizabetha found Phoebe in the kitchen. Phoebe's plump form was bent over the worktable rolling out pie dough, her black hands covered in a dusting of white flour.

As Elizabetha approached, she called Phoebe's name. Phoebe spun around with eyes wide; flour covered her nose like a marshmallow floating atop a cup of hot chocolate. Her kinky hair poked out all around the brim of her white mobcap. "Missus, you scairt me."

"I'm sorry, Phoebe. I just came to ask you to take some tea and a bit of the leftovers up to the guest room for the midwife, Mrs. Gruner."

Phoebe crinkled up her nose again but answered, "Sho' thing. How's Missus Anne doin'?"

"She and her new daughter are just fine, but Mrs. Gruner will stay the night to be safe."

Phoebe grinned widely and drew the back of her hand across her forehead, leaving a wide track of flour.

"I must go to the parlor and tell Joseph," Elizabetha said.

As she turned to leave, she heard Phoebe mumble under her breath as she resumed her work, "My, my white people sho' does walk light."

Martin was seated on the Windsor chair watching Joseph pace before the fireplace. Joseph stopped and searched Elizabetha's face, his eyes wide with fear of the worst. "How is she?"

"Mother and baby girl are doing fine," Elizabetha assured him.

He sank onto the sofa and put his head in his hands. "I don't know what I'd do if anything happened to Anne," he muttered.

Elizabetha marveled at the ways of men. A few hours earlier Joseph was lusting after her, and now he was lamenting the imagined loss of his wife. But then, was she so different? She loved Martin, yet she'd been attracted to Joseph as he'd been drawn to her. How did life get so complicated, and what could she do about it? She was too tired to think about it now.

In the morning, Anne was out of immediate danger and the

midwife accepted a smoked ham and a laying hen for her payment and left, but not before uttering an audible, "Humph."

⇒ 18 ⇐

The following week of Anne's recuperation, Elizabetha met Joseph in the hallway as she was about to enter Anne's room. He reached for her hand. "Thank you," he said.

She gave his hand a squeeze, then worried at how he might interpret it.

He put his other hand on hers and gazed into her eyes.

The longing was still there. She felt his gaze follow her as she entered Anne's room.

The next week, Elizabetha again met Joseph in the hallway. He reached inside his coat and handed her a book. "I meant to give you this earlier."

"Thank you," she said as she reached for the book.

His two hands encircled hers holding the tome. "Elizabetha." He gazed into her eyes with hypnotic yearning.

He pressed her against the wall, his chest crushing against her breasts, his loins hard against her through her skirts. She tried to push him back. He pinned both her wrists to the wall and kissed her hard, forcing her mouth open. She felt dizzy. She stopped struggling and felt their passion surging through her body. The book she'd been holding thudded to the floor.

"Elizabetha, is that you?" Anne called out.

Joseph stopped mid-kiss.

"Yes, Anne, I'll be right there," Elizabetha uttered.

Joseph kissed the hollow at the base of her throat, releasing her. He picked up the volume and handed it to her. Her hand shook as she accepted it. She took a deep breath to compose herself and went to Anne.

By the end of the week, Anne was rallying and able to come downstairs. Joseph and Anne prepared to return to their home. Molly, the new baby, was doing fine. Beth and Hannah had enjoyed their two weeks of constant companionship and fussed at the prospect of returning to their previous separateness.

Anne and Elizabetha hugged one another and said their good-byes. Martin accompanied Joseph and Anne to the carriage.

Joseph seated himself beside Anne and shook Martin's hand. Over Martin's head, Joseph gave one last longing look at Elizabetha standing at the front door.

That night in bed, Martin rolled over to Elizabetha and caressed her. Joseph's penetrating dark eyes flashed before her. She remembered the passion he awoke in her. She yearned for Martin to be more passionate, but his lovemaking remained gentle, controlled. Afterwards, she slept fitfully.

* * *

Six months later, Joseph crossed the bridge over the Clinch River, his rifle over his shoulder, his thoughts on Elizabetha as they were so often since Martin's birthday party and the stolen kisses. An aching ran through him as he recalled her soft body yielding to his. He loved her, loved awakening the physical passions in her, passions that met his own. He loved Anne's gentle ways, but, Elizabetha, he couldn't keep his thoughts off her.

He hadn't decided to fall in love with her, it happened in spite of himself. If only they were both free to follow their hearts. But they weren't. What a cad he was. He must never hurt Anne, or Martin, his best friend. He swore to control his feelings for Elizabetha. He must try.

The war cry of the Indians startled him. The overseer, Granger, and the four field slaves were working the fields closest to the river. The band of Indians was bearing down on them. Granger and the others ran toward Joseph.

Joseph returned across the bridge and opened the gate. He hoisted his rifle and fired. The tough and stocky Granger reached the stockade and hunkered down on the other side of the gate, firing his own rifle at the charging pack. The field slaves scurried through the gate, but not before Henry, the oldest slave, received an arrow in his back.

Joseph and Granger dragged Henry inside and yelled for Sarah. She was already running toward them with rifles and muskets for the slaves, her daughter, Prue, behind her.

Anne was at the doorway, crying and pacing back and forth. Joseph yelled to her, "Take the children to the cellar and stay there."

Anne darted into the house, reappearing with Hannah and carrying baby Molly. Anne's fingers fumbled at the cellar door latch. What's she doing? Joseph wondered. Finally, they were inside and the door closed.

Sarah and Prue dragged Henry toward his cabin. Joseph broke off the arrow shaft in Henry's back, gave Sarah his knife, and told her to cut out the arrowhead.

Joseph joined the others who'd already climbed the stairs and assumed posts along the wooden ledge on the stockade inner walls.

The Indians fired at the stockade, their ponies galloping around the exterior. One buck with one half of his face painted black and the other half painted red was ahead of the rest of the braves. Joseph figured him to be the leader. The brave turned to thunder past again; Joseph sited his rifle just in front of the Indian and fired. The black and red-painted man toppled sideways off his horse.

Indians galloped past shooting and yelling; one stopped and lifted the fallen leader onto the pony, mounted, and rode south. The other braves turned to follow.

A tall Indian aimed one last shot at the stockade. Granger

fired. The buck slumped forward on his horse. A comrade grabbed the reins and led the injured brave away. They were gone as quickly as they'd come.

Joseph assigned the shifts to stand guard in case the renegades returned.

Sarah and Prue finished bandaging Henry. He lay on his thin back holding the arrowhead. His tight hair was graying at the temples, making him appear older than his forty-some years. Joseph clasped Henry's hand.

"Kin I keep de arrowhead, Massa?" Henry asked.

"Of course, if you like. What will you do with it?"

"I's gonna' wear it 'round my neck for a 'membrance." His broad smile revealed several spaces from missing teeth.

Joseph smiled back. He was glad the arrow had missed any vital organs. He liked Henry.

Joseph strode to the cellar. Anne and the children were huddled in the dark.

Joseph lifted Anne who held baby Molly. He held them to his chest as Anne sobbed. Hannah threw her tiny arms around his leg. He cradled her head to his thigh.

"Thank God it's over," Anne said. "Thank God you're all right. Is everyone safe?"

"I'm afraid Henry took an arrow in the shoulder, but no harm to anyone else. He's doing fine." Joseph bent down and kissed the top of her head. No harm must ever come to his precious family.

❧ 19 ❧

1766 Five Years Later

The monthly visits between The Blakemores and the Kimberlins were riddled with stolen discussions between Elizabetha and Joseph behind Martin's back. She was relieved Joseph restrained his passions to fiery glances and an occasional touch of her hand when Anne was occupied. Without success, she had also tried to quiet the passions he stirred each time she saw him.

Elizabetha finished tucking her two children into the beds they were sharing with Anne's children. Anne waited at the doorway while Elizabetha gave a goodnight kiss to the five-year-olds her Beth and Anne's Hannah, her three-year-old Jacob and Anne's four-year-old Molly, and lastly, Anne's one-year-old James who slept alone in his crib.

Elizabetha and Anne joined their husbands in the Blakemore parlor. The men relaxed in their waistcoats and shirtsleeves before the fireplace. Joseph reclined in a Windsor chair to the side of the hearth. The firelight cast soft shadows across his tanned face. He read from the newspaper to Martin who rested on the sofa intent on Joseph's words.

"Listen to this, Martin, It's an unofficial transcript of Benjamin Franklin's testimony before the British Parliament February 13, 1766:

'... Question: If the stamp-act should be repealed, would it induce the assemblies of America to acknowledge the rights of Parliament to tax them, and would they erase their resolutions?

Answer: No, never.

Question: Is there no means of obliging them to erase those resolutions?

Answer: None that I know of; they will never do it unless compelled by force of arms.

Question: Is there no power on earth that can force them to erase them?

Answer: No power, how great soever, can force men to change their opinions.'"

He scanned down the rest of the item. "It says here that the Stamp Act was repealed in March, but the Declaratory Act still states Britain's right to tax the American colonies."

Martin got up and idly fingered a carving of Joseph's on the mantel. He stroked the back of the small cricket rendition. "I know the British thought they should have America contribute to the war debt after the French and Indian war and for their military defense of the colonies, but we expressed our willingness to be taxed by representatives in our own assemblies. When will they listen?" Martin stopped stroking the cricket and slapped his hand against the mantel. "Mark my words; this won't be the end of the matter."

Elizabetha asked, "Last year the acting governor of Virginia had dissolved Virginia's legislature for passing a resolution by Patrick Henry against the Stamp Act, didn't he?"

"Yes," was Martin's icy answer.

Joseph rose and turned to Elizabetha. "But the colonists organized the Stamp Act Congress that adopted the Declaration of Rights and Grievances, illegal in the sight of the British, but none the less, it proclaimed the colonists could not be taxed without being represented in Parliament."

Elizabetha started to speak again, but the scowl on Martin's face silenced her, reminding her how he hated it when she involved herself in the discussions of men. Sometimes she inadvertently spoke before she realized she'd been forbidden. How that word grated on her: forbidden.

"Don't you and Anne have some catching up to do?" Martin said.

"Why don't we go into the kitchen and talk, Elizabetha? Sarah and Prue are finished in there by now," Anne said.

Anne rose and led the way toward the kitchen. Elizabetha stood and glared at Martin. He turned toward the fireplace. Elizabetha's gaze was drawn to Joseph. He was staring at her. She knew he watched her all the way out of the room.

Anne and Elizabetha went through the door off the hall into the kitchen. Brass pans, a funnel, and a skimmer hung on the whitewashed brick above the large fireplace. An iron cauldron sat on the hearth. A long worktable held a lantern, wooden bowls, rolling pins, a horn spoon, lemon juicer, and skillet. A dresser to hold service ware stood in the corner behind the table that nestled cozily under a tall sash window.

Anne moved the iron balance with pans to the back of the table and pulled out a chair. "Have a seat, Elizabetha. I'll get us something to sip."

Anne lit the lantern on the worktable, brewed a pot of tea, and joined Elizabetha.

"So how have you been this past month?" Anne asked.

Elizabetha took a deep breath and released it. "Anne, I don't know what to do about Martin. He's becoming so strict in his religious beliefs. He's hard on Beth and me about it. If anyone utters a doubt or misses a prayer, Martin gets livid. He even gets upset if Jacob doesn't pay attention."

Anne rose, took two cups from the cupboard, and poured the tea. "I know you've always had your doubts about religion and you have such a curious mind. It must be hard for you to be married to someone as strict and pious as Martin."

"Having the church meetings in our hall every Sunday is wearing enough. He plans for it all week. Between that and tending the crops, he pays scant attention to any of us. When he's not busy with those, he is refining his drawings for that church he's planning to build. I get so lonely for someone to talk to about something besides religion. That's all Martin seems to talk about." Elizabetha gestured toward the parlor. "As you know, he doesn't allow my involvement in any important discussions. I'm just to be the dutiful wife, a pretty picture with no voice."

"What of your neighbors?" Anne asked.

"Oh Anne, you know I've never felt I really fit in with other women, except you, of course, but especially not those Lutheran women. I can't bear their chittering about nonsense."

Anne sipped her tea and gazed through the window into the night darkness. "This is such a wretched wilderness. I wish there was a group of Lutherans near us. Our Sunday services are usually limited to just our family, the overseer, and the slaves. Sometimes travelers who stop at our station join us," Anne lamented.

"You're an endlessly patient woman to put up with the wilderness out here. It must be so lonely for you. I hate not being able to see you as often as we'd planned. Thank goodness I have my journal to vent my troubles." Elizabetha took a sip and set the cup down. "At least you have Sarah and Prue. Sarah is so good with the children. Of course my Sudie is a treasure and Phoebe is a wonderful cook, but Sarah seems especially dedicated."

There was a knock and Joseph opened the kitchen door and stuck his head through, his mouth set in that devilish half-grin as he said to Elizabetha, "It's safe to return now. We're through talking politics. It's nearly time to retire. Martin wants to say a prayer first."

Elizabetha shot a glance at Anne. Anne patted Elizabetha's arm and said, "We'll be right there."

Anne walked past Joseph who stood by the door. As Elizabetha tried to pass through, he moved his body into her path for a moment, still grinning, before allowing her to pass.

Anne glanced over her shoulder just as Joseph blocked Elizabetha's exit. She wondered what it meant. She snapped her head around before they noticed she had seen. Elizabetha wore such a strange expression, and Joseph, why had Joseph done that? Was something going on between them? It almost seemed as if Joseph was deliberately baiting Elizabetha. Surely she must be imagining things. He was just teasing her friend. No harm.

⇒20⇐

The following summer, Elizabetha was pleased that Martin began building a log church on Reed Creek. Elizabetha knew it was to be temporary. Martin still planned to build a wood frame church one day. At least he had agreed to build the log one so the services could be held somewhere besides her home. She hoped, after it was completed, Martin's obsession with the church would be appeased and he would pay more attention to her.

Jacob liked to help his father with the building. When Elizabetha took Beth and Jacob along on the Saturdays they were constructing the church with a picnic for them all to enjoy, Jacob would swell his chest, his face beaming when he was allowed to drag small logs or carry mud for filling to his father or the slaves. This Saturday, Jacob was particularly pleased when his father let him put mud into the crevices himself.

Elizabetha and Beth spread the tablecloth on the ground and arrayed the food and lemonade before Martin and Jacob returned from washing their hands in the creek.

Beth was fidgeting while Martin said the grace. "Surely you can be still through grace, Beth," Martin scolded.

"But, Papa, can't you hurry, please?"

"Hurry!" Martin scowled at her. "We're thanking the Lord for our food. I'll not have my children fidgeting while we ask for the Lord's blessing. Now sit still!"

Tears spilled from Beth's eyes.

"Martin, she's uncomfortable. Perhaps you could hurry just a bit so I can help her be more comfortable."

"You, too? What kind of heathens am I harboring here?" Martin shouted.

Jacob began to sob.

"Now look. You have both of them crying. Please, Martin."

"Amen!" Martin jumped to his feet and whirled around, marching toward the church.

Just as he reached it, the overseer yelled, "Timber." Martin looked up just as the oak teetered toward the church. He turned to run, but the oak fell across the logs knocking them apart. One of the logs flew out, knocking Martin off his feet and pinning his right leg to the ground. He groaned.

Elizabetha screamed and ran to him. Beth and Jacob were right behind her. The slaves bounded to his aid, lifting the log off Martin's leg.

Martin tried to get up, but fell back with a gasp. "I think it's broken," he said, his mouth distorted in a grimace and his forehead rippled in a frown.

"Martin, I'm so sorry. It's all my fault," Elizabetha said.

"Papa, it's my fault. I shouldn't have fidgeted. I'm so sorry." Beth sobbed.

Jacob clung to Elizabetha's skirts and blubbered, "Me too."

"Massa, we's sho' sorry, Suh. We sho' thought dat tree would fall de other way," the towering slave, Big Jim, said as he shook his great, wooly head back and forth.

Charles, the slim and sedate overseer, though six feet tall, looked small beside Big Jim. Charles cut open the breeches and work boot on Martin's leg while Big Jim fashioned a splint.

Martin grimaced as Big Jim straightened Martin's leg, placing the wooden splints on each side.

Martin groaned as Big Jim lifted his leg and Charles tied rope around the splint to keep his leg in place.

"It's God's will. I'll be laid up for a couple of months, and it will soon be winter." Martin pursed his lips tightly together, clenched his eyelids shut, and frowned as Big Jim lowered his leg. "We'll have to postpone the building. Now no more tears, children. It's nobody's fault," Martin said as he grimaced again.

Martin gasped as Big Jim and Charles put him into the wagon.

Back home, Charles and Big Jim carried him into the house, up the stairs, and put him into bed.

Elizabetha thanked them as they went out the door, and she went upstairs to see to Martin.

"Please hand me my Bible, Elizabetha," Martin said.

Elizabetha fetched the Bible from the side table and handed it to Martin.

"God must have his reason for this delay. I'll study the Good Book to discover it."

Elizabetha watched him open it at the beginning. She went downstairs to her journal and left Martin with his Bible.

After a while, she heard the bell by the side of their bed frantically ringing. She raced upstairs. Martin was trying to get up.

"I have to use the outhouse," he growled.

"You can't manage the stairs. Wait a minute while I get the chamber pot." She held the pot steady and turned her head away while Martin aimed.

"I feel foolish," he grumbled, fastening his breeches.

Elizabetha tried to remain composed. "So do I." A grin sneaked across her mouth.

Martin glared at her. "It's not funny."

"I'm sorry. It's not." She laid a towel over the pot and took it to the hall before another grin betrayed her. In the hall, she called for Sudie to dispose of the pot's contents. She returned and helped Martin to bed.

In the evenings, Elizabetha ate her meals upstairs with Martin after seeing that the children were fed.

This evening, they played cribbage. Martin beat her the first game. "Ha, ha, take that," he crowed, placing his peg in the last hole with a flourish.

"Don't be so sure of yourself. We're not done yet."

When she beat him the second and third games, he frowned.

"Ha, ha, yourself, Sir. Now who has the last laugh?"

"As long as you don't laugh anymore when I need help with the chamber pot."

They both laughed.

Elizabetha went to his side. He pulled her head down and kissed her.

By the sixth week, Martin was able to resume his duties.

Elizabetha had enjoyed having his company and the extra attention from him while he was confined to the house. Now things would be getting back to normal, whatever that was.

Three weeks later, Elizabetha descended the stairs and found Martin returned from Evansham and in the parlor. He sat on the edge of the sofa, elbows on his knees and hands dangling between them. From his hands, hung a crumpled letter.

"What is it, Martin?" She knelt in front of him, placing her hands on his arms.

He glanced at her without recognition for an instant. He lifted the letter and handed it to her.

Elizabetha saw it was from his sister in Germany and quickly scanned down.

This was supposed to be a happy letter informing you of my recent marriage, but, alas, it is not happy.

A storm had developed soon after our parents left the marriage reception for home. There was an accident. It is assumed our parents' wagon horse was spooked by the lighting and stampeded. The wagon tipped over, and our parents were both killed instantly. I'm so sorry to ....

Elizabetha dropped the letter and embraced Martin's knees. She didn't know what to say, how to comfort him. Martin had worked so hard to amass enough money to bring them all to America.

Martin rested his head on top of hers. Neither spoke.

After a time, Elizabetha managed to say, "I'm so sorry your plans to bring your parents here have been lost, Martin."

Martin lifted his head and rested against the sofa back with his eyes closed. "My plans don't seem to have fit into God's." His eyes opened and he pondered a moment. "Papa would have been so pleased with the church I planned for him."

Martin stood upright and shook his head. "Faith must not falter. Faith is the answer, Elizabetha. I shall fetch my bible and read till supper."

With that, he was away and up the stairs. Elizabetha knew things had returned to normal.

⇒•21•⇐

A year later, Elizabetha received a letter from Joseph that Anne had miscarried. The baby girl was stillborn. Anne had lost a lot of blood and was run down. She'd contracted pneumonia and required complete bed rest. The slaves were occupied with the children and regular chores and Joseph had to run the farm. The doctor had said someone needed to tend to Anne during the days. Could Elizabetha come to help out?

Martin arranged for Big Jim to drive Elizabetha to the Blakemore station and stay until her return when Anne was through the crises.

Elizabetha and Big Jim left early the next morning. When they arrived, Joseph came out to meet them. "I'm so glad you could come, Elizabetha, thank you."

"That's what friends are for, Joseph. Can Prue give some food to Big Jim? I know he's hungry, and he'll need a place to stay."

"Of course. Let me see you to the guest room and I'll tell Prue. Big Jim can sleep in the second cabin."

"I'd like to see Anne right away. How is she?"

"The doctor said she's basically healthy and with enough rest she should recover in a few weeks. He left sedatives to help

her sleep at night. She's been distraught over losing the baby."
Joseph ran his fingers through his tousled hair. "She hasn't
wanted me close to her since it happened two weeks ago. She's
been cursing me and the wilderness in the same breath."

Elizabetha wanted to take him in her arms and comfort him,
but instead said, "Poor Joseph, don't fret, she'll soon come
around, you'll see."

Anne was flushed with fever and her breathing labored in a
fitful sleep when Elizabetha went into her room.

Elizabetha pulled a ladder-back chair to the bedside and
placed a wet cloth across Anne's forehead. She stirred.

"Elizabetha, you're here. Thank you. Joseph told you about
the baby?" Anne asked in a weak voice.

"Yes he did. I'm so sorry, Anne. You need your rest to get
your strength back. We'll have you feeling better in no time."

Prue brought in a tray of food for Elizabetha and broth for
Anne. Elizabetha was able to feed Anne most of it.

During the times Anne was awake, Elizabetha read aloud
William Falconer's *The Shipwreck* that Anne's mother had sent
her. Anne seemed to be less agitated knowing Elizabetha was
near.

Sarah stayed with Anne that night while Elizabetha and
Joseph took supper downstairs. The children had eaten in the
kitchen and were already in bed.

Elizabetha and Joseph sat at opposite ends of the table,
making only polite conversation. Perhaps it was the absence of
Martin and Anne that made them as uneasy with each other as
if they were strangers.

The second night was a repeat of the first, but by the third
night of Elizabetha's stay, Joseph had Prue establish Elizabetha's
place adjacent to his at the table. "I thought it more convenient
than talking across a vast space," he said and poured them each
a glass of Madeira.

Elizabeth lifted her glass in a toast. "To Anne's recovery."

Joseph raised his and clinked the rim to hers. His gaze held
her as if by magnetism.

The nearness turned their conversation to more familiar

ground. Once during a lively discussion of the political unrest in the colonies, Elizabetha's knee accidentally touched Joseph's under the table. A tingle shot up her leg. She wasn't sure if it came from him or her. She pulled away. His dark gaze searched her face as if looking for the answer himself.

He poured another glass of wine for each.

After supper, she put her napkin on the table and Joseph grasped her hand. His sensuous mouth wore that alluring half-smile as he drew her hand to his lips and kissed it, his gaze steady on her all the while.

She did not feel steady as her heart fluttered within her chest. She had better excuse herself before she did something crazy. "I think I'll go up to my room and read," she said.

She felt his gaze follow her out of the room and up the stairs. She hoped she wouldn't stumble. In her room, she went to bed and tried to read. After a while, she gave it up and blew out the candle. The house was quiet.

Her bedroom door opened and closed. She rolled over to find Joseph at the side of her bed. She jerked upright. "Joseph."

He lighted on the bed, gathered her into his arms, and rained kisses on her. His breath was ragged. He kissed her mouth, her eyes, her throat. Between kisses, she managed to ask, "Anne?"

"She's had her sedative. She's sleeping soundly."

"Joseph, don't, please."

"I can't help myself. I can't bear having you so near and not having you."

He lay her back on the bed and lowered himself onto her. He slid her shift off her shoulders, cupped her breasts and kissed them. She wanted to resist but was powerless. The smell of him, his heavy breathing, the weight of his body on her, his kisses, his caresses awakened every lustful fiber in her body. He paused a moment and scanned her face with his dark hypnotic gaze. He lowered his mouth to hers, gently at first, then with a force of passion that made her feel faint.

She wanted him. She knew this was the way he would take her, not sweet and gentle, but fused with lust. It was the only way it could be between them.

He slid off his shoes and straddled her as he removed his shirt over his head. His body engulfed her as his lips found hers.

He murmured, "I love you." He nuzzled her ear, the warmth of his breath titillating her as he said, "If only I'd met you before you met Martin and I met Anne." He ran his tongue along the side of her neck. "Things would be different." He kissed the hollow of her neck. "You and I were meant for each other."

She knew it was true. She couldn't deny her own love for him. Her hands couldn't resist stroking his bare chest. His skin was firm and she could feel his taut muscles beneath. She intertwined her fingers in his chest hair. She moved her hand up to his smooth jaw and caressed his lips with her fingertips.

He caught them in his mouth and gently sucked on them. He smothered her in more kisses and somewhere in the process removed his breeches, his hardness pressing against her.

She tasted the slight saltiness of his skin as her tongue traced small circles on his chest.

He pulled off her shift and their naked bodies felt as one. Their passion exploded in shared rhythm. Finally, they lay back, sated. Neither spoke. After a time, he took her hand and kissed it. He rolled over to his side and kissed her forehead. She couldn't voice her feelings. What they'd done was wonderful, and terrible.

Spending her days with Anne was a guilty torment for Elizabetha. Nights with Joseph were the utter abandonment of all she knew to be sane and proper. How could she go on living a double life? What was wrong with her? She must get away from Joseph. How could she get away from herself?

The second week Anne's fever broke. She became stronger. She was often able to sit up in bed while Elizabetha read to her. Elizabetha told Big Jim they would leave the end of the week. She knew she must get away from Joseph as soon as possible.

The last day, Joseph helped Anne downstairs to say her goodbyes. "Elizabetha, I can't thank you enough for all you've done for me. You're a true friend. You and Joseph have been so unselfish and caring through this ordeal. I can't thank you both enough."

Joseph and Elizabetha stole a guilty glance at each other. Elizabetha hated herself at that moment, and hated Joseph, and even Anne for making her feel so condemnable and miserable. How could she ever face either of them or Martin without shame? She remembered when she was younger, how she'd wished to not understand the feelings of others, to be totally selfish. Apparently she was successful at that. How could she have let this happen?

Tears formed behind her eyelids. Why did she have to like Anne so much? She brushed the tears away and kissed Anne's cheek. She nodded at Joseph and hurried outside to Big Jim and the waiting carriage. Safe inside the carriage, the tears flowed as Big Jim drove out of the stockade.

She freshened her upsweep and made sure her tears were dried as the carriage arrived home. Martin waited outside. Big Jim helped Elizabetha from the carriage. He carried her travel chest toward the house.

Martin said, "We've missed you."

As Big Jim entered, Beth and Jacob tore out of the house around both sides of the giant. They swarmed to Elizabetha who bent down to be engulfed with their kisses and hugs.

When she rose, Martin embraced her and kissed her forehead. He never kissed her on the mouth in front of the children. He held her at arms' length and said, "You look tired. Was it an awful ordeal? How is Anne?"

"I am tired, but no, it wasn't awful." If Martin only knew. She mustn't let herself think about it. "Anne has improved greatly. She'll be fine."

"And Joseph?"

"He's doing as well as can be expected. It was a trying time for all of us, but I'm home now, and everything will be fine." Oh, it would. She hoped it would.

⇒ 22 ⇐

Four months After Anne's recuperation, Martin put his Bible on his lap and studied Elizabetha while her fingers busily embroidered pink trim on a pillow slip. The warmth of the parlor fireplace felt good against the cool September evening. Beth and Jacob were tucked in bed.

There was something different about Elizabetha. He couldn't put his finger on it, but it was there. She seemed more withdrawn, as if she were wrestling with some insolvable problem. Ever since her return from Joseph and Anne's—no even before that—he'd noticed a difference about her. Could there be anything between Elizabetha and Joseph? He'd often suspected a secrecy lurked between them, as if they had been talking behind his back, but he had forbidden her.

She had everything she could want, two children, a comfortable home. She thinks too much. That's her trouble. Why can't she just go about her business and leave the problems to God? Martin picked up his Bible from his lap and began reading aloud.

Elizabetha's mind rebelled again at being subjected to his religious indoctrination. She dropped her work down on her lap and rubbed her forehead. "Do you really think I'll become a pious believer by you droning out the words of the Bible to me? I have such a headache, Martin."

"As Luther said, the Bible is '... the manger in which the Word of God is laid ....' Salvation is by faith alone, Elizabetha."

"So if one does some great good work it makes no difference?"

"Good works follow from faith as a good tree produces good fruit."

"What if one commits a terrible sin?"

"Sin is a fractured relationship between the people of creation and God. Every attempt to please Him falls short of the mark. Our failure to live up to God's just and loving expectation for creation reveals only our need for God's mercy and forgiveness. Faith, Elizabetha, you must have faith."

"You sound like my mother," she sneered. She rose and strode to the fireplace extending her hands to the fire.

"Jesus said in *John* 11:25 and 26: 'Those who believe in me, even though they die, will live, and everyone who lives and believes in me will never die.'"

Elizabetha turned toward Martin as he closed the Bible with a smug smile on his face. "Oh, Martin, no one really believes in heaven or why would anyone stay here and not go to be with God?" She turned to the fireplace, then back again, "What is heaven, anyway?"

Martin leaned his head against the chair back and recited, "Life with God persists now and after death. History moves steadily toward's God's ultimate fulfillment." He raised his head and peered at her. "It's not possible for a description of what life may be like beyond history."

"You talk in circles, Martin. I get the idea. Faith is the only answer to any question. Let's just drop it please."

"It angers me when you talk like that." Martin glared at her.

"It angers me when you talk faith, faith, faith. I'm going to bed. Are you coming?"

"No. I'll sit up awhile." He reopened his Bible. "I'll sleep in the guest room tonight," he added.

Elizabetha turned on her heels and stomped upstairs. He was so tedious.

The next morning at breakfast, she could tell Martin was still angry. He didn't kiss her cheek or greet her when he came to the table.

After breakfast, Martin announced Adam Cook planned to leave that day for business in Scott County. Martin would accompany him to visit the Klaus farm. They would be gone seven days.

That afternoon, Elizabetha sat in the parlor finishing the pillowslip. Martin hadn't even kissed her goodbye when he left. She was furious with him. He was so self-righteous.

* * *

By the sixth day of Martin's absence, Elizabetha missed him in spite of herself. She didn't like being alone, even if all he talked about was religion. When had he become so pious? Or had she just not seen it in the beginning, her girlhood romantic notions just glossing over it.

Sudie and Phoebe had taken the children down to Reed Creek for a picnic. Elizabetha had stayed at home to write a letter to her parents and update her journal. Outside, she heard a horse gallop to the house.

A knock resounded through the door. She opened it and Joseph Blakemore strode inside.

"Hello, Elizabetha. I rode over to see if Martin wanted to accompany me to Scott County."

"Martin's already there. He went with Adam Cook. They won't be back till tomorrow. I'm sorry you made the trip for nothing."

Joseph stood staring at her. "The house is quiet. You're alone?"

Elizabetha grew uneasy as she realized she was alone, alone with Joseph.

Joseph took his coat and hat off and hung them on a peg. He turned to her. His muscular body was silhouetted against the window, sunlight encircling him. His enchanting sable eyes held her gaze. Why did he have to be so handsome?

"Where are Sudie and Phoebe and the children?" he asked.

"They—they've gone on a picnic at the creek." She knew she must do something, but what? She backed up.

He had her in his arms before she could think what she should do. He held her close and kissed her and kissed her again, passionate, lustful.

She must stop him. She must. Each time she tried to pull away, he held her closer and kissed her harder. He swooped her up in his arms and carried her upstairs, kissing her all the while.

Afterwards, they dressed in silence. Joseph followed Elizabetha downstairs to the kitchen where she fixed tea. He sat at the table with his head in his hands. She knew he felt as rotten as she did. Neither of them spoke. She set the cups on the table and sat across from him, her hands folded on the table. She stirred sugar into her tea and passed the sugar bowl to him.

He took her hand in his. "Elizabetha, you know I love you. I'm sorry, but I can't resist you."

"I don't seem to do a good job of resisting either. What are we going to do, Joseph?"

"I don't know what to do. I love you, but I also love Anne. When I'm around you, I can't help myself. I want you." His gaze burrowed into her soul.

She lowered her head. "I know. I love you, and I love Martin. It's impossible. If only I were stronger." She raised her gaze to his. "You must be strong for both of us."

"I can't."

The sound of horse hooves outside broke their spell on each other.

Martin came into the house and hung his coat and hat on the peg next to Joseph's.

"Martin, in here," Elizabetha spurted. "Joseph has stopped by. We're having a cup of tea."

Martin came into the kitchen. "Joseph, when did you get here?" He shook Joseph's hand and joined them at the table.

"He just arrived," Elizabetha lied. "He wanted you to go to

Scott County with him, and here you are just back from there."

Martin and Joseph talked awhile as she poured tea. She kept thinking, what if Martin returned an hour earlier? She was relieved when Joseph finally took his leave.

As Joseph rode off, Elizabetha said to Martin, "You came back early."

"I was feeling badly about our spat and decided to come back a day ahead of Adam. Elizabetha, I'm sorry I behaved so self-righteously." He reached for the hand Joseph had held moments before.

"Martin, It's I who have behaved badly." She couldn't bring herself to speak more.

⟫•23•⟪

1775 Nine Years Later

Scarceness of opportunity to be alone together had confined Elizabetha and Joseph's relationship to brief stolen discussions with Anne present and Martin not, and clandestine touches and glances. Often Elizabetha found her daydreams filled with Joseph. She'd have to chase his image from her mind and find something else to distract her thoughts. She dreamed of the passions he'd awakened in her.

Elizabetha had resigned herself to the Reformed Lutherans in and around Mount Airy continuing to meet in the hall of her home for Sunday services since Martin had temporarily abandoned the log church. There was no preacher in the area, so members of the congregation took turns reading from the Bible.

After the death of Martin's parents, he had seemed to lose interest in finishing the church. He'd told her it was not God's will that he should build it yet. How could she argue with God's will?

Today, the Blakemores were expected for a visit. When Elizabetha and Martin had last visited the Blakemores, Joseph had told them he was going to attend the Virginia legislative convention March 23. A resolution to propose forming a committee to prepare the colony for defense against the British was to be proposed and Joseph had wanted to hear everything first hand.

After the Boston Tea Party, Britain had closed the Boston port to shipping and allowed British troops to be billeted in American homes. All the colonies were resistant and the Virginia legislature had called it a hostile invasion.

Fifty-five members were selected from the individual colonies and had met in Philadelphia in 1774, as a Continental Congress. Their goal was to unite the colonies to vote on fighting against the British tyranny, but there had been quibbling over the method of voting and whether it should be by colonies, or by the poll, or by interests. A Second Continental Congress was going to meet in May in Philadelphia.

Elizabetha watched for her company from the parlor window until she saw the Blakemores' wagon pull into the yard. She went out the door to greet them.

Martin came from the barn and joined her in the yard as the wagon came to a stop.

While Joseph helped Anne down from the wagon seat, their children poured out of the back. Martin and Elizabetha's offspring greeted them.

The four teenagers with James tagging behind them headed one way, Samantha, Magdalena, Samuel and Rachel headed another. The two toddlers, Catrina and William, were taken in tow by Sudie. The adults retired to the parlor.

After Phoebe served lemonade, Martin asked, "How did the convention go, Joseph?"

"It was a day to make every Virginian proud, I tell you. Patrick Henry was a fiery spokesman as he expanded on the duty of preparing for war. His ending words stirred me so greatly I was impelled to write them down as soon as he finished speaking." Joseph rose, reached into his waistcoat pocket, and opened a folded sheet of paper. "Here, let me read them.

'What is it that the gentlemen wish? What would they have? Is life so dear or peace so sweet as to be purchased at the price of chains and slavery? Forbid it, Almighty

God. I know not what course others may take, but as for me, give me liberty or give me death!'

"Isn't that eloquent?" Joseph said.

Martin rose and strode to the fireplace mantle. He appeared deeply moved. He placed both hands on the mantle and lowered his head. Abruptly, he turned. "Yes, we must join together to end the British oppression. Better to die in battle than in British chains. God is just. He will look after our endeavor."

"Amen," Joseph said.

Elizabetha tried to lighten the mood of the men. "There's no war today," she said. "Who wants more lemonade? Maybe we could play whist before supper. The children will be coming in soon."

Joseph nodded. "Of course."

Joseph and Elizabetha's gaze held each other one split second before each turned away.

Anne thought she saw something flash between Joseph and Elizabetha in that instant, but she was being silly. She must just be nervous with all this talk of war.

"Whist would be fun, wouldn't it, Martin? It's been such a long time since we've been able to visit," Anne said.

Martin studied Elizabetha and Joseph. Surely he was mistaken about the spark that had seemed to emanate from one to the other. After all, Joseph was his best friend. It was just the tension in the air from the threat of war.

Martin returned to Elizabetha's side and said, "Whist is just the thing."

≫·24·≪

1776 One Year Later

On July 4, John Hancock, president of the Congress and Charles Thomson, the secretary signed the Declaration of Independence that Thomas Jefferson had been selected to write. By August 2, all fifty-six signers had set their name to it. Their identities were kept secret for several months to protect them from revenge by Loyalists and British. In spite of this, some of the signers had been singled out for vengeance.

Martin and Joseph determined to enlist at once. Military recruiters were traveling the countryside searching for men willing to enlist. The recruiters were reported to be in Evansham.

Martin and Joseph entered the tavern door into a boisterous group of ruffians milling around and drinking with gusto the beer being purchased by an army captain, a corporal, and a lieutenant.

One boisterous brute in particular was growing insolent toward the military recruiters. "You fancy pants think you can waltz in, promise a few dollars, ply us with liquor, and walk out with a bunch of enlisted soldiers." The red-faced rowdy brawled. He wiped his hairy forearm across his beer-foamed mouth. "I've half a mind to punch you square in the face." He leered at the

Captain and drew back his fist.

Martin grabbed the cocked fist and reeled the roughneck around causing him to lose his footing. The hooligan stumbled backward and crashed onto the floor. His buddies circled him and jeered.

Martin turned to the Captain and said, "I'd like to enlist."

The young Captain abruptly stood, his mouth agape, his eyes wide. Martin spun around just in time to see the brute with a knife drawn high over his head and a murderous gleam in his eyes heading for him.

Joseph intercepted the ruffian and wrenched the knife away. The man grabbed Joseph by the throat and wrestled him to the floor. Joseph's eyes glinted with animal cunning. The man clutched his hands around Joseph's throat and squeezed with vicious force. Joseph tried to pry away his attacker's fingers, still holding the man's knife. Failing, he slit the rowdy's throat with one quick slash. Joseph leapt to a crouched stance and the animal glared at the rest of the rabble. To a man, they backed away. Joseph pulled himself erect and glanced at Martin. The beast had retreated behind sable eyes.

The Captain, Corporeal and Lieutenant all had drawn their pistols. Joseph dropped the knife.

Several from the crowd dragged the dead man out to the alley behind the tavern and threw the knife after as well.

The soldiers holstered their weapons.

Martin strode over to Joseph and clasped him on the shoulder. "You saved my life. I owe you."

* * *

By 1780, Martin and Joseph were with General Washington in Williamsburg, Virginia. The French fleet assisted by Admiral de Barras blocked the Chesapeake Bay. The French and Americans marched to Yorktown. They planned a siege of the fort. A direct attack would result in high casualties. The French and Prussians assisting the Americans were masters at siege warfare. The Americans had no such experience. They learned to dig zigzag trenches so artillery could be brought closer to the fort. General

Cornwallis tried to escape by transporting his men across the river at Gloucester Point.

Martin and Joseph were in the American defense line firing at the British. A lead ball struck Joseph in his right shoulder, the force spinning him around. He fell to the ground. Martin ran to him and pulled him out of the line of fire. He tore the bottom of his shirt off and bandaged Joseph's shoulder as best he could to slow the bleeding then took his position with the colonists, who were joined by the French. They fought harder. The escape failed.

October 19, the British surrendered. At first they tried to surrender to the French who insisted the British surrender to the Americans. General Cornwallis's second in command, General O'Hare, attempted to give Cornwallis's sword to General Washington. He refused the sword. He instead made the British surrender to the American second in command, General Benjamin Lincoln.

After the army doctor dug the ball out of Joseph's shoulder, Martin assisted Joseph on the long journey home. They stopped for Joseph to rest. Joseph's wound was bleeding heavily again, soaking his shirt and Martin's as he supported Joseph against his body under an elm. Martin helped Joseph into his saddle and led his horse by the reins. It was all Joseph could do to hang on. At last Martin spied lights shining from houses in the distance. "Not much further now," Martin said.

Joseph slumped on his belly in his saddle.

That evening after supper, Elizabetha heard horses ride up to the house. She fetched the rifle from its pegs, stood at the side of the window, and pulled a corner of the muslin curtain aside to peek out. Martin assisted Joseph from his horse. Big Jim reached the two just as Joseph collapsed. Elizabetha bounded to the front door and flung it open.

Big Jim carried Joseph inside. Both Joseph and Martin were covered in road dust streaked by sweat. Martin's eyes were red-rimmed. Joseph's shirt was soaked in blood. Martin's shirt was similarly stained. For an instant, Elizabetha thought both men were injured. She was immobilized, torn between which man to see to first.

Martin led the way and Big Jim carried Joseph upstairs to the guest room. Sudie and Prue followed to settle Joseph in bed.

Martin returned downstairs. Elizabetha threw her arms around him. "I'm so glad you're all right. Is Joseph badly hurt?"

"The surgeon dug the ball out of his shoulder. He's lost a lot of blood, but he'll survive. He'll need to stay here until he's strong enough to travel home."

"The overseer is making a trip to Scott County tomorrow. I'll send word to Anne with Charles. He can pass by there on his way." She scanned Martin's face. "And the war?"

"It's over. The British surrendered." Martin collapsed in the wing chair and Elizabetha helped him off with his boots. Martin patted her head as she knelt by him and laid her head on his lap. "You'd better see to Joseph's wound. Maybe Phoebe could make some tea."

Elizabetha kissed the back of Martin's hand as she rose. She left Martin in the chair, instructed Phoebe to make Martin's tea, and went upstairs.

Joseph was still unconscious on the bed. Sudie and Big Jim had removed Joseph's bloody shirt and his boots, and wiped the worst of the grime from his face. The room reeked of blood and sweat.

Elizabetha sent Sudie for the household medical supplies. Perching on the edge of the bed, Elizabetha traced Joseph's sensuous mouth with her fingertips. His wavy, sandy hair was pasted across his forehead. She smoothed it back from his brow.

Sudie returned with the supplies and they cleaned and rebandaged Joseph's wound. He stirred and grimaced once while they tended him before falling into a peaceful sleep.

* * *

Four days after arriving home, Martin prepared to attend the Sunday meeting at his St. Paul's Church. Two years before, in 1779, between battles, Martin and the other Lutherans had joined together to finish the log church Martin had started years before. So many new people had settled in Mount Airy, the congregation was too large for the Kimberlin's home. Martin named the church St. Paul's after the one in Schaefferstown. Elizabetha was relieved the meetings were no longer held in their hall.

Before leaving for church, Martin said, "Elizabetha, you should stay home and look after Joseph, he's still weak."

Surprised at being excused, Elizabetha found Joseph propped up against the pillows gazing out the window at the rolling hills as she entered the guest room.

Joseph turned his gaze to her. "You didn't go to church with Martin?" he asked.

"He said I should see to you because you're still so weak. Let me change the dressing on your wound." She arranged her supplies on the small table beside the bed.

Joseph remained still, observing her as she changed the dressing. As she started to rise, his good hand reached the back of her neck and pulled her face to his. He kissed her with more passion than she thought possible in his condition. He released her and his arm fell to the bed with sudden exhaustion.

"You seem to be gaining part of your strength back." She smiled.

"Elizabetha—."

She put her index finger to her lips. "Don't talk. You're to rest, and no more feats of exertion." She couldn't be angry with him.

⇒ 25 ⇐

After several weeks of recuperation, Joseph became stronger. Martin assisted him downstairs for supper and to sit in the parlor afterward. Soon Joseph could manage on his own.

The day before Joseph was to return to Clinch River, Elizabetha believed she was alone in the house as Sudie and Phoebe were hanging the wash while the four younger children played outside, Martin and Jacob were surveying the fields, and Joseph was asleep upstairs. Elizabetha rose from her writing desk. As she turned, she was startled to see Joseph standing there inspecting her. As she started past him, he grabbed her shoulders and held her.

"Elizabetha." He pulled her close, his arms enveloping her and kissed her, his mouth hungry on hers, hers hungry on his.

The back door to the kitchen slammed shut. "Mama, Mama."

Joseph and Elizabetha separated.

Five-year-old Rosanna ran into the parlor. "Look, Mama, a gas—a gashop—. Look, Uncle Joseph."

"Grasshopper?" Joseph asked.

Rosanna nodded her curly head. She started to open her

hand.

Joseph clasped his hand over hers. "Let's take it outside and look at it, all right?"

Rosanna ran toward the door and called over her shoulder, "Come, Mama."

Elizabetha and Joseph followed Rosanna to the yard. Elizabetha thought, *saved from ourselves by a child.*

* * *

In the summer of 1781, the Blakemores and Kimberlins celebrated the safe return of Joseph and Martin with a picnic on the precipice near Joseph and Anne's station. Joseph's shoulder had healed and only a little stiffness remained.

Martin lolled on the blanket on the ground with a full stomach, and Joseph did the same while Elizabetha and Anne put in a basket the remnants of the feast that Sarah and Prue had spread for them. The warm air was filled with laughter from the children, the earthy smell of green grass, and heady scent of wild flowers.

Martin could relax knowing eighteen-year-old sensible Jacob kept an eye on the teens, his brother Johanas and Joseph and Anne's Samuel and Rachel as they overlooked the precipice to the Clinch River below, mesmerized as they threw stones over the edge and watched them tumble off the rocky descent to the bottom and plop into the river.

Sarah and Prue stowed away the rest of the picnic items while the younger children scampered around an elm whooping and laughing while the slaves, Gim and Hany, chased them. Anne and Joseph's one-year-old, Thomas, dug in the dirt under Sarah and Prue's watchful eyes.

Beth and Hannah had spread a private blanket for themselves away from the nuisance of the children. At twenty, they were too grown up for childish play and too young for the likes of their parents.

Sarah and Prue had laid out a picnic for each group.

The lazy humming sounds of summer lulled Martin. His eyes

flashed open with a start. He realized he must have dozed off. Elizabetha and Joseph were in the middle of a whispered discussion. Anne lounged beside Joseph, smiling and glancing from one to the other as each debated in a low murmur. Martin bolted to a sitting position. What did Elizabetha think she was doing? "Elizabetha," Martin blurted. "How many times must you be told to not speak of men's affairs?"

They all snapped to attention with mouths gaping.

Elizabetha said, "But, Martin, I—."

"A woman has no place debating men's issues." He bore his glare on Joseph. "I blame you for encouraging her."

Joseph said, "Now wait a minute, Martin, there's no cause for anger."

Martin leapt to his feet.

Joseph rose and reached for Martin's shoulder, "Come on now, calm down. Elizabetha was just—."

Martin thrust Joseph's arm away with his forearm. "Mind your own wife, not mine."

Something switched on in Joseph's gaze. He glowered at Martin with the wild eyes of an animal about to pounce. Joseph's muscles tightened into springs eager to uncoil. His fist exploded into Martin's face.

The blow reeled Martin backwards. He rubbed his chin and exercised his jaw to be sure it wasn't broken.

Joseph covered the short distance between them and dove at Martin. He clutched Martin's throat with powerful fingers.

Martin gasped, trying to break Joseph's steel-like grip around his neck.

Anne screamed, "Joseph."

Elizabetha placed her hand on Joseph's shoulder and uttered, "Joseph."

The vicious glaze ebbed from Joseph's eyes and his grip eased on Martin's throat. Joseph bounded upright pulling Martin up with him by the hand. "Martin, I'm so sorry. Are you all right? I don't know what came over me. I just saw red. I'm sorry. Forgive me."

Saw red. Martin remembered Joseph had saved his life in that tavern when they enlisted, he had seen that same fierceness erupt in Joseph. "I forgive you, Joseph."

Joseph reached his hand to Martin.

"I'll remember to never knock your hand away again," Martin said as he rubbed his throat while he accepted Joseph's handshake.

"I'll remember not to reach for you when you're angry," Joseph said.

Martin spotted the children gaping at them and waved his arms in the air. "Everything's fine. No harm done. Time to go home."

On the drive home, Martin wondered what it was about Elizabetha placing her hand on Joseph's shoulder that bothered him. It had probably saved his life, but why had her touch affected Joseph so? Was there really something between them after all? No, if Joseph wanted him out of the way, he wouldn't have bothered to save his life. It was probably Anne's scream that brought Joseph's temper under control.

* * *

Two years later in 1783, Elizabetha and Martin's son Jacob turned twenty on the day of his sister Beth's marriage to Captain Bruce Spangler who served in the regular army. The treaty of Paris had been signed, officially ending the Revolution. It was a day of celebration on many counts, Elizabetha mused as she watched Jacob mingle among the wedding guests after the ceremony. Always the efficient one, he made sure everything ran smoothly.

Jacob noticed a young girl of about thirteen gazing at him every time he finished talking to one group of guests and moved on to the next. He wondered why she stared at him.

He finished chatting with what he thought was the last group, turned, and found himself staring into the pale blue eyes of the young girl he'd found watching him.

She offered a tenuous hand for a handshake that Jacob obliged.

"I'm Margaretha. You are Jacob," she said, blushing.

Her light brown hair was upswept and decorated with blue satin ribbons matching the color of her eyes, as did her dress. She wasn't exactly a beauty, but pleasant looking, nonetheless. "Yes," he answered.

"I thought so. Your sister Beth had described you."

"You know my sister?"

"I suppose I do since I'm here." She lowered her eyes, her complexion turning even a rosier pink.

"Of course," Jacob said. How could such a shy young girl make him feel so foolish?

A small smile quavered on her mouth as she said, "Actually my father is uncle to the groom."

"Your father is the Indian Agent, then?" Jacob remembered Beth telling him that.

"Yes. I help him," the petite Margaretha said.

"How interesting. You must know a lot about the Cherokee."

Her eyes widened in excitement and lit up her whole face in radiance. "Oh, I do. I do."

"Margaretha, there you are," a thin man with the same eyes and hair of the girl said behind her and moved to her side.

"Papa, this is Beth's brother Jacob."

Jacob smiled and shook his hand.

"Pleased to meet you, name's Sam Stringer."

"She was telling me she helps you in your duties of Indian Agent."

"Yes." Sam smiled down at his daughter. "Since her mother died when she was five, I have always taken her along."

"He's interested in the Cherokee, Papa."

"That so? Be happy to take you along sometime."

"I would enjoy that. Thank you." Jacob wanted to learn more about this strange little Margaretha who seemed to love the Indians so much.

❖26❖

1785

Just two years had passed since Beth's wedding and here Elizabetha was preparing for Jacob's. She plucked a gray hair from her temple and peered closer in the mirror. If she kept that up she'd soon be bald. She convinced herself the scant silver threads softened her otherwise dark hair. She finished her preparations.

Jacob at twenty-two was marrying a girl of just fifteen. The bride-to-be, Margaretha, was involved with the Cherokee Indians. Her father had been the Indian Agent, and Margaretha accompanied him on his visits to the tribe. After her father's death, she had followed in his footsteps and had become a quiet champion for the Cherokee cause. Elizabetha had been surprised at how easily the tiny fifteen-year-old wrapped Jacob around her finger. She might be little but she was mighty.

* * *

Two years after Jacob's wedding, Elizabetha received word from her mother that her father was extremely ill. The doctor had said it was his heart. At sixty-nine, her father's heart was failing.

Elizabetha and Martin made immediate plans to go to Lebanon. Their son Jacob and his wife, Margaretha, would stay at the house and look after the farm and the children.

While Elizabetha packed, she couldn't imagine her father ill. He'd always been invincible. What if he should die? Her mother was always dependent on him. She'd have to come live with Elizabetha that was all there was to it. Once Elizabetha decided that, she felt better.

They took the lighter wagon, traveling The Great Road, built to a width Elizabetha didn't remember twenty-seven years ago. They stayed at the numerous settlements and forts along the way.

At last, they pulled up to her parents' home. Her brother, Toby, greeted them. Elizabetha didn't recognize him at first. He'd been just a boy when she'd seen him last. Now he was a grown man, tall and lean like their father but with the sensitive features of their mother and her same dark, wavy hair.

Toby scooped Elizabetha up in his arms and twirled her around in his excitement. "You're as beautiful as I remembered," he said.

He set her down and turned to Martin. They clutched each other's arm in a warm handshake.

"Papa?" Elizabetha asked.

Toby's smile disappeared. The blue of his eyes turned a shade darker. "He's gone, Elizabetha. He passed away last night. I'm sorry." He held her to his chest as her body quaked with sobs.

Gaining control of her tears, she asked, "How's Mama?"

"She's holding up."

"I must see her." Elizabetha left the men to the luggage and rushed into the house.

She found her mother in the parlor, resting in a wing chair. The parlor was as Elizabetha remembered, the paint-laden canvas carpeting with blue squares still covered the center of the floor, the sofa at the left edge where it had always been. The open three-shelved cupboard display of porcelain Chinese vases next to it.

Her mother rose as Elizabetha hastened to her and embraced her. Her mother patted Elizabetha's back and smoothed her hair as Elizabetha wept. "There, there. He was so tired at the end. He's at peace now."

Elizabetha's mother sank back in her chair. Elizabetha pulled a ladder-back chair up beside her. Her mother wore a high-necked black dress with white lace above the necking that surrounded her throat. A white, lace-trimmed handkerchief peeked out of her sleeve cuff. Her dark hair was heavily streaked with gray, her slender figure still graceful, but thinner.

There were dark circles under her mother's eyes, and the blue veins in her wrinkled hands threatened to burst through the transparent skin covering them. Elizabetha always remembered her parents as they were when she was young. It surprised her to see how her mother had aged.

Toby and Martin came into the parlor. "This is my wife, Marcie," Toby said as Marcie deposited a tray of tea on the table. She shook Martin's hand and reached to shake Elizabetha's, but Elizabetha hugged her instead. Marcie was a pretty blonde, not plump, more cuddly. Her cheeks dimpled as she smiled. She was several inches shorter than Elizabetha. Strange that tall men often seemed to choose short women, Elizabetha mused.

The day of the funeral, the procession of family and friends followed her father's pine coffin to the town burying ground. A bespectacled Reverend Henkel from St. Paul's of Schaefferstown, his thick mane now grayed, delivered a sermon with eulogy and prayers. Elizabetha tossed the first sprig of rosemary into the grave. Goodbye, my beloved Papa. Shovelfuls of earth were cast. It was over.

Later that afternoon, Elizabetha found her mother, reclined in a rocker, alone in her bedroom in front of the open window. The sky was a clear cerulean and the songs of many birds filled the air. The rocker creaked as her mother rocked.

"I love the sound of birds singing. Your father and I listened to them by the hour," her mother said as Elizabetha came to her side.

Elizabetha held her mother's hand. Glancing around her parents' bedroom, she noted the four-poster bed across the room, much too large for one small woman. The wardrobe still held her father's garments. Maybe Toby could take those. She gazed upon her frail mother. "Mama, I want you to come live with Martin and me. You can't stay here alone."

"Thank you, dear, but Toby and Marcie have invited me to live with them. I am used to town, you know."

"But, Mama, I want to take care of you. I've made up my mind to it."

Her mother's eyes crinkled as a small chuckle escaped, then she grew serious. "I know when you make up your mind the thing is as good as done, Elizabetha, but not about this. I'm going to Toby's."

Elizabetha peered at her mother with wonderment. "I didn't know you had such determination. You never seemed to stand up to Papa."

Her mother chuckled again. "Children don't see or know everything, though they think they do." Her mother smiled. "When I disagreed with your father, I did it in private. The way of things were mine, as much as his."

"I never knew you had such strength."

"A woman needs strength to deal with a man. You've always had strength enough for two people." Her mother patted Elizabetha's hand.

On the trip home, Elizabetha's thoughts turned to Joseph. Maybe she could have strength enough for two people. She'd have to resist Joseph if they should chance to be alone together. She must do it for Martin and for her dear friend, Anne, and perhaps even for herself, and, yes, for Joseph's sake, too.

⇒27⇐

1789

After returning from Elizabetha's father's funeral, Martin had finally built his frame church and Anne's son, Samuel, planned to wed there.

Joseph was in Scott County on business, and Anne reminisced as she planned the guest list. The older children had all married Lutherans from Mount Airy, Evansham, or Scott County. All but Jacob and his wife Margaretha had moved away. Some had gone farther west and some further south.

Anne would just have Rachel and Samantha and her three youngest boys still at home, and Elizabetha had three young daughters and a son left, and, of course, Catrina, who at seventeen was a worry to them all, too curious and challenging like her mother, Elizabetha. The relationship between Catrina and her strict father, Martin, was often strained.

Anne marveled at how fast all their children were growing up and moving out. Where had the years gone?

Her daughter Rachel would probably marry the next year. Rachel's beau was brother to Samuel's intended.

Rachel and Samuel were on an outing to overlook the precipice two miles down the Clinch River. They'd no doubt talk about Samuel's wedding and Rachel's beau.

Anne's daughter Samantha and the slaves, Sarah and Prue, entertained the three boys with games in the parlor.

Anne heard the shots as Gim ran into the house and yelled, "Bes' git into the cellar with the chillun, Missus Anne. Dem's Injuns shootin'."

Prue, Samantha, and Anne gathered the boys and headed for the cellar. Sarah grabbed a rifle and ran with Gim to the stockade walls.

Anne's son Samuel and daughter Rachel stood at the precipice gazing down at the Clinch River below. Rachel and Samuel always loved how rugged the terrain was at this part of the river. At their family's station, the river seemed so tame in the flat, smooth land. Here, the river raged sixty feet below them at the base of the cliff. Throughout their childhood, they'd often begged their father to bring them here.

Samuel picked up a stone and hurled it over the precipice. He and Rachel followed its fall until it bashed into the rocks below and pieces bounced into the roiling waters.

They turned at the sound of horse hooves behind them. A band of Indians dismounted.

Rachel turned frightened eyes toward Samuel.

He glanced from her to the Indians and back.

An arrow struck Rachel through the heart. Samuel grabbed at her as she fell to the ground. Blood oozed from her mouth. Her eyes stared sightlessly.

"Oh my God, Rachel!" Samuel half rose as the Indian's tomahawk slashed across his scalp. He reeled and felt himself fall from the precipice. He felt himself floating down and down. His arms and legs thrashed for something to grasp. His own blood blurred his vision as he felt his powerlessness. At the bottom of his fall, he felt no more.

At the Blakemore station, Sarah spotted the Indian as he shimmied over the top of the stockade wall and darted behind a shed. The buck who'd given him a boost went down with her first shot. She reached into the possibles pouch she'd placed over her shoulder for a prepatched ball from the loading block, and with the ball starter, rammed the ball into the bore of her Pennsylvania rifle, a cross between the German jaeger rifle and the long English fowler.

She descended from the stockade wall. The Indian ran from behind the shed toward the cellar. Just as he reached it, he turned to fire at Sarah. She'd darted sideways and the shot only grazed her head. She dropped to one knee and fired. The Indian fell in a heap.

Sarah sank to the ground, shaking. Her husband, Gim, reached her and gathered her in his arms. She leaned against his broad form a moment, steadied herself, and headed for the cellar with Gim following after.

Anne and the others huddled together in the dark cellar. She held her young boys close to her. When would it end? Were Samuel and Rachel all right? She wished Joseph were here.

Anne heard a voice calling, "Missus Anne, Missus Anne." Sarah threw open the cellar door. Gim was behind Sarah. The graze across Sarah's temple was red with oozing blood. She didn't seem to notice.

"Missus Anne, is you en de chillun all right?" Sarah asked.

"We're fine. Have they gone? Is it over?" Anne and the children climbed out of the cellar. Anne squinted from the bright afternoon sun shimmering through the tree leaves, casting mottled shadows over the ground. Anne didn't know how long they'd been in the cellar.

"Yessem, de's gone," Gim said.

"Let me see to your wound, Sarah." Anne took out her handkerchief and daubed at the oozing blood of Sarah's head wound. "I'll need to bandage this. Let's go to the house."

"Gim, bes take some folk en fetch Massa Samuel en Miss Rachel." Sarah said, grabbing the hands of the two older boys.

Anne picked up the youngest and Samantha raced ahead to help Sarah with the boys. They hastened across the yard into the house.

The slaves Gim and Henry, and Granger, the overseer came across Rachel on the top of the precipice and Samuel at the bottom. They laid Rachel's body across Henry's horse, then backtracked about a mile until Gim and Granger could find an easier access to the river below to retrieve the body of Samuel.

When Granger and the others returned, Anne ran out the door to greet her children. She fainted as Gim and Henry lifted the bodies of Samuel and Rachel off the backs of their horses and laid them on the ground.

By the time Anne awoke, Joseph was beside her. She sat up in the bed. How had she gotten there?

Joseph slouched on the edge of the bed. As she stirred, he took her in his arms, sobbing into her shoulder. Anne sat life-lessly. It all came back to her. She was too numb to cry.

Granger, the overseer, read from the Bible at the gravesite. The black frock coat he wore on his stocky frame gave him an aura of solemnity. Gim and the other slaves lowered Samuel and Rachel's bodies into the ground.

As they shoveled dirt into the chasms, Anne screamed. Joseph grabbed her and held her steady. She pounded his chest with her fists. "I hate you. I hate this wilderness. I hate the Indians." He held her wrists and pulled her arms to his chest. She sobbed against him. "My poor babies. My poor babies," she moaned.

Joseph learned from his neighbor, Tom Kilgore, that the raid was done by a band of renegade Cree. Kilgore and his trapper friends tracked them and surprised the Indians in their camp. The trappers shot and scalped every last Indian in the band, leaving the scalps tied to stakes the trappers drove into the ground in a circle, a warning to future renegades.

Granger, the overseer, told Joseph what Sarah had done and Joseph personally thanked her for her bravery in protecting his wife and other children. He didn't tell her his intent to grant freedom to her, Gim, and their issue upon his own death and Anne's.

Joseph had seen too much of death in battles, and now two of his own children was more than he could abide. He was worried about Anne. She was distraught throughout the month. He decided to take her and the children to Elizabetha and Martin's for a few days. He hoped it would bring Anne some cheer and peace to be around Elizabetha and her family. He knew he needed to see Elizabetha as well. He needed her vitality, her passion. Anne was devoted to him and he loved her frailty and sensitivity, but Elizabetha met him as an equal. She had a lust for life as great as his own. He realized how much he'd been missing her.

❯❯28❮❮

The Blakemores arrived at Elizabetha and Martin's the next day. Elizabetha involved Anne in household matters. Elizabetha's brood soon had the Blakemore youngsters engaged in the business of being children. Anne's daughter Samantha was taken in tow by Elizabetha's daughter Catrina. Martin invited Joseph to help in the duties of the farm. After a few days, Anne began to retrieve a bit of her old self, until any mention of Indians was made. She would tremble with rage at the word.

This night was hot and Elizabetha couldn't sleep. She rose, put on her robe, and let herself out of the bedroom not wakening Martin. She tiptoed downstairs and into the night to catch the soft breeze. She strolled toward the barn, lifting her long hair and letting the breeze cool her throat and neck.

As she neared the shadows at the side of the barn, a hand grabbed her wrist. She started to scream. A hand clasped over her mouth. "Elizabetha," Joseph whispered.

"You frightened me," she said when Joseph removed his hand.

"I'm sorry. You couldn't sleep either?"

"No."

"I've missed you terribly." He pulled her close to him in the shadows and kissed her, her body responded to his passion.

The image of Martin and Anne crossed her vision. Her mother's face flashed before her and she heard her mother's words, "You've always had strength enough for two people."

No, I can't let this go on, she vowed. I must find the strength to stop it. I must. She pushed herself away from Joseph. "Joseph, Anne needs you now more than ever. I must be strong enough for both of us. I must. I've made up my mind."

Perhaps it was the sharpness of her words that made him stop. He gazed at her.

She fixed her jaw and firmed her mouth in determination.

"I love you. I'll always love you," Joseph avowed.

"I've locked my own love away in my heart, Joseph. Promise me you'll do the same. Promise for Anne's sake, for mine."

He gazed at her a long moment. "You can't mean it." He pulled her closer to kiss her.

She turned her head away.

"Elizabetha, don't do this to me. I need you."

She steeled herself. "Anne needs you."

Joseph's grip eased as his mouth gaped and his eyes widened. He gazed deeply at her. "All right. I'll promise. But I'll never stop loving you or hoping."

Elizabetha tore herself free and ran back to the house.

In bed, Elizabetha thought she'd finally done what had been needed, she'd resisted. It was the most difficult thing she'd ever done. Oh, Joseph, Joseph. She buried her face in her pillow to stifle her sobs.

* * *

One year later in 1790, Elizabetha and Martin's daughter Catrina met a Catholic young man named Jeremy Sutter from Evansham at the July celebration of independence from Britain. They danced many dances together.

Martin was livid when he learned the young man was Catholic. He forbade Catrina to see him again.

But a few months later, Elizabetha went to Catrina's bedroom in the morning. The bed hadn't been slept in. A note was lying on Catrina's pillow. Elizabetha picked it up and read:

Mama,
I love Jeremy so much. I can't give him up. I know you'll understand. Jeremy and I made plans to elope because Papa is being so unreasonable. Wish us luck and tell Papa I love him.
Love,
Catrina

Elizabetha plodded downstairs, note in hand. Catrina, gone. How was she to tell Martin? She trudged into the hall. Martin was on his way to the breakfast table. He turned as Elizabetha entered.

"What is it?" Martin asked.

Elizabetha couldn't think what to say. She handed him the note.

Martin read it. He glared at Elizabetha. "This is your doing," he sneered. "She's as pig-headed as you are."

Leaving no room for mourning the elopement of her daughter, Elizabetha's anger flared through her veins like wildfire. "*Me* pig-headed. You're the stubborn one, always ordering everyone around. You set impossible rules and demand everyone follow them, allowing no room for their feelings."

"Feelings," he roared. "Perhaps if you'd disciplined Catrina instead of catering to her feelings, we wouldn't be having this discussion."

Infuriated, she felt herself ready to burst into tears if she said another word. She would not let him see her cry. She would not. She turned on her heels and marched, trying not to run, up to her room.

⤚•29•⤙

1798

Eight years later, Elizabetha had resigned herself to Catrina's elopement. Over the years, Joseph had kept his promise and not approached Elizabetha in any intimate manner. It made her love him all the more. Anne and Joseph had accepted Martin and Elizabetha's invitation to dinner. As Elizabetha finalized her coiffure, she heard their wagon pull into the yard. With a last glance in the mirror, she tucked a stray stubborn wisp into place and hurried down the stairs to greet her guests.

As she passed the parlor door, she glimpsed Martin bent studiously over the desk and she stopped. Something was wrong in the way his shoulders tensed. Her breath caught in her throat as she remembered leaving her journal open to the day she'd begged Joseph to bury his love for her in his heart as she had.

Martin slowly turned toward her just as Joseph and Anne were let in the front door.

Elizabetha's hand shot to her mouth as she glanced wide-eyed from her guests to her husband.

Anne faltered at the door as if unsure whether to leave or stay.

Joseph strode to Elizabetha's side and grabbed her elbow just as she was sure she would faint.

"Well, if it isn't our old friends come to visit," Martin said. An ugly sneer made his face grotesque. "Do come in gentle Anne and her husband, my best friend, Joseph Blakemore and, of course, my loyal wife."

As Joseph and Anne entered the parlor, Elizabetha seemed unable to move her feet.

"Don't tarry, Elizabetha. You are among friends. Why I believe you know my best friend, Joseph Blakemore, quite well."

Elizabetha wobbled on rubber legs to the sofa and grabbed hold of the back for support.

"What's going on, Martin?" Joseph asked. He glanced from Martin to Elizabetha.

She could see from Joseph's shocked expression that he had guessed what was going on.

"Whatever is the matter, Elizabetha?" Anne asked.

"What is the matter, my dear Anne, is that our respective spouses seem to have been quite something more than friends for a good number of years." He glared at Joseph a long moment and then at Elizabetha.

"Joseph, what's he talking about?" Anne gasped.

"Calm down, Anne," he said and encased her shoulders with his arm. He turned to Martin. "This won't help anything, Martin. Let's talk reasonably."

"Talk reasonably?" Martin bellowed. "Reasonably?" He grabbed the journal and threw it at Joseph's feet. "Is this reasonable enough for you?" His brows arched high and his eyes wide, he blared. "Get out of my house you bastard. Get out."

Anne screamed. She glanced at Elizabetha with confusion and ran outside.

Joseph turned to follow her. As he passed by Elizabetha, he stopped. "I'm so terribly sorry. What can I do?"

"Go," she muttered. "Just go."

Martin and Elizabetha still faced each other as the door slammed shut.

In a small voice Elizabetha offered, "I put an end to it, Martin."

"You put an end to it," he said.

The hurt and anger mixed together in his gaze broke her heart.

"And that is supposed to make everything all right?" The anger overtook the hurt. His eyes widened and bulged, his face turning scarlet in uncontrolled rage. He glowered at Elizabetha. His mouth opened in a vile curse that came out in gibberish. He stared blankly at her and collapsed on the floor.

Kindly Doctor Marlowe of Mount Airy pushed his glasses higher on his large nose before speaking, as usual. The tufts of gray hair at his temples were even more unruly. "Martin's had a stroke," he said.

Elizabetha collapsed in a chair.

"If he survives the next few days, he'll have a good chance of recovery," Doctor Marlowe explained. "Will you need a sedative? Are you all right?"

Elizabetha gaped at him for a moment. "No, I'll be fine. Thank you for coming so promptly."

"I'll take my leave then. If Martin takes a turn for the worse, send one of the slaves for me." He donned his hat and departed.

Elizabetha remained in the chair for a long time after the doctor left, before she could bring herself to go up to Martin.

* * *

A year passed and Martin made slight headway toward regaining his speech, though he couldn't get his thoughts to express themselves in words. With the aid of a cane, he could shuffle from the bed to the armchair in his room. Elizabetha had thought it best to move into the guest room under the circumstances. She knew it was the practical thing to do, but she missed him lying next to her.

Everything had gone wrong because of her. Perhaps everything had happened for a reason. If only she could discover it. Maybe she was supposed to learn something from it.

Martin gazed at Elizabetha as she read from *Romeo and Juliet*. How he wished he could express his feelings to her. He'd had a lot of time to think these past months, nothing but time. These past months she had been so patient and attentive to his every need even when he was behaving his worst. Elizabetha always made sure Martin's Bible sat on the small table next to his chair, and he'd consulted it often.

She'd always been a passionate, strong-willed woman. He had known that from the beginning. And he had fallen in love with her anyway. She had strength. He'd give her that. Hadn't she turned her back on what she felt for Joseph? He knew she had. He had read it in her own words. He'd also read of her love for him, not only just in the beginning, but after Joseph. In his heart he knew he'd not been an easy husband, and he knew he loved her now more than he ever had. If only he could tell her that he loved her—that he forgave her.

As Elizabetha ended a poignant passage, she glanced over at Martin. Tears were at the corners of his eyes which held all the steel-blue glimmer of his youth.

"'Liz'beth'," he slurred.

She rose and went to his side. She kneeled at the side of his armchair and laid her head on his left arm which refused to do his bidding any longer. His right hand stroked her hair.

"Martin, I know, I know," she said. I miss you too, she thought. In the beginning he had been belligerent as she'd had to feed him every spoonful of food, bathe him, and assist with bodily functions; but with time, he began to accept her help without resistance; and, finally, had even seemed grateful for it, almost as if he were trying to make things easier for her. She was thankful for that.

He gazed at her as if from prison. She felt that inside he was still Martin, a Martin who no longer was able to express himself. He'd paid dearly for his zealousness and wrath. Her heart empathized with the frustrations he must feel, with the hurt she'd caused him.

Always she'd wanted him to change, be less this, be more that. If only she'd had sense enough to love him for what he was. She'd give anything to have him back to whom he'd been.

She rose and helped him to the bed, slipped off his robe, and tucked the blanket around him. She leaned over and kissed him on the mouth. When she stood, he smiled with the right side of his face and patted her hand. She caressed his cheek and turned to go to her room.

"'Night," he said.

"Goodnight, Martin," she hesitated at the door. "I love you." She closed the door and went to bed.

The next morning after helping Martin with his breakfast and making him comfortable with his Bible beside him, Elizabetha went downstairs to the desk. She had taken over the bookkeeping for Martin. Between their son Jacob and Charles, the overseer, the farm continued to prosper.

Her mother had passed away the same year Martin had his stroke. Elizabetha couldn't leave Martin. Toby had to handle everything himself. He said he understood. She missed her mother.

She thought how little she had really ever known about her parents' lives beyond her own needs. She didn't know what their inner thoughts, hopes, and fears had been. It struck her that her own children would never know her either. What a strange state humanness was.

At first the younger children had been afraid of Martin's disabilities, but soon they grew accustomed to him and didn't mind sitting with him occasionally. The children settled into their own routines once again. Life went on.

At least Martin had built his church before the stroke. He'd been so proud of it. He'd built it on top of a high hill by Reed Creek, complete with two towers with tall steeples just as Martin had planned it. The Lutherans had named it Kimberlin's Church. Perhaps, with Big Jim's help, she could start taking Martin to his church again. Yes, he'd like that.

⇒·30·⇐

A knock at the door interrupted Elizabetha's musings over Martin and his church. Sudie opened the door and Joseph Blakemore entered. Anne had not spoken to her since that fateful day Martin read the journal. She understood. Elizabetha was surprised to see Joseph here.

"Joseph," she greeted.

"I'm on my way to Scott County. I wanted to see how you were doing. How's Martin?"

"He's coming along as well as can be expected. He's upstairs reading his Bible."

"Can we go into the parlor?"

"Of course. How is Anne doing?"

He followed her in and closed the door. "Things are quiet around our house. She has moved into the guest room and only speaks to me when she can't avoid it. I've tried to explain that it's possible to love two people at the same time, but for different reasons. She just stares at me. She says she still loves me, that it will take time to forgive me if she ever can. It breaks my heart to have hurt her so much." He turned to Elizabetha. "To have hurt you."

He put his coat and hat across the back of a chair. Elizabetha sat on the sofa facing him. He paced in front of her, his brow knit in deep grooves. His graying hair lent dignity to his handsomeness. He still moved like a mountain lion, ready to pounce at any moment.

"Elizabetha, I must talk to you."

"What is it, Joseph?"

He stopped pacing and sat on the couch. He took her hands in his. "Elizabetha, I've been miserable since that day, and not just because of the hurt to Martin and Anne. I can't bear to think of my life without you. Please tell me you still have a thread of love for me. I know I've put you, Anne, and Martin through hell, but I still can't help loving you."

Her heart yearned for his comfort, his understanding. She wanted him to hold her. "I can't love you, Joseph." It was a hard thing to say.

He stared incredulously at her. He pushed her against the sofa cushions, his body pressing hers, and kissed her. She tried to push him away.

"You can't mean it. You love me, I know you do. You can't just stop loving, stop wanting." He kissed her again, deeply.

It took all her will to stiffen and not respond.

He stopped.

She glared at him.

He moved back and put his head in his hands.

She sat up and straightened her hair.

He lifted his head. His sensuous mouth drooped. The corners of his eyes seemed to droop as well.

"I can't deny loving you, Joseph, and wanting you—."

He turned to her, his gaze seeming to search her face for a sign of hope.

She held up her hand to dissuade him. "I am denying you and denying myself. What's gone on before can't continue. As long as Martin and Anne are here, you and I can never be. I once pleaded with you to be strong enough for both of us. You said you couldn't. Now, I have to be. I am."

"But Martin—."

"Martin needs me. He is my husband for better or worse. Remember the vows?" She winced at her own cruelty. She stood. She didn't dare let herself feel pity for Joseph, for herself. She steeled her body and her mind.

Joseph lowered his head. He rose, picked up his hat and coat, and moved to the parlor door.

Before opening it, he turned toward her. There were tears in his beautiful, sad, sable eyes. His gaze embraced her, held her fast.

She wouldn't run to him. She wouldn't.

He went out the door and closed it behind him.

Joseph mounted his horse and turned homeward. She couldn't mean it. She was still upset over Martin's stroke. She just needed more time. No. He was kidding himself. It had been ten years since she extricated his promise to hide his love in his heart as she had. And she had. There had been a hardness in her eyes. She meant it, but she must still love him as he loved her. You didn't just decide to stop loving someone, any more than you decided to start. Yet, she had just tucked her feelings away, hiding them from herself and from him. He vowed to continue to honor her wishes and keep his love buried in the deepest recesses of his heart. But perhaps somewhere in the future she would relent and allow her love expression. He would wait. He would hope.

* * *

Two years later in 1801, Joseph continued to honor Elizabetha's wishes and kept his desires to himself. She missed him, missed their stolen discussions, their intimacy, the passion they'd known, but always Martin and Anne's faces would crowd into her thoughts and she'd push Joseph's image from her mind. She missed her dear friend Anne. Elizabetha still hoped Anne would one day be able to forgive her.

Elizabetha sat in the kitchen sipping the tea she'd prepared for herself. She had come downstairs not wanting to wake Martin so early. She was sixty-one, she mused, and Martin sixty-six.

Where had all the years gone? One day had flowed into the next. Martin had remained stable and their lives moved on in a straight line of small routines, punctuated by visits from Jacob and Margaretha and the grandchildren.

Phoebe came into the kitchen. "Missus Elizabetha, why you up so early? Anythin' wrong?"

"No, Phoebe, I was merely reminiscing."

"I'll fix some nice breakfas'."

"Thank you. Then I'll go up to Mister Martin's room."

"I'll fetch his tray up after."

Elizabetha ate breakfast in silence. Phoebe had become the nearest thing to a friend Elizabetha had since Martin's stroke.

Elizabetha finished breakfast and smiled as Phoebe's plump hand patted Elizabetha's arm reassuringly. When had Phoebe's hair turned so gray?

"You takes good care a Massa Martin. You got de strength of two people," Phoebe said.

Thoughts of her mother came to Elizabetha's mind. "Thank you, Phoebe."

Elizabetha opened the door to Martin's room. His eyes were closed and his mouth was open as if in a snore, open too far. He wasn't breathing. She touched his arm. It was cold. She pulled her hand away, feeling that iciness would suck away her love as death had sucked away his life while he innocently slept. She settled on the edge of the bed and clutched her hands together in her lap. Oh, Martin, Martin. It did happen. How many times in their life together had she checked on him to make sure he was still breathing? And suddenly, he wasn't.

Phoebe entered with the tray.

Elizabetha said in a quiet voice, "We won't be needing the tray, Phoebe, he's gone."

Elizabetha went through the funeral in a daze. She couldn't have said who had attended. She was still dazed weeks later. She must gather up Martin's belongings. She would donate them to the slaves.

She went upstairs, opened the door to Martin's bedroom, and stepped inside. The room was as it had been, except for one thing. Martin was not in it.

She slumped on the edge of the bed and ran her fingertips over the pillow where his head had lain. Tears trickled down her cheeks. Through the blur, she noticed a piece of the embroidery on the hem of the pillowslip was unraveled. That would have to be mended. She grabbed up the pillow and crushed it in her arms. "Martin, oh Martin, I'm so sorry," she wailed. Sorry about the pillowslip, sorry that you died, sorry about Joseph, sorry she couldn't believe in God. Sorry she'd ever been born.

She didn't know how long she sat there sobbing before she realized she had come here for a purpose. What was it? Oh yes, Martin's things. She swiped the tears from her cheeks with her fingers, pulled her handkerchief from her sleeve, and blew her nose.

She removed Martin's clothes from the chest of drawers and wardrobe and stacked them on the bed. When she had everything piled, she gathered his belongings in her arms and glanced around. She spotted Martin's Bible on the table next to his chair.

She sauntered over and placed it on top of Martin's belongings. She ran her hand across the worn and tattered cover. To whom should she give the Bible?

She trembled and collapsed onto the wing chair and clutched the Bible and clothes against her bosom as the tears once again streamed down her cheeks. Where did all these tears come from? They kept spilling out at the most unexpected times. The sight of something, or the smell, or just a thought would bring on another torrent of tears over a remembrance of Martin.

At last the tears spent themselves, and she rose and placed the Bible back on the table. It wouldn't hurt anything to just leave it here—where it had always been. She let herself out and closed the door to the room behind her, never to enter it again.

⇉ 31 ⇇

1 8 0 2 O n e Y e a r L a t e r

A year later, Anne was furious. Her son, Thomas, was seeing an Indian girl. Jacob's wife, Margaretha, had introduced them. Anne didn't know with whom to be most angry. Margaretha was always championing the Indians. "Cherokee, not Cree," Thomas had said they were. What did it matter, they were all Indians. Thomas accompanied Margaretha on her visits to the Cherokee's village.

Anne had begged Joseph to forbid him, but Joseph had just said, "Thomas is twenty. I can't forbid him."

How could Thomas do this to her—after his own sister and brother—? How could he?

The Cherokee were a proud and handsome people. Thomas thought with their chiseled features and light complexions, the Cherokee could almost pass as whites if dressed appropriately. Many of them did wear parts of colonial clothing. Some still wore only deerskins. Most, too, had taken on English first names and surnames. There had been much intermarriage between the Cherokee and the white traders. Some passed these surnames along. Others anglicized their Cherokee names.

Thomas and Margaretha rode through the village which was

located along a stream. The Indians grew fields of corn, beans, squash, pumpkins, sunflowers, and tobacco. Thomas knew the Indians actually grew three kinds of corn or maize as they called it: one to roast, one to boil, and a third to grind into flour for cornbread. Colonists learned to do the same.

Thomas spotted Olive Poteet, the Indian girl Margaretha had introduced to him. Thomas had been visiting Olive for six months on Sundays since that day.

Olive added wood to the fire outside her family's summer lodge which was rectangular with a peaked roof, pole frame-work, cane and clay walls, and a thatch roof. The smaller winter house also served as a sweathouse. It stood over a fire pit with a cone-shaped roof of poles and earth. A warehouse and store-house made of poles and thatch roofs stood nearby.

Olive wore a blue dress. Her thick, long hair flowed down her back. Her large eyes were nearly as black as her hair. "I hoped you and Thomas would come today," she said to Margaretha. She lowered her head.

"You're wearing the dress I gave you. You look lovely, Olive," Margaretha said.

Olive smiled and glanced at Thomas.

Thomas dismounted.

Margaretha remained on her horse. She was a small woman, plain-featured with light brown hair and pale blue eyes, but her heart must have taken up the whole of her, she had been cham-pioning the Cherokee's lot for most of her life.

His mother had told him that Margaretha had married Jacob when Margaretha was just fifteen. Thomas had always thought the couple was a well-balanced combination, Jacob, rather stern like his father with the same steel-blue eyes, all business and no frills, and Margaretha, so kind and warmhearted, ready to help anyone in need.

Margaretha rode on to find the half-breed, Sequoyah, also known as George Gist, who had written a syllabary of the Cherokee tongue. Margaretha worked with him to teach it to those willing to learn it. Margaretha and Sequoyah would also teach them English in the process. Thomas and Olive attended as often as they could. They were able to communicate more easily.

Thomas sat cross-legged on the ground as he watched Olive place a piece of wood on the fire. Olive had invited Thomas to join in a game between the young men and women of the tribe. A feast would follow. Olive's mother would be cooking for it along with the other squaws. After the feast, there was to be dancing.

Olive rose from in front of the fire pit. "It's time," she said. "The game will start soon." She motioned for Thomas to rise.

He stood. Olive's ebony eyes gleamed. She returned his gaze. She gave a short giggle and ran ahead of him toward the plaza, a name carried over from the early Spanish invasions.

Thomas bolted after her and caught up. He was confused as usual by her contradictory behavior—the bold promise in her eyes—and her running away from him. She half skipped, half walked backward while she explained the basics of the game they would play. Dazed, he followed after her.

They arrived at the plaza already filled with young people. A tall pole stood in the center of the plaza. A tall, muscular brave in deerskin with two wide braids over his shoulders, passed a stick to each male player. One end of the three-foot stick was bent into a loop and a shallow pocket of animal skin was attached to the loop. The women, Olive had told Thomas, were allowed to use their hands. Whichever team hit the pole twelve times with a small ball of inverted animal fur, skin side out, would win.

The handsome Indian beamed as Olive approached him. She said a few words to him and nodded toward Thomas. The brave scowled and started to argue with her. She said a few more words and motioned for Thomas to join them. The man shoved a stick into Thomas's hand. Still glowering, the brave turned abruptly away from them and passed out the rest of the sticks.

Thomas asked Olive, "Who was that happy fellow?"

"Luke Aiken, but I call him Angry Bear. A few months after I'd met you, he told my aunt he would like to court me. On a prearranged morning, I set out a bowl of gruel in front of our lodge and sat beside it. When he came by and asked if he might have some of it, I told him no. It is an old Cherokee custom when a woman does not choose a certain suitor to let him know by refusing to let him eat the gruel. If she lets him eat it, they become lovers."

"No wonder he's so sullen."

"That's why I call him Angry Bear. He's always sullen. Come on, the game is about to begin."

An old man threw the ball into the air. Angry Bear caught it in his stick basket and the game began. Angry Bear threw and missed the pole. The women taunted him, and one grabbed the ball, tossing it to Olive. Olive threw and made the first point for the women.

Thomas scooped the ball off the ground and missed the pole so far that even Olive doubled over laughing. Thomas hit the pole the next time.

Angry Bear scooped the ball away just as Thomas was about to trap it in his basket. Angry Bear threw and made a hit.

The next time Angry Bear went after the ball, Thomas scooped it away from him. Angry Bear glowered at Thomas.

The men's team made many points, but the women managed to defeat them in the end, with much laughter and taunting. Angry Bear sulked as Thomas and Olive left the plaza together.

The feast was a lavish array of venison, bear, turkey, trout, rabbit, and cornbread, roast corn, squash, beans, nuts, and berries.

Margaretha left after the feast to return home before dark.

One man began beating a drum and another began shaking a gourd rattle for the Friendship Dance.

Angry Bear and another brave danced in a slow shuffle around the fire. After one circle, they chose two women as partners. Angry Bear picked Olive.

After the four shuffled the circle once around the fire, Olive picked Thomas and the other three chose new partners. So it went until, except for the musicians, the entire village was dancing.

The rhythm changed and two circles formed, one of the men and the other of women. These moved around the fire four times, the women dancing one direction, the men the other.

When the dance ended, Thomas took Olive aside to sit on the ground in the circle of people gathered around the dance area.

They watched the dancing men moving awkwardly and pawing the air in the Bear Dance.

The music changed and the women, with thorns in their hands, pricked the men as the latter circled the fire in the Mosquito Dance.

Thomas reached for Olive's hand. She didn't pull it away, but instead gazed at him with the firelight glinting in her irises.

When the festivities ended, Thomas walked Olive back to her lodge. They held hands. The moonlight glistened on Olive's tawny complexion and shimmered in her long, black hair as she moved.

Just before reaching her lodge, Thomas stopped and gazed at her a long moment. Her dark eyes twinkled with merriment. He bent his head down to her. She lifted hers upward and met his kiss. Their lips lingered in a slow kiss. Afterward, Olive said, "You will come again, Thomas, on Sunday?"

"Yes, I'll come again."

He mounted his horse and rode home alone.

On his way home, Thomas's mind replayed every dance, glance, and touch Olive and he shared during the evening, especially the kiss.

⇉•32•⇇

The next morning at breakfast after the feast, Thomas's mother, Anne, plopped scrambled eggs on his plate as she accused, "You were out late last night."

"Yes, Mama, there was a feast and dancing in the village." He shoveled some eggs into his mouth and took a long drink of buttermilk.

"Why must you associate with those savages? You know how I feel about them after—."

"Anne, leave the boy alone," Joseph muttered.

"I'm sorry you feel that way, Mama, but they're not savages. Olive is a wonderful girl. You'd like her. Maybe I could bring her here to meet you and you could see for yourself."

His mother shoved her chair back causing it to screech against the wooden floor. She stood. "Never! How dare you even think about bringing a heathen into my home!"

"Mama—."

"Never!"

"Now, Anne," Joseph said.

Anne glared at Joseph.

His father shook his head. He shrugged his shoulders as if in helplessness for his son's plight.

Thomas rose and went to his mother. He kissed her cool cheek. He studied her stony countenance a moment and said, "I'm sorry for you, Mama." He turned and left the house.

Thomas mounted his horse and rode to Tom Kilgore's station. Thomas had been fur trapping with Tom and Charles Boren a few days during the week for several years. This time, Thomas intended to stay out with them for the whole week. He'd told Sarah to let his parents know. He needed time to think. By Saturday, he'd made up his mind. He would ask Olive to marry him if she'd have him. Tom Kilgore had told Thomas he could stay at his place. He had an extra cabin.

On Sunday, Thomas went to the Cherokee's village. Olive was sitting in front of her lodge. Beside her sat a bowl of gruel. Thomas's heart raced. Would she say no if he asked to eat it? Had she changed her mind about Angry Bear and this was her way of letting Thomas know—what about the kiss? She had let Thomas kiss her, had kissed him back. Best get it over with at once.

"Is that gruel in the bowl?" he asked.

"Yes, it is," Olive replied. She was weaving a basket on her lap and didn't look up at him.

Thomas's heart turned over. "May I have some?" he ventured.

She thought a moment, a long moment. "Yes," she said and handed it to him.

His legs almost buckled with relief. He took the bowl and ate a bite of the gruel and squatted beside her. "It's delicious," he said, beaming with delight.

"I'm glad you think so."

"Will you marry me, Olive?"

"Of course."

They were married by a preacher in Evansham the following Sunday. Margaretha and Jacob accompanied them. Margaretha had given Olive more of her clothing. Olive wore a beige gown with lace at the bodice, and Margaretha had pinned Olive's hair atop her head. She was beautiful.

After the ceremony, the four drove to Elizabetha's for a small reception. Olive's parents, Tom and Jane Poteet, had given them their blessing, but did not attend the reception. They would have an Indian celebration later. Thomas's father, Joseph was there, but his mother, Anne, was absent.

Watching the couple at the reception, Elizabetha thought how beautiful a young woman Olive was. Elizabetha liked her immediately and invited Olive to visit whenever she could. Olive's black hair and eyes glistened. Her coppery complexion glowed against the white lace at her bodice. Standing beside Thomas with his wavy, sandy hair, deep tan, and good looks of his father, they were a striking couple.

The reception drew to a close. Joseph followed Elizabetha back inside after the young people drove away. Sudie and Phoebe had finished cleaning out the last of the reception dishes and Elizabetha and Joseph were alone in the parlor.

"I'm so sorry Anne wouldn't come. Was it because of me?" Elizabetha said as she picked up an errant napkin from the floor.

"Not altogether. She refuses to have anything to do with Olive," Joseph said. He turned and gazed out the window, his shoulders taut.

"It makes me sad to hear that. I hoped time would heal her heart against her hatred of Indians." She put the napkin on the table.

"I don't think there's enough time in the world for that." He turned to Elizabetha.

"It must be hard for you," she said.

"Elizabetha." Joseph moved toward her.

She held up her hand. "No, Joseph, please. I can't. I won't. You promised."

"I promised." He turned and left the house.

* * *

1804 Two years later, Olive was excited to finally be carrying Thomas's child. She'd used herbal remedies to postpone pregnancy. She'd wanted to learn as much of the ways of the whites as she could before bearing a child. Now she was ready.

She'd gleaned much about cooking and keeping house from Sadie Kilgore during the three months Olive and Thomas stayed at Tom and Sadie's station. She'd learned how to dress and fix her hair from Margaretha and Elizabetha. Olive regretted Thomas's mother still refused to meet her. She wondered if the child would bring Anne around.

Thomas had taken a job as surveyor, and they'd moved into a home of their own in Evansham near Jacob and Margaretha. Olive was convinced the future of the Cherokee people was in learning the ways of the whites.

Her musings were interrupted when Thomas arrived home. He'd been to his parents to inform them they were soon to be grandparents. Olive was anxious to learn Anne's reaction. Olive hoped the news would make a difference.

Thomas's solemn face when he came through the door revealed that it hadn't.

"What did she say?" Olive asked.

"Nothing, nothing at all. Papa was delighted, but Mama just stared at me when I gave them the news." Thomas held up his hands and shrugged his shoulders.

Olive's lower lip quivered. She'd hoped the expected child would change things. Thomas took her in his arms and held her to his chest. She tried to hold her tears back, but they spilled out anyway. "When our child is born, things will be better. She surely can't resist her own flesh and blood," Olive said.

"I hope you're right." Thomas bent down and kissed Olive's protruding belly.

❧ 33 ❧

In September, Olive was delivered of a healthy son. He was named Joseph after his grandfather, and Samuel for Thomas's slain brother.

When he saw his grandson at the baptismal, Grandfather Joseph beamed. Anne refused to come. Olive saw the hurt in Thomas's eyes. She felt so helpless to soothe his pain, to ease her own disappointment.

Elizabetha attended the service and she and Joseph Senior doted on young Joseph Samuel. The sight appeased Olive's heavy heart somewhat.

Elizabetha asked to hold the baby after the ceremony in the Kimberlin Church.

Joseph Senior smiled as he watched Elizabetha with the infant. "I'm glad you're here, Elizabetha," he said. "I wish Anne had come." He turned to Olive. "I'm sorry, Olive."

Elizabetha patted Joseph Senior's arm. "I'll have Big Jim drive me over to your place and I'll talk to Anne. It's been six years since that fateful day. Perhaps she'll agree to see me. We were friends once. Maybe I can make some difference. I'll try."

Two days later, Big Jim assisted Elizabetha from the carriage at the Blakemore station.

Anne emerged from the front door. Her expression grew rigid as she recognized her guest. "Elizabetha, it's you," she said through clenched teeth.

"It's important that I talk to you, Anne. It's about your son."

"It must be important for you to come here. Well, come in then. We can't be friends, but we can be civil."

When they were settled in the parlor, Elizabetha said, "You were missed at Joseph Samuel's baptism."

Anne's expression turned even stonier. "I can't forgive Thomas for marrying that heathen. I have no interest in her papoose."

"But he's Thomas's child as well, and your grandson. Olive is a very nice young woman. She doesn't even look Indian."

"I don't want to talk about her."

Silence followed.

Elizabetha changed the subject to safer ground. "It's hard to believe all of our children are grown and married. What do you hear from Samantha?"

After no response, Elizabetha brought up the birth of her latest grandson. "Catrina writes that she and Jeremy have a son. I've never seen him. If only Martin could have forgiven his daughter, but he'd shut her out of his life. Such a foolish thing to shove away one's own children from the heart. They're often taken from us so unexpectedly." She picked up her teacup and took a sip while she studied Anne's expression. Should she venture toward the subject of Anne's grandson again? She had to try. "Your grandson Joseph is a beautiful baby."

Anne's piercing glance at Elizabetha withered further attempts to soften Anne toward seeing young Joseph.

Elizabetha prepared to leave, but made one last effort before she stepped out the front door. "It would be wonderful if you could find it in your heart to visit your son. It would please Thomas very much. I'm sure."

Anne's expression hardened. She made no answer.

"Another time, perhaps." Elizabetha started to touch Anne's hand but instead just said, "Goodbye, Anne." She turned to board the carriage.

"Elizabetha," Anne said.

Elizabetha stopped and turned expectantly toward Anne.

"You needn't concern yourself with my family any further." Anne turned and entered her home.

* * *

In 1808, Anne recalled it had been four years since Elizabetha had tried to sway her to accept Thomas's wife and son, and Anne wondered that Elizabetha's words haunted her still: "Such a foolish thing to shove away one's own children from the heart. They're often taken from us so unexpectedly."

Usually she could push the words out of her mind, but not today. As if the words had seared themselves into her soul, she could not shake them. Today, the words made her think of Rachel and Samuel and how quickly she'd lost them forever. Samuel. Thomas had named his son Joseph Samuel. She rose and paced the floor. What had she done? She'd been right, hadn't she? Right to close Thomas out of her life, close out her grandson? What a foolish old woman she was. Of course it wasn't right. She had only hurt herself. Her grandson was four now and she'd never seen him. She'd set it right. She would.

Joseph trudged in early from the fields for dinner.

Anne stopped pacing and went to him. "Joseph, I want to see my grandson."

Joseph's eyes widened. He began to grin as her words sank in. "Now?" he said, as if hoping she meant what he thought she did.

"Yes, now. I've waited far too long." She lifted her cloak off its peg.

Joseph called out into the yard, "Bring the carriage, Gim. Hurry."

Thomas glanced out the window as his father's carriage pulled up. He called to Olive in the kitchen, "Better set another plate for supper, Papa's here." Thomas glanced out the window again as he started to rise to greet his father. "Oh my God!" he exclaimed.

Olive hurried from the kitchen, drying her hands on her apron. Young Joseph followed behind her. "What is it, what's wrong?"

"You won't believe it. I don't believe it."

"What won't I believe, what?"

"Mama is with him."

"Oh my God!"

They were frozen in their positions with widened eyes and gaping mouths.

Olive yanked off her apron and smoothed the straggles of hair that escaped her upsweep. "I must look awful. Quick, help me pick up Joseph's toys. She'll be in here any minute. Hurry."

Thomas grabbed a blanket from the armchair and picked up stray toys off the floor.

Anne waited on the porch while Joseph knocked on the door. She smoothed her hair and wrung her hands together.

Thomas opened the door, his arms filled with toys.

"Mama, come in." He stepped back for her to enter and seemed to realize he still held the toys. He tossed them in the corner and embraced Anne. "I'm so glad you came."

"It's been far too long," Anne said and kissed his cheek.

Thomas put his arm around his mother and guided her into the hallway. Thomas glanced at his father. Joseph Senior grinned broadly and followed them inside, closing the door.

A small head with wavy light brown hair and brown eyes peeked out from around his mother's skirts.

"This is Joseph Samuel. Come, Joseph, and meet your grand-mother."

Joseph approached his father, not taking his gaze from the stranger woman. He wore a simple tunic tied behind his back.

Thomas lifted the boy in his arms and said, "Joseph Samuel, I'm proud to introduce you to your Grandmother Blakemore."

Anne smiled at the child as she shook his tiny hand. Her heart welled with joy and instant love at the sight and touch of him. How perfect and precious he was. He looked so like his father at that age, wavy hair falling into his impish eyes. Young Joseph smiled back and hid his face in his father's neck.

When the boy peeked out again, he spotted his grandfather. "Grandpa." He clambered from his father's arms and scampered to his grandfather.

Joseph Senior bent down and accepted his hug from the boy. "You're a fine young man, Joseph Samuel!"

"Mama, this is my wife, Olive," Thomas said.

Olive's hands were clutched together in front of her waist. She made a small curtsy to Anne, a timid smile quavering on her mouth.

Anne curtsied back, her own smile unsure of itself as well. Why, Olive wasn't a savage at all.

Olive said, "We seem to have forgotten our manners in all this excitement, please come into the parlor." She turned and led the way.

Anne was impressed at the tidiness of the room as she accepted a seat on the sofa. White muslin curtains hung at the windows. There were fresh lilacs in vases on the cupboard and table. A linen doily edged in lace covered the top of the highboy, a candle box and a Bible sat on top. "You've made a lovely home here, Olive," Anne said, settling herself.

"You're kind. Thank you," Olive responded.

Anne watched Joseph Samuel playing on the floor with his spinning top while the polite conversation continued. She hoped she hadn't scared him. She would love to have him run up for her attention someday as he had with his grandfather.

Young Joseph walked over to her with a bilbo catcher and handed it to her. Anne wanted to impress her grandson and tried several times to make the ball on the string land atop the spike, finally, to her relief, she was successful. Young Joseph grinned at her.

Olive rose and said, "You will stay for supper, I hope. It's almost ready."

Joseph, Senior peered at Anne, as did Thomas.

Anne glanced from Joseph to Thomas. "We'd love to. Let me help you."

After supper and the dishes were done, the elder Blakemores prepared to leave. Thomas kissed them both on their cheeks.

Young Joseph insisted his grandparents both bend down to receive a hug and a kiss on the mouth. Joseph Senior kissed Olive's cheek, and Olive extended her hand to Anne. Anne accepted it and put her other hand on top with a small squeeze.

On the ride home, Joseph gazed at his wife and said. "I'm so glad you've accepted Olive and Joseph Samuel. Whatever made you change your mind?"

Anne paused a moment and smiled. "Oh, just something Elizabetha said once. It just took me four years to get it."

Joseph curiously studied his wife. He'd never understand women. He flicked the horsewhip above the ears of the carriage horse. "Giddyap."

≫•34•≪

1 8 1 0   T w o   Y e a r s   L a t e r

After supper in the parlor, Anne recalled the dark cloud that came over Joseph's face when several months after Martin's death she'd asked Joseph if he still loved Elizabetha. He had gazed deeply into her eyes a long moment and said, "I could no more stop loving her than I could stop loving you." Perhaps it was then she had begun to forgive him.

Joseph had that expression now as he stared into the fireplace as if absorbed in the dance of the flames. At seventy-two, his gray hair was still thick and wavy. His sable brown eyes hadn't lost any of their Welsh fire when he was annoyed, but his moodiness had increased.

Anne put down her knitting. "What's wrong, Joseph, you look as though your mind is in some faraway place."

"Huh? Wrong? Nothing's wrong. I was merely daydreaming."

"What about?"

"Can't a man have private daydreams?"

"Of course. I'm sorry." She fought back the tears that sprang to her eyes whenever Joseph was cross with her. She concentrated on her knitting of a sweater for grandson Joseph Samuel.

It was in a pale gray, heavy woolen yarn. It would keep him warm this winter. She inhaled to calm herself to keep her knitting gauge even.

Joseph glanced over at her, his brow furrowed. Anne watched the anger ebb from his gaze. "I'm sorry, Anne, I didn't mean to be gruff," he said.

"I understand. A man needs his private thoughts." She dropped a stitch and cursed to herself at her sensitiveness.

Joseph picked up the newspaper, scanned over it, and set it back on the side table. "I've been thinking, with Granger, the overseer, ailing in bed and me needing to supervise the cotton picking, that I'd have Arry, that youngest son of Sarah and Gim, start on the drying shed in the morning. The tobacco hung in the shed has been drying on low heat for twenty-four hours and it's time to stoke the fires higher."

"You know best," she said, retrieving the errant stitch.

Joseph rose from the wing chair and stretched his arms above his head. "Morning comes early. We'd best be off to bed."

"Yes, Joseph." Anne laid her knitting aside and followed him upstairs. So many things puzzled her about Joseph. She'd never understand the complexity of him.

The next morning as Joseph waited in the drying shed for Arry, he checked his old watch against the new one Anne had bought him for his birthday. He often made sure the new one kept the right time. They agreed again.

Arry arrived. He was in his thirties, tall and well built like his father, Gim, but Joseph knew Arry to be as efficient as his mother, Sarah. His birth had nearly killed her due to her age. Sarah and Gim doted on Arry. Joseph was confident Arry could handle the task he had for him.

"Mornin', Massa," Arry greeted, his smile wide and generous like Gim's. He looked around at the drying shed as did Joseph.

The tobacco leaves, impaled on sticks which were suspended one above the other in sets, hung from horizontal poles across the interior of the shed. The two brick furnaces on either side of the shed were arranged to be stoked from the outside of the building. Their flues extended nearly horizontally across the shed to economize heat.

Joseph checked the thermometer, 100% on the button. "Arry, you'll need to stoke the fires and check the thermometer often. The heat inside should only rise a degree an hour. If it rises faster than that, it'll blacken the stems and affect the color of the leaves."

"Uh-huh." Arry nodded his understanding.

Joseph showed Arry the markings on the thermometer indicating one degree. "When the heat reaches 125%, hold the temperature there for eight to twelve hours."

Joseph drew an arrow on the wall at the 125% marking. "After that, the temperature should be increased to 180% and held there about two or three days until the stems of the tobacco are thoroughly killed."

Joseph drew another arrow at the 180% marking. He handed Arry his old watch and explained when the big hand pointed straight up and the short hand reached the next number, an hour had passed. "I'll check back every so often. You understand everything?"

Arry grinned widely. "Yasser, Massa, one of those little marks an hour. Yasser," Arry said.

Satisfied, Joseph left his trainee to carry on and rode out to the field to oversee the hands.

His thoughts turned to the night before. He really hadn't meant to be cross with Anne. He'd been thinking of Elizabetha. Anne's voice had shocked him back to reality, was all. He thought of Elizabetha often. He felt so isolated since that terrible day of Martin's discovery of their love. Even after she'd extracted the promise from him to keep his feelings to himself, knowing she was there comforted him. He could still hope she might one day relent.

The field hands were already at the cotton crops. Gim, now as gray and worn as Joseph knew himself to be, handed gunny sacks from the wagon to each man. Joseph sat upon his horse and directed the men to the south fields. He watched as each hand, after filling his bag and bringing it back to Gim, waited as

Gim emptied it into the wagon.

After the fifth sack was emptied into the wagon, Gim paused and drew his shirtsleeve across his brow.

Joseph pulled out his pocket watch, three hours since he'd left Arry. He'd best go check on him. "I'll be back soon, Gim. Let the pickers empty their own sacks. We're both too old for this work."

Gim's large smile enveloped his face. He wiped the sweat from his brow with one of the empty sacks, "Yasser, I knows that all right."

Joseph rode across the fields, once again daydreaming of Elizabetha. He smelled smoke and jabbed his heels into the horse's flanks. As he approached the shed, smoke poured out between the wooden slats.

He descended from his saddle, cursing his boot for hanging up in the stirrup in his haste. He finally freed it and called out, "Arry. Arry."

No answer.

Joseph swung open the shed door. A wall of black haze greeted him. He pulled out his handkerchief and covered his nose, but it did little against the thick, acrid smoke.

He tied the handkerchief around his face and dropped to his belly, propelling himself forward with his forearms and elbows. He stopped every few feet and felt along the ground for Arry. He peered through the thick smoke. He thought he saw a shape ahead of him. Joseph pulled himself along faster. He felt a twinge in the middle of his chest. He couldn't think about that now. He must find Arry.

His hand groped along the damp dirt floor and felt cloth beneath its fingers. There was a body beneath the cloth. Arry was face down. Joseph turned him over and grabbed his underarm, tugging him toward the light at the open shed door. The twinge had spread to Joseph's left arm.

Joseph's coughing forced him to stop dragging Arry. Joseph tried to clear his lungs. They burned. Perspiration trickled into his eyes, stinging them. His heart raced. The stench of the smoke was unbearable. He felt dizzy and nauseated. He glanced at the door. It seemed no closer.

Joseph hauled Arry further. Joseph stopped again and pulled his shirt over the handkerchief on his face, gasping into it for air. His throat was raw. His chest felt as if a steel band were tightening around it.

He glanced toward the door again. Elizabetha stood there beckoning to him, her dark hair flowing around her head as it had on the pillow. She smiled.

He reached his hand toward hers and cried out in a hoarse gasp, "Elizabetha."

It was the last word he uttered.

Meanwhile, Gim drove the wagon while the slaves laughed and joked as they walked behind returning to the station for their dinner. Hany, Gim's daughter Prue's husband, sat beside Gim. Hany was as gregarious as Prue was shy. They struck a nice balance.

Hany sniffed the air. He pointed at the smoke billowing from the shed at the far end of the enclosure. "Look," he said.

Gim could smell the stench of thick smoke now. It spiraled into the air. Gim whipped the wagon horse to a gallop toward the shed. He clambered off the wagon and peered into the smoke. The other slaves gathered around him, handkerchiefs to their noses. Gim pointed to an outstretched arm on the ground about twenty feet inside.

Hany and several younger men rushed inside and carried the bodies out, carefully laying them on the ground dappled by the sunshine peeking between the tree leaves. It was too late. Joseph and Arry were dead.

Gim sank to the ground. He cradled Arry's head in his lap. Tears gushed down his cheeks. The other slaves stood by silently.

Two of the slaves lifted Joseph's body onto the wagon. Gim didn't want to let go of his son. At last, the others convinced him, and Arry was loaded into the wagon.

Gim and Hany drove their grim cargo back to the main house. All but two of the slaves followed. These stayed to dampen the fires. They would learn a flue had broken in half at a joint. Instead of the smoke traveling to the outside, it had filled the shed.

⇒ 35 ⇐

Anne heard the slave's wagon pull into the yard for dinner, then Sarah's scream followed by a crash. She threw down her knitting, and rushed outside nearly tripping on the tray of sandwiches and broken glasses and pitcher. The slaves from the fields huddled together off to the side of Gim and Sarah who were bent over a body, tears streaming down both their faces.

Anne's heart froze. Who was it? She stepped closer to them. She could see now it was their son Arry. Anne wondered what had happened to him. This was awful. She must find Joseph. Joseph, where was Joseph? She searched the yard.

The slaves' black eyes were rimmed in white fear as they gaped at her. There was a second body to the side of the group of slaves. She knew in a heartbeat it was Joseph. She screamed, "No!"

The trembling began in her knees and worked itself up the length of her body. She didn't know how she'd made it to Joseph's side, her whole being quavering jelly. She gazed down at him, flinging her head back and forth. "No, no, don't let it be true, God," she begged. Her knees gave way and she collapsed across his dead body, weeping onto his chest. "Joseph," she wailed over and over, "Joseph."

Elizabetha was surprised to see Thomas's carriage pull up in front. Thomas strode toward the door, but Olive remained inside the carriage. Elizabetha stepped out on the porch. The bright sunshine made her eyes water. She was greeted by a delightful chorus of singing birds.

Thomas reached the porch. There were no clouds in the sky, but a very dark one shadowed Thomas's face.

Elizabetha stopped. Her hand flew to her throat. "What is it, Thomas? What's wrong?"

Thomas gave her a quick hug and led her to the porch swing. He kneeled before her and took her hand. "I have bad news," he said. "Papa is dead."

Elizabetha's breath caught in her throat. "Joseph?" she uttered. "Joseph is dead? How?" Her heart sank to the pit of her stomach.

"An accident. He and the slave Arry were both suffocated from the smoke in the tobacco shed when a pipe broke."

"Dear God. How's Anne? How's your mother doing?" Elizabetha stammered. She felt weak as a kitten.

"She's beside herself with grief as we all are. I know you two haven't spoken in years, but you and she had been such dear friends. If you could attend the funeral, Olive and I would be pleased to take you in our carriage. Perhaps seeing an old friend would help Mama."

Elizabetha gaped at Thomas. He obviously didn't know why Anne had not spoken to her all these years. Of course, she wouldn't have told him. She was far too grand a lady to confide to her son that her husband and her best friend had an affair. That's how Anne must think of it Elizabetha was sure, an affair. But it had been so very much more than that. "I think it best if I stay away, especially at this time. There are many things I can't explain, but trust me, it's best." She patted Thomas's hand and tried to smile.

"As you wish," Thomas said as he stood.

As he turned to leave, Elizabetha put her hand on his sleeve.

"My deepest and most sincere sympathies." She almost asked him to convey her sympathies to Anne but caught herself in time.

She sat in the porch swing a long time after the carriage had driven off. She felt numb, dead inside herself. Martin dead. Joseph dead. And Anne as good as dead to her. She'd never felt so alone in her life. She tightened her arms around her shoulders, laid her head back, and closed her eyes. Tears streamed down her cheeks as she rocked herself in the swing, repeating a single word over and over in her mind, Joseph, Joseph.

* * *

The days grew into weeks and weeks into months. Thomas, Olive, and Joseph Samuel remained with Anne after the funeral. They sold their home in Evansham and Thomas took over the farming. The tobacco shed was refitted with new stovepipe.

Gim and Sarah stayed on with Anne in spite of the letter Joseph left granting their freedom and Anne offering their freedom before her death. "We's too old to be anywhere else, Missus Anne," Sarah explained. "'Sides dis is where Arry be."

Joseph's body was placed in the family cemetery. Each morning, Anne gathered wild flowers and placed them on the graves of Joseph, Rachel, Samuel, and the infant, Alissa, Anne had miscarried. Sometimes six-year-old Joseph Samuel accompanied her. He was the only bright spot in the dreary days of her grief.

This morning she was alone. After placing the flowers on each grave, she sat beside Joseph's as she always did when she was alone. Her fingers traced his name on the headstone. Fifty-two years together she thought. Fifty-two years and she'd never fully known him. Never truly understood him, but she had loved him. How very much she had loved him. He had always protected her.

But not from the one thing that he couldn't control, his love for Elizabetha. Anne had felt so betrayed, her best friend, Elizabetha, had loved Anne's Joseph. Her best friend. Her fingers traced his name again. Of course Elizabetha had loved him. How could she not? They were both so very much alike. Perhaps it was she, Anne, who had been in the way.

Tears streamed down her face. She couldn't make out Joseph's name on the headstone any longer. The whole of her being erupted in one anguished wail and she prostrated herself across Joseph's grave. "I forgive you, Joseph. I forgive you." She whispered into the earth, "Please come back to me. Please come back." Her body shook with sobs that wrenched from the pit of her stomach. She wailed, "Please, God, undo the done."

Later, Anne slowly strolled back toward the house. She had forgiven Joseph. Now it was time to deal with Elizabetha.

* * *

Elizabetha's hand absently caressed the worn leather cover of her journal as she lay in her bed waiting to die. She had written so many words over the years. If only in a string of words somewhere between a capital and a period, she had struck a chord that resounded through the hardest heart, she would have achieved some purpose to her life, but perhaps that was too much to hope. Perhaps they were just a foolish old woman's empty words.

It felt strange lying there knowing each breath might be her last. Death was something that happened to other people, not to her. Of course, she'd always known, as everyone does, that one day she would die, but it seemed so soon. Would she grapple toe to toe with the dark angel or quietly take his hand? Would she slip at once into oblivion or be aware of death happening? She drew her hand across her eyes as if to chase the thoughts away. Her hand plopped down upon the journal, its strength expended.

Her old friend Dr. Marlow had died years ago and his replacement, Dr. Kinney, a slender young man with fine features and long fingers at the ends of delicate hands, surprisingly firm in their touch, had told her that her heart was tired.

A tired heart, like her father's. She glanced down at her hands on the journal. When had her hands begun to look like her mother's? She *was* tired. Too tired anymore to lift those old hands with the bulging, blue veins seemingly intent on bursting through the papery skin that contained them. She closed her eyes.

Her son Jacob and his wife, Margaretha, had visited moments earlier to say their goodbyes. She'd told them she wanted her best friend, Anne, to have her journal. If she'd accept it.

Anne and her husband, Joseph. Dear, sweet, passionate Joseph, how Elizabetha had loved him. All of their lives would have been so different if only Elizabetha had met Joseph first—before Martin, her own husband. But she *had* met Martin first.

Elizabetha again gazed at the bulging blue veins of her hands. She had tried to live her life by logic and will, but her emotions and passion had nearly destroyed them all. Perhaps religion wasn't so much about being controlled by a greater power as it was balancing the powers that raged within. She wished she could tell Martin she understood, in her own way.

A small knock at the bedroom door brought her back to the present.

The door opened and a small woman sidled through it. The figure stood gazing down at Elizabetha.

Elizabetha strained to make out who it was.

Silence echoed off the walls as Elizabetha finally recognized Anne.

Elizabetha fell back against her pillows. "I'm already dying, Anne, in case you've come to kill me," she said.

Anne eased onto a small chair near the head of the bed and took Elizabetha's hand in hers. "Dear Elizabetha, I hadn't known. I'm so sorry," Anne said, tears filling her eyes.

Elizabetha closed her eyelids. She wasn't sure she could open them again, and they flew wide in panic. She studied Anne's face. "What made you come?"

"To tell you that I forgive you, and Joseph," Anne brought Elizabetha's hand to her lips and kissed the back.

Elizabetha could no longer see Anne's face for the tears welling in her eyes and spilling over her cheeks. "Thank you." Her hand slid out of Anne's and rested on the journal. It reminded her. "I want you to have this," Elizabetha said and closed her eyelids. "Perhaps it will help you to understand—everything."

Anne picked up Elizabetha's hand again and held it. "I shall treasure it always."

They were the last words Elizabetha heard.

Anne felt Elizabetha's hand go limp. She sat a long time letting the tears stream down her cheeks. Finally she laid down Elizabetha's hand, picked up the journal, and held it to her bosom.

≫36≪

After Elizabetha's funeral, a light April rain pattered on the window pane as Olive heaved a final push and her new baby, Annjanine, slithered into her mother-in-law, Anne's, waiting hands. One tiny slap of an able hand on a miniature bottom brought the first gasp for air and an indignant wail, the sound of which told Olive that another miracle had just occurred. A new generation was born.

She laid back against the pillows panting, sweat dripping from the tip of her nose. She wiped it away with the back of her hand and brushed her damp hair off her forehead.

She watched as Anne cleaned the baby and wrapped her in a soft pink blanket. Olive had been so sure it would be a girl. She had chosen the name Annjanine to honor Anne and Olive's Cherokee mother, Jane. Olive hoped the new child would lighten Anne's heavy mourning burden over the death of Anne's husband, Joseph, and so soon after, Anne's best friend, Elizabetha.

"Hello, Annjanine, my precious granddaughter," Anne cooed to the child as she brought the bundle of baby to Olive's bed.

The infant's eyelids fluttered and finally dropped closed over her coal black eyes, her chubby cheeks rosy. Black hair spiked out around her tiny head, truly a Cherokee baby. Olive's son, Joseph Samuel, resembled the white heritage of his father more. Olive made a solemn vow for the second time, that this child, too, would be raised in the ways of the whites.

Two years later, Annjanine took her first steps from Olive's outstretched protective arms to Anne's. "Those three short steps are no less an accomplishment than walking from Pennsylvania to Virginia," Anne said.

Anne gathered the child in an embrace and rewarded her with a kiss. "I regret having missed Joseph Samuel's first steps. I don't intend to miss anything with this grandchild."

Annjanine squirmed to be free and headed back to her mother.

"What a little minx," Anne said. "She's headstrong like her father."

"You mean like her grandmother." Olive countered.

"No, not me. Elizabetha was the determined one. She always seemed to know what she wanted and went after it. Did you know she was just eleven when she decided she would marry Martin? Though she always seemed to be searching for something else or something more." A past pain played across Anne's gaze. She shook it off and returned to Olive. "I was content to be Joseph's wife." Anne heaved a sigh. "I still miss him."

"I know." Olive patted Anne's hand. "But I do remember one time you were headstrong. When you refused to meet me and even your grandson, Joseph Samuel." Olive remembered her own past pain at that refusal.

Anne put her arm around Olive's shoulder. "Dear Olive, I'm so sorry for that wasted time. I know now the loss was mine more than anyone's. I hope you can forgive me."

Olive propped Annjanine on her hip and hugged Anne with her free arm. "I do. I'm so glad we've become friends."

"Me too. It's been so kind of you and Thomas to stay on after Joseph's—."

"It's where we wanted to be."

Anne brushed the tears from her eyes. She seemed to never

be able to stop the tears for long. "I'm so tired." She smiled at Olive and tousled Annjanine's mop of dark hair. "I think I'll go lie down awhile."

Olive watched Anne shuffle upstairs. Anne moved ever slower it seemed. But, then she was seventy-two. Olive guessed it was to be expected; still, she worried about her.

After a time of quiet play with Annjanine, Olive took her upstairs for her nap.

She placed the baby in the crib and stroked Annjanine's temple for several moments while the child fell asleep.

Several hours later, Olive's husband, Thomas, came in from the surveying fields. "Where is everyone?" he asked.

"Your mother and Annjanine are having their naps and Joseph is playing in the parlor. It's about time for Annjanine to wake up. I'll go check on her."

When Olive reached the top of the stairs, she heard the baby cooing in her crib.

Olive stepped into the nursery and was greeted by an endearing smile from Annjanine. Olive changed her, scooped her into her arms, and headed toward Anne's room to see if she was awake yet.

Olive cradled Annjanine on her hip, gently pushed open the bedroom door, and tiptoed to the bed.

Anne looked so peaceful. A small hand-painted portrait of Joseph lay on her bosom beneath her hand. Elizabetha's journal was beside Anne.

Olive slipped Joseph's portrait from beneath Anne's hand and put it on the table beside the bed. She picked up the journal to place it on the table when a piece of paper slipped out and fell to the floor. Olive retrieved it and saw her name on it.

To my Friend, Olive,
I hope you gain as much insight on life from Elizabetha's journal as I have. You owe her more than you know.
Love,
Anne

Dread filled Olive as she stood with the letter in hand before putting it on top of the journal. She shook Anne's shoulder.
Anne didn't stir. Olive shook her again, harder. Nothing.

Olive stepped back, her eyes brimmed with tears. She hugged
Annjanine to her. She picked up the letter and journal, walked
to the landing, and called down, "Thomas, you'd better come
up here."

Thomas bounded up the stairs. "What is it?" he asked.

"I can't wake her."

He stared at Olive blankly for a moment. He glanced at his
mother's open bedroom door. He left Olive and rushed into the
room. Olive heard him call, "Mama, Mama," silence followed.
"Oh, Mama, no."

⇒ 37 ⇐

Summer of 1812

After Anne's death, Thomas sold the Blakemore station and they returned to Evansham, keeping only enough slaves to run their home; the rest were sold. The money from the sale of the property was ample, and Olive enjoyed being able to entertain. The Thomas Blakemore family was becoming well accepted in the community of upper-class white friends and neighbors. Olive truly felt she fit into the white society as if she'd been born to it.

She clasped the hand of tawny-haired Joseph, and balanced the dark Annjanine, on her hip as they waited beside the storefront for the children's father to come out of the Evansham general store. Inside, Annjanine's tiny two-year-old fingers had grasped at everything in reach. In exasperation, Olive decided to wait outside for Thomas.

The rhododendron covering the Blue Ridge mountains cast a lilac-colored sheen across the rounded, parallel ridges reminding Olive of the folds in a satin gown.

Annjanine squirmed in her arms. Olive glanced up toward the sky. The September sun sat high enough to dry the morning dew and promised a warm and muggy day. She made a mental note that her and Thomas's tenth wedding anniversary was next week. She would throw one of those popular oyster parties to celebrate the occasion she decided.

She idly observed pedestrians, passing horsemen, and carriages stir up the road dust as they passed.

Olive spotted Luke Aiken, or Angry Bear as she still thought of him, walking with his wife and sons, one about the same age as Annjanine. The older boy by her side looked sullen.

As Angry Bear approached, he said, "Olive, it *is* you. I almost didn't recognize you; how easily you blend in with the whites."

Olive knew he didn't mean it as a compliment.

"You remember my wife, Sara," Angry Bear said.

Olive hadn't been to the village while they were with Anne at the Blakemore station and hadn't mingled much with others of their village when she visited her parents there since she'd been back.

Sara stepped to Angry Bear's side and extended her hand. "It is good to see you again. These are our sons, Kyle and this is Lance," she said, indicating the older boy last. Sara was petite with a small straight nose and the eyes of a doe, giving her a frail, fawn-like appearance. Her long hair hung loosely down the back of her fringed deerskin dress.

Joseph and Lance were about the same age, but Lance was larger than Joseph. They eyed each other.

Olive noticed Lance circled his foot in the soft sand, sending some to the top of Joseph's shoe.

In turn, Joseph circled his foot, making sure sand landed on Lance's moccasin.

"I'm pleased to see you, Sara. These are my children Joseph and Annjanine." In her full blue skirts, laced bodice, and her hair fashioned in a knot behind her head with waved short bangs in front, Olive felt herself a sharp contrast to Sara and to Angry Bear dressed in deerskin leggings and breechclout with his hair in thick braids. Angry Bear had always avoided the white man's clothing.

"Perhaps when you visit your parents you will stop by our lodge." Sara glanced at the boys still measuring each other.

"And the children could become better acquainted."

Olive felt guilty not having been friendlier in her own village. She should make an effort. After all, her friend Margaretha was the only white who visited the village besides Thomas, and both already knew Olive was born Cherokee. "I'd like that."

Angry Bear's proud smile twisted to a scowl at something behind Olive. She turned to see Thomas exiting the general store with the keg of nails he'd wanted.

"We must go," Angry Bear said. He nodded once at Olive and ushered Sara in front of him away from the approaching Thomas.

Thomas reached Olive's side and hoisted the keg on his shoulder. "Wasn't that Angry Bear? He certainly left in a rush."

"It appears he still doesn't like you much." Olive grinned.

With a wickedly raised eyebrow and lustful gleam, Thomas leered at Olive. "I still understand why." He put his free hand at the small of her back and escorted her toward their carriage.

The following week, before the guests arrived, Olive sneaked a broiled oyster to sample before her cook, Sassy, swatted her hand away. "Dat's for de party, Missus," the stout, heavy-breasted Sassy said. "Shame on you," she added after further indignant contemplation. She clasped her hands together at her ample aproned waist beneath her large bosom. "Humph."

Olive somehow managed not to grin as she said, "I apologize, Sassy." She plopped the oyster in her mouth. "Hmm, delicious," she muttered around the savory oyster taking up most of her mouth as she scooted out of Sassy's kitchen, licking her fingers.

Later that evening, Olive was delighted with her guests response to Sassy's array of oysters which were boiled, broiled, curried, deviled, fricasseed, fried, scalloped, steamed, and stewed. She'd tried each type and couldn't decide which was her favorite.

She felt a congenial glow on her cheeks as she ambled through the guests gathered in groups around the parlor, stopping to chat with each cluster. She meandered over to her friends

Margaretha and Jacob Kimberlin.

"What a wonderful party, Olive," Margaretha said as Olive approached.

"Thank you," Olive responded. At forty-two, Margaretha, like her father before her, was still as determined in her fight for the Indians as she'd ever been. Margaretha's eyes burned with dedication, lending an aura of brilliance to her plain features and pale coloring.

Margaretha's husband, Jacob, stood beside her and reminded Olive of the description in his mother's journal of Jacob's father, Martin Kimberlin, as stern, pious, and all-business with light-blue eyes the color of steel set in a determined countenance. The two families of Blakemore and Kimberlin still faithfully attended the Kimberlin Church built by Martin.

"Quite delicious," Jacob acknowledged as he downed the last fried oyster on his plate.

Olive's complacency was curtailed as the stocky Sam Brockton bawled out in his husky voice, "The British have been stealing our sailors and impressing them into their own navy far too long."

Someone else shouted, "I've heard they've taken between six and fourteen thousand men. They seize our exports if they think they're headed for France."

"A war will wipe out the shipping trade," a dissenter yelled.

"They're helping the Indians under Tecumseh keep us from expanding into the wilderness. Remember the Battle of Tippecanoe," someone roared.

Jacob stepped forward. "Remember the *Chesapeake*," he said in his low but commanding voice. "The British attacked her because her captain would not let the British board to search her crew for British deserters, a ruse they've blatantly used to steal our sailors. They broadsided her until her flag had to be struck."

Olive's husband, Thomas, came up beside her and spoke, "In the words of Henry Clay, 'What are we to gain by war? What are we not to lose by peace? Commerce, character, a nation's best treasure, honor!' I, for one, will fight for this nation's honor if we must go to war."

"Here, here," a chorus shouted.

A dark foreboding daunted Olive's festive mood and twisted her insides into a knot. She glanced at Margaretha.

Margaretha patted Olive's sleeve and gazed at Jacob.

A loud rapping at the front door was answered by the butler, Sassy's thin husband, Goral, who sought out Thomas and led him to the entry.

Thomas chatted several moments with the caller, closed the door, and turned toward his guests with a somberness Olive had not seen since his mother's funeral. When he reached the entrance to the parlor, all eyes were turned to him. He scanned the sea of faces before saying, "President Madison has declared war on the British."

The solemn hush that filled the room stung the eardrums as much as any cacophony.

⇒ 38 ⇐

1813

By December of 1812, a force of twenty-five British ships had blockaded near the Chesapeake Bay, and Thomas's militia company was mustered into service to join the Virginia State Militia and the few United States Army Regulars in defending the bay. Most of the United States regular forces present at Fort Norfolk were sent to the northern front when the war started, leaving Norfolk and Portsmouth virtually defenseless. Virginia's Governor Barbour decided to rotate the militiamen every three months for training and to man the forts in the area.

The January chill heightened the fish and salt aroma of the harbor which was to be the home of Thomas's militia company for their tour of duty. Thomas's company had just arrived at Fort Norfolk at the mouth of the Elizabeth River with Fort Nelson on the opposite bank, the Chesapeake Bay before them.

Thomas surveyed the serene countryside and beach of the snug harbor. It was hard to imagine it could ever be disturbed. Soldiers fished along the shore and in small boats. Some caught crabs with cut up eels, while others snagged eels with pieces of crab. Still, others hauled in oysters. Some soldiers played quoits or marbles along the grassy inland.

That night Thomas wished Olive was lying next to him. He rolled over on the hard cot, trying to find a comfortable position. This was going to be a long three months. He drifted off to sleep dreaming of Olive's delicate face and her mischievous black eyes.

* * *

In Evansham, Olive purchased some thread at the general store then walked along further to peek in the milliner's shop. She took her handkerchief from her sleeve and dabbed at the perspiration gathering at her throat. It was certainly a scorcher today. A crowd overtook her and jostled Olive along the main street. "Horse race," someone yelled.

She tried to reach her carriage where her driver the slave Booker awaited her return. She was glad she'd left the children home this day. If she'd known there was to be a horse race, she would never have come herself. She dropped her handkerchief and tried to retrieve it, but the crowd bore her away from it.

Someone grabbed her arm and yanked her into a nearby doorway. Her heart raced with fear at not knowing who had seized her. She faced forward with her savior or demon behind her clutching her arm. She held her breath as the madding crowd passed. She turned to glimpse Luke Aiken's dark eyes peering at her. "Angry Bear," she exploded in relief.

Angry Bear, still holding her arm and gazing at her, said, "You still call me that."

"I guess I do. I'm sorry."

"It's fine. I don't mind."

Olive thought his lips twitched with a smile.

"Your husband should not leave you alone among these savages." Angry Bear's almost-grin reappeared.

She rallied to Thomas's defense. "He's fighting the war against the British." She straightened her skirts with her free hand and wondered at Angry Bear's hand still encircling her other arm. She glanced back to his steady gaze. "My driver is waiting for me in the carriage."

"Allow me." Angry Bear guided her by the arm to her carriage and assisted her inside, closing the carriage door behind her.

As the carriage pulled forward, Olive peeked out the back opening. Angry Bear stood in the road with his arms folded across his chest, staring at the back of the carriage. He remained that way until she could no longer see him. She wondered if he still had feelings for her. Don't be silly. He was just being an old friend.

Angry Bear watched Olive's carriage jostle down the road and remembered the vision he had the night before. He had been standing on a grassy knoll in a foggy mist when he heard his name called. He turned and saw Olive running toward him with her arms open. He caught her in his arms and kissed her, and the vision vanished. It had been a long time since he had kissed Olive, since before Thomas came to the village and stole her from him. Through childhood they had been friends. He had loved her even then. But she turned her attentions away from him and could see only Thomas. Luke had grieved long over the loss of her. Sara had filled the void, but he knew one day Olive would again be his. He didn't know how or when, but the vision said it would be.

* * *

Thomas had signed up for a second stint because a British invasion was imminent and they were fortifying Craney Island in the bay, but it hadn't happened. Eight days before Thomas was due to leave the bay, the British made their move. Early on the morning of June 22, a long drum roll in the American ranks tumbled Thomas out of his cot on Craney Island. He pulled on his coat and boots, grabbed his musket and haversack, bolted out of the tent, and drew to attention before Captain Stanley.

The Captain announced that British troops of more than two thousand had landed two to three miles west of Craney Island and were marching toward Wises Creek on the island's south side.

The Captain glanced at the half-built blockhouse and gasped, "We're not displaying a flag. Get me a pole, someone, quick about it."

Thomas hastily hunted up a long slender tree trunk, and nailed an American flag to its top and raised it over the breastwork.

The commander of the post, ordered the artillery line be strengthened, and Thomas's company manhandled two twenty-four-pounders and one eighteen-pounder from the unfinished blockhouse on the southeastern side of the island to the opposite end.

The sky burst into a spectacular volley of British rockets. Thomas closed his eyes against the blinding glare and thought of Olive. "Let us all return to our families safely," he prayed.

When the barrage finally ceased, Thomas checked his body for damage and was relieved.

In turn, the American artillery commander battered the British troops with continuous volleys of grapeshot and canister. The British infantry, unable to ford the deep waters of Wises Creek, was driven back with heavy losses.

Thomas would have breathed a sigh of relief, but a double column of fifty British barges took that moment to make an amphibious assault.

The American commander of a light artillery division, waited until the British barges were well within range of his guns and said, "Now my brave boys, are you ready? Fire!" The result was lethal, and the barges were sunk and scattered with numerous casualties.

A column of boats veered off into a creek behind Craney Island. The captain of the fleet stood upright in the lead fifty-foot barge.

A volley of shots burst from Craney Island. The British captain's thigh exploded with blood as he collapsed on deck. His men carried him back to his ship.

When the Craney Island defenders regrouped, the Captain removed his hat and swiped his forearm across his brow. "We've not lost a man. It's over as quickly as it began."

The time between "over" and "began" had seemed an eternity to Thomas. And it was an eternity since he'd seen Olive. He was anxious to go home.

* * *

Olive hadn't received any more letters from Thomas since he wrote that he'd signed on for another three months. She perched on the sofa in the parlor embroidering a pillow slip with pink rosebuds and hoped nothing was wrong. He must be all right. He just must be. A prick of the needle caused her to plop her finger in her mouth to suck the tiny drop of blood away before it spoiled the pillow slip. She heard a noise in the hall and turned her head.

She jumped to her feet as Thomas strode into the room in his handsome though dusty uniform. He leaned his musket against the wall and turned to her with arms open.

The embroidery fell to the floor as she bounded to his waiting arms. He was safe. She encircled his midriff with her arms and buried her face against his chest. He smelled of sweat and dirt from the long march, but she didn't care. He was home. She covered his cheeks, eyelids, nose, and forehead with kisses as she stood on tiptoe.

"Did you miss me?" he teased. With his hand at the back of her head, he leaned forward, bending her backward and immersed her mouth in sweet ecstasy.

That night in bed Olive remained snuggled against Thomas's clean, soap-smelling body long after they'd made love. He'd only been gone six months, but she'd been so lonely for him she'd thought she would die. Whatever would she do if anything ever happened to him? Funny that she'd always thought there wasn't anything she couldn't do if she put her mind to it, but the thought of having to live without Thomas petrified her. Damn the war for making her realize he was vulnerable, and, therefore, so was she.

The Chesapeake Bay had remained safe and the war moved northward. Thomas would not have to fight any longer. She was relieved by that. Hard times remained on the land as the war with Britain became increasingly unpopular until it finally would end in December of 1814, when the Treaty of Ghent was signed by both sides, essentially restoring territories captured by each. But before news of the treaty would reach the United Sates, its victory in the Battle of New Orleans weeks after the signing of the Treaty, would lead it to proclaim the war a United States victory.

⇒ 39 ⇐

Thomas recalled the first time he arrived at the Cherokee's village as he drove Olive and the children to visit Olive's parents, Tom and Jane Poteet, to celebrate Joseph's ninth birthday. That first visit was when he'd met Olive with the huge black eyes that twinkled with devilment.

As he reined the carriage horse to a stop beside the Poteet lodge of cane and clay with a thatch roof, his son, Joseph, scrambled out of the wagon and bolted to his grandfather.

Tom Poteet bent down to the boy, handing him a wooden flute he'd fashioned, the copper bracelet on his wrist reflecting the sun.

Joseph beamed as he took the flute in his hands. A wide grin at his grandfather and a huge hug told Thomas how happy Joseph was.

Joseph hugged his grandmother, Jane, as she came out of the lodge. He plopped down under a willow tree to play the flute.

Olive handed the squirming Annjanine to Jane. Annjanine immediately tried to grab one of the dangling beaded earrings her grandmother wore.

Thomas had always been fond of his in-laws. Olive's father,

Tom, had taught him how to hunt small game with the blowgun made out of a hollowed cane.

Three-year-old Annjanine squirmed her way out of her grandmother's arms and headed toward the stream as fast as her chubby legs would carry her.

Thomas darted after, catching her in his arms just before she reached the river. He twirled her around and carried her to the shore. She loved water. He sat with her on the bank while she plopped down on her belly and splashed her hands in the tantalizing liquid. "You must never come to the stream alone," he warned. "It can be dangerous." Annjanine glanced up at him and giggled. So much for warnings.

Later that afternoon while Annjanine napped, Thomas invited Olive, and young Joseph to stroll through the village. Joseph asked to join a group of boys playing in the plaza. "All right," Olive said. "But mind your manners."

As Joseph scooted off, Thomas asked, "What are they playing?"

"Shinny," Olive said. "The team that kicks the buckskin ball across a line scratched in the dirt the most times, wins. The ball can't be touched by the hands."

They watched the boys play. One team wore a green strip of cloth around one leg of each boy, and the other team's players each wore a red strip. The members of one side tried to intercept the team with the ball by kicking it to a boy of their own side. Joseph, wearing a green strip, and Lance, in red, eyed each other. Joseph managed to kick the ball away from Lance, and over the line at the last minute.

Lance shoved Joseph. Joseph punched him in the stomach. Their fists flew at each other.

Thomas bolted to the fight and grabbed Joseph by the arm, pushing Lance away just as the boy's arm was grabbed by his father, Angry Bear.

Thomas and Angry Bear each held their sons apart. "Don't shove my son," Angry Bear spat.

"Your son started the fight," Thomas retorted.

Angry Bear glowered at Thomas.

Thomas felt guilty when he glimpsed the two boys glaring at each other. "Let's have the boys shake hands," Thomas said and offered his to Angry Bear.

Angry Bear slapped it away.

The color red exploded before Thomas's eyes. His fist flew into his opponent's face without Thomas having thought of it.

Angry Bear reeled backward from the blow.

He pulled a knife from his legging and raised it, glaring at Thomas.

Thomas hunkered to a crouch for the attack.

Olive reached her hand to Angry Bear's weaponed arm and ordered, "Stop it both of you. You're behaving like children, worse. What kind of example are you setting?"

Thomas and Angry Bear glanced at their sons' gaping mouths.

Angry Bear peered hard at Olive. He returned the knife to his legging, grabbed his son's arm, and led him away.

Olive turned to Thomas. "Whatever has gotten into you?" she scolded.

Thomas didn't know what had gotten into him. He hated when his temper overtook him. Now he felt foolish. "He started it."

That spring, Thomas hadn't returned home from his hunting by suppertime. Olive and the children ate alone. "Joseph, sit up straight," Olive snapped.

"Yes, Mama."

Olive picked up her fork and laid it down again. She couldn't eat. "Annjanine, close your mouth when you chew."

Annjanine's large, dark eyes filled with tears.

Olive screeched her chair back, rose, and paced while the children finished eating in silence.

After the children were tucked in bed and her apologies given, Olive tried to occupy her mind with her embroidery. Every so often, she went to the front window and peeked out, hoping to see Thomas strolling home.

At ten, she went upstairs and prepared for bed. She climbed

in under the covers and stared sightlessly at the ceiling. Where could he be? Perhaps he'd gotten lost. Calm yourself, Olive, he's hunted all his life. He can handle himself in the woods. It probably turned dark, and he decided to camp out instead of taking a chance. He was always level-headed. She listened the whole night in vain for his footfalls.

Meanwhile, Thomas didn't know how many times he had blacked out. He glanced down at his left foot. The huge rusty steel trap dug its ugly jaws into his boot and flesh. It was nearly dark. He must free himself. He cursed himself again for being so careless.

If only he hadn't tried to steal some honey to take home for the children. He had seen the trap at the side of the tree and knew he could avoid it, until he couldn't quite reach the honeycomb, had disturbed it, and several bees swarmed out to investigate. He inadvertently stepped out of the bees way and into the trap.

He tried once more to pry open the steel jaws. Sweat ran into his eyes as his arm muscles quivered. He couldn't pull it apart far enough from this angle to free his foot. He had to release it again. He gasped at the excruciating pain and fell back in the underbrush.

He awoke to a rustling in the leaves. His gun, where was it? He pulled his torso upright and scanned the ground. The fowling piece had fallen a few feet away. He had to get hold of himself, build a fire, get his gun.

An Indian emerged from the trees.

Thomas exhaled, relieved that it wasn't a bear.

My God, it was Angry Bear. He'd rather see an animal.

Angry Bear towered above, stared down at him, and took out his knife.

Thomas prepared for the thrust. Angry Bear would finish him off once and for all this time. At least it would be quick.

Angry Bear stepped toward him.

Thomas held his breath.

It would be easy to kill him Angry Bear thought. But he knew he wouldn't. He would never deliberately hurt Olive like that. She loved Thomas. He would spare him for her.

Angry Bear bent, stuck his knife in the ground, and released the trap. He cut off Thomas' boot and sliced his trouser leg open.

Thomas groaned from the movement to his leg or perhaps from relief at the sparing of his life. He fainted.

When next he awoke, Thomas found himself in the lodge of his in-laws. Angry Bear must have carried him there. He lifted his head enough to see his foot and ankle wrapped in soft doe-skin.

"It's a poultice of the root of comfrey and trillium to heal the bone and prevent gangrene," Olive said as she brought a small bowl to his mat and kneeled before him. "Drink this—a tea of the same," she said. She supported his head as she put the wooden bowl to his lips. It tasted strangely bitter but sooth-ing. He swallowed and lay back.

"How did you know I was here?" he asked.

"When Angry Bear found you, he brought you here because it was closest, then he came for me."

"Is it broken?"

"The medicine man didn't think so, but badly bruised and cut. You were lucky Angry Bear found you," she said.

Lucky he didn't kill me, Thomas thought. He wondered why Angry Bear had helped him, but he was grateful he had. "I'll have to thank Angry Bear."

Olive glanced at him. "He knows you are thankful."

➤•40•◄

The September morning briskness hinted at the colder months to come. Olive led seven-year-old Annjanine through the village toward Sara and Angry Bear's lodge so Annjanine could play with their youngest son, Kyle. Olive's daughter was the only child who wanted to come to the village with her these days. Her son, Joseph, at thirteen, was too involved in school work to be bothered. He was a good scholar. He would make a fine lawyer as was his dream. He spent most of his time poring over books. She was pleased he had such ambitions.

"There's Kyle," Annjanine yipped. She pulled her hand from her mother's and streaked to Kyle.

"Annjanine, come back here." Olive scolded, but her daughter paid no heed. Olive marched over to her wayward child and tugged sharply on a raven tress of Annjanine's hair.

"Ow," Annjanine said. She glanced up to her mother's scowl. "I'm sorry, Mama."

"Sorry is as sorry does. Don't run away from me like that again."

Young Kyle, slim and delicate like his mother, but with an impish air, led Annjanine by the hand to a patch of soft dirt beside the lodge. His black eyes twinkled. He drew a circle in the dirt and placed a flat stone in the middle then gathered pebbles and gave half to Annjanine. They took turns throwing the pebbles into the circle, trying to hit, or be closest to the flat rock.

Sara slouched on a rough-hewn bench in front of her lodge with a large wooden bowl on her lap and a grinding stone in her hand. There were dark smudges beneath her eyes, and she ground the corn slowly as if too tired for the task. She gazed at the children and said, "Those two are quite a pack of trouble all by themselves,"

"They certainly are. What one doesn't think of, the other does." Olive settled beside Sara. "Have you been ill, Sara?"

"Just fatigued. I have made a tonic of Indian Sage. That will help build my strength soon." A feeble smile tried to curve her mouth.

Sara's oldest son, Lance, strode past his brother and Annjanine and into the lodge, returning seconds later with his bow and arrows. He was tall and well-built like his father. Young Annjanine's gaze followed his every move.

Kyle said, "Can we come with you?"

"No. I'm joining the warriors in a man's game." Lance lifted his chin half an inch and marched off as quickly as he had appeared.

Sara wagged her head side to side. "That one, so stoic like his father, but without the patience."

Annjanine's gaze followed Lance's departure. He was so much older. She wished she would hurry and grow up so he would pay attention to her. She noticed Kyle watching her. "Your brother's very tall, isn't he?" she said.

"Yes," he said as he glanced after his brother. "Very tall and very full of himself."

* * *

That summer, Angry Bear knew his wife, Sara, and son Kyle had smallpox. Sara had stayed at the lodge of her parents while she tended to them for the few days before they died of it, even though she wasn't well herself. She'd said the tonic would help her, but it hadn't. She seemed tired all the time.

Angry Bear hadn't known Sara's parents had smallpox until he went to bury them. Sara had never allowed him inside her parent's lodge during their illness.

As a child, he had heard of the smallpox epidemic that devastated his people before he was born. He remembered the stories of the proud warriors who had survived the illness but upon seeing their disfigurement from the disease killed themselves. The depth of their shame was such that they shot themselves, cut their own throats, stabbed themselves, or some, in madness, threw themselves into the fire, utterly divested of the power to feel pain.

Angry Bear and Sara had burned the lodge of her parents, but it was already too late, within days Sara had gotten sick and then Kyle.

Angry Bear had ordered Lance to stay at the lodge of Sara's sister, and Angry Bear tended to his wife and youngest son.

The medicine man had danced, chanted, and wafted burning sage throughout the lodge, but nothing had helped.

Angry Bear dabbed water on his young son's feverish forehead. Kyle opened his red-rimmed eyes and gazed into Angry Bear's face. "Papa," he said. His young body shuddered and his eyes stared sightlessly.

Angry Bear eased his son's eyelids over the fixed glaze. Angry Bear dropped his head and wept.

With leaden limbs, he rose and went to his wife's mat.

Since Sara had been stricken with the disease, she had insisted on keeping her blanket over her face to hide the pus-filled blisters from Angry Bear. She'd said she didn't want him to see her ugliness.

He gazed down at her. She was so still, Angry Bear was hesitant to touch her for fear her skin would not be warm.

He forced himself to take her hand. It was deathly cold. In honor of her wishes, he left the blanket over his wife's face, and prepared to do what he must.

Olive went to her village alone. Annjanine had accompanied her father to Evansham and Joseph was engrossed in his studies. She had the slave Booker drive her in the carriage. He sat stiffly erect in front of her, his broad back interfering with her view, she contented herself with the side scenery, as usual. The lazy summer sunlight flickered through the trees making her sleepy.

As the carriage approached her parent's lodge, Olive spotted Angry Bear and Sara's son Lance standing alone beside the stream. He threw stones into the waters with great force as if he were tying to punish the river. Whatever could be the matter?

She smelled smoke, scanned the village, and saw smoke and flames billowing up from Angry Bear and Sara's lodge. "Hurry Booker," she urged.

Her parents were among the villagers watching the lodge burn. Why wasn't anyone trying to put out the fire?

Angry Bear stood in front of the group. His shoulders sagged and his arms dangled at his sides as he stared into the flames. Something was terribly wrong. "Stop," she said to Booker. She jumped from the carriage as it halted and rushed to her mother.

Her mother glanced at her and hurried to meet her.

"What is it?" Olive asked. "What's happened?"

Her mother held Olive's hand and shook her head back and forth in sadness. "Smallpox," she said. "Sara and young Kyle, both gone. Luke is burning everything to keep it from spreading." The reek of burning flesh should have told Olive.

"I must go to him," Olive said and threaded her way through the crowd.

She put her hand on Angry Bear's shoulder. "Luke, I'm so sorry."

He turned slowly toward her. He had cut off his braids in grief. Dark smudges under his red-rimmed eyes told her he hadn't slept in days. He placed his hand on top of hers and turned back to the fire.

Together, without speaking, they watched the flames devour the lodge and all of his possessions until, starved of sustenance, the flames flickered slowly into ashes. The rest of the villagers had long since dispersed to their homes.

Weeks later, Angry Bear worried about Lance. He'd started hanging around with some rowdy older braves in Evansham. He was becoming more surly every day. He refused to talk about his mother or Kyle as if he blamed them for leaving him, or maybe he blamed Angry Bear for not having saved them.

Angry Bear glanced up from the deer he had finished dressing out and was preparing to hang from an oak limb as Lance approached their new lodge. Lance's left cheek had a swelling cut under his eye. "What have you been doing? Where have you been?" Angry Bear asked. "What happened to your eye?"

Lance shot his father a glowering sneer.

"Answer me," Angry Bear ordered.

"A fight," Lance yelled. "I got in a fight, in Evansham, all right?"

Angry Bear's open hand struck the boy's face leaving a streak of deer blood across his cheek. "I am your father. Do not speak to me like that again."

Lance's fingers touched his cheek, and he stared at the blood his fingertips came away with, probably unsure if it was the deer's or his own. He glared at his father, turned, and stomped into the lodge.

* * *

That spring, unbeknownst to Thomas, Lance was again in Evansham. Thomas sauntered down the side road toward his carriage parked on the main street. His mind was on The Missouri Compromise that had passed on the third of March. The country had been growing since the Revolution, from thirteen states to now twenty-two, half being free states without slavery and the other half being slave states. The balance of power between the North and the South had been equal except for the House of Representatives where the more populous North held one hundred five votes to eighty-one for the agrarian South. The South resented this inequity.

Lost in his thoughts, Thomas was unprepared for the collision with Lance who tore around the corner as if his life depended on his fleetness. Thomas held him by the shoulders to keep both of them upright.

Lance glanced over his shoulder. "They're after me," he said and tried to push past Thomas.

"In here," Thomas said. He opened the back door of the tavern, shoved Lance inside, and followed, closing the door behind him. Stacks of crates shielded them from the patrons.

Thomas heard voices outside. "Which way did he go?"

Thomas slipped the door latch into place.

Someone outside rattled the handle. "It's locked. He must have gone somewhere. Come on."

Sounds of feet scuffling away, allowed Thomas to resume breathing.

Thomas waited for five minutes before saying "Come on, my carriage is around the corner. I'll take you home."

On the road out of town, Lance peered suspiciously at Thomas. "Why did you help me?"

"I owe your father," Thomas replied.

Lance gazed ahead at the road. "I didn't do it," he said.

"Didn't do what?" Thomas said, staring at the road himself.

"Steal that man's wallet."

Thomas glanced at Lance. He was clothed in only a breechclout, leggings, and moccasins. "Where did they think you could put it, I wonder?"

Lance peered at him again and turned his gaze back to the road.

Thomas turned the horse into the Cherokee's village, and Lance pointed to the new location of his lodge.

Angry Bear stepped outside as Thomas halted the horse and carriage.

Lance climbed out of the carriage and started for the lodge.

Angry Bear scowled at his son. "What trouble have you been in, now?" he said.

Lance glared at his father.

"He didn't do it," Thomas said from the carriage seat.

Lance glanced at Thomas. "Thank you."

Angry Bear turned his gaze to Thomas and studied him. "Thank you," he said.

Thomas returned Angry Bear's steady gaze. "Thank *you*," he said and turned the carriage horse toward the road home.

⇒ 41 ⇐

Three Years Later 1822

In August, the slave, Booker, drove Missus Olive and Miss Annjanine to the Cherokee's village.

"There's Lance, Mama," Annjanine said.

"Yes. I see him, dear. Don't pester him."

Booker reined the horse beside the lodge and assisted Missus Olive and Miss Annjanine from the carriage. He glanced toward the stream.

Milly waved her arm to him.

"Missus, I should water dis ole horse," he said.

"Of course, Booker, go on ahead."

Olive peered after Booker leading the horse to the stream. She noticed the pretty young Milly smiling and watching his every move. Booker, you sly devil.

Olive turned back and saw Annjanine gazing at Lance in the distance with the same expression as Milly. Annjanine was too young for such an expression, at least not for an Indian. Olive wanted Annjanine to one day marry in the white world. Goodness, she's only eleven.

Olive remembered the words from Elizabetha's journal: "Today, I met the man I will marry, Martin Kimberlin." That was

1751 and Elizabetha was eleven. Annjanine was as anxious to grow up as Elizabetha had been. Olive would have to watch her daughter closely, maybe introduce her to some nice boys from white society.

While her mother visited her grandparents, Annjanine sauntered over to Lance squatted on a stump preparing arrows by binding a leather strip around the point, attaching it to the notched shaft.

Annjanine picked up a finished arrow, holding it lightly in her hands and blowing on the feathers to make it spin as her grandfather had taught her. She was impressed with the arrow's straightness.

Lance warily watched her out of the corner of his eye. "Leave them be."

She set the arrow back. "You needn't be so grumpy." Her lower lip protruded in spite of herself.

He peered at her a moment. "Don't pout. It makes you look like a baby."

His sullenness was infuriating. "There you go again." Tears welled in her eyes as they always did when she was angry, making her angrier. She turned away. She wouldn't give him the satisfaction of seeing her cry. Why couldn't he ever be nice?

Lance put his hand on her shoulder. "I'm sorry. I guess I should be kinder to you."

Annjanine faced him, wondering why he'd said that, but liking the thought of his being kind to her.

"After all, your father stood up for me when he didn't have to." Lance tousled her hair. "Come on. You can help put some feathers on the arrows."

Annjanine believed she'd never had a happier afternoon. Lance had never before allowed her to be around him. She gazed up to his handsome face, her heart feeling so full it might burst. He smiled at her. Oh, it would burst. She knew it would.

* * *

Annjanine dreamed every night of Lance. She dreamed the

same dream. They were married and lived in a lodge of their own in the village. She saw herself dressed in deerskin and moccasins tending a fire. Lance sat on a log across from her with a small child on each knee and gazed adoringly at Annjanine. She always woke at that point.

The following Saturday when they went to the village, she hurried to Lance's lodge as soon as her parents were distracted with her grandparents.

Lance was carving something from a piece of oak. As she approached and plopped down breathless, he shoved the piece under his sitting mat and stood.

"What are you making?" Annjanine asked.

"Nothing," he barked and sat back down.

"Well, it looked like something. Oh, do let me see, please?"

"No, it's nothing," he mumbled.

Her lower lip started to push forward, but she remembered he'd said pouting made her look like a baby. She pulled the lip back. "You promised to be nice to me, remember? Please let me see it, Lance."

Lance studied her a moment. "You'll laugh. It's my first attempt."

"No, I won't. I promise."

"Cross your heart."

She made a cross sign over her heart and gazed at him with what she hoped was a mature pleading in her eyes.

"All right." He reached under the mat and pulled a small bird shape out and handed it to her.

She turned it over delicately in her fingers. The little figure was exquisite with its wings outspread at its sides. Its head was turned sideways, showing a tiny beak. At the bottom, its tail flared out. He was just beginning to carve in the feathers. "It's beautiful," she said.

He grabbed the carving back. "You're just saying that."

"No, Lance. I really mean it. I would love to have such a beautiful carving."

"It's not beautiful. It's just a silly bird." He stuffed the lovely little creature under his mat again.

The next week when she saw Lance, he had the finished carving around his neck. He had polished it with animal fat until it had a warm golden sheen, and had poked a hole into the spot where its eye would be and threaded a piece of rawhide through it.

Before she had to leave, Lance slipped the bird necklace from his neck and put it around hers. "Because you didn't laugh," he said.

Three years later, fifteen-year-old Annjanine dallied in her bed Sunday morning daydreaming and toyed with the bird carving Lance had given her. She didn't know just when Lance had begun to be interested in her the same way she had always been interested in him. But she was glad that he had. Ever since she could remember she had wanted him to like her. Now there were small hints that he liked her very much, like the carving and yesterday, when she'd caught him gazing at her when he thought she wasn't looking. And last week when he took her hand to help her cross the little creek that crept through a remote area of the village as they walked together there.

She hadn't said anything to her mother because of the way her mother always tried to steer her toward white society and discouraged any interest she showed in her Cherokee heritage. Her mother always talked about her meeting some nice white boys. Annjanine knew her mother wouldn't understand that the only boy that had ever held her interest was Lance. She never felt comfortable in her mother's white society. Annjanine was proud she was half Cherokee. It was with Lance in the Cherokee's village that she felt most comfortable.

"Annjanine, it's time to leave for church soon. Hurry every chance you get," her mother yelled up the stairs.

"Coming, Mama." She tumbled out of bed and decided she'd wear her yellow dress. The one Lance had said she looked nice in. Maybe she'd see him afterwards. He often hid behind the church to meet her after services while her parents visited with church members out front.

After arriving at the Cherokee's village the following Saturday,

Annjanine hurried to meet Lance at the river. She'd told her mother she was going to meet her friends, Maggie and Emma. Well, Lance was a friend. She hadn't really lied.

She didn't see him at first. She glimpsed a rock skipping across the water, and turned toward the trees. Lance leaned against a poplar, and with a flick of the wrist held out at his side, he skipped another rock. It almost made it to the center of the river. He caught sight of her, threw down the rocks, and motioned her over.

She sat down on a blanket Lance had spread. He traced her chin and jaw line with his forefinger, slid his palm over her ear, and undid her hair. "I like your hair down. It looks more natural, like a Cherokee."

"I am Cherokee, silly."

"Yes, you are." Lance gazed at the river. "Not like your brother."

"You don't like Joseph much do you?"

"You have always joined in with Cherokee ways whenever you visited. I can see in your eyes that you feel comfortable here. Your brother has always stood apart, not one of us. He thinks he is better."

"But that isn't true. He just wants to be a lawyer."

"Let's not talk about your brother." Lance lay back on the blanket and pulled Annjanine beside him.

She snuggled up to his side with her head resting on his bare chest as he stroked her long hair. She was enchanted with his firm muscles and loved the smell of him. He smelled of wood smoke and pine and a sweet aroma all his own. She thought she'd be able to recognize him by his scent alone. They didn't talk a lot when they were together. They didn't need to. She was totally comfortable just holding his hand or gazing into his eyes, or just lying together like this. She knew he was comfortable, too. They were meant for each other. They would be together forever.

The sound of her mother's voice calling, "Annjanine, Annjanine," caused her to leap to her feet. Her mother mustn't find them together. "Run, Lance, run. It's mother."

Lance rose and stared deeply into her eyes. "No, I'll not run away as a frightened squirrel runs."

"Lance, please, for me, please."

His reluctance lingered, but he said, "For you, I go," and ran toward the woods.

Just as her mother reached the river, the last of Lance's feet flew behind the trees. She hoped her mother hadn't seen him.

⇒•42•⇐

But Olive had seen Lance dash into the woods. She determined to confront Angry Bear on the very next visit. She must break up this fascination between her daughter and his son. It would ruin everything for Annjanine—all of Olive's plans.

Today was the day of that visit and she'd purposefully come alone. As soon as she alighted from the carriage, she marched to Angry Bear's lodge.

He was chopping wood and stopped to wipe his brow. As he spotted Olive, he buried the axe blade into the chopping block and propped his foot on the stump as he waited for her approach.

"Angry Bear, I need to speak with you."

"Apparently."

"You must make Lance stay away from Annjanine."

Angry Bear appraised her from toe to head. "He's not good enough for a half-breed?"

Olive should have known he wouldn't make things easy for her. "Of course that's not it. But she's soon to debut into society and I don't want her being involved with a—a...."

"Savage?"

"Don't put words in my mouth. You know what I mean. The white ways are the ways the Cherokees should go. It's the future."

"The Cherokees are going that way too fast to suit me. We have our own ways. One day, you'll regret the path you've chosen to forsake your people."

"I haven't forsaken them."

He fondled the lace at the end of the sleeve of her fine linen gown. "Haven't you?"

She snatched the lace from his fingers.

"You will regret one day," he said again.

"Is this one of your famous visions?"

"No vision, just a knowing." He gazed into her eyes. "My vision shows me that one day you will belong to me and love me as you once did." He grabbed her by the arms and pulled her against his chest. "I'll help you remember." His mouth crushed down upon hers and his arms held her tight.

The kiss was long and ardent. The more she tried to free herself, the firmer he held her. She felt the tautness of his body through her garments. Her heart pounded. She struggled to be free from his grip, his kiss.

He released her.

"Don't ever do that again," she ordered.

"I'll be waiting."

"Oh, *you!*" It was useless to appeal to his decency. He had none. She lifted her skirts and marched back to the carriage, trying to wipe the kiss from her mouth with the back of her hand.

The next week, Annjanine made conspirators of her two Cherokee girl friends, Maggie and Emma, by bringing them ribbons, beads, and brooches from her assorted possessions. "You must promise to keep my secret about meeting Lance from my family."

The tall, slim Emma placed a silver bracelet on her arm and admired it reflecting the sun. "Yes, yes, of course," she promised.

"What are we to say if one of them asks why you are not

with us?" the practical Maggie asked.

Annjanine pondered. "Tell them we're playing a game, and I've gone to gather treasures from the woods that you must guess when I return with a full bag, or some other errand you've sent me on, like gathering pebbles for a game of toss. Since I am younger, I would be the natural one to fetch."

The next few visits to the village, as Annjanine and Lance had agreed, she spent her time with Maggie and Emma, making a point to be seen often with them to throw off her family. Soon, her family did not check on her whereabouts any longer.

In the spring, Lance grabbed Annjanine's hand as soon as she arrived at the elm behind the council lodge where they had agreed to meet. "Come, I have something I want to show you." The excitement dancing in his gaze aroused her curiosity.

He led her through the woods until he stopped in front of a rock face among the foothills of the Appalachians. Perplexed, she glanced at him and then back at the rock. "You wanted to show me a rock?"

He laughed and started pulling the underbrush away from the base of the rock. An opening was revealed. "Come on," he said as he entered through it.

When they were both inside the narrow cave, Lance said "Wait." She stopped and he pulled the brush in front of the opening. "Follow me," he said when he was finished.

The lowness of the ceiling of the cave caused them to crouch down. After a few feet, the cave opened up into a large room of stone. There were ledges around the sides of the stone where he had placed the many carvings he had made and shared with her alone since the bird carving that she always wore under her shift. She only took it out to run her fingers over it when she was alone in her room or with Lance. But she could always feel it next to her heart beneath her clothes.

He had laid cedar boughs upon the rock floor and covered it over with a bearskin. She sat on it and inhaled the sweet scent of cedar. She ran her fingers across the soft fur of the bearskin and gazed up to Lance's beaming face.

"It is the first bear I ever killed," he said and sat beside her on his prized possession.

She scanned the room again and saw a small opening in the roof of the cave. Lance had the makings for a fire beneath it. The smoke would travel up and out the opening. Lance bent to the fire and lighted it.

"Lance, this is beautiful. Our own private hideaway," she said.

"For just the two of us. No one else knows of it. I keep the brush in front of the opening so no one suspects. Your family will not find us here." Lance laid back against the bearskin and pulled her to his side.

"I shall bring some candles of just enough length to last four hours. That way we'll know when I have to leave," she said. She laid in the crook of his arm and put her head against his chest. This was the nearest thing to heaven that she could ever have imagined. It was as if they had their own lodge just as she had dreamed. She hoped this day would never end.

Four months before Annjanine's sixteenth birthday, she accompanied her mother to the Cherokee's village. She would see Lance. Their clandestine meetings for more than two years while her mother visited Annjanine's grandparents had not lessened no matter how much her mother tried. Since Lance had discovered their cave, Annjanine met him there as soon as she could slip away on each visit. They talked of marriage—and sometimes—not anything wrong, just kissing and cuddling.

Booker reined the carriage horse in front of her grandparents' lodge.

Annjanine visited with her grandparents for an extra long time while her mother did an errand. She hoped Lance wouldn't tire of waiting for her.

"I'm back," her mother said as she returned to the lodge.

Annjanine waited five minutes or so before rising. "I'd like to see if I can find some of my friends. When do you want me back, Mama?"

"Well, uh, I guess as the sun meets the top of the trees would be fine, dear." She worried that Annjanine was seeing Lance on their visits, but what could she do? She couldn't order Annjanine to stay at home and deprive her own parents the joy of their granddaughter, and Annjanine's joy of them. She could only hope and pray that as Annjanine grew older, she would see what her mother wanted for her was best.

As soon as Annjanine cleared the village, she raced to the cave. Out of breath, she scrambled through the small entrance that opened into a large room.

Lance was lying on the mat made of cedar boughs and bear-skin.

"I'm sorry I'm so late," Annjanine said as she lowered herself beside Lance. His dark eyes were smoldering as he gazed at her. His forehead was creased with small lines.

"I was worried." Lance studied her. "You're beautiful, you know." He'd been trying to fight the passion that grew stronger in him every time he saw her. He could fight it no longer.

Annjanine was startled as he sat erect, cupped the back of her head in his hand, and lowered her body against the fragrant bed as he kissed her mouth hard, more passionately then ever before. Exhaling into her mouth, he took her breath away. She felt light-headed.

His hand moved across her breasts and then beneath her skirts. She pushed her fists against his chest to make him stop. He was scaring her. But he kept on, and she began to enjoy his fondling. Before she knew what was happening, they were both breathing heavily, the fondling turned to passion. After the initial thrust, she thought she would surely die of her pleasure.

Afterward, he sat erect against the cold cave wall and pulled her upright all in one move. He still held her hand. "I love you, Annjanine. I want you. I want you too much. I shouldn't have let this happen." His fiery glance turned to her.

She felt afraid again. She'd made him angry somehow. "Lance, I love you as well," Annjanine said, her heart pleading for forgiveness.

The fire in his eyes turned to a warm glow as he gazed at her. "I'm sorry I frightened you." He held her by the shoulders. "We could be married right away in the Indian custom," he said.

Thank goodness he still wanted to marry her. "It would break my parents' heart for me not to marry in Kimberlin Church. In four months, I'll be sixteen. You could ask my father for permission."

"What if he doesn't give it?" Lance sulked.

"If he doesn't, we'll marry in the Indian fashion."

"In four months, I shall ask." He kissed the tip of her nose. "Till then, we will meet in the village—around others."

⇒·43·⇐

Two months later, Annjanine had missed her monthlies for the second time and knew for sure that it wasn't because she'd had a slight cold. At first, she'd thought the nausea she suffered was from the cold as well, but now she was ravenous and had heard enough about being with child to know that she was.

As soon as she and her mother arrived at the village, she had found an excuse to leave her grandparent's lodge and seek out Lance. She now waited nervously beside the elm where they met as she pondered how to tell Lance and worried about his response.

Lance snuck up behind her and tugged at a tress of hair.

She jumped and turned toward him, grabbing his hand. "Lance, we must go to the cave. I need to talk to you." Before he could answer, she started off. She glanced over her shoulder to be sure he was following. He was.

Neither spoke until they were inside the cave.

"What is it," he asked.

"Oh, Lance," she answered and threw her arms around his middle and sobbed.

He held her for a moment and lifted her face. "What is it,

Annjanine?" he asked in a low voice.

"We're going to have a baby," she said through her tears. Her heart felt so heavy she feared it would crush the baby growing inside her. What if he were angry with her? What if he wanted her to take some Indian potion to get rid of it?

He held her without speaking. He dropped to the cave floor, pulling her down beside him and turned her by the chin to face him. "Then why are you crying? You should be joyful. It's a boy. I know it is." He laid his hand on her belly and stroked it.

* * *

In April, Olive helped Sassy prepare the picnic basket for Annjanine's sixteenth birthday. Annjanine insisted they go to the Clinch River for a picnic. She missed being able to swim in the river as she had as a child.

Joseph had promised he would come home from the University for his sister's birthday and would meet them at the river for the picnic.

Annjanine burst into the kitchen, her long black wavy hair flying around her face. "Mama, I'm so excited."

Olive straightened, arms akimbo, and studied her vivacious daughter. "Why haven't you pinned up your hair yet? Your father is seeing to the wagon. We're almost done here."

"I'll hurry." Annjanine shook out her thick mane and tied a yellow ribbon around her ebony hair. "When is Joseph coming?"

"He said he'd meet us at the river. He had some errands to run."

"I can't wait to show him how well I can swim." Annjanine stole a pickle from the jar Sassy was about to pack in the basket.

"I swear, child, you've the appetite of a horse lately. Get on now and fetch your things while I load this basket in the wagon," Sassy said and swatted Annjanine's hand away as if she were truly angry with her.

Annjanine hiked up her bright yellow skirt and bounded up

the stairs for her swimming clothes. "Wait for me," she yelled across her shoulder, the half-chewed pickle muffling her words.

Olive and Sassy wagged their heads at each other and carried the picnic items out to the wagon.

In her room, Annjanine placed her hand on her stomach and whispered, "I'll teach you to swim like a little fish, my son." She had been ecstatic ever since Lance had been pleased that she was pregnant. They had made endless plans for their marriage and the future of their son.

Olive and Sassy set the baskets in the carriage. Goral took the reins today as driver as Goral and Sassy would attend the family at the picnic. Sassy climbed up beside Goral on the driver's seat.

Thomas and Olive climbed inside the light Dearborn wagon. Olive pulled back one of the window curtains and watched for Annjanine.

Annjanine came flying out the door and scrambled in beside her mother. "We're off," she said and kissed her mother's forehead.

The spring rains had swollen the Clinch River. Red, yellow, and white wild flowers and tall green grass covered the banks. Olive watched Annjanine pace the bank while Sassy laid out the picnic fare. Olive called Annjanine when everything was ready.

Annjanine scurried from the bank and plopped down on the quilt Sassy had spread on the ground. "I'm starved. Can we eat?"

"I wonder what's keeping Joseph," Olive said to Thomas.

"He'll be along soon. Don't worry."

Annjanine snatched another pickle from the jar.

"Yes, we might as well eat. Joseph can catch up when he gets here," Olive said.

Annjanine grinned and heaped potato salad and chicken on her plate. After dinner, she helped herself to a second piece of double chocolate cake.

Annjanine sliced two pieces of cake and took them over to where Sassy and Goral had spread their picnic beneath a nearby elm. "It's delicious cake, Sassy."

"Thank you, Missy."

"I'm going to put my swimming clothes on."

"You'd best wait after eating."

"I'll be all right. It will take a while to change." Annjanine smiled.

"Let me help you." Sassy started to rise.

"No, finish your dinner. I can do it." Annjanine skipped off to the wagon.

Ten minutes later, she emerged covered neck to ankle in her navy cotton bathing outfit with matching ruffled cap on her head. She paused to kiss the top of her mother's head as she headed for the river. She was so happy this day to be sixteen at last. Lance said he would ask her father for her hand when they returned from the picnic for her birthday. Everything was wonderful. They would soon be married and have a baby. She stroked her stomach as she dashed to the river.

"Annjanine, you need to wait after eating," her mother admonished.

"I'll stay close to the bank. Don't worry."

"That child," Olive said to Thomas. They watched their daughter perched amidst the wild flowers on the bank dawdling her feet in the river. Annjanine slipped into the waters and splashed along the bank.

"She's a good girl, full of life," Thomas said.

"I worry about her, still. She's so willful. Last week in the Cherokee's village when we visited my parents, I found her flirting with Angry Bear's son, Lance. I do try to get her interested in the nice white boys we know, but she insists on going to the village with me as often as she can. I suspect she meets Lance."

"There's nothing wrong with an Indian mate," Thomas said. He took Olive's hand. "I understand they make wonderful spouses." He grinned. His wavy, sandy hair fell across his handsome face.

Annjanine decided to wade out a little further into the river. She ducked her body under the water. She thought she would float a while in this shallow part before she swam. She hadn't noticed the eddy until it sucked her under water. She fought to rise to the top.

A scream erupted from the river. Thomas and Olive jumped to their feet.

Annjanine's head bobbled in the middle of the swift current and disappeared. She reappeared further downstream.

Thomas yanked his boots and coat off and bounded to the river.

Olive and Goral chased after him, with Sassy waddling behind as fast as she could.

Thomas dove into the river and the current carried him along at a fast pace toward Annjanine.

Joseph Samuel arrived. On seeing the commotion, he leapt from his horse and raced to the group on the bank.

Olive pointed down the river at the two heads bobbling in the current.

Joseph darted along the bank through the thick underbrush. Goral was just behind him, and Olive chased after with Sassy huffing behind her.

Thomas spotted Annjanine ahead of him, her head disappearing then reappearing. His throat tightened. He kicked harder. When he finally reached her, she was flailing wildly at the current, panic filled her eyes. He tried to grab her arm, but she was crazed with fear and thrashed out erratically at her rescuer.

They both went under. She writhed and fought, trying to get to the top as he tried to subdue her. He was running out of breath. He thought his lungs would burst.

Joseph and Goral rounded a bend in the river where an elm had fallen across the river. They both halted abruptly. The gnarled limbs held the figures fast against the raging current.

"Stay back," Joseph yelled to his mother.

Olive tried to follow, but Sassy had caught up to her and held her back with strong black arms.

Joseph and Goral sloshed into the river and pulled the bodies from the branches. His father's arms encircled Joseph's sister. The men laid the still figures on shore and tried to pump water from their lungs. Neither responded to the effort. His father's sandy hair was matted against his bronzed skin, as were Annjanine's dark tresses.

Joseph's mother broke free of Sassy's grip and ran, screaming, "Nooo...!"

Joseph caught her in his arms and twirled her away from the sodden bodies. "Get the wagon, Goral."

Still in a daze, Olive was returned home. She ran up to her and Thomas's room, and grabbed her Cherokee knife from the dresser. She glanced at her image in the mirror and didn't recognize the anguished face reflected there. The thought of slitting her throat with the knife edged its way into her mind.

Grief-driven anger erupted like a flame engulfing her from the inside out. How could they leave her? Damn them. Damn the river. Damn everything. Gone, gone. She grabbed her hair down from its upsweep and chopped it off at ear level. She threw the knife across the room. With tears streaming down her face, she swept her arm across the dresser top removing Thomas's belongings into a heap on the floor. Gone, he was gone. She pulled Thomas's clothes from the wardrobe and threw them atop the pile.

She spotted the knife, grabbed it up, and rushed to Annjanine's room. She pulled out all of her daughter's gowns. She held Annjanine's favorite yellow gown against her face and sobbed wet splashes of tears into the soft folds. Annjanine would never wear it again. No one else shall have it. She held the dress away from her and slashed it into strips and did the same with every gown.

At last spent, she plopped down amid the tatters and pulled them into her lap. She bent her head and sobbed. She prostrated herself in the rags and wailed. Everything she had held dear, ripped from her heart in an instant of time. It wasn't fair. It just wasn't fair.

* * *

Lance kept saying Annjanine's name as he hurled stone after stone into the stream. First, his mother had died and his little brother, Kyle, and now, Annjanine and their baby with her.

He had loved her, wanted her, wanted to make her his wife. It wasn't fair. He threw all the rest of the stones at once with a violent fling. He felt a hand on his shoulder and spun around with clenched fists.

His father, Angry Bear, gazed steadily into his eyes. "I know what you're feeling, son."

"How could you know? At least you and mother lived as man and wife many years before she died." Lance wrenched his gaze from his father's empathetic eyes.

"The loss of anyone we love is difficult, no matter when, no matter how. Whether they die, or marry another, it is all the same loss. The pain will ease with time. Believe me, Lance. I know."

"I'll never forget her, no matter how much time passes. There will never be another Annjanine."

"Son, you have your life ahead of you. This pain will ease."

"Maybe for you, but not for me. I've decided to leave here. I can't bear the places she and I shared. I see her image everywhere. I'll join the Seminoles in Florida."

Pain shot across Angry Bear's forehead. He rubbed his eyes to ease the burning ache behind them.

"I'm sorry, Father," Lance conceded. "But I must go away from here."

Angry Bear watched as the last person he had ever loved turned and walked out of his life.

⇒·44·⇐

1 8 3 0 F o u r Y e a r s L a t e r

.

Joseph Samuel came home from his law office and entered the parlor of his mother's home where he had stayed on after returning from the University. It was dimly lit and felt solemn. His mother's eyes were closed and she rested her head on the back of the maroon sofa.

He kissed his mother's forehead and sat across from her in the flowered wingback chair beside the fireplace. Sassy brought in Joseph and his mother's supper. They often ate something light in the parlor. He ate in silence watching his mother lost in her thoughts and hugging his father's coat around her.

After eating, Sassy removed Joseph's dishes and brought him a cup of coffee. He took a sip and settled into reading the paper he'd not had a chance to read at the office. His mind wandered.

Since his father and Annjanine's deaths, his mother had lost interest in life itself, all she did was sit in the parlor.

The house was quiet without Annjanine's trilling laughter and their father's quiet humor. It pained Joseph to see his mother so desolate. Her dark hair had grown back since she cut it short in the Cherokee's custom over her grief. She no longer pinned it up but wore it long down her back, perhaps in memory of Annjanine. In the chill of the evenings, his mother often wore his father's coat and hugged it around her as she stared blankly into the fireplace.

Sassy moved with silence and efficiency through the house tending to the meals and chores. Goral, too, had little to say, unlike his usual talkative self. A great cloud hung over them all.

Joseph returned to his paper.

Olive had found Elizabetha's journal and read it again each evening before the fire, wrapped in Thomas's coat.

Sassy picked up the remaining dishes, placed her free hand on Olive's shoulder, and gave it a squeeze as she headed for the kitchen.

Olive gazed into the fireplace. She missed Thomas so terribly. How could she go on alone? Her beloved husband gone, and her baby, beautiful and spirited Annjanine. Olive once had such hopes for her daughter and now she was gone at just sixteen. All she had left now was Joseph and her parents. Olive glanced at Joseph. He was such a fine young man and now he had his own law practice. He certainly didn't need her care anymore.

Olive returned to Elizabetha's journal:

After Anne and Joseph's children Samuel and Rachel were killed by Indians, Anne seemed to have lost all incentive to live. Part of her had died in that massacre as well. My heart weighed heavily for my dear friend's pain. Would that I could carry the load for her and ease her heart. How devastating to lose two loved ones at once.

Anne clung to their memories to the exclusion of everything else including the children she had left, and her husband, Joseph. She focused all of her hatred on the wretched Indians who had wrenched her babes from her arms.

When Martin died, I felt death's grim grip on my own heart and could relate to Anne's pain. Death seems cruel to obliterate a way of life with a single swath of the scythe. Perhaps it's meant to cleanse our hearts and make way for new endeavors. Perhaps it's meant to focus our attention on others' needs we

have not seen, to open our hearts to ease another's pain.
Ourselves, our own, through life we focus on,
not seeing others' pain, nor looking yon.
Death strikes one scythe slice laying bare
our soul, and suddenly we are aware
the one good thing we have left in life
is to ease the pain of another's strife.
To hold each hand and treasure each glance
as we try to master the steps to life's dance.

Olive closed Elizabetha's journal, leaned her head back, and mulled over Elizabetha's words.

Joseph surged upright in his chair nearly upsetting his coffee.

His mother's eyes flew open. "What is it, Joseph?"

"It says here President Andrew Jackson has signed a bill to remove all Indians east of the Mississippi and transport them to an Indian Territory west of the river."

His mouth slackened as he stared at his mother. In 1827, the Cherokee founded their own nation under a written constitution based on the whites, electing a principal chief, a senate, and a house of representatives. In 1828, through Sequoyah's syllabary, they published the first Cherokee newspaper, the *Cherokee Phoenix*, printed in their own language. The whites forced the Cherokee to sell their lands for next to nothing, plundered their homes and possessions, and destroyed the printing press of the *Cherokee Phoenix* because it published articles opposing Indian removal.

Now in spite of the great Cherokee orator, John Ross, winning their case before the Supreme Court, and despite the support of Daniel Webster, Henry Clay, and Davy Crockett, President Jackson ordered the eastern Indians' removal. All because of the white man's lust for land. "So far the removal is voluntary and it's being fought in the courts," he said.

Olive's hands flew to her face. "My parents," she exclaimed. "They'll need me."

Olive recalled Elizabetha's words, "... the one good thing we have left in life is to ease the pain of another's strife ...." She knew now what she had to do.

"I'm going home, Joseph, to be with my parents. If this can't be won in the courts, we'll hide in the Appalachians. The Cherokee say there's a valley up there."

Joseph studied his mother. She was only forty-eight, but she'd seemed much older since the accident. Now her eyes were bright and cheeks rosy, the first sign of animation she'd shown in four years. "Of course," he answered. "When do you want to leave?"

She pondered a moment. Had she been too hasty in her decision? Was she ready to go back to the Indian life? What else did she have now that Thomas and Annjanine were gone? Joseph would probably soon marry, and she remembered the old saying: A son is a son till he takes him a wife, but a daughter's a daughter for all of her life. Annjanine's short life was over and Joseph would be moving on with his own. No, she really had nothing else to live for except what she could now do to help her parents. "Next week will be fine. We'd best leave early morning on Monday." Yes, the morning was a good time to start a new life.

When Joseph and his mother arrived at the Cherokee's village of her parents, there was much talk about the Indian Removal. The villagers were nervous.

Soldiers were beginning to round up the Choctaws in Alabama, Mississippi and Louisiana, it was said. The Cherokee people prayed their case would win in court against the Removal Act.

Joseph tied the reins of his horse to a tree and watched his mother alight from her horse. She had dressed herself in a wrap-around soft leather skirt and full, long-sleeved, calico blouse tied around her waist with a sash woven from mulberry tree bark. Her long thick hair flowed down her back. She hugged her mother and father in turn.

In their seventies, Joseph's gray-haired grandparents wore deep wrinkles in their leathery faces. How long had it been since he'd visited, eight, ten years? He'd been so busy with his studies and new practice. He hugged his grandfather then his grand-mother.

His grandmother, Jane, stroked her worn and rough fingers across his cheek and kissed his hand, holding it between her two. Tears filled her eyes.

When her belongings were settled, Olive approached Joseph as he readied his horse for the return trip. "Joseph, you must promise not to visit here until this Removal mess is cleared up. You have a life to live as a lawyer in the white world. Please don't jeopardize it."

Joseph dropped the reins and took hold of both her hands. "But, Mama, I can't just stop seeing you."

"You must do it for me. It would break my heart if you were labeled Indian and denied your place in the white world after all the work you've done. Promise."

"All right. For you, I'll promise."

"When this white man's foolishness is ended. Everything will be all right," Olive said.

After Joseph returned home and Olive was preparing the corn gruel for her parents' supper, Angry Bear visited her fami-ly's lodge approaching her from behind. He squatted beside her and poked at the fire with a thin stick.

"I'm glad you've rejoined the tribe," he said, not looking up.

Olive studied the simmering gruel. "It is good to be home."

⇒•45•⇐

Early the following winter, Olive's father became ill. The medicine man said it was consumption. It was hard for her to watch his large frame grow thin and frail. Her mother sat beside him through the long days and tried to feed him broth. He was too weak to sit up. Her mother poured what little she could into his mouth as she propped his head on her lap. His rasping cough allowed for little sleep within their lodge.

Angry Bear came to visit every day. He sat on the ground beside Olive as they watched her mother tending to the dying man she had loved all her life.

"I'm worried about my mother's health. I pray if my father is not to recover that he will not suffer further. It is breaking my mother's heart," Olive whispered.

Angry Bear placed his hand on top of hers that lay in her lap.

Days later, her prayers were answered one night when her father's soul slipped away to join his ancestors. His spent body was wrapped in his blanket and the head of the coffin pointed east in the grave dug by Angry Bear.

Olive's mother was despondent after her husband's death.

She sat wrapped in her blanket and rocked her body as she moaned. With the will to live buried with her husband, she grew weaker and weaker. Her heart gave up. She did not see spring, and was buried beside her husband in a second grave dug by Angry Bear.

Afterward, Olive glanced around the empty lodge. Her heart filled with grief. She sank to her knees and let the tears gush forth. She had lost nearly everyone she ever loved, except for her son, Joseph, whom she couldn't see by her own insistence. How long she wailed alone, she didn't know or care. Exhausted, she finally fell to sleep.

The days crept on with her feeling she had nothing to live for. She was so very tired. She knew she wasn't well, and she didn't care. She forced herself through her chores.

Today, she didn't even feel like getting up from her sleeping mat. She rolled over and went back to sleep, hoping the world would finally go away. Sometime during the day, the fire must have gone out because she was chilled. She pulled the bear skin over her shivering body, too tired to rebuild the fire. She dozed off again.

When next she woke, Angry Bear was there building a fire. It was night. She closed her eyes again, too weak to thank him. She drifted in and out of consciousness. Once she felt his hand stroking her brow. Another time she smelled the scent of sage, and briefly glimpsed Angry Bear smudging her lodge and dancing in a circle. She woke again to daylight pouring through the lodge doorway and caught sight of Angry Bear stirring something in a pot over the fire pit.

At times Angry Bear would bring her broth and spoon some into her mouth. She didn't know how long he had been there, but every time she opened her eyes, there he was. It seemed even when her eyes were closed she saw him in her dreams. He was the only thing she was aware of, as though he constituted her whole world.

At length, she was able to keep her eyelids open a little longer each time she woke. One of these times, Angry Bear carried her outside and laid her in the shade of an elm. He sat by her side and tried to feed her huckleberries. She waved his hand away, not caring if she ever ate again.

"You must get your strength back. Your fever has broken, but fresh air and food will help you grow strong."

"I don't care."

He gazed at her a long moment. "I care." He slipped a berry between her lips and continued to watch her.

She dutifully chewed and swallowed, hoping that would satisfy him. It didn't.

The days wore on and in spite of herself, she improved. As soon as she could stand without support, Angry Bear insisted she go for walks with him. Her stamina increased more each day. She guessed she would live after all.

When Angry Bear allowed her to stop and rest on a grassy knoll, he still held her by the upper arm and turned her to face him. "The color is back in your cheeks," he said. "It looks good there."

"You've spent a lot of time and care to put it there."

"Time well spent."

She gazed into his eyes and read such tenderness in them, It almost elicited tears.

He stepped nearer and gazed down on her, holding her by the shoulders. He bent his head toward her and kissed her mouth gently.

As she allowed his kiss, it became more insistent and she felt a dizzying tingle run through her body. A body she thought was dead to such feelings.

That evening alone in her lodge, she remembered how Angry Bear had always looked after her when they were children. Just as he had that day she was trapped in the horse race crowd in town and he had pulled her to safety. She remembered when he had saved Thomas's life that day Thomas had been caught in the bear trap. Angry Bear had helped her bury both of her parents. She remembered the days, or was it weeks, he had just spent bringing her back to the world she had wanted to leave.

He, too, had suffered loss with the death of his wife and youngest son. The leaving of his oldest son, Lance, had been the hardest blow. She and Angry Bear had a great deal in common.

The following day, Olive set out a bowl of gruel. Angry Bear came to the lodge as he did every day. He stopped and stared at the gruel set beside her. "Is that gruel?" he asked.

"Yes," Olive answered and continued husking the corn she would prepare for supper.

Angry Bear gazed at her. "May I taste it?" He ventured.

Olive picked up the bowl and handed it to him.

Angry Bear tasted the gruel and set it back upon the ground as he squatted on his haunches before her. He took both of her hands in his. "You know I've always loved you."

"I know," she said. "You, too, have held a special place in my heart, before Thomas and now after Thomas."

They exchanged token gifts of corn from her and deer meat from him and became husband and wife.

Three months later, a miracle happened. Olive was overcome with the joy of knowing she would give birth. She would turn forty-nine before it was born. She had never expected to bear children again.

The night she told Angry Bear, he wept. They knelt upon the ground, holding hands, to silently give their thanks for the fruit-full womb of the universal mother, the Earth, where the embryos of plants and men lay hidden. Later, they slept wrapped in each other's arms.

At dawn, Angry Bear was the first to walk down to the stream to greet the morning alone, as was the Cherokee ritual. After his return, Olive made her way to the water's edge. She knelt and dipped her hands into the icy waters, splashing it on her face. She stood erect before the advancing dawn and gave her thanks to the universal father, the Sun, who sparks the principle of growth in nature.

Olive chose her father as a model for the child. She daily called his spirit to mind. She gathered the painted pictures upon a dried skin which noted her father's deeds and daring exploits that her mother had kept and rehearsed them whenever she was alone. During the days, she wandered prayerfully in the stillness of the woods with an eye to the impressions of the beautiful scenery that her unborn child might, from the beginning, be filled with the majesty and grandeur in nature and behold in awe the Divine in all creation.

So went the days and nights of her pregnancy until the morning of her day of days, the birth of the child, was begun. She ground the root of Blue Cohosh with water and sipped it. She walked alone into the woods. The Squaw Root helped along a smooth delivery as she knew it would.

When she returned later to the lodge with her small bundle, Angry Bear was sitting on a wooden stool carving a small trinket. Olive handed him the precious package from her arms. He lifted the blanket from the infant's face. His eyes filled with tears as he looked up to Olive's gaze.

"I wish to call him Luke," Olive said. She didn't know which of them was prouder, she or Angry Bear.

"Luke," he said and smiled.

Olive was pleased she had borne well her part in the great song of creation.

As the child grew, Olive would stop in her chores or meanderings through the woods to point her index finger to nature at a flock of Chickadees or the rising sun to show her precious gift, and young Luke flourished.

She told him the stories of her father's deeds, and, if he chanced to fret, she raised her hand and said, "Hush! Hush! The spirits may be disturbed." She bade him to be still and listen to the silver voice of the aspen, or the gurgling waters of the rippling stream. Silence, love, and reverence were her early teachings. As he grew, she added generosity, courage, and chastity in the Cherokee way.

She pointed out a large oak tree in early spring. "See the tenacious grandparent leaves clasped to the tops of the branches? They are waiting to instruct the next generation in the stately ways of oakism."

Luke laughed and clapped his hands together. He picked up a leaf from the ground. "And what of the fallen leaves, Mama?"

"They make a soft landing spot for the time the young leaves grow old and it is their turn to make a place for the leaves that will come after."

Luke acquired the attitude of prayer and reverence of the Powers. He understood all living creatures were his blood brothers and sisters. He understood that the storm wind was just a messenger of the Great Mystery. He'd become a Cherokee.

≫•46•≪

Meanwhile, Joseph read that Congress had passed another tariff, moderating some of the duties that the Tariff of Abominations of 1828 had imposed but continuing the protective system. The 1828 tariff had exacerbated the notion that states had not surrendered their ultimate sovereignty to the federal government. When South Carolina proposed they had the power to make null and void the new tariff in the state, President Jackson sent Congress the Force Bill reaffirming the President's powers to call up state militia, the army, and the navy to quell insurrections. There was growing unrest in the South.

Joseph's attention was distracted from his country's troubles when a middle-aged man entered Joseph's office and introduced himself and his daughter. Joseph invited them to sit down and took a seat behind his desk. He couldn't keep his eyes off the pretty daughter. She wore a fashionable pink and black dress with a pointed bodice and full skirt over a small bustle in the back. Her bonnet was pink silk trimmed with black ribbon and a black feather. Black lace edged the front, and her blonde ringlets peeped out all around. Her blue eyes were the color of a robin's egg.

He was glad he'd worn the newer long pantaloons reaching to his ankles and half-boots instead of the breeches which were going out of style.

Her name was Susannah and she'd accompanied her father to Joseph's office. Her father, Charles Hamblen, was the descendant of a Blakemore ancestor.

Joseph wasn't sure how this made them related, but it seemed enough for Charles Hamblen to come calling, and Joseph was glad he had, and brought his lovely daughter with him.

Susannah's hands felt as if they would take flight at any moment under the young man's intense gaze. She reposed her hands one atop the other on her lap to ensure their stability. She tried to regain her composure as her father told the young man, Joseph, about their distant familial connection. Her father had remembered the Blakemore family name from his stepmother who had been much younger than her husband and often spoke of her family to the young Charles. At the conclusion of his explanations, Susannah's father invited Joseph to supper on Sunday.

Joseph glanced her way again. His soft brown eyes searched her face, perhaps for confirmation. His collar-length thick sandy hair surrounded his head in a casual curl.

Susannah's gaze met his and she smiled, she hoped demurely.

Joseph acknowledged her smile with a charming one of his own and returned his attention to her father as he accepted her father's invitation.

Susannah allowed her gaze to wander around the tiny office. Rows of dark, ominous-looking books lined the bookshelf along the wall behind Joseph's desk. She marveled that anyone could read any of those, much less want to. There was a neat stack of papers on the side of the desk and a second, not so neat, pile just in front of him. The stiff wooden chairs upon which she and her father sat, the desk, Joseph's chair, and the bookshelf were the only items of furniture. A pile of newspapers was stacked in the corner. The room smelled of printer ink and dust.

Susannah's father rose and offered his hand to Susannah.

Joseph walked around the desk and shook her father's hand. Joseph turned to her.

Susannah extended her hand, "It's been a pleasure to meet you, Mr. Blakemore."

"The pleasure's been mine." He kissed her fingertips.

And to think she'd been reluctant to visit this grandnephew of her father's stepmother. She'd been so sure, because he was ten years older than herself, he'd be a stodgy old bookworm. Instead, she looked forward to Sunday.

Three months later, Susannah especially enjoyed the usual after-supper walk with Joseph on Sunday. Susannah glanced back at her Aunt Mattie, a buxom and jolly widow of fifty. Aunt Mattie had moved into Susannah's parents' home after her husband had died. She had taken it upon herself to chaperone when Joseph came to call. She always followed several paces behind Susannah and Joseph on their strolls. Aunt Mattie's small Pekinese dog, Pookie, accompanied her, darting all around as usual at the end of his red velvet leash. Pookie's light fur complimented the curly blonde hair of his mistress.

Joseph stopped and, with a turn of his head to be sure Aunt Mattie was occupied with Pookie. He reached inside his coat and handed Susannah a jonquil.

She knew the flower indicated, "Will you return my affection?" and she blushed.

The previous Sunday he had given her an iris meaning, "My compliments." He called flowers, "... the alphabet of angels," and had given her a lexicon indicating the meaning of each one.

Her heart raced as she accepted the jonquil with its long slender leaves and fragrant yellow flowers. She clutched it to her and smiled.

Joseph's sensuous mouth curved into a smile as he tilted his head and winked at her.

When they returned to the house, Susannah's parents were in the parlor. Aunt Mattie followed her dog, Pookie, who scampered into the Victorian room ahead of everyone else to claim the hearth.

Susannah entered after setting the jonquil on the small ornate table in the hall to later save the jonquil inside her Bible when she was alone.

Susannah's mother perched in a brightly stenciled Boston rocker beside one end of the fireplace, crocheting a dainty white doily. She glanced up and smiled, her long thin fingers never missing a stitch. Joseph and Susannah sat on opposite ends of the brocade sofa.

Aunt Mattie plopped onto a Hitchcock chair which miraculously withstood her heft, and Pookie quickly leapt onto her lap and settled there.

Susannah's father was engrossed in the paper. He rubbed one hand down his side whiskers as he concentrated. Seeming to realize he wasn't alone, he planted his paper on the table next to the wingback chair and said, "Ah, I see you're back."

"Yes, Sir," Joseph said, "Sir, I wonder if I might speak privately with you a moment."

"Why of course, Joseph." Susannah's father rose and Joseph followed him out of the parlor.

Susannah's mother smiled as she busied herself with her crocheting and Aunt Mattie gave Susannah a wink. Susannah hoped Joseph was asking her father for her hand in marriage.

When the gentlemen returned, Susannah studied her father and Joseph. Neither gave indication of the content of their talk. Her heart sank. Polite conversation was bantered around the room, but Susannah felt such disappointment she could barely participate.

When it was time for Joseph to leave, her hopes once again pinned themselves to some display of his intentions, but he only bowed graciously to all and took his leave.

That night in bed after carefully pressing the jonquil in her Bible, Susannah wondered if Joseph was just toying with her affections. She sobbed into her pillow.

The following Sunday, Joseph came again to supper and afterwards asked Susannah on a walk. With Aunt Mattie and

Pookie several paces behind, they leisurely strolled along the stream that wound its way across the back of her parents' land.

Joseph stopped and ran his fingers through his sandy hair lifting it off his tanned forehead. He seemed about to say something.

Susannah gazed expectantly at him. She wondered what he would say. Perhaps he would tell her that he didn't want to see her anymore. She would die if he said that. She fiddled with a ringlet at her neck.

He reached inside his coat producing a bouquet of ivy, blue morning glory, and straw.

She mentally consulted the lexicon and recalled this bouquet meant, "Let the bonds of marriage unite us." Her heart fluttered. Maybe she was mistaken about their meaning. She peered into his soft brown eyes, "Does it mean what I think it does?"

"Yes, if you'll have me."

She buried her nose in the morning glory and breathed in their fragrance. She threw her arms around Joseph's neck. "Oh, yes, Joseph, yes." She didn't care if Aunt Mattie saw them kissing or not.

⇒·47·⇐

1835

Marriage was not to be for Lance. He hated the Florida swamps. He hated everything except the Seminole war. The white man's leader, Jackson, was behind trying to evacuate all of the Seminoles out of Florida. The Seminole would not go. They hid in the swamps and attacked the white man at every chance. The Seminole would drive every last one of the whites off their land.

Lance was now one of them. It suited him. Seminole means runaway or wild. He had tried to run away from himself when Annjanine and their baby—their son—he knew it was a son—died. It had been eight years since then, and he knew he'd only grown more bitter. The only pleasure he took was in battle. There he could forget how much he missed her, how much he still loved her, how angry he was they'd never see their son. Her laughing eyes and ebony hair surrounding her delicate face danced through his dreams every night.

Lance gazed out from his chickee made from palmetto trees with pole foundations, thatched roof, raised platform, and open walls. The sun had not yet risen as he remembered when the Federal Officials tried pressuring the Seminole leader Osceola to sign a treaty to agree to removal of the Seminoles to west of the Mississippi River. One of the agents had said the runaway slaves that lived among the Seminoles would remain in Florida.

Osceola had said, "So they can be returned to slavery." He thrust his knife into the treaty, shouting, "Am I a Negro slave? My skin is dark, but not black! I am an Indian, a Seminole. The white man shall not make me black. I will make the white man red with blood, and then blacken him in the sun and rain, where the wolf shall gnaw his bones and the buzzard shall live on his flesh."

After that day, they had ambushed the new Indian agent Thompson who threatened force to remove the Seminole. They next killed Chief Emathia, who was helping Thompson recruit Indians to go to Fort Brooke where they would be sent to the reservation in Oklahoma. This dawn they would attack the government troops before they united with those at Fort King on the trail where Chief Micanopy's town, Okahumpy, intersects the military road. Chief Micanopy was still undecided. They would soon know which way the old chief would choose, death or to join the fighting.

At daybreak Lance set out with the Seminoles. They assembled at the point of intersection on the military road. As the troops appeared in sight, Osceola said to Micanopy, "You must decide if you are with us or against us."

Micanopy answered, "I will show you." He took a position behind a pine tree about thirty yards from the road. The rest of the Indians lay down in the high Savannah grass.

An advance guard of an officer and eight men were two hundred yards ahead of the main body. A mounted officer joined the guard. As he arrived opposite to where Micanopy had taken his stand, the chief raised his rifle, took aim, and fired. The officer fell dead from his horse. The horse reared and headed back to the troops behind.

Hidden by the tall grass, the Seminoles made short work of the guard and made their way toward the main body of soldiers. They arrived with war-whoops just as the officer in charge commanded his men into line and unlimbered a six-pounder. The

Seminole returned fire from a semicircle the range of their rifles and concentrated their firing upon the troops. The soldiers discharged canister-shot to different quarters of the semicircle.

After an hour of fighting, the Seminoles held council a short distance from the soldiers' position. Micanopy and Osceola bickered for a time about continuing. Osceola convinced the others they must wipe out these soldiers, and the second attack advanced more fiercely than before. The Seminole war-whoops rang through the woods, and the crack of rifles was an incessant peal of ringing accompanied by the loud booms of artillery and sharp reports of musketry.

The Seminole's council had allowed time for the soldiers to throw up a log breastwork. The Seminole were unrelenting and fired from behind the trees. They out-manned the soldiers twenty to one. When the soldiers at last ran out of ammunition, the Seminole entered the little fort to dispatch with their knives some few in whom a ray of life may still glimmer. As they entered, a very handsome young man, dressed in a blue frock-coat offered his sword. Osceola drew up his rifle and shot the young officer dead.

Something about that handsome young officer touched Lance. A handsome young man like his and Annjanine's son would have been one day, killed in the prime of his life, like Annjanine and their son, and his own life wasted because of their deaths. Tears filled his eyes for the first time since they'd died. He caught a glimpse of a wounded captain leveling his pistol at Osceola. Lance shoved Osceola aside. Lance felt the ripping crash of a bullet tear into his chest. He fell forward on his face in the bloodied dirt, his lips mouthing a single word, Annjanine.

⇝•48•⇜

In the Cherokee's village, Olive lay beside Angry Bear listening to his even breathing. She couldn't sleep. She had been with him for six years and loved him more with every passing year. She certainly hadn't forgotten Thomas or Annjanine, but that now was a closed chapter in her life. She glanced over at where their son, Luke, now five, was sleeping. How lucky she and Angry Bear were to have been blessed with young Luke.

Angry Bear jerked up with a start. He rose and clutched his heart then his head.

"What is it Luke?" Olive asked as she sat up, fearful that he was sick.

"It's Lance. I had a vision. He's dead." He sat down on their sleeping mat. His eyes were clouded in mourning. "It was on a battlefield."

"Perhaps it was just a bad dream," Olive said not really believing it. Angry Bear had these visions before. They were seldom wrong. She wrapped her arms around him.

He laid his head against her chest.

She rocked back and forth cradling her husband in her bosom.

* * *

Susannah was content in Virginia. Young Charles turned two. Marriage was just as she'd hoped. Joseph opened a law practice in Wytheville previously called Evansham where they lived. He said he had lived in the town during his youth. Susannah's mother and father and Aunt Mattie visited often as well as friends. It seemed the house was seldom empty. Joseph still lavished attention on her and often brought her flowers.

Today was Saturday and tonight they would visit Johan Kimberlin and his wife Magdalena. Johan was the son of Jacob and Margaretha who were friends of Joseph's family. Magdalena was forty and expecting again. Susannah was worried about her. Magdalena's other children, four boys, were in their twenties or fast approaching. Magdalena had told Susannah she just had to try one more time for a girl, before she was too old.

Joseph and Susannah sipped their afternoon tea in their Hepplewhite style parlor. They sat on the oval-backed slender chairs and gazed at each other.

A sharp knock at the door broke their tranquility. They both set the teacups on the mahogany table and rose simultaneously looking one to the other with curiosity. Who could be calling?

With Susannah by his side, Joseph opened the door. Johan and Magdalena's youngest son, Nathan, burst inside. He was out of breath as if from riding fast. His eyes were wide. Road dust covered him from head to toe.

Nathan yanked off his hat, swatted at his dusty clothes, and panted trying to catch his breath.

"Whatever is the matter, Nathan?" Joseph asked.

"Come and sit, dear boy, you look awful." Susannah gestured toward the parlor.

Nathan just stood there in the hall shaking his head. He held up his hand in decline to her offer and inhaled deeply.

When he could speak, he blurted, "Ma had twins. She didn't make it. One of the twins didn't either. The other one is yelling its head off. Pa said to ask if you'd come."

"My God, man, that's awful. Of course we'll come," Joseph gasped.

"Of course, I'll get our things. We'll leave at once. Nathan, I'm so sorry. Please do come into the parlor."

"Can't sit, ma'am, I'll just wait here."

Nathan stood in the hall nervously twirling his hat in his hands as Susannah rushed upstairs.

On the carriage ride over, Susannah couldn't grasp the fact that Magdalena was dead. Poor Johan. What will he do?

When they arrived, Johan was sitting on a straight-backed chair in the darkened parlor with his head in his hands. His sons stood around him. Nathan joined them.

The house felt as cold and gloomy as Susannah's heart felt. The family's grief was overwhelming.

Johan glanced up, tears streaked his cheeks, but he rose to greet them.

Joseph clasped his hand and put his arm around Johan's slim shoulders.

Susannah hugged him. She uttered her condolences. The words seemed so meaningless. No words could express her sympathy for his loss, for her own loss. Tears welled up and tumbled down her cheeks.

The wail of an infant caused her to glance at Johan.

"Up there," he said, gesturing.

Susannah followed the crying and entered the bedroom from which it came.

The heavy stench of blood filled her nostrils. She glanced around the room.

A pile of blood-soaked sheets and rags were piled on top of a wooden rocker. There were still some blood spots on the floor that had been missed. The four-poster bed stood solemnly beside the highboy.

A sheet covered two forms on the bed, one large and one tiny one in its arms.

Susannah had to turn away.

The plump midwife was dipping a cloth in milk and squeezing small drops at a time into the baby's mouth trying to get it to suck. She puckered her mouth and made sucking sounds as if the infant would learn from watching her. She glanced up at Susannah.

"It's been several hours since the baby was born. I thought some warm milk might soothe him," the midwife said.

The infant wailed loudly.

Susannah's heart nearly broke at the pitiful sound. She said "Let me try. I haven't quite weaned my own son yet."

Susannah prepared herself as the midwife brought the baby to her. Susannah put the baby to her nipple and inserted it into the baby's mouth. The infant turned its head and lost the nipple. Susannah placed it back in the baby's mouth and held him closer. She felt pressure. The tiny mouth began sucking. She was glad she hadn't totally weaned Charles. She smiled.

After the baby was settled into the feeding, the midwife said, "The other twin was a girl."

"Magdalena finally had the girl she'd always wanted. She said she'd name it Barbara if it was a girl," Susannah remarked.

"A shame only the boy survived. There was so much bleeding. I couldn't save his mother." The midwife dabbed her eyes and blew her nose.

Susannah cuddled the small bundle in her arms.

"I don't know how that poor man and those boys will be able to take care of this baby. Mr. Johan's parents are far too old to be of any help," the midwife said as she shook her head side to side.

Susannah hadn't thought that far ahead. She did now. The infant had stopped sucking. He was sound asleep. Susannah gazed down at the tiny form. She still had breast milk. She could take care of the baby. She knew Joseph would want her to. If only Johan will agree.

Susannah placed the sleeping baby in the waiting midwife's arms. "If Johan agrees, perhaps I could take care of the child," Susannah said.

"Missus, that would be so good of you. God bless you." The midwife cradled the baby in one arm and dabbed her eyes with her apron with the other hand.

Downstairs, Susannah motioned for Joseph. She explained the situation.

"Of course," Joseph said. "Of course, it's the best way. We

must propose it to Johan at once."

Together they walked over to where Johan sat.

"Johan," Susannah began. "Have you thought about how you will take care of the baby?"

Johan stared at her blankly not seeming to grasp her words.

"I still have milk and can feed the baby. If you'd allow Joseph and me to take him home with us, I could care for him until he's old enough."

Johan gazed at her as if she were a stranger.

"You could visit him as often as you like. And bring him home for visits as he gets older. What do you think?"

Her words seemed to finally sink in. Johan's eyes brightened. He smiled at her. "Susannah, you'd do that? You'd do that for me, for Magdalena? Joseph, You'd agree to this?"

"Of course," Susannah and Joseph replied as one.

Johan took Susannah's hand and patted it. "His name is Jacob, Jacob Abraham Kimberlin." Tears filled his eyes.

⇒·49·⇐

Several months later, Joseph had occasion to visit Fort King in Florida while investigating a property dispute for one of his clients. The claimant was a captain in the Army stationed there.

When he arrived at Fort King, Joseph heard a voice from behind.

"Massa Joseph, is dat you?"

Joseph turned to the voice. "My God, Booker. How in the world did you get here?"

"I lives here now, with the Seminoles." Booker fidgeted then said so quietly Joseph could barely hear him, "I run off wiff Millie an we's married." Booker glanced around. "Don't tell nobody," he added.

Joseph clasped Booker on the shoulder and said in an equally whispered tone, "Don't worry, Booker. I won't give you away." In his normal voice he said, "But how do you come to be at the fort?"

"I was wiff de Seminoles a few months back when dey attacked dem soldiers." Booker fidgeted again then added, "I wasn't no part of it, but I seen it all. Dat Lance was wiff 'em too. He got kilt saving dat Osceola chief. I got grazed in de shoulder so I come to de fort. I didn't want to be wiff dat crazy wild pack of fightin' Indians." Booker rolled his eyes.

"Come over into the shade of that old oak, Booker. You have to tell me every detail." Joseph had already decided that he would have to break his mother's wishes and visit the Cherokee's village as soon as he returned. It was only right that he let Angry Bear know what had happened to Lance.

On his return to Virginia, Joseph was careful that no one followed him as he wound his way to his mother's village.

His mother and Angry Bear were tending a crop of corn. As he approached astride his horse, his mother glanced up from her hoeing and shielded her eyes from the bright sunlight. She dropped her hoe and ran toward him.

Joseph alighted from his horse and ran to meet her. He scooped her up in his arms and twirled her around. She threw back her head and laughed as he set her on the ground. Crinkles danced merrily at the corners of her eyes. Her long dark hair sported several silver strands, but she was as beautiful as he remembered. He held her by her calloused hands and kissed each one.

"Joseph, it's so wonderful to see you." She glanced behind him. "No one followed you, did they?"

"I was careful, Mama. No one followed."

Angry Bear joined them and Joseph shook his hand. "Glad to see you, Luke."

"You can call me Angry Bear, I've grown fond of it." Angry Bear glanced adoringly at Joseph's mother.

A small boy ran up to them. "This is our son, Luke. Angry Bear and I are married," his mother said. Her gaze searched Joseph's face for a clue to his reaction. She moved beside Angry Bear and put her arm around his waist. She gazed up at him with eyes brimming with her open love.

Joseph grabbed Angry Bear's hand and pumped with enthusiasm. He kissed the top of his mother's head. He picked up the young spitting image of Angry Bear and twirled him around. "Congratulations is all I can say. We must celebrate." His heart was full for his mother's happiness. It quickly emptied as the reason for his coming filled his mind. "I'm afraid I've come with bad news."

Angry Bear's expression turned solemn as if he knew what news Joseph brought. "We will go to the lodge and talk."

Joseph's mother took young Luke in her arms and followed behind Angry Bear.

Joseph soberly brought up the rear, leading his horse.

Joseph's mother poured cool water in clay bowls as Joseph related the story of the battle. When he told the part of Lance bravely shoving Osceola out of the way and himself taking the bullet meant for his chief, Angry Bear rose and gazed outside, his hand against the doorjamb.

"My vision was correct," he simply said. He turned to Joseph, raised his chin and squared his shoulders. "Thank you for coming to tell of my son's bravery."

After supper and dragging out from Joseph everything about his wife, Susannah, and son, Charles, Olive lay beside Angry Bear. Both he, young Luke, and Joseph were asleep. Olive was happy Joseph was wed and she had a grandchild. She wanted so much to see them. She had been shocked to learn of the death of her friend, Magdalena, but grateful that Joseph and his wife would care for the surviving twin. She prayed for Johan.

Outside, a cricket chirped loudly breaking the night silence. As when she was a girl, she wondered how such a tiny creature could make such a loud noise. He must be happy to be alive and proclaiming all the wonderful deeds his life would hold. She wondered what the rest of her life would hold. She was getting sleepy. Time to turn the page in this chapter of her life and see what was written for tomorrow.

* * *

The future did not bode well for the Cherokees. On a spring morning in late May 1838, white, uniformed soldiers entered the village with guns drawn. Olive had just stepped from her lodge carrying Elizabetha's journal which she planned to read after she shook out the night's sleeping blanket and hung it up to air when she saw the dust cloud from horses hooves billowing around the village. Her son was playing with friends in the yard beside the lodge. "Luke, come here at once," she yelled. The other children ran home.

Seven-year-old Luke scampered to her side with eyes wide with fright. He threw his arms around her skirt. "What is it, Mama?"

"I don't know. Stay close."

The soldiers dismounted and began knocking in doors to the lodges and chasing the people out of their homes. Three soldiers brandishing guns rounded up Olive and Luke toward the horses at gun point. There she found her cousin Willow frantically looking for her husband, Jake. Willow was a few years younger than Olive. She clasped her two braids at her shoulders and stretched her short frame to peer over the others. "Where is he, Olive? Have you seen Jake? He went off with Angry Bear."

Olive searched the crowd for their men. She spotted Angry Bear and the tall, thin Jake being prodded by bayonets toward the gathering crowd of captives. Angry Bear and Jake rushed to hers and Willow's side. Jake bent his gangling frame to kiss the head of Willow. Angry Bear scooped up Luke. Olive held onto Angry Bear's arm with one hand and clutched the journal and blanket she still carried with the other.

They were forced to walk for many days. Mothers carried and dragged their children along, afraid to let them out of their sight. Old women wailed. Children cried. The men huddled together in groups and spoke in low angry tones.

"How can they uproot other human beings like this, tearing us from our homes, and forcing us to leave all worldly possessions behind, as if we were no more than wild animals?" Olive asked Angry Bear.

An angry scowl was her answer.

The white soldiers herded the Indians like cattle into the pen of the stockade. Olive counted thirty families from her family clan the corn, and the beaver clan of Angry Bear among the villagers. Days and weeks passed as more and more Cherokee from other villages were herded into the stockade, all with few if any possessions. Some were barefoot. The stockade was crowded beyond capacity.

The leaves began falling from the trees and the nights grew ever colder. There were not enough blankets. There was not enough food. The earth of the pen was frozen in the morning and sloppy mud by noon. Every Indian was encrusted with dried mud. There wasn't enough water to drink much less to wash in.

During the days, Olive wrapped the journal in the blanket and tied it around her neck with the journal resting on her back. At night, she lay the journal beneath her head and snuggled into the arms of Angry Bear, tightly holding Luke against her. They covered themselves in the lone blanket. Luke trembled with the cold and Olive placed her chin on his head and cuddled him closer. "There, there," she said. She could feel his soft breaths on her arm, and Angry Bear's on her neck. It was the only time she felt safe.

As suddenly as the soldiers had appeared in the village, they now came in force to the stockade and rounded the Indians into a westward trek away from the stockade toward a destination they did not know and had not chosen.

They walked for days until the mountains were behind them. As they passed the white towns, the townspeople came out to stare at the Indians passing by. "I wonder if the whites feel any compassion at all for us, scantily clad for a winter march to a place we don't wish to go, while they stand gawking, dressed in their warm coats and blankets?" Olive asked.

"Their eyes do not hold pity, only scorn," Angry Bear answered.

"I hate them," Olive stated. "I regret I ever wanted to fit in with them, or thought that their way held the future for the Cherokee. It holds nothing but death and misery for the Cherokee."

Olive was glad that Joseph had not come to the village that fateful day the soldiers came. She knew he would be fighting against the taking of the Cherokees lands. She wondered if he knew of their plight.

* * *

Joseph could only pray that his mother and her new family would survive the Indian Removal and make a new life for themselves.

With the signing of the Treaty of New Echota by a few dissenters of the Cherokee position, giving Cherokee land to the federal government, the situation was dire. Things were brought to their worst when Martin Van Buren took over the presidency and ordered the implementation of the Treaty in 1838.

Gold had been discovered in Georgia and that state claimed sovereignty over the Cherokee Nation. The words of Georgia governor, George Gilmore, enraged Joseph: "Treaties were a means by which ignorant, intractable, and savage people were induced to yield what Civilized Peoples had a right to possess."

Joseph's heart sank at the Cherokees' fate. In spite of the fact that the Cherokees had adapted their clothing, farming, housing, and even government patterned after the white people, it was clear that the white government did not intend to honor any of the treaties giving the rights of their own land to the Cherokee.

He was burdened further by the fact that he could not share his concerns with anyone for fear it would be learned that he was half Cherokee. His practice would be ruined and he would be sent westward. He dared not even tell his wife and family.

≫·50·≪

The Removal wore on. Olive trudged beside Angry Bear on the westbound trail. Her stomach rumbled from lack of food. It felt like it was devouring itself and trying to eat its way through to her back. Rough stones tore through her moccasins, adding fresh blood to stale. She didn't believe she would ever be clean again. She couldn't remember the last time she had washed her face and hands, much less bathed.

The last drop of water she'd drank was stagnant. She was cold, hungry, and weary. The snow and icy rivers they'd crossed had cut and froze her feet. She felt like she was walking on stumps. Sometimes as many as fifteen or more people died in a day, and the Indians were forced to leave the dead along the trail. Some would carry or drag them along until the captives were allowed to camp at night.

Young Luke developed a cough and grew more feverish each day. Olive knew it was pneumonia. He became increasingly weaker. Angry Bear and Olive took turns carrying him. Sometimes Willow or Jake would take a turn at carrying Luke. They had no children of their own.

At night, Olive would cuddle him and stroke his hot head.

The warmth of his feverish body next to hers did not relieve the cold that built in her heart. She had grown to hate the whites more every day. They were killing her son as surely as if they held a gun to his head. They were killing him because he was the wrong color. And through him, they were killing her.

Olive walked beside Angry Bear who was carrying Luke while Olive held Luke's hand. She felt it go limp.

Angry Bear sank to his knees holding the boy. "He's gone," he said.

"Nooo!" Olive wailed and buried her head against the still body of her son in Angry Bear's lap.

Angry Bear's head dropped to her shoulder and she could feel his warm tears soaking her tattered calico blouse.

A soldier rode up to the grieving couple and told them to leave the boy and march.

Angry Bear rose with his son in his arms and said, "I'll carry him till we camp. He'll have a proper burial."

At camp that night, Angry Bear scooped out a shallow grave from the frozen earth with his bare hands as Olive gathered stones into her blanket and hauled them to the grave site, tumbling them onto the ground beside the body of young Luke.

As if all her tears had evaporated, she watched with gritty, dry eyes as Angry Bear stoically lowered Luke into the small grave. She knelt beside Angry Bear and together they placed the stones with care to cover Luke in his final sleeping place. They held each other through the long, cold night.

The dreary days of marching through the wilderness dragged one into the other for Olive. Angry Bear had become preoccupied with his own thoughts and spent more and more marching time with Jake. She wondered what they talked about.

A few nights later, she was to learn when Angry Bear lay beside her under the blanket. "Olive, we must escape," he whispered.

"What?" She turned toward him. "That's impossible. We're guarded." He must be losing his mind. The trek, the loss of Luke has been too much for him. She shivered.

He held her close. "No, it's not impossible. Dead are left along the road all the time. We'll pretend to be dead."

He's surely lost his mind. With the loss of Luke, she already felt dead inside. But his words were crazy.

"The rumor is that we'll soon reach the Mississippi River. We'll have to accomplish it before we lose the cover of the wilderness," he whispered. "Jake and I have figured it out. First he will die and hide in the woods later. Then Willow will pass on and meet up with Jake."

Olive tried to turn toward Angry Bear again, but he held her tight and whispered in her ear.

"Next, you will be left and find them in the woods. I will come last."

"But how will we know where to meet. Where will we go?" Fear restricted her breathing.

"Jake and I will find the right place as we march. We'll point it out to you. We will go to the Appalachian Mountains. You know of the valley high up in the mountains. The place no white man would believe possible to go."

"But we'll surely die."

"We'll have a better chance out there—" He gestured slightly with his hand under the blanket, "then here on this Godforsaken march to hell. At least we can forage for our own food and water. We can return to our beloved homeland. The whites have taken our son. I'll not stand by doing nothing and let them take you away, too."

The next days found the four walking as a group, each moving ever slower toward the back of the pack and with more fatigue and coughing fitfully as they prepared for their deaths. As they passed by a waterfall far off the trail, the men brought the attention of the women to the spot. "There is where we'll meet," Angry Bear whispered to Olive. "Watch for landmarks along the way until it is your turn to die. Jake will go tonight. Two days later, Willow."

Late that afternoon, Jake stumbled and fell to the ground at the side of the road on cue and gasped one last breath. He lay still. Willow ran to his side wailing and prostrated herself atop Jake. Angry Bear hurried over with Olive at his heels and felt

Jake's pulse. He rose and pulled Willow to her feet. "He's dead," he said.

A bearded soldier rode up behind them and said, "Move along."

"He's dead," Willow wailed.

"Roll him off to the side. Keep moving," the gruff soldier ordered.

They did as they were told. Olive put her arm around Willow's shoulder to comfort her as best she could as Angry Bear rolled Jake safely out of the way of horse hooves. They trudged on, making sure they walked among different people by the second day.

Willow's demise went smoothly and in two more days it was Olive's turn. It was easy to tremble and be unsteady on her feet as her heart was frozen in fear. She fell to the ground in great agony and flopped over to her stomach, lying still. Angry Bear's wails sent chills through her spine. She dare not move, dare not breathe as Angry Bear rolled her to safer ground before a soldier prodded him to move along.

Angry Bear watched the young blond soldier turn and glance back at Olive. Angry Bear prayed the soldier would not decide to go back to her. Finally, the soldier turned forward in his saddle and prodded his horse past Angry Bear. Angry Bear let out a low whistle.

Olive lay motionless until dark. She wanted to be sure there were no stragglers behind. Slowly she opened one eye, then the other and glanced along the empty trail. She gradually lifted her head and scanned the landscape. She bolted for the trees. Her heart pounded so hard she feared it would leap out of her chest. She ran through the woods at the edge of the trail searching for landmarks and finally reached the designated meeting spot exhausted. As she slipped behind the falls, first Willow and then Jake hugged her. With greetings over, Olive took a long drink of the abundant fresh water.

After a supper of winter berries, Willow helped Olive out of her filthy clothes while Jake stood watch with his back to the women. Olive slipped into the quiet pool of water at the base behind the falls and scrubbed every inch of her body with her hands. "It's freezing cold, but it feels so good to be clean of months' worth of dirt and grime," Olive told Willow.

"I know." Willow washed out Olive's clothes and dried them before a small fire Jake had built behind the falls so the smoke mixed with the mist of the cascading water and could not be seen.

After bathing, Olive wrapped herself in the blanket.

That night, Olive fretted for Angry Bear. Who would roll his dead body safely out of the path of the soldiers' horses? Who would declare him dead? What if something went wrong? She hugged Elizabetha's journal to her and tried to sleep.

Angry Bear did not show up the second night and Olive was sure his escape had failed. She might as well have really died.

Willow had gathered winter berries for their breakfast. There was plenty of water to drink. Olive sipped the cool liquid and tried to force a few berries down. Willow sat beside her and patted her shoulder as Olive hugged the journal and wept.

⇉51⇇

Angry Bear lagged behind the other marchers on the trail towards the Mississippi River until only a few remained behind him. He broke into a fit of coughing and fell to the side of the road and laid still. The dust of the marchers and soldier's horses choked him, but he did not move. There was no one left to announce that he was dead and roll him to safety. He held his breath, half expecting to feel horse hooves upon him at any moment, but the last of the Indians and soldiers passed him without incident. Still, he did not move a single finger.

The young blond soldier that had prodded Angry Bear to move along when Olive died had seen Angry Bear fall. As he rode on further, he thought how odd that the husband died just a few days later. He would just go see that the fellow was really dead, if not, he'd make sure of his demise.

Angry Bear heard but did not see the soldier ride up to where he lay in the same position as when he fell to the ground. He sensed the soldier dismounting and felt the soldier roll him over to get a good look at him.

Angry Bear intuited the soldier leaning over him. His eyes flew open in time to see the soldier's knife about to slash his throat. He surged his body upward and head-butted the soldier. With the soldier's shock, Angry Bear easily wrested the knife away and sank it deep into the soldier's heart.

Angry Bear hunkered in a crouch. No one had followed the soldier. Angry Bear inserted the knife into his legging and reached for the reins of the soldier's horse. He loaded the soldier on top and led the horse into the woods, tied the horse to a tree, and went back to the road with a pitch pine branch to brush away the tracks leading into the woods.

Once sheltered from sight, It took the whole night with only his hands and the knife to dig out a hole large enough to hold the stripped clothes and gear of the soldier. He buried everything including the saddle and guns and covered it all over with leaves. Whatever hunting they did on the way home would have to be of the silent type by traps and knife. They couldn't afford to risk bringing any attention to themselves with gun powder. He dragged the soldier deeper into the woods and left his burial to the animals as he led the horse away.

Olive froze at the sound of horse hooves. She gaped at Willow and Jake who stood motionless with eyes wide. Without further warning, Angry Bear was beside her and lifted her to her feet. Tears of gladness tumbled out as he kissed her eyelids then her mouth with the tenderest of kisses. Thank God he was safely here. After the telling of his ordeal, Olive thanked God again for sparing him. If he had died, she would have also.

After two days of rest, they began the long trek back to the Appalachian Mountains and the valley atop which would be their new home, staying off the trail and concealed by the woods as they feared meeting up with other captives being herded west.

After many weeks of foraging for food and stealing their way to the Appalachians, Olive, Angry Bear, Willow, and Jake were greeted by the majestic mountains of the Appalachians. A blue mist hovered at the summit.

The little group began its secret ascent up the arduous trail. They stopped often to rest. Soon the trail through the mountains became too steep and precarious for stopping. Angry Bear led the horse at the front of the group. Olive held onto its tail and Willow's hand behind. Jake brought up the rear.

The trail wound around the mountain like thread around a spool. At some places, the climb was almost a forty-five-degree angle. Olive avoided looking down at the potential drop, concentrating instead on the heavens they seemed to be headed for. The horse occasionally kicked out loose stone as they stumbled upward.

Finally the trail splayed out into a broad valley with lush green meadows forded by great forests as if the land were opening its arms to receive the outcasts. Here the group would make its home in land considered worthless and inaccessible by the whites.

As they made their way through the valley, they spotted a small group of lodges. They appeared to be empty. There was no sign of life around. They hesitatingly approached the dwellings. Just as Olive felt sure the lodges must be abandoned, a dozen or so Indians came out of the woods.

The Indians welcomed them immediately. They, too, had avoided the trail where the people cried. The new neighbors prepared what Olive could only think of as a feast of yams and venison and corn. Afterwards, they all gathered around the fire in the middle of the small settlement.

The medicine man, an old man with straggly, gray hair and a bent back, rubbed black ash onto his hawk-like features and slowly danced his way around the fire giving thanks for the arrival of newcomers to help the tiny village.

Olive and Willow began the very next day to gather materials for the lodges that would house them through the next winter as Angry Bear and Jake made crude axes from stone and boughs. The only tools they had were the knife, what they could borrow from the other stragglers, and what nature provided.

Olive put the deer hides from Angry Bear's kills to quick work, soaking them in wood ash and water, scraping them with a beveled deer antler to remove flesh and hair as they were draped over a fallen tree trunk, then placing them in the rafters of their lodge over the winter allowing a good smoking. In early spring she mixed the animal brains of new kills with water and soaked the skins several times. Soon she could sew new clothes for herself and Angry Bear.

She glanced across the flames at Angry Bear sharpening his knife blade on a stone, his forehead furrowed in concentration, his lips slightly pursed. She liked to watch him work.

She busied herself with her sewing. How peaceful their lives were again at last. It was an open and honest life lived in the bosom of nature which provided food, shelter, and clothing—all that was really needed. An owl hooted hauntingly in the distance.

She glanced again at Angry Bear. Slivers of silver in his hair glinted in the firelight. He had grown patient and kind. She felt kinder, too. Living brings that about she guessed. Living and surviving the loss of loved ones finally brings us to realize that life is short, and that being kind is more important than being right.

Angry Bear rose, and gazed through the narrow doorway of their lodge at the last glimmer of the setting sun. He turned and stretched, his muscles rippling across his back. He glanced to Olive and reached his hand out to her.

She folded the deerskin and rose, taking his hand.

He led her to their sleeping platform of split white oak saplings and cane covered with mats of cane and skins.

Angry Bear nuzzled his nose through her long hair and kissed her neck.

As she lay with Angry Bear's arms wrapped around her, she watched the smoke swirling up to the vent hole in the thatched roof. Contentment caused her eyelids to grow heavy.

⇌ 52 ⇌

1 8 5 0

Also content with her life, Susannah reminisced that her oldest son, Charles was now sixteen and her youngest son, William, was just two. Her daughter, Olivia, was nine, born five years after they'd taken in fourteen-year-old Jacob. Olivia constantly followed after Jacob through the years. When younger, she'd often cried whenever Jacob went to stay with his father. Those occasions got oftener as Jacob got older and could help out at the farm.

Joseph named their daughter Olivia after his mother. Susannah had never met Olive. Joseph just said she was in isolation, but would not elaborate. Surely he knew best.

Her thoughts returned to the present as Jacob came into the parlor with Olivia following him, pulling the dark brown hair at the back of his head and saying, "Please let me come with you."

Jacob swatted at the back of his head. "Make her quit, please Ma'am." The eyebrows above his steel blue eyes arched in pleading.

"Olivia, leave Jacob's hair alone."

Free of his tormenter at last, Jacob asked, "Charles and I want to go fishing at the creek, is it all right?"

"I want to go, too," Olivia chimed in.

Charles, entered the parlor, "We want to go without Olivia."

"Without Olivia," Jacob added, lowering his head.

Olivia's lower lip slightly protruded.

Susannah studied the children. "Yes, you boys can go alone."

When the boys had left, Olivia plopped on the sofa beside her mother. The dark lashes around her large robin's-egg-blue eyes glistened with moisture. "It's not fair."

"Sometimes boys need time just for themselves." Susannah patted Olivia's knee and tucked a stray strand of sable hair behind Olivia's ear.

"Jacob's nice to me and we have lots of talks when Charles isn't around, but when Charles wants Jacob to do something, Jacob tells me. 'Go away.'"

Susannah knew it was hard for Olivia to be excluded from any activity of Jacob's. Olivia nearly worshiped him. Susannah smiled and patted Olivia's head against her chest as she hugged her, "One day maybe he won't say that anymore."

Several days later, Susannah and Joseph talked in the kitchen over morning coffee. Joseph said, "There's a law firm in Nashville, Tennessee that Steve, from college, wrote me about. He wants me to go into partnership with him. He said the town's been rapidly expanding since it became the capital in 1843."

Susannah's mouth involuntarily gaped and Joseph set his coffee cup on the table and took her hand.

"Steve says he has more business than he can handle. You know how slow it is for me here. It would be a wonderful opportunity. What do you think?"

"I don't know. There is so much to consider, the children, young Jacob, friends and family—." She wasn't at all sure she liked the idea of moving away. "What about young Jacob? Would he want to move away from his father?"

"I know there's a lot to consider, but do consider it. After all, you could be the beautiful wife of a wealthy man." He tilted his head and winked.

By the end of the month, Joseph convinced Susannah to move. He was so eager and excited when he talked about it, she couldn't disappoint him. Now all they had to do was tell the children.

Susannah greeted Johan as he and Joseph joined her and the children in the parlor. Johan had come by to take Jacob to the farm for the weekend.

Susannah rose from the rocker and motioned for Joseph. She put her hand on Joseph's sleeve and whispered, "Would now be a good time to tell everyone about Tennessee?"

Joseph smiled and bent down to kiss her forehead. "Of course it would. Thank you for being you."

Johan, now in his sixties, was still thin. His hair was nearly white and somehow softened his sharp features. He stood before the fireplace conversing with Charles and Jacob. Charles was nearly as tall as Johan and Jacob was to his shoulder. Both boys had dark hair, but Charles had the brown eyes of the Blakemores while Jacob had the steel-blue eyes of the Kimberlins.

Olivia was on the sofa with her pillowcase embroidery. She sullenly watched the boys and Johan talking together and excluding her again.

Young William played on the floor with his toy soldiers. His sandy-colored hair hung in his eyes.

Joseph led Susannah to the center of the parlor and announced, "Since we're all gathered together to say good-bye to Jacob as he goes to his father's for the weekend, we thought it a good time to tell you of a decision we've reached." He glanced at Susannah and squeezed her hand. "As you're all aware, we've been discussing moving to Tennessee. We've agreed that's what we want to do."

Susannah held her breath as she waited for Johan and the children's reactions.

Johan came forward and shook their hands. "I'm glad for you. It's a grand opportunity." He cleared his throat and put his hands in his pockets. "Jacob and I had our own announcement for this evening. Jacob is coming to live permanently with me at the farm."

Jacob came up beside his father and said, "I can be a lot of help to Pa on the farm. Since now all of my brothers have married and moved away, Pa needs me." He gazed up at his father and beamed.

Susannah exhaled. At least that has worked out fortunately.

Jacob held out his hand to Joseph, but Joseph hugged him instead.

Susannah wiped at her eyes with her hanky before hugging Jacob.

"We knew this day would come soon. We'll keep in touch with you. Good luck," Joseph said.

"Best wishes to you, Jacob. I know you'll do a fine job on the farm." Susannah dabbed at her eyes again. "Be sure to keep your room neat."

It startled Susannah when everyone laughed. Remembering what she just said, she joined in.

Charles shook Jacob's hand. "I'll miss the heck out of you, but I'm happy for you."

The boys each put a hand on the other's shoulder and gave an embarrassed quick hug.

"I'm looking forward to Tennessee. I'm nearly seventeen, maybe I can get an apprenticeship," Charles said as he glanced at his father.

"Maybe, indeed." Joseph winked at Charles.

Susannah smiled. Another fortunate outcome. She knew young William wouldn't care one way or the other.

As she turned to her daughter Susannah asked, "Olivia, don't you want to say anything to Jacob?" Susannah's smile disappeared at the redness of Olivia's face and neck. Olivia's embroidery was cast aside on the sofa and she clenched her fists glaring at Jacob.

Olivia rose and dashed out of the room, turning to yell, "I hate you, Jacob. I hate you all."

After good-byes were said all around, Susannah tucked William into bed for the night and she and Joseph headed toward their bedroom as Charles went to his. Susannah paused at Olivia's door and turned to Joseph, "I need to talk to her."

"Want me to go in with you?"

"No, but thank you. I'll speak to her alone." She thought she knew what the outburst was all about.

❯❯53❮❮

Three months later, Susannah surveyed her Tennessee home. It was a townhouse within walking distance of Joseph's law office.

She straightened the doily on the side table next to the wing-back chair for the third time. Charles was serving an apprentice-ship with a merchandiser and seemed to enjoy it. Olivia had moved beyond her anger at Jacob for leaving, after she wrote him her apology and he'd written back that he forgave her. Olivia attended the Lutheran school during the day and Susannah found herself alone much of the time, just she and young William.

Susannah looked forward to Joseph's return home each mid-day for dinner and each evening for supper.

At supper that night, Joseph said, "Did you notice the bulletin posted at church about a quilting bee for ladies on Wednesdays?" He picked up his fork laden with green peas. "Why don't you go? It will be good for you to get out of the house and see people."

Susannah lowered her glass and smiled. "You're all the people I need to see."

"Nonsense. It's a great community. You should get involved."

"If you think so. I'll try it." Susannah had always relied heavily on the directions and suggestions of her parents. Now she had only Joseph. He was ten years older. He knew what was best.

Susannah found the quilting bees disconcerting. The main subject the women discussed was the first women's rights convention held two years ago in New York. She hadn't thought of it much, but she was of the mind that a woman's place was taking care of her family. What do I need rights for? Joseph provides everything I need.

Cynthia Bailey, a thirtyish, attractive woman was eager to answer her question. "By depriving women of the first right as a citizen, the vote, men have oppressed her totally."

Susannah had learned that Cynthia had attended the convention as well as countless abolitionist conventions.

"Women are no better off than the slaves," Cynthia continued. "As married women, we are civilly dead. We are compelled to promise obedience to our husband in all matters. As single women we must pay taxes on any property to support a government in which we have no representation. We are treated as subordinate in all matters."

Cynthia scanned the ladies around the room and then rested her gaze on Susannah. "How can you purport to believe you have all the rights you need? How can you willingly submit to this absolute tyranny?"

Susannah didn't know what to say. "I-I guess I never thought much about it," she mumbled. She wasn't sure she was going to think about it now either. She just wanted to get home to Joseph.

That evening after supper, Charles was in his room reading, and Susannah put young William to bed. She joined the rest of the family in the parlor. Olivia worked on her embroidery sitting on the sofa. Susannah knitted a pale yellow shawl while Joseph read the paper.

Joseph glanced up from the paper to Susannah. "Listen to this. The Compromise of 1850, which took seven months to reach conclusion, calls for the admission of California as a free state, provides for a territorial government for Utah and New

Mexico, establishes a boundary between Texas and the United States, calls for the abolition of slave trade in Washington, D.C., and amends the Fugitive Slave Act." He shook his head. "The North is not in favor of having to return runaway slaves to the South, and the South is not happy with the continued and growing imbalance of representation in the government and unfair taxes benefiting the North at the South's expense. The North is trying to destroy the South and its economy. How can the South survive without slaves?"

The mention of slaves reminded Susannah about Cynthia's statements that women were no better off than the slaves. She related Cynthia's statements to Joseph and concluded, "She said women should have the right to vote."

He looked up from his reading. "To vote?" He chuckled. "I don't think that will happen any time soon." He glanced at Susannah. "Whatever got women started on that?"

"Apparently the two leaders of the convention Cynthia attended were Elizabeth Stanton and Lucretia Mott. They had attended the World Anti Slavery convention in London and were forced to sit on a balcony covered by a curtain and were not to speak a word. This sexist behavior of the men got them thinking they had no more rights than slaves themselves, that men held tyranny over women by demanding obedience in all matters. They began recruiting and eight years later held the first women's rights convention."

"The papers made a mockery of that convention. Don't take Cynthia's rantings too seriously." Joseph smiled and returned to his paper.

"You're right of course, Joseph."

Olivia attended her parent's conversation. She couldn't agree less with them. She didn't know women weren't allowed to vote. It didn't seem right. Women were just as good as men. It had chilled her blood to hear of the tyranny men had over women. Obedience to a man in all matters. She'd see about that.

⇒·53·⇐

Meanwhile, the young Jacob Kimberlin contemplated, while lying in his bed at his father's farm that first night, that he didn't remember his mother, Magdalena, who'd died giving him birth, or even his grandparents, the elder Jacob for whom he was named, and Margaretha. They had both died before he was five. He only knew them through his father's eyes. He didn't even know his older brothers who had all married and moved further west before he'd turned fourteen. After all, there were nineteen years between Jacob and Nathan, the youngest of his older brothers. His father, Johan, was the only family he really had and at sixty-four he needed Jacob's help to run the farm. He was fourteen, a man now, and he would do a man's job of taking care of his father and the Kimberlin farm.

Several weeks later, Jacob received a letter from Olivia pleading his forgiveness for her behavior the night they had last seen each other. He would have to answer her right away, of course. She could be pesky sometimes, but she was so sensitive, it disturbed him to think of her suffering on his account.

Jacob paid close attention the next morning to everything his father taught him about running the farm.

"I want you to get the hang of the books and take them over. That's the first order of the day." His father showed him the stack of ledgers piled beneath the drop-front desk.

Jacob sat down with his father at his back. His heart swelled with pride at the trust his father was bestowing on him. He opened the first ledger to the first page and saw the writing of his great-grandfather, Martin, who had initialed each page he entered. He skimmed through the rest, noting the initials of all who entered information into the ledger after Martin: his great-grandmother, Elizabetha; his grandfather, Jacob; and his own father, Johan. Soon his own initials would fill the pages.

"Take a few days to get familiar with them, and then you can start making your own entries."

After several weeks, Jacob became proficient with the books, and his father said, "Now, we will review Martin's master plan of rotation of the crops. You know, your great-grandfather brought those farming skills from Germany. It was how his father planted. His father was a fine farmer in the old country. When Martin found this land with good limestone soil, he knew this was where he would carry on his father's farming."

Jacob studied the rotation written in his great-grandfather's hand of how to keep the soil healthy: Limestone soil is best, first plant hay, then corn, next tobacco, then wheat or barley, and use plenty of manure.

"Now, we also plant cotton and then repeat the rotation," his father said.

Jacob spent every day memorizing the rotation that had kept the Kimberlin farm soil healthy and productive nearly a hundred years. The thought of that awed him.

"Tomorrow you'll start working in the fields so you get a good feel for the land and the crops," his father said.

He also learned to give orders to the Negroes, and he learned about the selling of the crops while accompanying his father on his trips to the buyers at the railroad yard.

Three summers passed, and Jacob was proud of his skills and of the new muscles he'd developed. He was happy, until the morning he turned seventeen.

Jacob woke at dawn feeling a strangeness he didn't recognize. Somehow, for no-good reason, he was anxious. The foreboding continued as he performed his morning ablutions. It followed him down the stairs to the breakfast table. It sat upon his shoulder as he took his seat and saw his father was not yet down from his room. Jacob sat down and waited for his father to join him.

His breakfast was served him by Mattie, the house slave. Her usual amicable smile was missing this morning. Her stocky form reached out a well-rounded arm and placed a plate of scrambled eggs before him. He glanced up at her. "Thank you, Mattie."

"Welcome, Massa." Mattie's eyelids lowered.

He thought her white head bandana was tied tighter around her head this morning as if she, too, felt the same misgiving. It seemed to pinch her plump face into a worried frown as she glanced upstairs. Like himself, she seemed to be wondering where his father was. He was usually the first one downstairs. As Mattie left Jacob's side, she placed a warm hand on his shoulder as if to comfort him.

It didn't. He took three bites of the eggs before him and shoved the plate back. Something was wrong. Where was his father? Jacob sat and wondered what he should do. Should he continue to wait for him? Or should he go to his father's bed chamber and see what was the matter? The grandfather clock hanging on the wall ticked. The mesmerizing beat of the clock's heart transfixed Jacob into a stupor. He jumped as the clock gonged the half hour. It was seven-thirty.

He could put it off no longer. He rose and ascended the stairs, concern pushing him from behind, and misgiving shoving against his chest. He stopped in front of his father's room, took a deep breath, and rapped on the door.

He had known there would be no answer. He placed his hand on the doorknob. The hand refused to turn it. He stared intently at the wayward hand and ordered, "You must open the door, you must." The hand obeyed, and Jacob entered his father's bedroom.

His father, Johan, lay peacefully under the quilt. One hand

was laid across the top of the covers and the other one flopped above his head which was turned to the side facing the door with closed eyes. His father did not stir at Jacob's entrance.

Jacob approached the bed and forced his hand to touch his father's brow. It was cold as he knew it would be. Jacob pulled the ladder back chair to his father's bedside and took his father's hand into his own. Jacob's head bowed and the hot tears he had felt beneath his lids all morning flowed freely now. He didn't know how long he sat holding his father's hand before he finally rose, went to the door, and called down the stairs for Mattie and the other house slaves.

Months after the funeral, Jacob mused about the letters he always received from Olivia. She told him all about the Woman's Rights Movement that she faithfully followed in the papers. She related every incident of her school life and her friends. He felt he knew her through and through. He tucked the last letter he'd received into his pocket and rode out to the south field of cotton in the low land.

He reined his horse at the edge of the field and watched the two dozen slaves and their children picking cotton with their long sacks slung over their shoulder and both hands plucking cotton balls and shoving them into the bags as fast as they could. The cloth containers of the smaller children dragged on the ground behind them.

Jacob turned in his saddle and surveyed the Kimberlin farm. It was his responsibility now. When his brothers had returned for their father's funeral, they had said they wanted no part of it. Well, Jacob did. He would see to it that the farm remained as prosperous as it had been under his father's, hand, and before him, his grandfather, all the way back to his great-grandfather, Martin, who had created it. The farm and the Kimberlin Church that his great-grandfather had also created were as much a part of Jacob as if he himself had built them.

* * *

Tension was building in the South. Joseph Blakemore read the passage of the 1854 Kansas-Nebraska Act with a sinking feeling in the pit of his stomach. It included an amendment repealing the Missouri Compromise which had said territories above a certain line were banned from slavery and those below could choose slavery. The Act allowed Kansas and Nebraska to be two separate territories. The assumption being that one would be free and one slave. The North and South were exerting full pressure on Kansas to determine the popular sovereignty issue in their favor. A new political organization called the Republican Party was founded by the opponents of the bill. The chasm between the North and the South was ever widening.

➤ 55 ◀

1858 Four Years Later

Olivia was elated that the distance between her and Jacob would at last be closed. Her family was leaving Tennessee and moving back to Virginia. Her father had always considered Evansham now called Wytheville as his home and wanted to rebuild his old practice there now that he had the money. Her brother Charles had married a sweet girl named Mary and had moved back to Virginia three years ago. The following year their son, Guy, was born.

A few months later, Olivia's mind wandered as she waited for Jacob's move in their game of checkers. The first time Olivia saw Jacob when they returned to Wytheville, she had thought how much he'd changed. No longer was he a slim boy, but now he was well-muscled, tall, and tanned. Farm life had agreed with him. He had the sharp facial features and piercing blue eyes of his father, but they were more handsome on Jacob.

He had stared at her all through supper that night as if he didn't really believe she was the Olivia he once knew. She had felt awkward and had wondered if he did also.

Jacob visited for supper many Sundays after that and she had felt less awkward with each visit. Things had slipped into a more comfortable routine where she and Jacob played checkers after supper while her father read the newspaper and her mother mended, knitted, or the like. William would usually be in the barn until dark, tinkering with some project or other. He loved building things.

Jacob broke Olivia's train of thought with, "It's your move."

"What? Oh, I'm sorry, guess I was daydreaming." She reached to move her man.

Jacob put his hand on top of hers. He gazed into her eyes. She felt her heart skip. He gave a squeeze to her hand and let go.

She made a foolish move and Jacob promptly removed the last of her men and sat back in his chair watching her. "So, tell me all the things you've done and seen in Nashville. It's a long time since we've talked together," he said.

Things were just like before the move away, Olivia mused, only now he didn't say, "Go away," whenever someone came around. Her mother had been right.

Jacob didn't know just when he had started falling in love with Olivia. Was it when he first saw her, or several weeks ago? Or was it only tonight? He watched the animation of her features as she related everything her letters had held. She was a strong-minded woman. A woman like he needed to help him on the farm. He realized how lonely he had really been, and how much he had missed her trailing after him as she had when they were children.

* * *

Meanwhile, in the small village atop the Appalachians, Olive prepared for the journey down. Years before in 1849, the tribe was brought word that the government had allowed a reservation in North Carolina in which the remaining Cherokee's could live and stop hiding. Olive and Angry Bear had decided to stay in the mountains. The rest of the hideaways had opted to go to the reservation, and she and Angry Bear were the only ones left.

But she recently realized she had contracted the same consumption from which her father died, she begged Angry Bear to take her to the reservation. Perhaps she could get word to her son, Joseph, and she would be able to see him one last time before she died. Angry Bear relented and agreed to leave.

She took one last look around the valley. For twenty years she and Angry Bear had lived here in peace since the Indian Removal had torn everything they had possessed away from them, including their only son together, young Luke. They had given much to the mountains and taken much. But she was very tired. She knew her health was failing fast.

She hoped Joseph was still in Virginia and would come. She hoped to meet her grandchild or perhaps grandchildren by now.

Olive looked up from her packing at Angry Bear's approach. She turned. His once dark hair was now gray and he wore it loose, but he still held himself with pride.

"Come, my wife, it is time to leave," he said.

* * *

When Joseph had left Tennessee and returned to Virginia, he had heard of the reservation in North Carolina and decided to search there for his mother. He feared his mother and Angry Bear were in the Oklahoma reservation, or dead. Either way, he had thought he would never see her again. But he had to try in the outside chance that they had escaped the Removal.

The next Saturday, without telling his family what he was about, he left Wytheville and rode to North Carolina. At the reservation, he wandered through the people asking here and there, "Have you seen Olive Poteet or Luke Aiken called Angry Bear?" and "Do you know the clan of the bear or the corn from the Virginia Cherokee's village?" Each time there was a shaking of the head in the negative, and Joseph moved on to the next group.

Joseph was beginning to think his search was folly. As he stopped by an old woman to ask the same questions he always asked, he was surprised when she nodded yes and pointed to a lodge.

Joseph led his horse to the lodge and tied it to the hitching post. He knocked at the door. Could the old woman possibly be right? Did his mother and Angry Bear actually escape the Removal? His palms were sweaty as he waited for a response to his knock.

The door was opened and the tall, proud frame of Angry Bear with long, gray hair filled the opening. Joseph felt his jaw slacken. Was Angry Bear alone? Had his mother not escaped? Fear for his mother again caught in his throat. "Is mother—?" he mumbled.

Angry Bear stepped aside and allowed Joseph to enter the lodge. In the dark, Joseph could barely make out a form lying on the mat atop the wooden bed.

The figure sat up. "Joseph," his mother said in a frail voice.

Weeks later on Saturday, Joseph rode back from the reservation after his visit with his mother as he did every Saturday since he'd found her. Seeing his mother again brought him a joy he hadn't realized he'd been lacking. She seemed so grateful for his visits.

She asked all about his family. He'd admitted that he'd never told any of them about his mother being Indian. It wasn't that he was ashamed, he'd said, he'd been afraid of losing everything when the Indian Removal began, and later he just had always lived so much in the white man's world, he didn't think of being half Cherokee any longer, and then it seemed awkward to tell them so much later.

Why hadn't he been honest with his family in the first place? Because he feared not being accepted in the white man's world, he knew.

He would tell them tonight. His mother was so frail and weak, if he didn't tell his family soon, they might never have a chance to meet her.

Unexpectedly his son, Charles, was beside him.

"Blazes, where did you come from?" Joseph asked.

"I'm afraid I followed you, Papa. Mama told me you went

somewhere every Saturday morning, but she didn't know where. This morning, I decided to follow you."

"I see," Joseph said. He didn't know if he was angry at Charles for following him or ashamed of himself for not revealing his secret.

"That Indian woman you visited, you seemed close to her. Who is she?"

"My mother," Joseph said. He watched Charles out of the corner of his eye.

Charles rode along without saying anything for a while, staring straight ahead.

"Why didn't you ever tell us? Were you ashamed?" Charles asked quietly.

"I don't know, maybe. It's hard being a half-breed. You're never sure where you belong. I always tried to belong in the white man's world, so I ignored my Indian heritage. I was wrong."

They rode on in silence.

"I'd like to meet her," Charles said.

"I'd like for you to."

Joseph reached over and laid his hand on Charles's arm as he said, "Thank you," and righted himself in his saddle as he blinked away the tears of pride in his son's generous nature.

≫•56•≪

Joseph hoped the rest of his family would be as generous that evening after supper when he told them he was part Indian. His palms were sweaty in anticipation.

He rose from his chair and paced. The women weren't paying any attention to him. Both were sewing. William was sitting cross-legged on the floor whittling, being careful to keep the shards of wood on a spread out piece of newspaper.

Joseph pondered various ways of getting their attention without being obvious. He couldn't think of anything satisfactory. He just turned and faced them. "Ahem."

They looked expectantly at him.

"I have something to tell you," he said. "Something I should have told you long ago."

Olivia put down her embroidery and Susannah set her knitting aside. William glanced up from his project. They peered curiously at each other and back at him.

"What is it, Joseph?" Susannah straightened the folds of her long maroon skirt.

Joseph paced a few steps as he contemplated how to begin. "I have discovered that my mother is here in Virginia."

Susannah and Olivia peered more intently at him. Even William seemed curious now.

He certainly had their attention. There was no turning back now. "She had lived with her people in a remote part of the Appalachians in hiding until recently."

"With her people?" Olivia asked. Her eyes widened and her mouth fell open.

"Yes, her people that have now been allowed to move onto the reservation. They had been hiding to avoid being removed from their homeland to the Indian Territory west of the Mississippi. She's Cherokee."

Joseph stopped and waited for their reaction. He glanced first at Olivia. She sat dumbfounded, her mouth still agape.

William's face revealed nothing but mild curiosity.

Susannah rose and threw her arms around Joseph's neck. "Poor Joseph," she said. "You were afraid it would make a difference to me? You could be Chinese for all I care. I love you. I always have. I always will."

Joseph buried his face in her neck and held her tightly. "Thank God for you." He glanced again at his daughter.

She also rose, but she stood where she was.

Joseph straightened. He didn't like the way her eyes were flecked with sparks, like fire.

"How dare you? How could you? Indian! What will people think? How could you ruin my life like this?" She turned and ran upstairs.

Joseph's shoulders sagged as he exhaled a heavy sigh.

Susannah put her hand on his shoulder. "Give her some time, Joseph, she'll come around, you'll see."

He hoped so.

The following Saturday, Susannah and William accompanied Joseph on his visit to the reservation. Olivia refused to come. She barely spoke at all to him, and did so only when it was absolutely unavoidable. Charles and Mary and their son followed behind in their carriage.

His mother sat in a wooden chair. She was gray-haired and

frail looking dressed in calico with an Indian blanket of reds and yellows on gray wrapped around her shoulders. Her skin was thin as parchment, and her eyes were glazed. Her husband, Angry Bear, stood at her side protectively. Joseph introduced them to Susannah, Charles and his family, and William.

Joseph's mother motioned them to sit in front of her. "Sit," she said. "Let me get a good look at you. These old eyes don't see as well anymore."

They all took a seat on the rough-hewn stools placed in front of her.

In a voice less strong than younger years she said, "Joseph had told me all about you. I almost feel as though I know you. It is good to put faces to the names. But where is your daughter, Olivia?"

"I'm afraid she's having a difficult time adjusting to the news," Joseph said.

"Oh, I see. I'm sorry for that," his mother answered.

They visited for more than an hour and Joseph could see his mother was growing weary. Angry Bear had stood at her side the whole time without speaking. He was Joseph's mother's age or older, yet Angry Bear stood protectively there in case she needed anything.

"It's time we left, Mama. You need your rest. We'll be back." He bent down and kissed her goodbye. When he stood, he offered his hand to Angry Bear. Angry Bear gave his hand one shake and nodded his head one time toward Joseph. It had become their ritual goodbye to each other.

Susannah, Mary, and Charles each clasped Joseph's mother's hand and nodded toward Angry Bear as he had done.

William bent down and kissed his grandmother on the forehead.

She patted his sandy hair. "You look so much like your great-grandfather Joseph," Olive said.

William smiled and said, "Thank you." He stepped toward Luke and shook his hand vigorously.

"Wait," Joseph's mother said. "Angry Bear, please fetch the journal for me."

Angry Bear returned with the journal and handed it to her.

Olive presented it to Susannah. "Give this to Olivia. I know I will die soon—." She lifted her hand to stop Joseph's protest. "And it is fitting that my granddaughter, named after my name, should have my most precious possession."

Susannah held the journal to her bosom with tears in her eyes and said, "Thank you. I'll see that she gets it."

"Good, it was given to me by my mother-in-law, Anne Blakemore, who had received it from her dearest friend, Elizabetha Kimberlin. I hope it helps my granddaughter accept life as much as it has me." She leaned back. "Now, go. I am weary." She closed her eyes and fell asleep.

Days passed and Olivia kept eyeing the journal but didn't open it. She spent most of her time in her room. She even took her meals there. She hadn't wanted to see Jacob. She couldn't face anyone right now. She was too ashamed. Indian, kept ringing through her head. If only her grandmother wasn't Indian. If only her father had at least told her sooner. If only things were different.

Curiosity finally got the better of her and she opened the journal and began reading.

She spent the whole day reading until she came to a passage that particularly caught her attention.

Life is so fleeting and relationships so fragile; it behooves one to carefully knit each wound closed, to carry each relationship on a satin pillow of forgiveness. Not to judge and try to change them, but to accept them as they are while there is still time. I had tried to change Martin so many times, resenting him for things he did, or things he didn't do. How I would give anything to have him back the way he was, now that it's too late.

Olivia, dressed only in her pantalets and chemise, had been sprawled across her bed as she read. She sat up and wrapped her arms around her knees. She thought of her father. She couldn't go on forever not talking to him. He hadn't meant to hurt her.

He loved her, she knew. She couldn't go on avoiding Jacob. She'd been so afraid he'd shun her. Well, she'd just have to tell him and if he didn't want anything to do with her, she'd just have to accept it. She couldn't stay in her room forever.

She dressed and went downstairs for supper.

Olivia sat down in her place between her parents on each end of the table. William sat across, one eyebrow lifting ever so slightly as she seated herself. Olivia passed the corn bread to her father. "Here, Papa, you start."

Tears welled up in his eyes as he took the plate and said, "Thank you."

That evening, Jacob came to call. Olivia's parents and William went into the hall to give them privacy in the parlor.

"Why have you refused to see me, Olivia? What have I done?" Jacob asked as soon as her parents left.

"It isn't anything you've done, Jacob, it's me."

"I don't understand."

Olivia pulled herself up straight. She had to face it. She had to tell him. Whatever his reaction, she'd have to accept it. "My father's mother—my grandmother—is Indian."

Jacob gazed at her dazedly, his mouth slightly agape.

She prepared for the worst.

"I know that," he said.

"What?"

"I've always known. My father was friends with your grandmother, remember? He told me long ago. I just assumed you knew."

Olivia felt her own mouth widen in surprise. His words suddenly dawned on her. She ran to him and threw her arms around his neck.

"What a silly little goose you are," he said catching her. "But you're my silly goose. Will you marry me?"

"Yes, yes, forever yes." She had never felt more silly or more happy in all her life.

≫•57•≪

The following Saturday in late April, Olive didn't know her granddaughter would bring her happiness as she pulled her gray and yellow blanket a little further up under her chin. She waited for Joseph and his family, or at least most of it, to come for their visit. She wanted to see her granddaughter, Olivia, but guessed that would be too much to ask. She heard the carriage pull up. They walked to her side. She asked Angry Bear to prop her up with blankets which he did. One by one they came beside her cot.

First came dear Joseph, then his lovely wife, Susannah, then kind and loyal Charles and his family, and lastly, the dashing young William, and—what's this? A girl. Olive strained her eyes to see clearer, her heart beat faster. Could it be Olivia, dare she hope?

The girl leaned down and whispered in her ear as she held her hand, "Thank you for the journal, Grandmother."

It *was* Olivia. Thank God. What a beautiful child she was with nearly black hair, blue eyes, and a small, angelic oval face with gently pointed chin. Olive motioned to Olivia to come closer.

Olivia bent down on her knees and put her ear to her grandmother's lips.

"Remember to always be true to yourself. Never let the desire of fitting in dissuade you from your truth," Olive said.

On the following visit, Olivia brought Jacob along. Her grandmother talked about the Trail where the people cried and how she and Angry Bear had escaped. "I hated the whites at that time. They had taken our son, Luke, from us."

"Do you hate us, Grandma?" Olivia asked.

"No, I have no hate left in me. The years Angry Bear and I spent in the valley chased all the old hatreds away." She glanced over at Angry Bear talking with Joseph. "When your heart is filled with love, There is no room for hatred. Besides you are family. You remind me so much of Annjanine. How could I hate you?"

"But what about Jacob? He is not family—yet." Olivia gazed at Jacob and squeezed his hand. "We're going to be married soon."

Her grandmother leaned forward and took Olivia's and Jacob's hand in hers. "How happy that makes me. The Blakemores and the Kimberlins at last intertwined in marriage. Think of that, after all these many generations." She sat back as a coughing spasm gripped her. When she was able to get her breath, she said. "This consumption is getting worse. Soon Angry Bear's and my time will be gone. We are old. I am glad you will marry and people the earth with more generations to follow."

* * *

On the third of March in 1861, Olivia donned her white gown, her orange-blossom wreath, her bridal veil, and marched down the aisle to become Jacob's wife. Her grandmother was too ill to attend. After the ceremony, Olivia begged Jacob to take her to her grandmother so she could see them in all their finery and be a part of their joy. The whole family decided to join them.

Olive squinted at the late afternoon sun as Angry Bear tucked her gray and yellow Blanket around her shoulders. With each day she grew weaker and coughed up more blood. She had wished she could attend the wedding of her granddaughter Olivia. But she was far too weak. It would not be long now she knew. She reached her hand up to Angry Bear's and he brought it to his lips with a tender kiss. She gazed up to his face. Did she see a tear there? "It has been a good life," she said in a hoarse voice. "You have brought me much happiness."

"You have been my life, my happiness," he said.

A carriage pulled up to their lodge and Joseph and Susannah along with Charles and William alighted and came to her. Each bent down to kiss her where she lay on the cot Angry Bear had brought out so she could warm her old bones in the sunshine.

Through her blurred vision she glimpsed Olivia and Jacob. Dressed in their wedding clothes, they walked hand in hand to her side and kissed her forehead. My, didn't they look fine.

Her granddaughter was married. Tears ran down Olive's cheeks. All was well. She could die in peace. New generations were waiting for their turn under the sun. She smiled at the beautiful Olivia who so resembled Annjanine, and closed her eyes for the final time.

Joseph dug the grave for his mother's burial in the cemetery set off at the back side of the reservation, while Angry Bear wrapped her body in her gaily colored blanket. Joseph and Charles placed her inside the pine coffin obtained from the coffin maker of the reservation and lowered her into the cavity with her head pointed east as Angry Bear requested.

Joseph felt cold tingles run up his spine as Angry Bear chanted over the grave while Joseph and his family stood in a semicircle around him.

Afterward, Angry Bear took Joseph aside as Joseph's family boarded the carriage. "I am old and alone. I wish to die in the valley in the mountains," he said. "Will you help me?"

Angry Bear's black eyes had lost their sheen. On closer inspection, Joseph could see the rheumy look of them. "Of course. I'll be back first thing in the morning."

Angry Bear nodded his head once to Joseph and turned to the lodge. Joseph watched Angry Bear's proud bearing as he strode at a slightly slower pace than as of old with shoulders not quite as squared back as in his youth. Joseph knew Angry Bear had loved his mother very much. Her death had knocked the fierceness of his pride to a sullen sobriety.

The next morning, the traverse up the Appalachian mountains was a quiet one. Joseph wondered that Angry Bear did not tire on the steep hike more than he did. Joseph felt himself winded by the dizzying heights of the trail.

When the top of the mountain splayed into a wide valley, Joseph's breath caught in his throat at the beauty of it. No wonder his mother and Angry Bear had not wanted to leave. No wonder this was where Angry Bear wanted to die, the place where Angry Bear and Joseph's mother had finally found their peace together.

After Angry Bear settled his things in the old lodge, he returned to say goodbye to Joseph.

Joseph clasped Angry Bear's hand with both of his. "I'll come to look in on you from time to time." Joseph said.

"There will be no need of that. I won't be here that long. I am old; the animals will see to my burial," Angry Bear said as he placed his free hand atop Joseph's hands. "Thank you." He studied Joseph's face. "Your father once said 'thank you' to me. He was a good man. He once helped my son. Now his son has helped me. You, too, are a good man."

≫·58·≪

1861
Rural Retreat, Virginia

Olivia jostled on the hard wooden seat beside Jacob as her
thoughts lingered on the death of her grandmother. They'd both
been quiet on the bumpy wagon ride from Wytheville to Jacob's
farm in Rural Retreat. It was not until they arrived at the edge of
the Kimberlin farm that the excitement of the new life she would
begin with Jacob as her husband set in.
She gazed along the valley of grassy hills nestled in the sentinel
of the Blue Ridge mountains covered with mountain laurel, dogwood, rhododendron, trailing arboreta, and violet that would
be her home.
   She could see Jacob out of the corner of her eye sitting
straight-backed and deftly handling the reins, his straight nose
and firm jaw silhouetted against the blue sky. His dark hair curled
slightly below his ears. She didn't have to see his eyes to know
their steely blueness. From the fine crinkle lines, she knew those
eyes were twinkling.
   They wound their way along the wagon track on the Kimberlin
acres passing fields of cotton, corn, tobacco, and wheat. Vast
patches of green were dotted with cattle grazing. It had been so

many years since she had visited here with her parents, she had forgotten how large it was.

At last she could see the house set atop the highest hill among the acres. As they approached, the upstairs windows flashed the reflected sun as if winking to her. The wide porch with its stately pillars seemed to stretch its arms in welcome.

Jacob turned to smile proudly at her as he reined the horse to a halt in front of the porch. A uniformed slave rushed out of the house and took the reins. "Mornin', Sam," Jacob called to him. Jacob gestured to Olivia as he alit from the wagon. "This is my wife," he called over his shoulder as he walked around to her side of the wagon. "Olivia, this is Sam."

Sam bent his tall, lanky frame in a nod to her. "Welcome, Missus."

Olivia took Jacob's hand as he helped her from the wagon. "I'm very pleased to meet you, Sam," she said.

A broad grin spread across Sam's face.

With a flourish, Jacob lifted her from her feet and carried her across the threshold into their home. He set her down inside a very great hall. "My great-grandfather built it large to hold all the parishioners. Sunday services were held here before he built his first church."

In the parlor, Jacob strode over to a mahogany drop-front desk and laid his hand on it. "This is where all the inside business of the farm is handled." He beamed down at it and slid his hand along the worn wood.

"It's beautiful, Jacob. Everything is beautiful." She, too, stroked the antique desk. She would live in the same house that Jacob's great-grandparents, Elizabetha Kimberlin and her husband, Martin, had built. Olivia and Jacob were the fourth generation of Kimberlins and Blakemores in America. The two families had been intertwined in each others' lives for all these years and now, with their marriage, the families were one.

Olivia glanced around the comfortable parlor furnished in French Victorian. Several chairs with balloon-shaped backs along with whorl-footed tables with oval-shaped tabletops of marble were strategically placed for conversation around a large, upholstered sofa with a cartouche-shaped medallion comprising the center backrest. A winding staircase led to the upper floor.

Olivia twirled around to survey the entire room, nearly knocking over a slave woman who had entered with a tray of refreshments. "Oh my, I'm sorry," Olivia said as she reached her hand out to help the slave steady the tray.

Jacob came to their rescue, took the tray, and put it on the nearest tabletop. "Olivia, this is Mattie, head house slave. Mattie, meet the mistress of Kimberlin farms."

"Pleased to meet you Missus. It's been a long time since dey was a missus on de place. Not since dis boy's mama died when he was jes borned. I was jes a young gal then. Long before me and my man, Sam, jumped the broom."

Olivia instantly liked the talkative Mattie who seemed to be of an age somewhere between thirty and forty. A black bandana matching her uniform was neatly bound around her head. She was full-bodied and nearly as tall as Sam, and had an infectious, generous grin. "I'm truly pleased to meet you, Mattie," Olivia said and meant it.

Later that day while alone in the master bedroom, Olivia's heart was still full of the tranquility of the myriad generations this house had held. What stories these walls could tell. She glanced around and spotted the four-poster bed. The bed that she would tonight share with Jacob.

Olivia kneeled before the dresser and tucked the journal of Elizabetha Kimberlin that her grandmother had given to her into the bottom drawer.

Tears streamed down her cheeks as she mourned the loss of the grandmother she had only known for a few months but had come to love. Her death had cast a menacing pall on their wedding day. What if it portended disaster for their marriage?

Jacob entered the room and set down the last box of her belongings. He stood and turned to her. "Olivia, you've been crying." He strode to her side and embraced her. He held her head against his chest. "There, there. I know how much you miss your grandmother. I do too."

Olivia nestled against Jacob's solidness and breathed in the fresh smell of his starched white shirt. She tilted her head back and gazed up into his steel-blue eyes. "Oh, Jacob, tell me my grandmother's death on our wedding day was not a bad omen. We will have a long and happy marriage together, won't we?"

"Of course, we will, my silly goose. Your grandmother gave us her blessing, didn't she? With that blessing, nothing can go wrong." He kissed the tip of her nose.

But things were not going well for the country. Soon after Abraham Lincoln became President, South Carolina seceded from the Union. Six other southern states quickly followed. These states joined together and formed a new nation which they named the Confederate States of America. They elected Jefferson Davis as the first president. More and more southern states joined the Confederacy. Virginia as a border state between the North and South was torn over whether to join her southern sisters in seceding or remain loyal to the Union they had been so instrumental in forming. Talk of war was everywhere.

⇒• 59 •⇐

But Easter Sunday came in spite of the talk of war, this year on March 31. After services at the Kimberlin Lutheran Church, Olivia anxiously awaited the arrival of her family for Easter dinner. It was the first social event she was to conduct since becoming mistress of the Kimberlin farm.

Olivia followed Mattie around from kitchen to parlor to hall, straightening an arrangement of gladioli here, surveying the savory dishes arrayed on the sideboard there, bumping into Mattie as she turned to head another direction.

"I swear, Missus, you's gonna be the death of me. Go get yo'self prettied up and out of my way. They's gonna be here any minute," Mattie said, thrusting her splayed hands upward.

As if on cue, there was a knock at the front door, and Sam went to answer it just as Jacob joined Olivia in the hall.

She just had time to check her upswept hair in the hall mirror before her family entered en masse.

Her father led the group. Only his gray-streaked sandy hair hinted at his age. His brown eyes twinkled as he escorted Olivia's mother into the hall with his hand at the small of her back. "Come along, Susannah." He bent his tall frame down to kiss Olivia on the forehead.

Olivia's mother gave her a hug and removed her bonnet and brushed back a strand of blonde hair tinged here and there with wisps of gray that had fallen across her blue eyes.

Her oldest brother, Charles, approached Olivia next. "Hi, Sis, you look great."

His warm, plump wife, Mary, gave Olivia a peck on the cheek. Her pale blue eyes scanned the hall with obvious approval. "It's lovely, Olivia."

Their slim five-year-old son, Guy, trailed behind Charles and Olivia's thirteen-year-old brother, William, a spitting image of their father with sandy hair and brown eyes and equally as tall. He had the skin coloring of their grandmother Olive, giving him a swarthy, devil-may-care appearance.

Guy stood for a moment just inside the hall. His brown eyes went round in awe of the wide space within. He hurried to catch up with his mother's skirts.

After enjoying their noonday Easter feast of ham, deviled eggs, glazed yams, and sundry dishes, the meal was concluded with William plopping a pitted olive atop Guy's nose, much to the amusement of everyone except Guy who buried his face against his mother's sleeve.

"Olivia," Jacob said. "Why don't the ladies and children enjoy some games in the parlor while we gentlemen discuss a bit of politics?"

Olivia was taken aback. Jacob had never dismissed her like this before. "But, Jacob, you know I'm certainly aware of politics."

"Yes, dear, but war is an indelicate subject and since women don't have the vote, your opinion is only of interest to me." A broad condescending smile crossed his face as he said this.

Olivia rose to her feet. Impervious to the wink Jacob sent her. "When women do get the vote, political discussion certainly wont center around war." She turned and trounced out of the room.

When the last of the ladies and youngsters had left, Jacob whistled. "I'll pay for that statement a long time, won't I?"

"Yes, you certainly will," Joseph answered and grinned.

"Tell us, Papa, how the Virginia Convention is moving on the question of secession," Charles said.

"They've been arguing it back and forth since February and seem to be no closer to a resolution. Lincoln's Inaugural Address infuriated those who wish for Virginia to join the Confederacy."

"How so?" Charles asked.

Joseph Blakemore drew a deep breath. "The secessionists believe that southern institutions, namely slavery, have lost all protection in the federal government due to Lincoln's election. Being a border state, it is not an easy decision for Virginia. The members of the convention have focused a great deal on amending and adopting the resolutions from the report of the Committee on Federal Relations. Hopefully in April the document will be finalized and submitted to the federal government."

But before the document could be finalized, the sight of the United States flag flying on the Union's Fort Sumter at the mouth of Charleston Harbor was an affront to the South. President Lincoln alerted South Carolina in advance that he was sending supplies to Fort Sumter. South Carolina feared a trick and demanded the surrender of the Fort. The Garrison commander refused. On April 12, 1861, the Confederate States of America opened fire on Fort Sumter. On April 13, the Fort surrendered. The South saw this incident as an act of coercion by the North. A few days later, Virginia seceded from the Union. The war was on.

Jacob and Olivia were visiting her parents in Wytheville when Olivia's brother Charles and his wife and son arrived at the house to bring the news. Charles finished with the words, "I hoped Mary and Guy could stay here with you, Mama, I'm going to join the fighting."

"Not without me," Jacob said and clasped a hand on Charles's shoulder.

Olivia ran to Jacob's side and clutched his arm. "Please, Jacob, no. We've only been married a little over a month."

Olivia's father rose from the sofa and said, "I'll join you."

"Joseph, no," her mother cried out. "Please don't. Leave this nasty fighting to the young men. Think of your age. You're fifty-seven after all."

"The fighting won't last long. The North doesn't have the heart for it. Once they see we mean business, it will all be over in no more than ninety days," Olivia's father pronounced.

That afternoon, the three returned from enlistment. Olivia's father was the only one looking glum.

"What's wrong, Joseph?" her mother asked.

"You'll have your wish after all, Dear. They said I'm too old, and, oh, something about a heart murmur or some such."

Susannah's eyes flung wide.

"Now don't you worry," Joseph said. "I'll be staying home."

"Thank God." Susannah threw her arms around Joseph and brushed a tear from the corner of her eye.

When Jacob returned later that afternoon with his belongings, he looked so determined and proud as he sat his horse, sword and pistol at his sides. His steel-blue eyes glinted in the sun and his brown hair glistened. Olivia held onto his thigh as if she could deter him from his stated determination to join the southern forces.

Olivia's brother Charles sat high astride his horse. His wife, Mary, wrung her hands. Guy, hung onto his mother's skirts.

Olivia's brother William was being cradled against the hip of their mother. Olivia knew her mother was giving silent thanks that her thirteen-year-old was too young and her husband was too old.

As the two men rode off, Olivia prayed that it would all be over quickly as her father had said. She felt very certain that all of them standing there waving and watching the men in their lives ride off to war were praying the same thing.

Joseph and the women stood silently for a long time after the men were out of sight. Olivia's father broke the silence. "You must fetch your things and stay here, too, Olivia. You shouldn't be alone way out there on the farm."

"No, Papa, our overseer, Kendricks, can see to the fields, but I'm needed to see to the house and the slaves. I'll be going home."

⤞60⤝

A month after arriving home, Olivia knew she was with child. She had been delighted to learn that her sister-in-law, Mary, was also expecting. Wouldn't Jacob and Charles be surprised when they returned in a few months?

But the months came and went and the men did not return. No longer did anyone believe the war would be over quickly. Blockades reduced the imports into the South to a trickle.

The stocky overseer, Kendricks, was standing at the bottom of the porch stairs waiting for Olivia to instruct him as to how to handle the planting with the loss of field hands that had run off. He brushed a stray strand of mousy-brown hair off his forehead, held his finger to the side of his nose, and blew. A habit that turned Olivia's stomach. She interlaced her fingers across the top of her swelling belly and said, "We'll need to turn the fields into vegetable gardens to feed the army." She knew that was what most of the farms had been doing. "And to feed ourselves," she added.

On January 2, 1862, Mary was delivered of another son, Lewis. The following month, Olivia's mother and Mary and the children came to the farm to stay with Olivia until she gave birth. Olivia greeted them at their carriage. She could tell her mother had been crying. "What is it, Mama?"

Susannah hugged her daughter to her. She stepped back and wiped at her swollen eyes with her hankie. "It's William, Olivia. He's run off to join the fighting. He left us a note. I'm so worried. He's just fourteen. Your father is sick about it too."

Olivia's heart weighed heavily in her chest at the news of her younger brother fighting in this awful war. She put her arm around her mother's shoulder. "There, there, William's a feisty fellow. Those Northerners will wish he hadn't joined the fighting. Don't you worry." But Olivia knew her mother would worry just as she would.

Two weeks later, Olivia's labor began early in the morning. The pains gripped her hard and she called for her mother. Her mother sat by Olivia's bed through the day, wiping at Olivia's perspiration-soaked face and neck throughout the long afternoon. But it was Olivia's sister-in-law, Mary, who assisted with the delivery. With deft hands, Mary gently held the newborn and lightly smacked its bottom then gave the child to Susannah to be cleaned and swaddled while Mary saw to Olivia. After Olivia was cleaned up and helped into a clean shift by Mary, her mother handed her the baby. She carefully peeked beneath the swaddling and checked that he had all of his digits. Satisfied her son was perfect she settled back with him cradled in her arm. Her first child, Emmet.

Olivia had written Jacob about the birth of their son, but she had no answer back. The mail to and from the troops was often delayed for months. The war wore on and on.

Too bad that women didn't have the vote. Wouldn't they put an end to the foolishness of war? Olivia thought. The Women's Rights Movement seemed to have been put on a back burner since the war started. But the caring of her small son, Emmet, and the demands of the Kimberlin farm kept her focus on the war. Equality for women must wait.

⇛•61•⇚

1865

By April, after four years of war, Jacob couldn't remember being more scared than he had been since joining the fighting. He and Olivia's brother Charles occupied a section of a trench filled with Confederate soldiers, a sea of gray and butternut uniforms supplemented with items of Union blue taken from the enemy. Each soldier's knapsack, haversack, and ammunition boxes were piled beside him. Their .57 caliber Enfield rifles and a few smoothbore muskets were stacked against the dirt sides of the muddy trench.

The trench was deep enough for a man to stand erect and not be exposed to enemy fire. A fire step to stand on while firing was propped against the trench wall beside each man. The stench of unwashed bodies, including Jacob's, hung like an ominous fog above them. They were among the infantry of General Lee's Northern Virginia Army.

The Confederate soldiers faced the Federal soldiers who formed a semicircle more than forty miles long; the northern tip, opposite Richmond and the southern tip curling around Petersburg. The Yanks were trying to cut the railroads that led south and had spread their troops to the west. The Confederate army was stretched thin trying to cover them.

Jacob perched on a chunk of log, scraping idly at his mud-encrusted boots with his spiked bayonet. It had been a year after the birth before he had received Olivia's letter that he was a father. He still couldn't fathom it.

The acrid smell of stale sweat pierced his nostrils. Jacob stood and poked his nose into the air that wafted over the trench. It was moist and smelled of wet dirt, reminding him of his farm back home. He envisioned Olivia rocking beside him on the porch in the coolness of an evening. A lifetime ago.

Someone beside him in the trench coughed and spit, just missing his boot. Jacob kicked dirt—Bor rather mud—over the phlegm. It had rained steadily for days and finally had let up. The Virginia mud oozed everywhere.

Jeremy, the unit gagster, was a thin, buck-toothed kid from Tennessee. He called out his favorite comment, "Slim, If ever anybody was to ask us if we'd been through Virginia, what could we say?"

"Yes, sir! In a number of places," the chunky Kentuckian, Slim, dutifully replied. The two clowns laughed raucously. The Virginians just smiled.

Jacob sat back down on his log, his thoughts turning back to more serious considerations. He'd been thinking of the camp rumor that General Lee intended to make a sudden attack on the Federal center lines now that it was spring and they could move again. The Union army was nearly double their own. If they could punch a hole in the Union army and break the military railroad that supplied General Grant's army, the Union's left flank would have to be pulled back to avoid being cut off.

The Confederates could march south to join General Johnston in his fight against General Sherman. After that defeat, General Lee and General Johnston could return and fight General Grant on equal terms. It was unlikely, but it was their only chance. The South was losing the war. They seemed to be fighting out of sheer will as if in a trance.

Jacob's stomach growled. He reached into his haversack and unwrapped a greasy slab of salt pork, its rancid smell nauseating. He pulled out a chunk of coarse corn bread. There were chewed holes in the wrapper. The vermin had gotten to it before him as usual. He bit off a mouthful of the salt pork and followed its saltiness with a bite of the stale, dry cornbread, washing it all down with a swig from his cold cup of acorn ersatz coffee. There hadn't been much meat and no fruit or vegetables available for a long time. The army couldn't supply them and the land was too devastated to yield them.

Early in the war, the Army issued sacks of flour and rations the soldiers had to prepare themselves. Most had no idea how to make a meal from the raw components. Some of the wealthy officers and large plantation owners had brought slaves with them to do their cooking. Jacob and Charles's unit had pooled their rations and hired a cook, as many of the other units did.

It was March 25, Jacob remembered, Olivia's birthday. He wondered how she'd celebrate. She would be twenty-three today. God, how he missed her sweet face with its turned-up nose. The vision of her brown eyes swam before him. They'd had little more than a month together before he went off to war. Jacob missed the clean smell of her and her sweet low laugh. All he smelled now was sweat, mud, fear, and the sulphur smell of gun powder. First thing he wanted to do when he got home was to bury his face in Olivia's thick brown hair and inhale until the stench of war was forgotten.

Sergeant Gable appeared at the trench. The Sergeant was a burly Virginia trapper. His butternut uniform was splattered with mud around the trouser bottoms. He always wore his kepi tilted sideways on his head. It was a blue Union kepi, one he'd taken off a dead Yank, the same as Jacob had replaced his kepi. The sergeant's beard and mustache were stained from tobacco juice from a time when tobacco had been available. His husky voice barked, "General Gordon has been ordered by General Lee to attack the Federal Fort Stedman. Get your gear ready. We'll strike at daybreak."

At dawn, the fiery young Georgian General Gordon ordered the attack. He waved his sword above his head as he led his men into battle. As they ran toward the fort, Jacob ripped open a paper package of powder with his teeth, poured it down the muzzle, stuffed in a minie' ball from his pocket, and rammed it down. He put a percussion cap on the weapon lock nipple, cocked it, and squeezed the trigger, dropping a Union soldier who had poked his head above the fence. The confederates stormed through the gate. The surprise attack had caught the Yanks off guard and the Confederates easily carried the fort. General Gordon ordered Jacob's patrol to head back toward the railroad to seize a portion of Federal trenches.

The Kentuckian Slim and his buddy Jeremy each tossed a grenade into the first trench they came to. They were the only two who had any grenades left. Jacob leaped into the trench, shoving dead Yanks out of his way, with Charles right behind him. The rest of the patrol jumped in behind them.

The surviving Yanks in the trench attacked the intruders with bayonets and knives. A Yank lunged at Charles with his bayonet hoisted as Jacob whacked the back of the Yank's head with the butt of his rifle. The Yank rolled over onto his back. His eyes stared sightlessly. He was dead. He wasn't more than sixteen. That would be the age of Olivia's brother, William, now. Jacob knew that Charles had received a letter from home that William had run off to join the war. Jacob said a silent prayer for him.

Heavy artillery from the Union Rebs soared overhead. Yanks from both ends of the trench swarmed down on the patrol. Panic surged through Jacob's veins like ice water, chilling his entire body. The Confederate patrol began to desert the trench. Jacob and Charles glanced at each other. At the same instant, both abandoned their position.

When Jacob cleared the trench, he winced as he felt a hot searing pain tear into his left calf. He fell to the ground. It felt as if his whole leg had exploded. He could see Charles running ahead. He tried to drag himself, but the leg wouldn't work, it just hung there as if the bone were gone. The pain traveled up from the leg, engulfing his whole body in a cold sweat of agony.

Someone was lying on the ground next to him, face down in a pool of spreading blood. Jacob rolled the soldier over and saw it was Slim. Half of the front of his head was blown away. Jacob tried not to gag. He had liked Slim. Damn the war.

A soldier ran past Jacob's shoulder and pivoted in midair from the impact of the minie' ball which caught him in the back and came out his stomach. The soldier's entrails oozed from the gaping hole and he tried to stuff them back. Jacob recognized him. It was Jeremy. Jacob tried to crawl to him. Another minie' caught Jeremy in the throat and he fell to the ground and didn't move.

Any minute Jacob expected the Yanks to finish him off. He thought of Olivia and remembered how funny she had been when she found out she had Indian blood, as if he didn't know. He reached down to his calf and stared at the bloodstains his hand came away with. He hoped Olivia would find happiness with someone else. When would that next shot come? He was just lying here waiting for them to kill him. There was nothing left to do now, but pray it would be quick. The pain in his leg was excruciating.

A soldier crept along the mud toward Jacob, taking cover behind fallen soldiers as he came. It was Charles. He'd come back for him.

Jacob managed a faint smile. "Thank God," Jacob uttered. Even if he'd had the strength, he couldn't find words to express his gratitude for Charles's bravery and loyalty.

Charles secured Jacob's arm across his shoulder by the wrist and supported his back as he dragged him through the mud. Jacob helped push himself with his good leg, until at last they reached the Confederate lines.

⇉•62•⇇

Safely in Reb territory, Charles got Jacob to the outside field
hospital and laid him on a blood-slippery door that had been
placed atop barrels. Jacob spied the tub underneath nearly full
of dark red blood. The sickly sweet smell made his stomach flip-
flop. A grotesque pile of arms and legs stood to the side. Jacob
cringed at the gore. He leaned over the edge of the door and
vomited. He wiped his mouth with his sleeve and shakily settled
back against the bloody slab.

The surgeon wiped the sweat from his high forehead as he
strode toward Jacob. The surgeon put a finger to the side of his
hawk-like nose and graced the ground with its contents. Only
then did the tall, gangly surgeon turn his attention to Jacob.

Jacob didn't like the way the surgeon studied his leg. The surgeon shook his head. "That minie' ball has shattered the shin."
The surgeon set his finger to the other nostril and blew. "I'll have
to amputate."

Jacob's mouth went slack. He screamed. "No. Don't take it
off. No." But a hand from nowhere put a foul-smelling rag over
his nose and mouth. He didn't see anything more.

Hours later Jacob woke up on a cot in the infirmary tent. For an instant he didn't know where he was. Then he remembered. The surgeon said he'd need to amputate. He must have been wrong for Jacob could still feel the pain in his leg. Surely he'd know if it was gone. He forced himself to look down at his legs. There was only one full-length lump under the thin blanket. Hot tears trickled from his eyes. He tried to stem the flow, but he couldn't help it. How cruel to lose the leg and still have the pain.

Jacob pushed himself up on his elbows and scanned the infirmary. Cots filled with wounded soldiers crowded the tent. One man had bloody bandages around his eyes and was being led by another soldier with only one arm. Another, had a sheet propped up above his burned body. The man made low moaning noises over and over. Jacob leaned back and squeezed the tears from his eyes. What a sorry bunch of Southern gentlemen they were, none of them fit to fight or even fit to live.

Charles approached and put his hand on Jacob's shoulder.

Jacob peered up through his tears at Charles's dark brown eyes with their dark circles beneath as if he hadn't slept for a long while. Charles's dark hair hung limply across his forehead.

"You look as bad as I feel," Jacob said.

"You don't look so good yourself, but at least you're awake, and safe now." Charles smiled down at Jacob.

"Thanks for coming back for me, but you probably should have just left me. I'll not be good for anything now." Jacob glanced at the lump and a half beneath the blanket. Tears gathered in his eyes again. He brushed them away. He wouldn't cry, not anymore, not ever.

Screams came from outside the tent.

"They've run out of chloroform. It's only whiskey and a bullet to bite on now for amputations," Charles said.

Jacob shuddered. He was exhausted and must have fallen back to sleep before Charles even left.

When he woke up the next morning, Jacob looked down at his legs. Still only a leg and a half. He'd hoped it had only been a nightmare. He'd rather be dead than be an invalid. How could Olivia ever let him touch her again? He was only half a man. It would have been easier just to die out on the field. How could he bear to see Olivia look at him with pity in her eyes instead of the love that had glowed from them? He cursed the surgeon. He cursed the Yanks. He even cursed General Lee.

On the evening of April 2, Charles came to Jacob and said, "General Lee has ordered evacuation of Petersburg and Richmond. General Grant has broken through the Confederate lines. We're marching on to join General Johnston's fight against General Sherman, but you're going home with the other wounded."

* * *

Olivia glanced up from her hoeing. The last of the slaves had run off last year and she had been able to keep up with only one small patch of garden. Three-year-old Emmet was asleep inside the house. The sunshine was so bright her eyes watered. Someone was walking up the willow-lined lane toward the house. It was a soldier, a Confederate soldier she thought, but couldn't be sure. Part of his clothing was a dirty Confederate gray, but part of it was Union blue. He walked stiffly.Then she noticed the wooden leg strapped to where his left calf should have been. This awful, awful war. All those poor soldiers on both sides, maimed or dead. He'll probably want something to eat. She'd see what she could give him, poor soul. She peered closer. Her breath caught in her lungs and refused to exhale. There was something familiar about the figure. Jacob. It was Jacob. A swallow lodged in her throat. Her heart seemed to pound its fists against her chest to be free and run to him.

Olivia threw down the hoe and ran up the lane. Jacob was home. Her Jacob was home. He was alive.

When she neared Jacob, he stopped.

Olivia hesitated. There was something different in Jacob's appearance besides the mismatched clothes and the new chin whiskers and mustache he now wore. It was the eyes. They were harder somehow with dark circles underneath. He frowned, perhaps from the bright sunlight filtering through the willows.

Jacob yanked off his kepi and opened his arms to her, his oily hair matted to his head.

Olivia ran to him and threw her arms around his neck. "Jacob," was all she could say. Her heart thumped in her chest as if doing leaps into air. His bony ribs poked into her flesh. He reeked of sweat and dirt. His clothes were but filthy rags, hardly a uniform at all. She didn't care how he looked or smelled. He was home at long last and in her arms.

Jacob unloosed her hair, burying his face in it. As someone who'd just crossed a long, hot dessert, he inhaled the scent of her hair as if it could quench his thirst.

They stood clutching each other for several moments, neither of them able to speak. Olivia's whole body trembled. He was home. He was alive.

Jacob broke away first. "It's good to be home. First thing I need is a bath."

The rancid smell of him again engulfed her and her eyes watered. She waved her hand in front of her nose and laughed. "Yes, I think a bath is in order." The tears kept coming—not from the stench of him—but from her pure pleasure that he'd returned safely to her.

Jacob hauled water from the pump. Olivia dragged out the tub and poured some of the water into a large pot in the kitchen fireplace and poured the rest of the water into the tub. While the water heated, Olivia went upstairs for clean clothes for Jacob. She looked in on Emmet who was still sleeping. His tousled dark hair had fallen across his eyes. She lightly stroked it off his face and planted a kiss on his head. "Your father is home," she whispered.

When she returned, she found that Jacob had already poured the hot water in the tub. He had pulled a ladder-back chair to the side of the tub and was removing his rags.

After undressing and removing the wooden leg, Jacob swung his good leg over the rim of the tub, grabbed each side with his hands, and lowered himself into the water. The water instantly turned a murky gray and smelled of rancid soil.

Olivia tried to keep busy and not look at the stump, but she couldn't help it. A shiver ran up her spine. Poor Jacob. She distracted herself by pouring water over Jacob's matted hair.

After his bath, Jacob dressed and started to strap on the wooden leg as young Emmet came into the kitchen.

Emmet stopped mid step and gawked.

Jacob glanced from the boy to Olivia, puzzlement written across his face.

Olivia gathered Emmet to her and said, "Jacob, this is your son, Emmet." Olivia bent down in front of Emmet. "Meet your father, Emmet. Remember I told you he was fighting in the war? Well, he's come home."

Jacob finished strapping on the leg. He held out his arm toward Emmet. "Come here, son," he said in a low tone.

Emmet searched his mother's face as she nodded her agreement. Finally he made his way to the man whom his mother had said was his father.

Jacob embraced Emmet. Tears welled in Jacob's eyes as he glanced over his son's head at Olivia.

Later that night as they prepared to retire, Olivia was uneasy as she brushed her long thick hair. Jacob had stared at her all through supper and the evening. She felt as if she were walking on broken glass, fearing she'd say or do something that might upset him. She held a hank of her dark hair to brush the tangles out of the ends.

Jacob removed his shirt and put on his nightshirt. He undid the straps on his wooden leg, gazing over at her occasionally as if to see if she were watching. Olivia concentrated on her brushing. Jacob removed his trousers and climbed into the four-poster bed. Olivia finished brushing her hair and slipped in beside him. She felt tense. From her peripheral vision, Olivia could see Jacob staring up at the ceiling as she was.

"Relax," Jacob said. "You could be mistaken for a bed slat you're so stiff."

Olivia hadn't meant to be so rigid, but she couldn't help it. And she couldn't stop it.

Jacob grabbed her arm and forced Olivia's hand to the stump. "Feel it. It won't bite you," Jacob ordered.

Olivia tried to be nonchalant as she gingerly ran her finger-tips across the scar. Jacob gazed intently at her the while.

Jacob grabbed both Olivia's shoulders and roughly lowered himself on top of her. He smothered her mouth and neck in kisses. She put one arm around his back, and with the other ran her fingers through his clean-smelling hair. They kissed passion-ately for several moments. Jacob ran his calloused hands under her shift and caressed her breasts and hips. Her body ached for him. It had been such a long time. She savored the warmth of his touch on her. He spread her legs with his good leg and stump. Just as she prepared for him to take her, he rolled off her and onto his back. She gaped at him and thought she saw one tear glisten at the corner of his eye, but then it was gone. "Jacob?"

"I can't," he said and rolled to his side facing away from her.

Olivia lay still. She remained afraid to move until she heard Jacob's heavy, even breathing. He was asleep at last. Olivia turned to her side and put her pillow against her face to muffle her sobs.

The next morning Olivia ate her grits at the kitchen table. Jacob had finished his and watched as she ate. Several times he started to speak.

Olivia avoided his gaze. She was unsure of what she should say or do. She felt as if they were strangers.

As Olivia rose from the table, Jacob grabbed her hand and held it tightly.

Olivia turned to him. She didn't know what to expect. The pain she saw in Jacob's blue eyes tore at her heart.

"I'm sorry for last night."

Olivia put her other hand on top of Jacob's and said, "It wasn't your fault. It's just that we've been apart so long. It'll take time to get reacquainted."

"Yes, time," Jacob said.

≫•63•≪

In May, Charles had returned home from the war as well. Jacob and Olivia planned to visit Charles and his wife, Mary. Jacob fastened on his wooden leg, a contraption of wood strips which extended up his thigh and was kept in place with leather straps. The wood strips extended down and joined at the bottom into a single unit upon which to stand. The leg stump rested on a padded, wooden platform in the middle of the wood strips, secured by a wide leather band. It was clumsy, but at least Jacob could get around. Each day he cursed the loss of his leg.

Jacob pulled on a brown brogan and stood. He put his black vest over his white cotton shirt, donned his tie and black frock coat, and secured his pocket watch before clumping downstairs.

Jacob found Olivia in the parlor. She looked handsome in her dark-green full skirts with matching jacket, pleated in front with long sleeves puffed at the shoulder. Beneath, she wore a light green blouse with a high collar and cameo pinned at the throat. Both of them were dressed in clothes from before the war. Material as well as everything else was hard to come by now.

"Are you ready to go?" Jacob asked. He still hadn't been able to make love to Olivia and hated himself. What if he never could again?

After supper, Olivia and Mary and the children retired to the parlor. Charles and Jacob stayed in the dining room for a second cup of coffee and conversation.

Jacob had been anxious all through supper to learn from Charles about the ending of the war. "How bad was it at the end, Charles?"

"I tell you, Jacob, those last days were hell. With the confusion around the Richmond evacuation, the army's rations never got to us. We pushed on, though, staying with the colors only because of General Lee himself, I think. The Federals were at our flanks and our rear all the way as we tried to join forces with General Johnston and they finally attacked at Sayler's Creek, taking half our army as prisoners."

Charles rose and walked to the buffet and removed a bottle of brandy from the top. He decanted the brandy and poured some into two glasses, handing one to Jacob. "Last of the lot I'm afraid," Charles said gesturing a toast in mid air with his glass as he handed the second brandy to Jacob.

Jacob gestured back with his glass and inhaled the fermented peach aroma. He took a sip, letting the warm golden liquid slide down his throat.

Charles continued, "On April 9, at Appomattox Court House, the few of us left were surrounded. We were worn-out. Then General Lee flew the white flag and a sudden quiet descended on the battlefield. It was hard to comprehend that the war was over." Charles gazed off into space.

Jacob interrupted Charles's reverie, "I wonder why Lee surrendered instead of telling the troops to disband, take to the hills, and carry on guerilla warfare as long as there was a Yank below the Mason and Dixon line."

"That would have caused an enduring bitterness and hatred, I think. Descendants on both sides forever after would keep committing atrocities on one another. No, it's better this way. General Lee knew what he was doing."

Charles reached for the coffee pot. "Warm up your coffee?"

"Thanks," Jacob said.

Charles filled both cups and set the pot down. "The Confederacy had been fighting for an accepted place in the family of nations, but that fight was finally lost. Now we must make the best of what remains to us and become one nation. General Lee made the right decision." Charles raised his glass in a toast. "To General Lee," he said.

"To General Lee," Jacob said raising his own glass. "The papers say General Grant wrote the pledge the Union and Confederacy signed so that General Lee and, therefore, no lesser Confederate could be hanged. The South would have never forgiven the hanging of General Lee."

"Doesn't it make you pause to ponder that the fate of a nation can hang on the decisions of two generals on the battlefield, one victor and one surrendering, and both war-weary?" Charles asked.

"Amen," Jacob agreed. "God willing, may there never be such a war again."

Charles took a long sip of brandy. He bent his head. "Now with President Lincoln dead, I'm afraid there will still be a lot of hatred and hard times for us all. Nothing in this war has gone the way men planned it. The Almighty had His own purposes."

⇒·64·⇐

1866

Susannah Blakemore had no purpose left in life. The few old Negroes who'd chosen to stay after the Emancipation held the reins of the horses hitched to carriages beneath a spreading elm. Susannah stood silently as the gray Virginia mist wrapped wispy tendrils around the small group gathered at the graveside and watched as the headstone was set in place:

Joseph Samuel Blakemore
beloved husband and father
born 1804 died 1866

A lifetime, Susannah thought, summed up in so few words. Tears streamed down her face under the heavy black veil. How could she survive this? How could she go on without him? Her husband had been her life. She was devoted to him. He was ten years older and ten years wiser than she. He had counseled and consoled her their whole life together. She felt so—alone—so empty. Oh, Joseph, why did you go?

Her thoughts went back thirty-three years to the day Joseph had proposed to her. How he had courted her with flowers. She remembered the Sunday he proposed, and the bouquet of ivy, blue morning glory, and straw. She had felt such happiness.

She had been so glad when he'd not been able fight in the war. But his heart failed him in the end. How she missed him!

Susannah swayed. She glanced around at family and friends gathered at the grave side and her vision grew smaller and smaller as the darkness crept in. She fainted in a heap of black, billowing skirts.

Susannah awoke in her bed to the sound of Dr. Wellings telling her family she needed rest. The ordeal had been too much for her. He would leave a sedative. What ordeal? She wondered. Then she remembered. She sobbed into her bed covers, "Joseph. Oh Joseph."

A few weeks later, Mary and Charles arrived. They or Olivia and Jacob came each day to look in on Susannah and try to get her to eat and talk. None of them understood that she didn't care about eating or talking. She missed Joseph terribly. Nothing else mattered.

Charles pulled the rocking chair up to Susannah's bed and sat down. Susannah tried to sit up, but Charles put his hand on her shoulder and said, "Mama, just lie there a minute, you're getting so weak, we're all worried about you."

Charles patted Susannah's hand. "I wanted to prepare you that I've asked Dr. Wellings to stop in to see you. He'll be here in a short while."

"Charles, don't bother about me. I'm just weary."

Charles smiled at Susannah. "It won't hurt for him to examine you, will it? Here, let us help you to sit up so you'll be all ready."

Charles got up, moved the rocker back, and leaned her forward while Mary placed a second pillow behind Susannah's head. Susannah shook with cold. "I'm so chilled, Mary, please fetch my shawl."

Mary, came back with the shawl, wrapped it around Susannah's shoulders, and said, "There, the doctor should be here soon."

Susannah closed her eyes and rested her head against the headboard. She had awakened this morning drenched in tears again. She remembered her dream. She and Joseph were standing beside Wallen Creek. She smiled up at him. Joseph put his arms around Susannah and kissed her forehead. He said, "Everything will be all right, my darling." Joseph embraced Susannah for a moment, then took her by the shoulders, held her a bit away, and gazed into her eyes. "Let's go for a walk," he said.

Joseph took Susannah's hand as they ambled along the path. He stopped and picked some morning glories and handed them to her saying, "The alphabet of angels, remember?"

"Yes. They're beautiful," Susannah said and cradled them against her breast. Oh, yes, how she remembered.

Joseph took Susannah's hand again. They walked along, the creek on their right and the woods on their left. Joseph whistled the popular tune, "Jim Crow," as they strolled. Susannah smiled at him, and Joseph squeezed her hand for a silent I love you. Susannah squeezed his back for her own "I love you, too."

There was a low wailing as the wind ruffled through the thick growth. An uneasiness ran through Susannah's heart. The wind grew stronger, and the woods loomed larger. The woods became denser and darker. The back of Susannah's neck tingled. The wind howled. The world turned black. Joseph disappeared. She was left wandering alone in the blackness searching for him. She called and called his name, "Joseph, Joseph." But there was no answer. Susannah woke up frightened. She'd had that dream so often.

Susannah opened her eyes, startled by the knock on the door. Charles let Dr. Wellings into Susannah's bedroom. She attempted to straighten her shawl and bed covers but didn't have the energy. Even the tears that filled her eyes seemed too difficult to wipe away. She blinked to keep them from falling, to no avail.

"How are you feeling today, Susannah?"

Dr. Wellings was a kind middle-aged man with a paunch. His black, bushy eyebrows formed a continuous line above both eyes. Between his brows and his muttonchops, he seemed mostly hair. He meant well.

"Tired," she answered.

"Well, let's take a look at you." Dr. Wellings listened to her heart, took her pulse, and said, "How's your appetite?"

Mary answered for her, "She barely eats a thing, Doctor, just sips a bit of tea."

"I think it's best if you just stay in bed until you feel stronger, Susannah. Promise you'll try to eat some soup along with your tea."

"I don't care about eating. I'm so tired. I just want Joseph back. I miss him so."

"I know, I know," Dr. Wellings said and patted her shoulder.

Mary removed the second pillow under Susannah's head. Susannah settled back in her bed. The big four-poster bed she and Joseph had always shared and brought with them from Tennessee.

Dr. Wellings walked out of the bedroom, and Charles and Mary followed him. "There's not much we can do for her except try to get some food in her," Susannah heard Dr. Wellings tell them. "Hopefully, you can find something that will spur her into wanting to go on."

Go on, she thought. How could she go on? She had nothing to go on for. She just wished they'd leave her alone. Oh, Joseph.

Mary brought in a tray after Dr. Wellings left. Susannah took a small sip of tea.

Mary had set a sprig of lilac in a small glass on the tray to cheer her, so Susannah managed a wan smile and said, "The lilac smells nice."

Mary grinned.

Charles had followed Mary in. Charles's forehead was furrowed with worry. His brown eyes gazed tenderly at Susannah. Susannah wished she could make him understand. She gestured away Mary's offering of the soup spoon and allowed her hand to flutter down to the bed covers.

Charles paced the length of the bedroom and back. He was tall and straight like Joseph. Charles stopped beside her bed and said, "Mama, please try to eat." You've got to get your strength back. When you're feeling better, we can drive over to Wallen Creek, and you can dip your feet in the cool water. You used to like that, Mama."

Susannah remembered her dream with Joseph. She smiled wearily and said, "I don't think so, Charles. I'm so tired. Let me be."

Mary took the tray out and returned with her crocheting. She sat on the rocker across from Susannah's bed and held up the pale green baby afghan she was making. Mary smiled. Her soft brown hair was pulled back in a bun at the nape of her neck. Her pale blue eyes gazed tenderly at Susannah and she said, "Look, Susannah, I'm nearly finished with it. Don't you think Olivia's new baby will be pleased when it's born? You'll be a grandmother again."

Susannah inclined her head toward Mary. "It's lovely, dear. I remember when Charles was born. Joseph was such a proud father. He grinned every time he looked at his son. His chest would swell with pride. I miss Joseph so." Susannah closed her eyes and slipped into reverie.

Several weeks passed and Susannah heard Charles, Mary, Olivia, and Jacob murmuring in the kitchen. Probably at the kitchen table discussing their worry over her. They didn't understand, she knew. Susannah didn't know how long she'd been asleep. Her head rested on her down pillow on her side of the big bed. Her eyes were closed. She slid her right arm over to the side where Joseph should have lain. Tears filled her tired eyes and slipped down her hot cheeks. She didn't bother to brush them away. She was so exhausted. She couldn't keep on with this emptiness, this awful aching in her heart. When would it ever stop?

Susannah's thoughts turned back to her and Joseph's youth. She saw him sitting on the grass beside the winding stream at her parents' home. Susannah's head rested on Joseph's lap, and he stroked her brow with his long fingers and gazed down at her. Joseph bent down and kissed Susannah. She returned his kiss and smiled. "I love you, Joseph."

"And I love you, my darling." Joseph took her hand, brought it to his lips, and caressed each finger. "Come on, let's take a carriage ride to Wallen Creek."

Joseph pulled Susannah to her feet. They ran to the waiting horse and carriage, and he helped her up onto the high seat. Joseph cantered to the other side and climbed up beside Susannah. They rode in silence for several miles, content just to be together.

Joseph flicked the whip. The sun broke up the gray mist and cast mottled shadows of the forest leaves across the dirt road and heavy haunches of the carriage horse.

Joseph stopped the carriage. Joseph and Susannah held hands and basked in their love. Overhead, two cardinals perched on a bough, their bills touched briefly as the female accepted her lover's offered morsel.

Joseph smiled and said, "Those cardinals are like us, Susannah, together forever."

Susannah gazed at Joseph. Her heart swelled with love for him. He was so wonderful, so handsome. He was radiant. A bright glow shone all around him, as if all heaven approved him. The glow brightened and brightened. It grew so bright, Susannah couldn't see Joseph any longer. Suddenly, she was back in her own bed. She searched for Joseph. Her heart raced.

But—wait, she could see him again now. Joseph floated just above her. He glowed and floated. And he smiled. His outstretched arm beckoned her to follow. Susannah reached her hand out to Joseph's. She smiled and whispered, "I'm coming, Joseph. I'm coming."

⇒ 65 ⇐

1871

A year after burying her mother, Olivia had given birth to Susie and in 1870, John was born. Olivia worried about what would become of them all. She had planted mostly vegetables during the war to sell to the Confederate army for the soldiers. Now the selling of the few vegetables to locals and Jacob's blacksmithing, which he'd learned from his father, barely sustained them. They couldn't handle the cotton crops without slaves, not with Jacob's wooden leg, and they couldn't afford to pay wages. They'd had to sell some land.

The noon sun shone through the kitchen window over the table where Jacob sat across from Olivia after dinner, his elbows on the table and his forehead propped up on his fists. He slammed one fist hard against the table top. "Damn the War. Damn this wooden leg. It's killing me to sell off papa's land bit by bit like this. This farm has been in the family since Martin Kimberlin first bought it," Jacob said.

"But we have no choice. We've three children to feed." Olivia walked over to the wood stove and poured more hot tea into their cups and sat back down. Olivia knew Jacob felt less than a whole man since the amputation. It had taken nearly three months after his return before Joseph could make love to her, and it hadn't been the same, he seemed as far away from her as he'd been during the war even though now he was home. She still didn't know how to reach him. She could feel him distancing himself from her more every day. It was as if the war had shattered their intimacy, not just Jacob's leg.

"We could always head for Texas," Olivia said, watching Jacob's reaction. She'd been thinking for a long time about her younger brother William who'd moved to Texas soon after the war and had tried to convince Jacob to consider moving there.

Jacob's eyebrow rose.

"William always writes how grand it is there and how he's doing so well. He says his grocery store is thriving and the community is growing."

Both Jacob's eyebrows were raised now.

"Maybe we should go to Texas and make a fresh start." Olivia hoped Jacob would listen this time. They needed a change.

"Texas, again." Jacob raked his hand across the top of his head from back to front then smoothed it back. "I don't know anymore. I just don't know."

The next week, Olivia and Jacob had invited her brother, Charles, and his wife, Mary, over for supper. Jacob had killed a chicken that morning for the occasion. Olivia had boiled it with red potatoes, carrots, and onions and prepared a thick chicken gravy.

At supper, Olivia washed the last bite of the tender breast of chicken down with a sip of water.

Charles pushed his plate back and said, "That was a fine supper, Olivia."

"Delicious," Mary said.

Jacob, still chewing, nodded his head toward Olivia and saluted her with his glass of water.

"Thank you all." Olivia grinned.

"I've received a letter from William in Greenville, Texas. Did you know his grocery store is going strong?" Charles asked Jacob.

"That's what Olivia's been saying." Jacob wiped his mouth

with his napkin and cast a suspicious glance at her.

Charles continued, "My general merchandise store has not done well since the war. So few goods are available that it's hard to make a living in the South these days."

"Time's are hard," Jacob agreed.

"William has invited me to join him in running his store. He wants to expand it to include general merchandise as well. I've been thinking about taking him up on it," Charles said.

Jacob glanced at Olivia.

"That's wonderful, Charles, I've been trying to convince Jacob to move to Texas. William says it is beautiful and the town is growing and is full of opportunities," Olivia said.

Olivia turned to Mary, "What do you think of it all, Mary?"

"I have some doubts, but all in all, I think Charles may be right." Mary reached over and put her hand on Charles's sleeve.

Charles patted her hand and turned to Jacob. "You should consider it seriously, Jacob. The three of us had some good times growing up together. We would make a great team in Texas."

"I'll think about it," Jacob said.

"I've been talking with a Mr. Murphy who's been in the store stocking up for a wagon train he's been putting together. They have ten wagons so far going to Arkansas in a few months. Greenville, Texas is just across the border."

Jacob fingered his water glass before taking a long sip.

At the breakfast table a week later, Olivia couldn't stand the suspense any longer. She said, "Jacob have you thought about Texas?"

"I've thought about it."

"In Texas we'd have a new start," Olivia added.

"Guess it couldn't be any worse. I could always do black-smithing there as well as here." Jacob drummed his fingers on the table. "What with Charles going and William already there, I suppose it wouldn't be so bad." Jacob stopped his drumming and peered at Olivia. "If you're so all-fired set on it, we'll go."

Olivia couldn't believe what she was hearing. It was the first

354

positive thing Jacob had said since he returned from the war. She went around to Jacob's side of the table, put her hands on his shoulders, and kissed the top of his head. "Things will be better in Texas, you'll see."

"Can't be any worse." Jacob put his right hand on top of the hand Olivia had on his left shoulder. Did he squeeze her hand, or was it just wishful thinking?

By the end of the month, Jacob had sold the last of the farm to a cousin. Jacob had been relieved that the bulk of the farm would stay in Kimberlin hands. Charles had sold his store to his wife's uncle. Charles and Jacob had made the arrangements to join the ten wagons heading to Arkansas. Jacob and Olivia could stay on at the farm until they left for Texas.

⇉•66•⇇

A few days later, Olivia, Jacob, Charles, and Mary were on their way to a meeting Mr. Murphy had arranged to provide them with details they would need on the trip to Texas. They drove in Charles's carriage out to the Murphy farm, and up a long winding drive to the Murphy's rambling home with its massive oak front door.

Mr. Murphy greeted them and invited them in. "Charles, Jacob, good to see you." Mr. Murphy shook their hands then turned to Olivia and Mary. "I'm Frank Murphy, ladies."

"This is my wife, Mary, and Jacob's wife, Olivia. Olivia is my sister as well," Charles said.

"Pleased to meet you. Come into the dining room and have a seat at the table and we'll get started."

The table was a heavy mahogany piece of simple lines. It smelled of lemon and pine soap. Olivia and Jacob sat on the brocade-covered seats of the mahogany chairs and Mary and Charles sat across. Mr. Murphy took his position at the head of the table.

"The wagon train elected me to be wagon master," Mr. Murphy explained. "I was a sergeant in the Confederate army."

Frank Murphy was a tall, broad man with hair and mutton-chops the color of carrots. He looked to be in his forties. He seemed quite capable and level-headed. He was straight to the point. Olivia thought he would be a good wagon master.

"Your two wagons can travel with the train as far as the Red River where you and the wagon of the scout for the train, headed further west, will go on alone," Mr. Murphy said.

There was a knock at the door, and Mr. Murphy rose to answer it. He returned to the dining room with a stranger. "Folks, this is the wagon scout, Mr. Shane. I asked him to drop over to give you his expertise on wagon trains. He's made the trip four times. He's heading back to Texas after delivering his cattle in Virginia."

Mr. Shane was a wiry, lean young man, not much older than Olivia's twenty-eight years. He sported a blond, drooping mustache and no beard. His face was pockmarked and wore a disdainful expression. Even when he smiled, his hard eyes did not. His shaggy straw-colored hair peeked out beneath his sweat-stained cowboy hat, a Stetson it was called. He did not remove it.

A square-jawed, and obviously independent woman strode into the dining room.

"Here is my wife, Amanda," Mr. Murphy said and half stood.

Amanda Murphy wore her hair, brighter red than her husband's, in a loose bun at the nape of her neck. Curly stubborn wisps escaped all around her head. She had a face full of freckles.

"Pleasure to meet you." Mrs. Murphy gave Olivia's hand a firm handshake and did the same with the other guests. She sat at the foot of the table.

Frank Murphy reclaimed his seat.

Mr. Shane remained standing. "Will you be taking covered farm wagons or Conestoga wagons?" he asked.

"Covered farm wagons," Jacob replied.

"Good, they're lighter and easier to handle. First thing is to patch any holes or rips there may be in the canvas. The winds will get rough on the open plains. Take along extra canvas if you can."

"We've done that. And I've repaired all the iron work on the wagons," Jacob said.

"Good. Mr. Murphy told me you were a blacksmith. Those skills will come in handy on the wagon train." Mr. Shane paced the length of the table then stopped and turned to face them. His right eyebrow raised as his cold gaze studied each person. "First, for the most important thing of all. Take only what you absolutely need. The lighter you keep your load, the better on the horses. It's a long, slow trip."

"Well, yes," Olivia said. "But surly we'll need to take all the belongings we can. After all, I'm sure your wife would want her things around her."

Mr. Shane peered at Olivia. "I'm a single man, Mrs. Kimberlin. I wouldn't know what a woman may want about her."

Olivia felt a surge of revulsion at his fish stare.

Mr. Shane continued, "As I was saying, It's a long, slow trip. Best keep your load light."

Amanda Murphy cleared her throat and added, "Be sure to pack your chairs and table so you can easily get to them. You'll need them for cooking and eating and plain resting." Mrs. Murphy tucked a stray wisp behind her ear. "You'll need dried meat and beans, whatever canned goods you've put up, lots of flour, and your sourdough starter of course."

"Don't forget your first aid box for the trail. You never know what can turn up. Take along extra rifles and ammunition," Mr. Murphy added.

"Take along as many water barrels as you can. There will be many a dry day on the trail," Mr. Shane advised. He touched the brim of his Stetson and abruptly left.

Olivia couldn't say she was sorry to see him go.

Two months later, Olivia was glad she had already collected her new wild sourdough by setting a jar of flour and water covered with a thin piece of mesh outside. She had a nice batch fermenting. By making extra dough and adding equal parts of flour and water to the bit left over from time to time, the sour-dough would last indefinitely, she mused while preparing for the children's baths. It was a few days earlier than usual. They were heading for Greenville, Texas in the morning, and who knew when they'd get another bath. She and Jacob had their baths earlier. The water was still warm, just right for the children.

Nine-year-old Emmett climbed into the tub on his own, his skinny body all shivering. "It's cold. Brrr."

Olivia made him climb back out as she poured more hot water into the tub. After she tested it, Emmett climbed back in. His steel blue eyes gazed up at Olivia in appreciation. She tousled Emmet's dark hair. Those Kimberlin eyes, Olivia thought. How odd that the firstborn of any Kimberlin always had blue eyes. The other two of her children had the brown eyes of the Blakemores.

Olivia lifted four-year-old Susie into the tub. Susie immediately had to splash water on her older brother as she sat down.

Last of all, Olivia picked up one-year-old John. John-John they called him because he repeated everything he said: "Go, go. Up, up. Kiss, kiss." He was always so good-natured, plump as a plum, and drooling constantly while he teethed. He'd just begun taking his first steps.

Olivia handed Emmet and Susie each a soaped washcloth and soaped her own cloth to wash John-John. She started with John-John's hair.

As the time grew closer to leaving, Olivia had become more unsure of their move to Texas. The packing of their belongings was time-consuming and tedious. She had to leave so much of her belongings behind. Only the necessities were allowed in the wagon load: food, water, weapons, clothes, dishes and pans, mattresses and bedding, table and chairs, and her few linens and prized possessions she stored in the big trunk, and, of course, Elizabetha's journal that Olivia's grandmother had given her. Yet, she was excited as well. It would be wonderful for the children to see so many new places. She bet even Jacob will enjoy the adventure. And when they got to Texas, well, everything would be perfect then.

Susie yelled, "Soap, soap." She rubbed frantically at her eyes and stood up.

"Emmet, hold on to John-John, quick." Olivia passed the plum to Emmet and grabbed Susie. "Here, Let me wash them out with water. It will be all right." Olivia poured a cup of water over Susie's eyes and wiped them gently with a clean washcloth. "Is that all better now?"

Susie buried her face against her mother's apron.

"Just keep them closed for a minute then try to open them."

After a minute, Olivia wiped Susie's eyes again with clear water. "Now try to open them," Olivia coaxed.

Susie gingerly lifted her eyelids and snapped them shut. Again she lifted the lids and this time kept them open. She smiled at her mother. "Thanks, Mama, I'm all fine now."

Olivia cuddled Susie against her apron before taking John-John from Emmet. Yes, Olivia thought, we'll all be fine now.

⇒•67•⇐

It was a fine day the next morning for the trip to Texas. Olivia glanced back at the farm house one last time as they pulled out of the lane to meet Charles and Mary's wagon. Jacob kept his gaze straight ahead. They were to meet with the wagon train at the Murphy's ranch.

Mr. Murphy was at the head of the wagons that had already assembled, and Mr. Shane was there as well, accompanied by an Indian and a Mexican.

Jacob, Olivia, Charles, and Mary climbed down from the wagons to receive their instructions from Mr. Murphy and Mr. Shane. Olivia managed a civil smile as Mr. Shane introduced his hands, Long Blade and Cholo.

The Indian, Long Blade, had a jagged scar from his left temple to the corner of his mouth which caused his upper lip to wear a perpetual sneer. His eyes were jet black and his gaze bore through Olivia like hot coals on snow. He wore dirty buckskin trousers, shiny from use, and had a Bowie knife inserted into his rawhide belt. His calico shirt, rolled to the elbows, was open in front revealing a leather pouch hung around his neck by rawhide. His black, straight hair hung to his shoulders and a wide, sweat-stained headband encircled his forehead. His buckskin vest was as darkly shiny as his trousers.

Cholo, the Mexican, leered at Olivia with a scraggly-toothed grin. He wore a filthy, red shirt and his paunch stuck out over his wide, black leather belt which sported a huge, silver buckle. The further Olivia could remain from either of these two, and the cold-eyed Mr. Shane as well, the better she'd like it.

The Kimberlins and Blakemores took their places in the train. Jacob at the reins, was fifth in the long line of wagons. Charles and Mary were in the wagon behind them. Olivia perched excitedly beside Jacob and glanced back at Emmet, Susie, and John-John riding in the back.

Behind the train, there were fifty head of cattle and twenty horses which belonged to Mr. Murphy for the ranch he would have in Arkansas. After last minute instructions to his three sons herding the stock, Mr. Murphy road to the front of the train and yelled, "Wagons, ho!"

Amanda Murphy in the first wagon deftly handled her six-horse team and pulled the Murphy wagon onto the road. The rest of the wagons fell in behind.

Dust from the wagon wheels and myriad of horses and cattle hooves filled Olivia's lungs as the wagon train started rolling out. She drew up her apron across her nose. Jacob coughed and spit off to the side.

Olivia glanced back at the children. They didn't seem to notice the dust. They were on their bellies atop the mattress on the table at the rear of the load and peered out the back of the covered wagon, John-John between Emmet and Susie, and all propped up on their elbows with chins on their fists.

At noon, the wagon train stopped for a rest and dinner. Jacob, Emmet, and Susie walked beside the wagon when they started again. Olivia drove the four-horse team with John-John on her lap. They would all take turns walking beside the wagon to spare the horses.

By late afternoon, Olivia was exhausted. Her hands were sore and blistered from the reins, and her feet ached from walking. When the wagon train stopped and circled for the night, she was relieved. But there was still the unhitching of the team, fixing supper, cleaning up the dishes, and bedding down the children to be done before she could rest.

Olivia had been walking the last stretch, holding John-John's hand while he toddled along sometimes, but mostly carrying him.

Jacob climbed down from the buckboard and swatted his felt hat at his dusty, wool trousers. He had tied a red bandana around his face to keep out some of the dust. He wiped the sweat from his forehead with it and ran his fingers through his hat-matted hair. Susie and Emmet scurried down from the back of the wagon.

The noise from the cattle and all the wagons circling was deafening. "Emmet, watch John-John while we unhitch the horses. Susie, you help him," Olivia shouted as she removed her sunbonnet. Her blue cotton dress was covered in dust. She shook out her skirts.

"Yes, Mama," Emmet shouted.

Olivia was glad Emmet was so responsible for his age and so good with the baby. Susie loved to play with her younger brother but wasn't as mindful of him as Emmet was. But then, Susie was only four.

Jacob adjusted the straps on his wooden leg and unloaded a small work table on which to prepare food, then brought out the wooden table and chairs from the rear of the wagon. Olivia opened the trunk that had been stored under the table and removed her dishware and pans. She prepared a supper of bacon and beans in a large kettle over the cooking fire Jacob had started.

After supper, around the large campfire in the middle of the circled wagons, Olivia lolled a while in her ladder-back chair beside Jacob's before she would put the children to bed. The children played quietly beside them.

Mrs. Haines of the wagon train roosted on a chair to Olivia's right and Mr. Haines perched on his wife's other side. Mr. Haines was a gentle, sweet man. He had sandy hair streaked with gray and the kindest green eyes. He never raised his voice. He was tall and slim and stooped at the shoulders as if he carried a heavy burden.

Mrs. Haines was short and bone thin. Her mousy brown hair was drawn so tightly in a bun atop her head that her eyes tilted up slightly at the corners. She turned to her husband and nagged in a nasal whine, "Mr. Haines, do sit up straight."

Mr. Haines said, "Yes, dear." He pulled his shoulders back for an instant and let them sag as his wife turned her attention from him.

Mr. Shane and his two companions, Long Blade and Cholo, sauntered up to the campfire in front of Olivia and Mrs. Haines view. The men slowly lit their cigarettes with a long twig from the fire.

"Well, I declare," Mrs. Haines whined loud enough for the interlopers to hear. "Some folks have no manners." She leaned toward Olivia. "Have you ever in your life seen such a pack of ruffians? I can't fathom why that nice Mr. Murphy allows such riffraff in this wagon train." Mrs. Haines sat back with a smug grin on her pinched face.

"Mrs. Haines, that really is uncalled for," Olivia said. "Those men have as much right to be here as the rest of us." Olivia didn't think much more of those three than Mrs. Haines did, but Mrs. Haines superior attitude annoyed her.

Mr. Shane turned, touched the brim of his Stetson with two fingers, and nodded ever so slightly toward Olivia. The other two men gave a slight nod also, and the three sauntered toward their wagon.

Olivia spotted John-John toddling toward the fire, fascinated by the bright flames. Olivia jumped to her feet. "John-John," she cried.

Emmet dashed over to his brother and steered him away from the fire.

Jacob had risen as well, and Susie stood with her hand across her mouth.

Emmet led John-John back to Olivia. She scooped John-John up in her arms. "Thank you, Emmet, thank you. But don't ever let him near that fire, you hear?"

"Yes, Mama," Emmet said. He stared at his feet. One shoe traced a circle in the dust.

Olivia could have bit off her tongue. "I'm sorry I yelled at you, Emmet. It just scared me. It wasn't your fault." She bent down and kissed the top of Emmet's head.

"That's okay, Mama." Emmet's blue eyes glistened with unshed tears.

"Thank you again for running after him. You're much quicker than I am."

Emmet grinned at her.

"Time for bed, tomorrow's another day." Olivia headed for the wagon carrying John-John and Emmet and Susie scampering after her.

By dawn the next morning, they'd eaten breakfast and hitched the team. The cattle had been rounded up, and the wagon train was ready to roll out. Olivia climbed up on the buckboard and took the reins in her blistered hands. She wondered how long it would take to get to Greenville.

Nearly a week later as they arrived at a verdant valley, a local resident wandered up from a path in the woods to the wagon train as it set up camp. Jacob greeted the gray-haired gentleman who had a fishing pole on one shoulder and a string of bass on the other. "Looks like good fishing. What is this place?" Jacob asked.

"The bass are jumping all right. This here is the Holston River near Bristol or Squabble State." The old man laughed to himself. He said, "This half of Bristol is in Virginia and that half's in Tennessee and the states have squabbled over it since the days that section of Tennessee was considered part of North Carolina. Holston Lake's over yonder."

"I think I'll try my hand at some bass a little later," Jacob said.

"Good luck. There's plenty for the taking." The old man strolled on toward the town.

Olivia helped Jacob unhitch the team. While Jacob fed and groomed the horses, Olivia took the children and followed the winding path through the woods down to the lake to wash up.

At the shore, Olivia inhaled the spring-crisp Appalachian mountain air and watched a gull swoop lazily over the tops of the oaks, poplar, and yellow pine. A few yards out in the lake, a large bass splashed out of the water and disappeared again. At places along the lake, the foothills dipped their feet into the blue waters.

Olivia's feet ached so, it would feel so good to dip them into the water, too. She glanced around her. No one was in sight. They were all busy tending the animals and setting up camp. It wouldn't hurt for her and the children to wade just a while.

Olivia slipped off her shoes and stockings and tied her skirt into a knot around her hips then helped the children.

Emmet, with his pants rolled up to his knees and Susie, with her dress tied like her mother's, splashed the cool waters at each other. Olivia held John-John above the lake while he kicked his chubby legs back and forth in the water, soaking Olivia's legs.

"Wash your faces and hands," Olivia said to Emmet and Susie as she took her hanky from her bodice, wetted it, and proceeded to clean John-John's face.

Olivia stopped in a sudden dread. She could feel someone watching her. It could be Indians. How could she have been so careless, so stupid? What should she do? Slowly, she turned around.

Long Blade stood so close Olivia could see the pores in his face. She stepped backwards and clutched John-John closer.

Long Blade's steady gaze traveled down to Olivia's bare legs. She quickly undid the knot and let her skirt down. To hell with a wet hem. She wouldn't have this savage ogling her. Her heart pounded in her chest. Why had he followed her? What was he going to do?

Long Blade gazed into her eyes a long moment. Olivia stood frozen before him, her throat felt dry as dust.

Long Blade took one step to the side and pointed his long index finger toward the wagon camp. "Go back. Not safe alone," was all he said.

"Come, children. Grab your shoes," Olivia managed to utter.

She grabbed up her and John-John's shoes and stockings and herded the children back to camp. They'd wash their dirty feet when they got there. Olivia looked back over her shoulder. Long Blade stood watching their departure, his hand on the Bowie knife.

Back at camp, Jacob had finished tending the horses and was washing up at a basin filled with water. He looked down at their bare feet and Olivia's wet skirt hem. "Where have you been?"

"To the lake. To wash up," she replied, feeling foolish as she felt the grime between her toes from the dirt path.

"Looks like it didn't take."

"Something scared us and we hurried back."

"It's dangerous to go wandering the woods alone," Jacob said, his steel blue eyes glinting in the sunlight.

"I know." Olivia washed up their feet, and as she tied up the last shoelace, she saw Long Blade enter the encampment from the woods. She exhaled audibly. She glanced at Jacob. He scowled at Long Blade and then at her.

⇒ 68 ⇐

After crossing the Clinch River, the wagon train headed across the Cumberland Plateau which started out with level to gently rolling terrain, then became mountainous with steep bluffs in places. It held many mountain streams and breathtaking waterfalls. The spring forests were filled with wildlife. By late afternoon, they made camp beside a rocky stream.

Mr. Shane had killed a deer that day, and tonight everyone was to have a share of venison for their supper. Olivia's mouth watered at the thought.

As Olivia stirred her flour and water for sourdough biscuits, she reserved a quarter cup of sourdough starter adding a tablespoon each of water and flour to it, stirred it vigorously and resealed the jar—not too tightly lest it should burst—and stored it in a small wooden crate along with the other three jars she'd brought. At its next feeding she would add a tablespoon of rye flour, too, for extra flavor. She checked the older jars for caked flour and poured them into clean jars. She placed the biscuits into the iron pot buried in the coals of the cooking fire and placed the lid on top.

She gathered the dirty jars and the family under garments

and shirts along with a bar of homemade lye soap and her scrub board and sauntered down to the creek.

As Olivia returned with the washing, she saw the flaming arrow strike Charles and Mary's wagon. The fire caught quickly. Olivia set her wash down, grabbed the water bucket, ran to the wagon, and threw the water on the flames. The flames sputtered and died leaving a hole as large as a frying pan in the canvas.

The next few minutes brought a terrifying hail of arrows and bullets. A gray dust splattered up from the barrage. Olivia gathered the children. "Lie flat under the wagon," she ordered. Jacob and the other men were shooting back at the Indians. Rifle bullets whizzed past Olivia's head. The stench of sulphur hung in the air.

Ned Murphy, the youngest son of the wagon master, spun sideways from a bullet in the shoulder. His mother, Amanda, grabbed the rifle from him and pushed him to safety. She took Ned's position on the firing line and aimed at the Indians circling around the wagons. Dust and war whoops filled the air.

Olivia turned to see an arrow strike Mr. Haines in his chest. Mr. Haines glanced down at the arrow in surprise. He dropped his rifle, grabbed the arrow with both hands as if to break it, and fell forwards in a heap onto the ground.

Mrs. Haines ran to his side. "Dirty, rotten Indians," she screamed. She plopped on the ground and gently rolled her husband over and placed his head on her lap. She lovingly stroked his brow. Tears streamed down her cheeks. It was the first time Mrs. Haines had done anything Olivia could like about her.

The Indians turned abruptly and rode away from the wagon train, herding Mr. Murphy's twenty horses in front of them. Billowing dust was all that was left behind.

The Murphy's oldest son, Randy, ran to his horse, leaped on, and jumped his horse through an opening between wagons, waving his rifle above his head as he chased after the Indians.

Mr. Murphy darted for his horse.

Mrs. Murphy tended to Ned's wound.

At Olivia's side, Jacob said, "That boy is going to get himself killed."

A single shot rang out in the distance.

Mr. Murphy looked up from the horse he was about to mount then dropped his head to the saddle.

Shortly, Mr. Murphy, Mr. Shane and Long Blade and Cholo rode out to find Randy.

There were two burials before anyone ate supper that night.

Ned's shoulder was bandaged and his arm was in a sling as he stood beside his father who threw several shovel's full of dirt on Randy's grave. Mr. Murphy stopped and wiped his eyes with the back of his hand. The Murphy's middle son, Jason, standing across the grave, started toward his father. But Mrs. Murphy took the shovel from her husband and threw on the last of the dirt before Jason could cover the distance.

Mrs. Haines clutched her arms around her shoulders and wailed over the grave of Mr. Haines, Mrs. Haines whiney, nasal lament shrilling the night air above the rest.

Several weeks later after traveling through miles of rolling hills, woods, and farmlands, the wagon train arrived at the widest river Olivia had ever seen.

"The mighty Mississippi. We'll cross her by ferry," Mr. Shane said.

Only two wagons and teams at a time would fit on the barge. The ferry master and his sons poled the barge across the muddy Mississippi waters.

The horses were uneasy as Olivia and Jacob's wagon, along with Charles and Mary's, made the crossing. Jacob held the sides of the reins of the lead horses in one hand and alternately rubbed their long noses with the other hand. Olivia held John-John in her arms on the buckboard and Emmet and Susie crowded behind her back to get a good look at the river. Olivia would be glad when they reached shore. This ferry trip was even longer than the one across the Tennessee River. The Mississippi was huge. She had never seen such a river.

After a long day of ferrying the wagons and cattle across the river, the wagon train made camp on Arkansas soil where the wagon train would disband.

The next morning, Olivia cleaned up the dishes after a breakfast of sourdough pancakes and coffee. She looked around for John-John. When had he wandered off? Emmet was helping Jacob hitch the team, and Susie was watching them.

Olivia spotted John-John toddling toward the cooking fire where Olivia had prepared breakfast. The fire was out, but Olivia knew the coals were still hot. She threw the coffee pot she was holding to the ground and ran, calling out, "John-John, stop. John-John!"

John-John turned around and waved his chubby arm at her. He turned back to his toddling and tripped over the rocks surrounding the fire. He landed face first in the coals.

Olivia scooped him up from the fire pit. As she frantically swiped at the hot coals covering his face, they came away taking his skin and features with them. Olivia screamed.

Long Blade was beside her and poured his canteen of water on top of John-John's head and face. The coals fell away. John-John didn't cry. He just made awful moaning sounds.

Jacob came and led Olivia with John-John back to the wagon.

Mrs. Murphy met them at the wagon and helped Olivia smear lard on John-John's burns and wrap him in clean cotton strips of sheeting. His whole stomach, arms, and hands were badly burned and blackened. But his face was the worst, beet red with raw meat where the skin had pulled away. "Best not hold him," Mrs. Murphy said. "He'll be more comfortable."

Olivia lay down beside John-John, stroking his soft baby hair and cooing to him. John-John only whimpered. How could she have let this happen to her baby. Her stomach felt like her heart had fallen into it. She bit her lip until she tasted blood. Hot tears slipped down her cheeks.

Jacob said he would sleep with Emmet and Susie outside under the wagon.

Off and on through the night John-John moaned and whimpered. Sometime in the night Olivia had dozed off. It was quiet when she awoke with a start. Her heart raced so fast she thought she would surely die. She rifled through the covers for

John-John. She found his shoulder. He was cold. Olivia screamed an endless wail.

Jacob scrambled into the wagon with a lantern, his wooden leg thudding on the wagon boards. He felt for John-John's pulse at his throat. The sag of Jacob's head told Olivia that John-John was gone.

"My baby, my baby," Olivia wailed. She picked up John-John and rocked him back and forth, back and forth, cooing to him all the while. She didn't know how long she rocked there with John-John.

Sometime later, Jacob returned to the wagon and said, "It's time, Olivia."

Olivia stared blankly at Jacob. Time? For what? she wondered.

"Give me the baby, Olivia, it's time to bury him."

Olivia looked down at the tiny bundle in her arms. "No, oh no."

Jacob took the baby from Olivia's arms. He wrapped John-John in his soft green, crocheted baby afghan. Jacob climbed out of the wagon with the baby and held his hand out to Olivia.

Olivia followed Jacob in a trance to the waiting grave. She stood holding her shawl tightly about her shoulders as John-John was placed in the deep pit. She felt as though her heart had been ripped from her chest and thrown into the grave with John-John. Poor sweet John-John. How could she stand not seeing his lovable, plump little face smile up to her each morning? Emmet and Susie clung to her skirts, but all Olivia could do was clutch her shawl around her. The world began to spin as her vision narrowed. She fainted.

* * *

Emmet was worried about his mother. It had been weeks since John-John died. His mother hadn't spoken or paid mind to any of them. She just sat in her rocker and didn't seem to know where or who she was. Emmet had felt terrible about John-John. He should have been watching him. Then maybe it wouldn't have happened. But it did happen, and John-John was an angel in heaven now. Emmet was beginning to fear his mother would never get better.

Emmet perched on the ground after supper, with his arms hooked around his knees, watching his mother as she sat motionlessly in her rocker. Her eyes were closed, and she clutched her shawl around her. Susie sat on the ground in front of their mother with her head on Mama's knee. Mama didn't notice.

Emmet tried to help his father as much as he could. And he tried to care for Susie. Whenever Emmet couldn't find Susie, he panicked, but he would always find her sitting like this by their mother.

Long Blade appeared again in the shadow of the wagon and watched Emmet's mother. Long Blade's hand was around the leather pouch that hung from his neck. Emmet watched Long Blade through slitted eyes. He had seen Long Blade do this often these last few weeks. Emmet wondered if Long Blade was putting some kind of spell on his mother.

Emmet prayed to John-John up in heaven to please send Mama back to them. Every night when they went to bed, he and Susie prayed to John-John.

➤•69•◄

A pistol shot startled Olivia. She jumped to her feet and peered the direction of the sound. She saw Cholo holding Susie and Long Blade beside them with his pistol pointed at the ground. They had Susie. My God, they had Susie. Olivia held up her skirts and ran to them, her shawl slipping to the ground behind her. In front of her, Emmet was emerging from behind a bush.

Cholo set Susie down then lay on the ground.

Long Blade took out his Bowie knife.

Emmet ran to Susie and put his arm around his sister.

By the time Olivia arrived, Lang Blade had cut open Cholo's trouser leg and tied his belt around the top of Cholo's thigh. Long Blade made two slits crisscross on Cholo's calf then bent down and sucked at the wound, spitting the blood out on the ground. Olivia saw a dead rattlesnake, minus its head, sprawled on the ground.

Emmet and Susie threw their arms around their mother as she bent to them. "Susie was trying to find me when I heard her scream. A rattler was poised ready to strike, and Cholo scooped Susie up just in time, but the rattler bit him," Emmet said. His blue eyes were round with fright.

Long Blade helped Cholo to his feet. Cholo was sweating profusely. They hobbled toward their wagon.

Olivia stared after the men. She must thank Cholo for saving Susie, and Long Blade, with John-John. Olivia buried her head between Emmet and Susie. Thank God her Susie was okay. She couldn't have borne losing another child. This damnable wagon train had taken too much from her already, too much from many of them. She clutched Susie closer. "I'm so glad you're all right, Susie."

"I'm so glad you're back, Mama," Susie said.

That night after Emmet and Susie were asleep, Olivia and Jacob walked to Mr. Shane's wagon to convey their thanks to Cholo and Long Blade. Olivia was ashamed of herself for having thought she didn't want them anywhere near her. What a school girlish fool she had been.

Cholo lay on the ground by the campfire covered in blankets, but shivered from the cold though he was sweating. He was breathing shallowly. Long Blade and Mr. Shane were beside him.

Olivia bent down beside Cholo and put her hand on his shoulder. "Mr. Cholo, I want to thank you for saving Susie. That was a brave thing to do."

Cholo's glassy eyes gazed at her and he smiled a straggle-toothed grin. He shivered. Olivia feared the worst for him. His skin was a ghastly yellow-gray.

Jacob leaned over and took Cholo's hand. Jacob put his other hand on top. Cholo grinned up at Jacob.

Olivia stood and walked over to Long Blade. "I want to thank you, too, for what you did with John-John."

Long Blade's coal black eyes burned through her a moment. "Sorry your baby die. It is good you come back to the living. I called upon the spirits for you." His fingers lightly touched the pouch around his neck.

"Thank you," she said.

Jacob approached and offered his hand to Long Blade. Long Blade stared at the hand and then at Jacob. Long Blade took Jacob's hand and gave it a firm shake.

Cholo shivered one long last time, then was still.

Mr. Shane bent down to feel his pulse. "We will bury him in the morning," Mr. Shane said as he pulled the blanket over Cholo's head. Mr. Shane stood and touched the brim of his Stetson, nodding slightly to Olivia. "Night, Ma'am, thank you for your kindness." He turned to Jacob. "Night, Sir."

A week and a half of crossing hilly, densely wooded countryside, brought what was left of the wagon train to the Red River. Throughout Arkansas, members of the wagon train left to begin their new lives. Only the Murphy's, the Blakemores, and Kimberlins remained in the train along with Mr. Shane and Long Blade. The Murphy's would leave them at Red River to head for El Dorado. And Mr. Shane and Long Blade would see the Blakemores and Kimberlins to Greenville then head to their own ranch along the Trinity River near Dallas.

The camp was quiet that night. After supper, Olivia lazed in her chair along with the others around the center campfire on this last night together. Ned Murphy played a melancholy strain on his harmonica. No one seemed to feel like dancing. Olivia closed her eyes and listened to the river lapping at its banks.

Her thoughts turned to John-John and tears streamed down her cheeks. She took her handkerchief from her bodice and dabbed at her eyes then blew her nose. She mustn't allow herself to wallow in her grief. Emmet and Susie needed her. At least she still had them, and Jacob.

Jacob called for her. Olivia rose and went to him. Jacob had removed their trunk from the wagon and was searching through it. Her best linens were slopped over the side and hanging in the dirt. "What are you doing? You're making a mess of things." She scolded.

Jacob straightened and glared at her. "Where did you put the tweezers? I can't find them anywhere. Can't you be more organized? I've got a goddamned sliver in my thumb."

Olivia reached inside the wagon and grabbed the medicine box. She opened it and slapped the tweezers into Jacob's hand. "There," she said.

Jacob glowered. "Thank you, Madam." He turned on his heel, grabbed the lantern, and clumped away from her.

Olivia stared after him. Jacob had been as withdrawn from her through the journey as he had been in Virginia. He had become even more so after losing John-John. He hadn't cried Olivia remembered. She wondered if he blamed himself for John-John's death, or her. She didn't understand Jacob. Maybe when they arrived at Greenville he would find some happiness again. Maybe she could find a way to bring him back to the way he had been before the war: warm and caring, easily laughing, and even crying.

As Olivia reorganized the trunk, she spotted Elizabetha Kimberlin's journal. It had helped her through the time she found out about her Indian grandmother. Maybe it could help her again. Olivia picked up Elizabetha's journal, went back to the campfire, and began reading.

Olivia came to a passage that immediately caught her attention:

After the Revolution, Martin was a different man, as if the war had somehow annealed him. Not until my father died and Anne lost two of her children in that Indian raid, did I realize how death can so alter a person's life. I began to understand a little of what had made Martin so withdrawn from me. And then when Martin had his stroke and subsequently died, I fully realized the impact of the grief from losing someone, the guilt for having survived them, and the numbness that besets the heart and changes us into a different person than we were before. I think of the veterans who have fought in wars and wonder how any of them can survive with such a heavy load of death to carry.

Olivia stared off into the night sky and remembered the events of the wagon train journey. She closed the journal and went to find Jacob.

Jacob was standing at the table Olivia used to prepare meals. He was tending to a harness. The tweezers were on the table.

Olivia laid the journal on the table. She reached out her hand to Jacob's arm. "Jacob, I'm sorry I was snippy with you."

Without glancing up, Jacob muttered, "Uh huh."

Olivia put her hand on the journal. "I was reading about how Martin had changed after the Revolutionary War in Elizabetha's journal. Jacob, I think I know what you've been feeling since you came home."

Jacob lifted his head and gazed at Olivia questioningly. "You know how I've felt? When were you last in a war?"

Jacob's words crashed into the pit of Olivia's stomach and lay there in a heap of dead letters. Hot tears stung her eyes. She had to get away from Jacob. She turned to run from him.

Jacob grabbed her wrist before she could leave. "I'm sorry. That was cruel," he said.

"Why do you always push me away?" Olivia sobbed, the tears now streaming freely down her cheeks. She swiped at them with the back of her hand, angry with herself that she cried when she was angry. He could make her feel so stupid. How could she think she would ever understand him?

"Olivia."

"Let me go." Olivia tried to pull her wrist free.

"Olivia, wait." Jacob pulled her against his chest and held her head there.

Olivia's tears gushed from her eyes with a pent-up torrent of their own. Her body shuddered with heaving sobs of despair.

Jacob loosened her hair and stroked it, resting his head on top of hers.

"I just thought I understood the grief you've had from the war," Olivia blubbered through her sobs. "Losing John-John—."

Jacob held her closer.

"This journey has shown me death and how it comes so quickly and changes the ones who survive—Mr. Haines, Randy, Cholo, and our own John-John gone." Olivia couldn't go on. A refreshed torrent of tears engulfed her.

"I've felt the grief and the guilt that goes with it." Olivia shook with renewed sobs. She buried her head in Jacob's chest.

When her shuddering eased, Jacob untied his neck scarf and

wiped at her eyes.

Olivia took the scarf from him and blew her nose. "I'll never be the same person I once was," she said.

"Perhaps you do know." Jacob stepped toward her and took her in his arms. Olivia's tears resoaked Jacob's shirt front. It was the closest she'd felt to him in such a long time.

⇒•70•⇐

The next morning, the Murphy's prepared to leave for El Dorado while the rest prepared for the journey into Texas. When they were ready to pull out, Mr. Murphy solemnly shook hands all around as did his sons Ned and Jason. Mrs. Murphy did the same.

When Mrs. Murphy got to her, Olivia noticed the determined set of Mrs. Murphy's jaw. She's sworn not to cry, Olivia thought. I shall not either.

Mrs. Murphy shook Olivia's hand then abruptly gathered Olivia into a bear hug. "I'm so sorry for the loss of your baby," Mrs. Murphy said.

Olivia patted Mrs. Murphy's back, "Thank you. I'm so sorry for your loss of Randy."

Mrs. Murphy straightened and smoothed her skirts. She smiled bravely. "At least I still have Ned and Jason."

Olivia put on the best smile she could and said, "Yes, and I have Emmet and Susie."

"Also, unlike poor Mrs. Haines, we still have our husbands," Mrs. Murphy said. She turned and headed for her wagon.

Olivia waved until long after the Murphy's pulled out with

Mrs. Murphy at the reins on the buckboard, her bright hair vying with the red of the morning sunrise. Ned, Jason, and their father followed on horseback herding the cattle behind the wagon.

Two weeks later the remaining wagons had crossed level to gently rolling semi-wooded farmland and reached the black land prairies covered with tall waving grass where cattle ranches dotted the Texas countryside.

Mr. Shane halted just outside of Greenville. The Blakemores and Kimberlins alighted from their wagons and joined Mr. Shane and Long Blade on the dusty trail. Olivia had never seen Mr. Shane all scrubbed and fresh looking as this.

Mr. Shane said, "Folks, we'll be leaving you here and heading for the Trinity. It's been mighty fine traveling with y'all." He shook hands with Jacob and Charles and touched the brim of his hat and nodded to Mary. She curtsied back.

Jacob and Charles approached Long Blade and shook his hand. Mary made a small curtsy to Long Blade as well.

Long Blade came to Olivia and shook her hand vigorously. "You have a good life in Greenville." He stood back and smiled, cracking his face into unfamiliar creases.

Mr. Shane turned to Olivia and said, "It was a fine thing you did for Cholo, to thank him, and Long Blade, too, Ma'am."

"It was the least I could do. I'm sorry about your friend Cholo."

"Thank you, Ma'am."

"Best of luck to you back on your ranch. Perhaps you'll even find some nice woman to marry and rear a family." Olivia smiled.

Mr. Shane gazed at her a moment. "Ma'am, if all women were ladies like you, I'd surly marry me one." Mr. Shane took off his Stetson with a flourish and bowed to her.

Olivia's eyes widened in disbelief. The neatness of the center part in his blond hair surprised her.

* * *

A year later, Olivia strolled down Lee Street in Greenville with

Mary. A few hundred residents lived in and around the town in the Texas prairie. Woods dotted the land east of the town square. A large cistern was located on the west.

Along the rutted dirt road, they passed Colonel Bayne who owned the weekly newspaper *The Greenville Morning Herald.* The portly Colonel tipped his hat as he passed by and mumbled, "Ladies," around a cigar clenched between his teeth.

Olivia glanced up at the Methodist Church. The children would be getting out of school soon. The church served as schoolhouse, town hall, and courthouse as well as church. She and Mary would be done shopping in time to meet the children and give them a carriage ride home. Olivia and Mary crossed the street and entered the general store.

After arriving in Greenville, Charles and Jacob joined forces with William and expanded William's grocery store to include general merchandise as they had all planned. Jacob occasionally worked in the store when he wasn't blacksmithing behind it. Olivia could hear him pounding on his anvil in the background. Since the wagon train, he had become more content and not shutting her out as before.

Various canned goods lined the nearly floor to ceiling shelves on the wall behind the counter. Between the support beams in the center, boxes of assorted goods were stacked. At the front, open boxes of apples wafted their fruity aroma into the air. Barrels of pickles and flour lined the sides. A black potbellied stove commanded the back wall.

Mary helped herself to a red apple and polished it on her bodice before taking a juicy mouthful, as she and Olivia went to the bolts of cloth on a table at the back of the large room. They planned to buy material to make themselves each a new dress for William's impending wedding.

William approached them in his usual good humor. "Afternoon, ladies, how can I help you?" He wiped his hands on the bottom of his clean white apron and picked up a bolt of cloth. "Here's a pale blue velvet we just got in this week. How lovely it would look with your eyes, Mary," William teased.

"How you do go on, William. You'll have Ida Mae scratching

my eyes out if you don't watch out." Mary's cheeks glowed with a rosy blush.

"Ida hasn't a jealous bone in her body," William said as he winked at Mary. His coppery complexion was enhanced by his starched white shirt and apron. Olivia thought he resembled their Indian grandmother more than either Charles or she did.

"Don't you feel just a bit like you're robbing the cradle, William?" Olivia chided. "After all, she's only sixteen and you're seven years older."

"Ida's just the right age for providing youngsters. She's got gumption, that one. You should see her plow a field, better than a man," William boasted.

Olivia had liked Ida Mae the moment she met her. She reminded Olivia of a younger and darker Mrs. Murphy, square jaw and all. Ida Mae had rough ways of talking, but she was as big a tease as William. Between Ida and William's bantering, it was impossible for one to have a serious thought.

Olivia remembered even Jacob laughing at the pair of them. She was so glad she and Jacob had reclaimed their intimacy. She knew change was inevitable, but right now, everything was going well. She crossed her fingers behind her back and made a wish that it would continue.

≫•71•≪

1892

At thirty, Emmet was amazed at how Greenville had grown. Thanks to the coming of the railroads, it was now a cotton producing area and had a population well over three thousand. The new King Opera House was erected in Greenville at the rear of the old one that had burned to the ground. Over the years Susie had performed in several plays at the old King Opera House and before that at the Rainey Opera House. The King had drawn many famous actors. Emmet and Susie's father had never allowed anyone to speak to him of Susie's acting, but he did not forbid her. He never attended her performances either.

Emmet escorted his sister Susie to the opening night of her play. Susie had a small part as a maid but would appear in most of the scenes. Emmet fidgeted in his seat until the curtain finally rose.

In the very first scene, Susie entered on stage wearing a black dress with ruffled white apron and mob cap set on her high-piled brown hair. His sister was a handsome woman. She went up on her first line. Emmet knew because he'd helped her rehearse. After that, she settled down and did a fine acting job. When the play was over, Emmet went backstage to collect her.

Susie had already changed to her street clothes and was talking excitedly to a young woman about Susie's own age whom Emmet recognized from the play. Emmet sauntered up to the two women and put his hand on Susie's shoulder. "Good job of acting, Susie," Emmet said while gazing at her companion.

"Emmet," Susie trilled. "Thank you. This is my friend Effie. Effie, meet Emmet."

Effie shook Emmet's hand. She was petite with dimples. Her large green eyes gazed steadily into his. Her dishwater blonde hair was piled atop her head. Her alabaster skin reminded Emmet of a porcelain doll. The high collar of her dress did not succeed in hiding her long, slender neck. Emmet found himself fascinated by her.

Two months later Emmet dressed in his new store-bought charcoal gray suit with a white collared shirt. He tied his pale yellow necktie in a half Windsor knot and rubbed bay rum into his dark hair, carefully parting it on the left and smoothing it back from his forehead. He gazed at his image in the mirror hung over his dresser and adjusted his tie. He'd seen worse looking men he decided. He gave a final dusting to his shined black leather shoes with his handkerchief. He took a deep breath to calm himself and left for Effie's. Whenever he thought about asking Effie to marry him, he got nervous.

Effie lived with her father in a small clapboard house on St. John street. When Emmet's runabout arrived at Effie's home, he saw Susie rush out the front door and hurry down the street away from him, with a furtive glance over her shoulder. He tied the horse and carriage to a hitching post and walked up to the house.

As Emmet approached the front door, Effie's father barreled out of it. Emmet sidestepped just in time to miss being plowed over. "Evening," Emmet said.

Effie's father paused long enough to murmur, "Evenin'," as he stormed down the walk. He was a burly man with wiry blond hair covering his arms and sticking above the neckline of his shirt in front. He bartended at McGraw's tavern. He worked most nights. Effie's mother had died when Effie was nine. Effie had mostly raised herself, she'd told Emmet. She'd also told him her father drank considerably and sometimes turned mean afterward. The smell of whiskey hung in her father's wake.

Effie opened the door at Emmet's knock. She was dressed in a tailored white blouse with sleeves puffed at the shoulder and a long black skirt. Her blonde hair was piled high atop her head. She wore a black velvet ribbon around her slender neck and had an ugly fresh red bruise on her left cheekbone. She was crying.

Emmet entered and took her in his arms. "Did your father do this? Tell me what happened." He patted her head buried against his chest. He led her to the parlor sofa and sat her down, seating himself by her side.

"He'd been drinking all day." Effie wiped her eyes and blew her nose on the handkerchief Emmet handed her. "I hate him." She folded the handkerchief and handed it back.

"Why did he hit you?" Emmet stuffed the handkerchief in his jacket pocket.

"He'd lain down for a nap and I hoped he'd sleep it off. Susie came over. When papa awoke and found Susie and me downstairs, he was furious." Effie reached up and gingerly touched her cheek. "He ordered Susie out, and then he slapped me with the back of his hand and walked out. I hate him." The tears tumbled down her cheeks again.

Emmet took the handkerchief, blotted the tears away, and crammed it back in his pocket. He took Effie's hand in both of his.

"I want to get away from here—away from him," Effie sobbed.

Emmet gazed at her. He'd thought of it for a long time, why not now? "Marry me, Effie," He said.

Effie gaped at him. "Oh, yes, Emmet. Yes. Let's do it tonight. Right away. Please."

"Tonight?" Emmet asked.

"I don't want to be here when he returns. Please, Emmet. I'm afraid of what he'll do." Effie started to cry again. A huge tear trickled down her delicate cream-colored cheek.

Emmet took Effie in his arms. "Of course. We'll do it tonight. We'll take the train to Dallas. I'll just go and pack a few things and come back for you."

"Thank you, Emmet. Thank you. I'll pack my things." She kissed his forehead and jumped to her feet. "Hurry."

At home, Emmet entered through the back door. He didn't want to run into his parents or Susie. He was in a hurry. He could hear them talking in the parlor. He could reach the stairs without being seen. Upstairs he packed enough for the weekend and left a note on his pillow explaining the marriage and that he'd be back to work at the store on Monday.

A short time later, Emmet returned to Effie's. She let him in. A large suitcase was packed and standing in the hall. Effie had put on a short jacket, tapered at the waist. She had tried to cover the bruise with face powder. It almost worked. "Ready?" he asked.

"Ready," Effie answered.

Emmet loaded the suitcase beside his in the back of the carriage and helped Effie up to the seat. They rode in silence to the Dallas and Greenville Railway. Emmet's thoughts raced. Everything was happening so fast. One minute he was planning to ask Effie to marry him and the next, he was off to his wedding.

⇒·72·⇐

Five years later, Emmet whistled a tune he couldn't even name on his way home from the store. It was Effie's birthday. He had left early and bought her a bouquet of roses which lay on the seat beside him. He flicked the whip above the ear of the gray mare pulling his runabout as he turned onto their tree-lined street. The sun through the trees cast lazy shadows across the dappled lane. His and Effie's daughters, four-year-old Minnie and three-year-old Myrtle, would probably still be napping. He'd be able to be alone with Effie until the girls woke up.

He hitched the carriage a house away from his own. He wanted to surprise Effie. He lifted the roses from the seat and walked home.

As he cut across the front yard, he glanced in the parlor window. He stopped in his tracks. His heart sank to the pit of his stomach. Effie and Susie were embraced. They kissed. It wasn't an innocent peck on the cheek. It was a kiss full on the lips. His head reeled. He felt that he was going to be sick. His vision blurred. He stumbled. He rushed past the window and through the front door before he knew he was going to.

Both women gaped at his sudden explosion into the doorway.

Their mouths slackened in sickening shock. Their arms dropped to their sides.

The roses slipped from Emmet's hand and landed at his feet. He trod across them into the parlor.

"Emmet," Effie uttered.

Susie started toward her handbag. "I'd better go," she said.

"Wait," Emmet thundered.

Susie perched precariously on the edge of the sofa.

Effie wrung her hands together. She gazed at Emmet without blinking. Her eyes were round as saucers.

"Tell me it isn't so." Emmet glanced from one woman's astonished face to the other's.

"I—I," Effie began.

Susie lowered her head.

"My God," Emmet screamed. He dug the heels of his hands into his eyeballs as if he could push the pain out.

"Emmet," Effie started again.

"Shut up." Emmet peered at her as if he could understand it all if he searched her eyes. All he saw was fear.

"Emmet," Susie said.

Emmet turned on his heels toward her. His thoughts reeled. Lovers behind his back, his wife, his sister—his very flesh and blood. How could Susie have done this to him? He felt sick again. "Get out. I don't want to ever set eyes on you again," he roared.

Susie grabbed for her handbag and clutched it to her as she slowly rose.

Effie stepped toward Emmet.

He glared at her. "You. Pack your things and get out, too."

"The children—," Effie started.

"You'll leave the children," Emmet bellowed. "Get out of this house. Get out of this state. Get out!"

Susie scooted out the front door. Emmet glanced out the window and saw her waiting up the lane.

Effie raced up the stairs.

Emmet flopped onto the sofa and put his head in his hands. He gazed up dazedly as Effie returned downstairs.

Effie carried one bag. She had donned her jacket and hat. She hesitated before the front door and peered with uplifted brows at him. "Emmet?"

"Get out."

With elbows on his knees, Emmet's hands shook as he plopped his spinning head back into them. He didn't know how long he sat there before he heard his daughters stirring upstairs. What was he going to do? How would he care for his daughters alone? He tried to organize his thoughts. He'd have to hire someone to be with the girls while he was at work. Let's see, today was Friday. On Saturday, he would ask his neighbor Mrs. Grover if she would be willing.

Early Monday evening, Emmet walked through the front door of his home after a long day at the store. He was exhausted. He hated having to explain about Effie's leaving. He'd made up the story that she had run off with her lover. Not entirely a lie.

Minnie chased her younger sister around the corner. She nearly collided with her father as he entered the hall.

Myrtle turned in her flight and screamed at Minnie, "Leave me alone." Tears streamed down her reddened cheeks.

"What's going on here?" Emmet asked.

"Minnie's mean to me," Myrtle moaned. "When's Mama coming home?"

Emmet put his arm around Myrtle's shoulder. "Remember we talked about it, honey? Mama has gone some place very far away and she can't come back, but she still loves you."

"I miss her," Minnie said.

Emmet reached his other arm out to Minnie. She allowed him to embrace her.

"It's just the three of us now. We're going to be just fine, you'll see."

Mrs. Grover entered the hall from the parlor. She carried her hat, purse, and coat. She was a stout elderly woman with mousy hair mottled with gray. Her starched cotton blouse was stretched tight over her massive bosom. "They've been at it all day, Mr. Kimberlin." She plopped her hat on her head and put on her coat. "I'll have to leave now and get back to my own chores and my husband."

After Mrs. Grover left, Emmet kissed each daughter on top of her head and went into the kitchen.

He rummaged through the cupboards for something to fix for supper. He decided on a can of baked beans and warmed them on the wood stove. At least Mrs. Grover had got that going.

⇒•73•⇐

1899
Two Years Later

Olivia studied Emmet out of the corner of her eye during supper on Sunday. She was glad she had suggested that he ask Mamie Blakemores, Ida and William's youngest, to take care of the girls after that first year when Mrs. Grover fell and broke her hip and couldn't look after them any longer. "Is it still working out with Mamie and the girls, Emmet?"

"It's a pleasure to have Mamie looking after things. The girls adore her. Mamie always has them spruced up when I get home, and she has our supper all ready for us every evening."

"That's nice." Olivia glanced down at the head of the table where Jacob sat, his granddaughters on each side of him. The two young girls, Minnie and Myrtle, now age six and five, were always fascinated with their grandpa's artificial leg. Jacob was so pleased to be able to wear a shoe on the new one he'd gotten years ago. Jacob still wore his beard several inches long even though clean-shaven had been in vogue for some time. Now, mostly gray at sixty-six, to her he was as handsome as ever. Olivia smoothed her hair which she was vainly proud had remained dark. Poor Jacob suffered from rheumatism and was often unable to get out of bed. She was glad this was a good day for him. She turned her attention back to Emmet. "I was sure Mamie would work out. She's a fine young woman, twenty-two already. That makes me feel so old."

"You'll always be young in my eyes, Mama." Emmet winked at her.

"Susie writes me that she's moved to California," Olivia said before she remembered Emmet didn't want her name spoken in front of him.

Emmet paused his fork in mid-bite and set it back down in his plate.

"Emmet, I'm sorry. I'll say no more about it." Olivia had never known what had happened between Emmet and Susie. Susie had just written that she wasn't coming home. She had left around the time Effie had left Emmet. Olivia had never understood Effie's leaving either. Minnie and Myrtle were such darling girls in their large satin bows and dimples, blonde like their mother. Olivia wondered what could ever cause a mother to leave her children like that. A lover, Emmet had said. Olivia would just never understand some people.

"The dinner was delicious, Mama. Thank you," Emmet wiped his napkin across his chin and inched his plate back.

"Why don't you take Papa out on the porch and smoke your pipes, Emmet? The girls can help me in the kitchen," Olivia said.

* * *

Several months later, Emmet drove home from the store thinking how Mamie did such a fine job raising the girls, maybe she would take it on as a permanent situation. After all, the girls needed a mother full time. He could look after Mamie and the girls financially. Why Mamie's father, William, himself had just mentioned Mamie was of marrying age and no prospects in sight. William said Mamie was just too particular. But this was ridiculous, what would Mamie want with a man fifteen years older than her?

Emmet was greeted on his arrival home by Minnie and Myrtle in brand new pink crocheted dresses with matching satin bows in their hair. "Why wherever did those beautiful dresses come from?" Emmet asked.

"Mamie made them," his daughters said in unison.

"Just 'cause she loves us," Myrtle added.

Mamie stood behind the girls, smiling. Her brown eyes were arched by generous dark eyebrows. A square jaw lent her face a quiet determination. Her chestnut hair was gathered in a loose French twist at the back of her head, and she wore a long navy blue skirt with a white blouse striped in a faint blue pattern. A navy blue ribbon encircled her neck and ended in a bow at the side of the ruffled yoke of her blouse. The sight of her made Emmet's heart catch in his chest a minute. He tore his gaze away and bent down to his daughters gazing up at him. "Is it a special occasion?" Emmet asked.

"It's my birthday," Mamie said. "Supper is ready on the stove." Mamie picked up her bonnet from the hall table.

"Your birthday," Emmet exclaimed. Why hadn't he remembered? "Are you off on the town, tonight?"

"Oh no. I'm just going home." Mamie turned to the mirror above the table and placed the plumed bonnet on top of her hairdo.

"Stay and take supper with us," Emmet blurted. "We should celebrate such an occasion." She did look exceptionally lovely tonight.

Mamie hesitated and gazed steadily at Emmet. "I suppose I could. My parents won't be home for a few hours. They've gone to Dallas—for my present I think—yes, perhaps I could stay awhile."

"Yes, yes, please do," Minnie and Myrtle said in unison.

Emmet held out his hand to Mamie. "Yes, please do." He grinned.

After dinner, Mamie cleared the table. Emmet had gone upstairs to tuck the girls into bed. Mamie poured the heated water into the sink full of dishes and scooped in soap. She rolled up her sleeves as Emmet came into the kitchen.

"I'll help you with those," he said. "It's the least I can do for the birthday girl. By the way, that was a delicious chicken dinner." Emmet took a dishtowel from the drawer and with a flourish of the towel, prepared to do the drying.

Mamie's hand brushed against Emmet's as she placed a plate into the drainer just as he reached for one. An electric shock sparked through her arm directly to her heart. Her breath caught in her chest. She glanced at Emmet to see if he'd felt it. He busily dried the plate and set it in the cupboard. She busied herself in the dishwater. Silly of her to think he felt anything. She must have just imagined the sensation. After all, she was just the hired help.

"You're a very good cook you know," he said. "The girls are fond of you." Emmet reached for another plate.

"Thank you." Mamie made sure she waited until his hand was gone before adding the next dish to the drainer.

"You've made a big difference in all of our lives." Emmet placed the dried plate on the stack in the cupboard.

"I'm glad I've done my job well," Mamie said.

Emmet took a deep breath. "Maybe you'd be willing to think about making a permanent job of it."

Mamie froze with her hands immersed in the dishwater. She yanked them from the steaming heat and wiped them on her apron. She gazed curiously at Emmet. Make a permanent job of it? What could he mean?

"I've been thinking about it." Emmet deposited his towel onto the counter. "I know you're much younger, but I could provide well for you." His gaze searched her face.

Mamie stared at him. It sounded like—no, it couldn't be—she was imagining things again.

"At least tell me you'll think about it." Emmet picked up the towel and dried a coffee cup.

"I don't understand—," Mamie began.

"It could be a good marriage. The girls already love you like a mother."

Mamie's heart pounded against her chest. Surely it would explode from its frantic beating. "Yes," she said.

"What?" Emmet asked.

"Yes, it would be a good marriage."

"But you haven't even thought about it," Emmet fumbled.

"I've thought about it my whole life," Mamie said.

Emmet peered at her curiously. "Well then, that's settled."

⇒• 74 •⇐

The following Sunday, Olivia watched Mamie at supper. Emmet had just announced they were to be married. Mamie's gaze had never left Emmet's face. It was obvious from her adoring gaze that Mamie idolized Emmet. She had as a young girl.

"Congratulations. That's fine news," Jacob said. He reached over and patted Mamie's arm.

Emmet beamed at his father and his fiancé. He turned to Olivia. "Mama?"

"It's marvelous, Emmet. Mamie is a wonderful young lady. I'm sure you'll both be very happy."

"Thank you," Mamie said.

Emmet's grin grew even wider.

Olivia rose to gather the dishes.

Mamie scooted her chair back and reached for hers and Jacob's plates. "I'll help you."

"Thank you, Mamie," Olivia said.

After finishing the dishes, Olivia and Mamie joined the others in the parlor. Pungent apple-flavored pipe smoke wafted above the heads of Jacob and Emmet who each sat reading the newspaper. Minnie gazed through the stereoscope, and Myrtle turned the kaleidoscope round and round before her eye.

Olivia and Mamie perched on opposite ends of the sofa. "Tell me how is Susie doing these days?" Mamie asked Olivia.

Emmet lowered his newspaper.

Olivia glanced from Emmet to Mamie. "She, uh, she's fine," Olivia stammered.

"That name is not to be spoken," Emmet seethed in a low ominous tone.

"Why ever not? She's my cousin and your sister," Mamie said.

Olivia fiddled with the ruffle on her cuff.

Jacob slowly lowered his paper and glanced from Emmet to Mamie to Olivia. He looked so much older these days. Olivia didn't want him upset.

Even Minnie and Myrtle sensed the tension in the room hovering like a vulture waiting for something to die. They nervously peered from one adult to the other.

Emmet stared steadily at Mamie and said in a slow monotone, "I do not wish her name spoken."

Mamie's gaze did not waver under Emmet's icy blue eyes. "Very well—for now," she replied.

Their gazes locked around the silent battle being waged between them. No one had won, but no one had lost. Olivia sighed her relief. The Kimberlin men could be stubborn. It was a good thing the Blakemore women had gumption.

Elizabetha and Martin Kimberlin along with Anne and Joseph Blakemore had been the start of it all. Their combined offspring would now be united for the second generation. It would be fitting to pass Elizabetha's journal to Mamie. "Mamie, come upstairs with me a moment will you? I have something I want to give you."

"Of course." Mamie rose and followed Olivia. As she passed by Emmet, Mamie placed her hand on his shoulder.

Emmet gently patted it, a smile snuck across his stern countenance in spite of himself.

Upstairs, Olivia said, "Have a seat on the bed, Mamie. I'll just be a moment."

Mamie plunked down and straightened her skirts. Her dark brown eyes reflected a catlike satisfaction with herself.

Olivia removed Elizabetha's journal from the bottom drawer of her dresser and placed it on Mamie's lap. Mamie peered at her curiously.

"It belonged to Elizabetha Kimberlin, the best friend of your great, great-grandmother, Anne Blakemore. At her death, Elizabetha had passed it on to Anne. It remained in the Blakemore family until I married Jacob, when it once again became part of the Kimberlin family."

Mamie caressed the old worn leather cover with the tips of her fingers. "It's beautiful."

"Once again, the Blakemores and Kimberlins are to be intertwined. It is fitting that you should have the journal as a wedding gift. I hope it will bring as much help to you as it has to previous Blakemore women," Olivia said.

Mamie hugged the journal to her, and turned her gaze up to Olivia. "Thank you. I'll cherish it always."

"Lord knows you'll need it. Emmet can be quite a stern man, like his father and all the rest of the Kimberlin men."

"My mother says we Blakemore women are strong. I've strength enough to handle him. I've strength enough for two."

Olivia laughed. Yes, her niece had the same kind of strength and wisdom of Elizabetha Kimberlin as well as the patience of Anne, and the endurance of Olive. She'd also inherited the sweetness of Susannah, and maybe Olivia's own determination. All the previous generations had come together in this girl. She remembered the poem from Elizabetha's journal:

> The clouds of time creep across
> the field of generations
> leaving one row of golden grain
> illuminated by the sun a while
> and then move on to give
> another row its time to shine.

It was Mamie's time to shine.

ISBN 141209580-8
9 781412 095808